JADE STREET
PROTECTION SERVICES

BLACK MASK

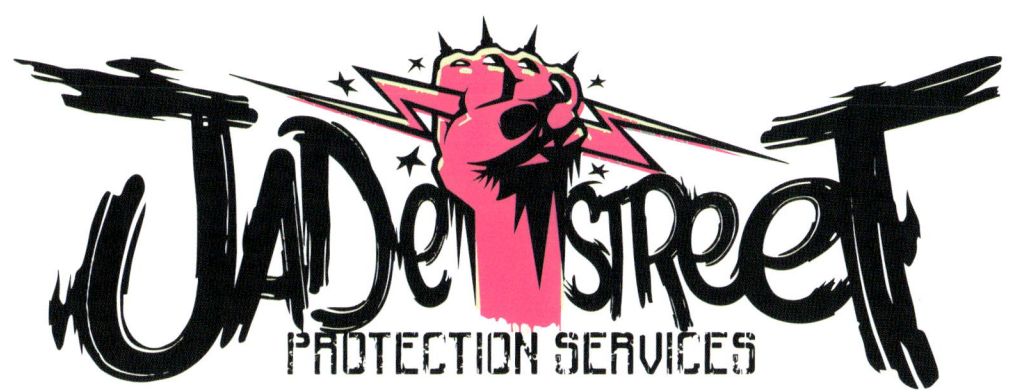

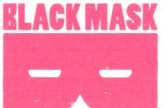

KATY REX
STORY

FABIAN LELAY
STORY + ILLUSTRATION

MARA JAYNE CARPENTER
COLORIST

MAGDALENE VISAGGIO
EDITOR

TAYLOR ESPOSITO
LETTERER

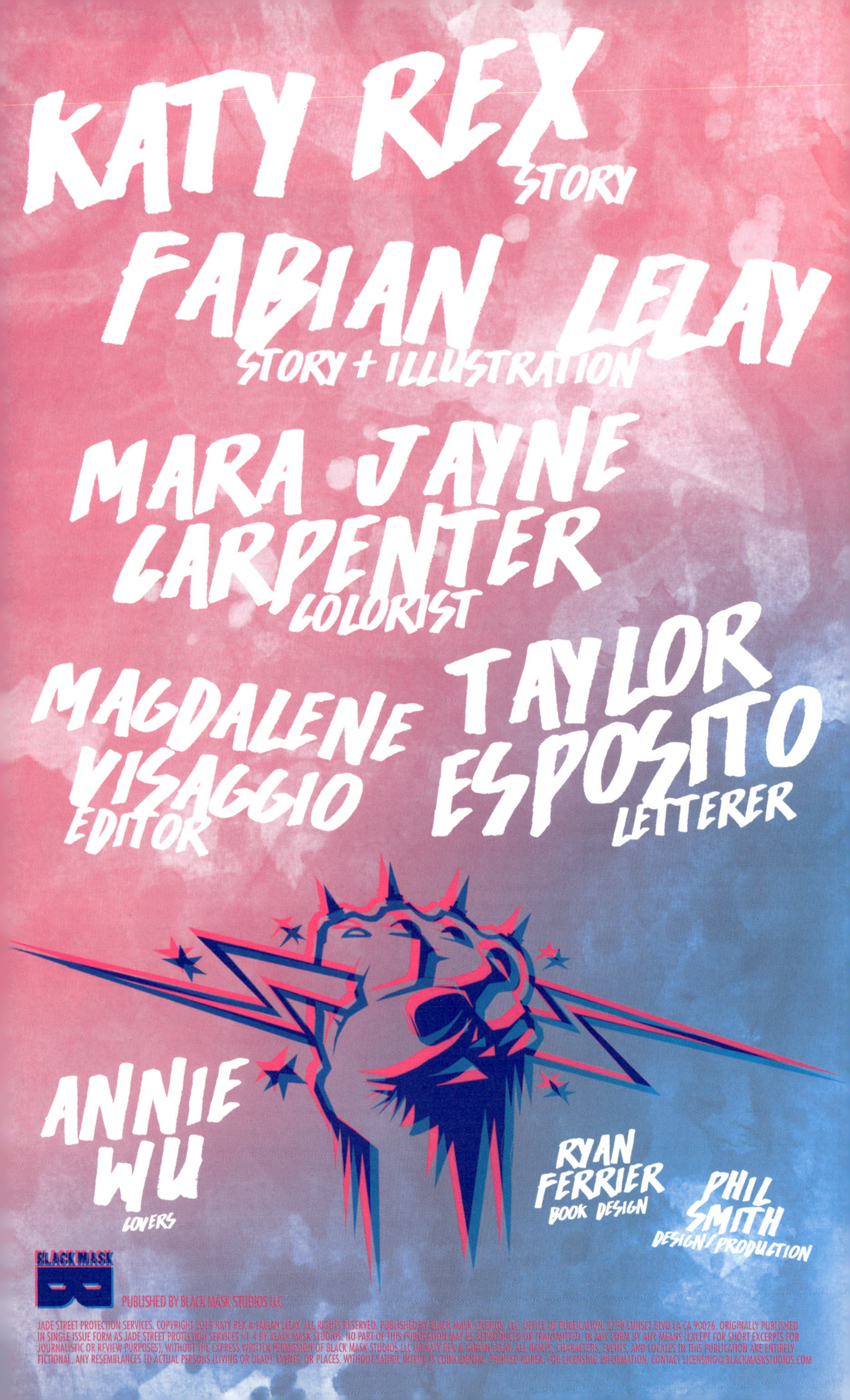

ANNIE WU
COVERS

RYAN FERRIER
BOOK DESIGN

PHIL SMITH
DESIGN/PRODUCTION

PUBLISHED BY BLACK MASK STUDIOS LLC

GIRLS ARE MAGIC

It's a truth commonly known, frequently spoken, but so rarely actually accepted at face value by the rest of the world. The world works to hide that magic, suffocate that magic, and make you hate that magic. We live in a time when young women and girls are constantly at risk of being shouted down, discouraged from excellence, or flat out attacked should they dare to shine independently.

And then, once it's removed from the girl and the girl is no longer allowed to shine, if it can, the world will happily commodify that magic.

"Jade Street Protection Services" is a book about magical girls that fight exactly this.

Now, if you grew up anywhere near the time I did, the phrase "Magical Girls" automatically inspires certain images of astronomy themed teenage girls in uncomfortably short pastel skirts. You remember these girls facing off against some evil monster that lured them in with the promise of a particularly pungent perfume that would surely attract that boy they liked, before shattering that dream of romantic bliss and challenging them to battle. That DNA is in Jade Street Protection Services, but it's only part of a much more amazing hybrid.

The girls of Jade Street are not here for cosmetics and they don't fight using tiaras and magic rods. They are highly trained magical girls with a lust for life and a thirst for combat. And when things go south, they're the ones you want looking out for you. And they have that great strength that some other groups of magical girls lack, real honest diversity.

Because here's the thing. ALL girls are magic. You can't say girls are magic and just mean one type of girl. And Jade Street has it all. Whether it's the bookish sword wielding Hindi speaking over-achiever Divya, the tattooed asymmetrical haired magic rock star Noemi, the face-punching lady-flirting bruiser with her heart on her sleeve Kai, our super-bright mute narrator Emma, or – my personal favorite – the giant hammer wielding hijab wearing trapmaster, prankster, and friend to insects Saba, there is a character here that you will not only relate to, but that you will love. These magical girls come as amazingly real and beautifully complex as the magical girls you're sure to have met in your own life.

And it's that fact which makes the comic you hold in your hands valuable in a way that other comics aren't. It speaks the amazing truth that magical girls come in all shapes, sizes, races, religions, disabilities, fashions, sexualities, and types. Whether you carry a sword, a hammer, a guitar, brass knuckles, or a sniper rifle – did I mention that one of these girls carries a magical sniper rifle – you have the power to fight back against a world set on beating down, stealing, and commodifying your magic. You can fight for yourself. You and your friends can be your own protection and you can beat the everloving snot out of anybody who tries to take your magic.

Because girls are magic. All girls. And that knowledge is powerful.

Jeremy Whitley
Writer of *Princeless*, *The Pirate Princess*, *The Unstoppable Wasp*

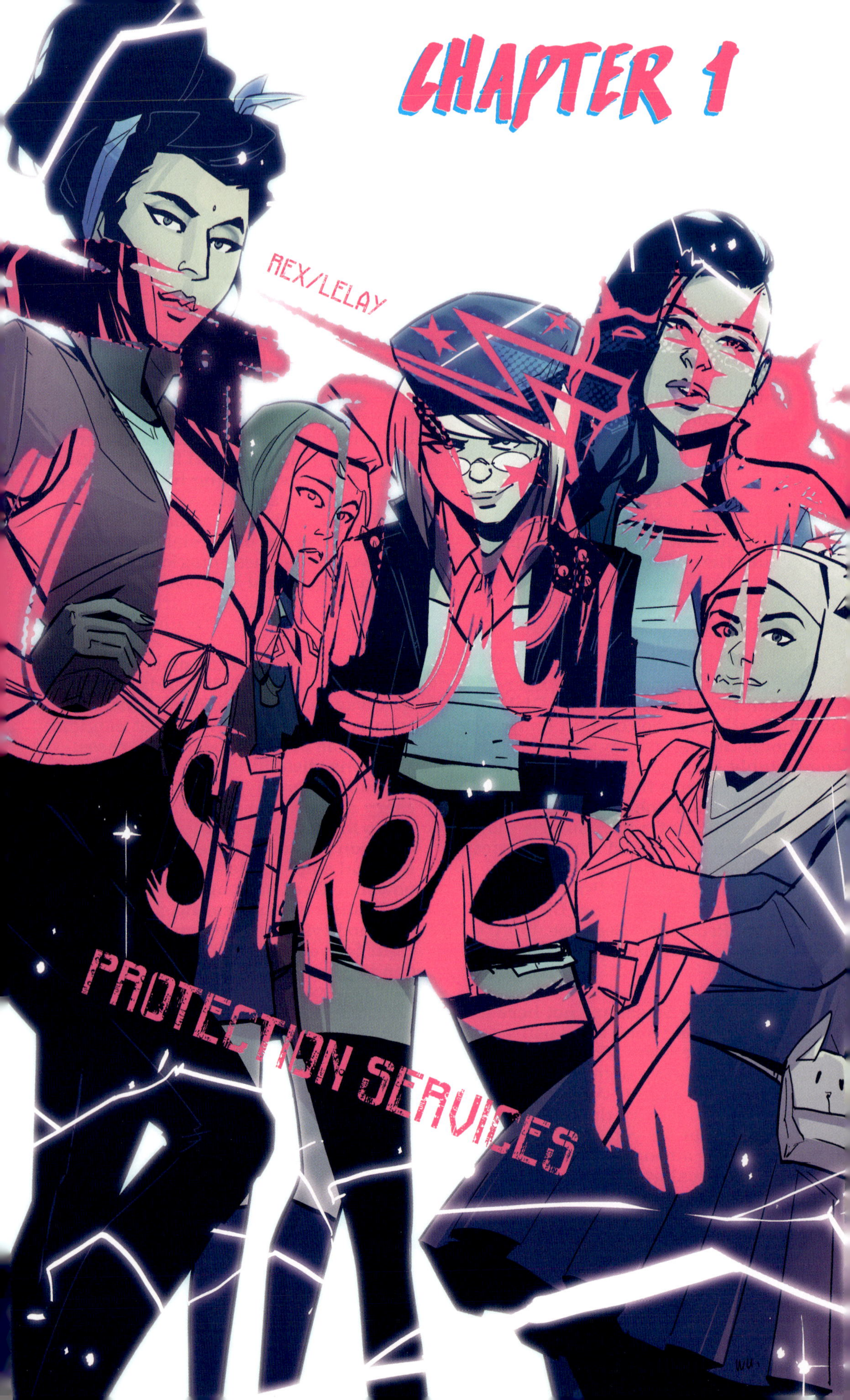
CHAPTER 1
REX/LELAY
PROTECTION SERVICES

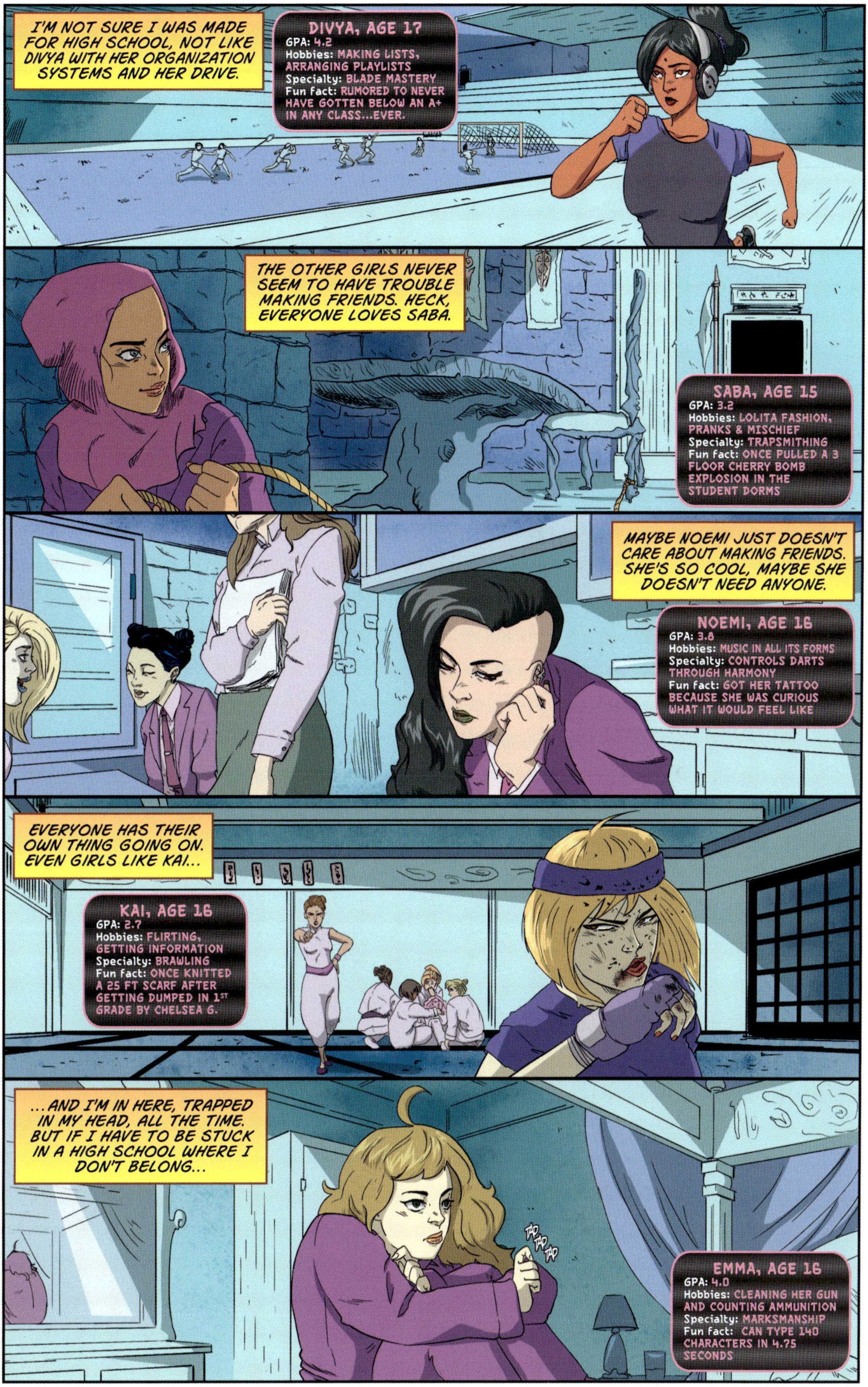
I'M NOT SURE I WAS MADE FOR HIGH SCHOOL, NOT LIKE DIVYA WITH HER ORGANIZATION SYSTEMS AND HER DRIVE.
DIVYA, AGE 17
GPA: 4.2
Hobbies: MAKING LISTS, ARRANGING PLAYLISTS
Specialty: BLADE MASTERY
Fun fact: RUMORED TO NEVER HAVE GOTTEN BELOW AN A+ IN ANY CLASS...EVER.
THE OTHER GIRLS NEVER SEEM TO HAVE TROUBLE MAKING FRIENDS. HECK, EVERYONE LOVES SABA.
SABA, AGE 15
GPA: 3.2
Hobbies: LOLITA FASHION, PRANKS & MISCHIEF
Specialty: TRAPSMITHING
Fun fact: ONCE PULLED A 3 FLOOR CHERRY BOMB EXPLOSION IN THE STUDENT DORMS
MAYBE NOEMI JUST DOESN'T CARE ABOUT MAKING FRIENDS. SHE'S SO COOL, MAYBE SHE DOESN'T NEED ANYONE.
NOEMI, AGE 16
GPA: 3.8
Hobbies: MUSIC IN ALL ITS FORMS
Specialty: CONTROLS DARTS THROUGH HARMONY
Fun fact: GOT HER TATTOO BECAUSE SHE WAS CURIOUS WHAT IT WOULD FEEL LIKE
EVERYONE HAS THEIR OWN THING GOING ON. EVEN GIRLS LIKE KAI...
KAI, AGE 16
GPA: 2.7
Hobbies: FLIRTING, GETTING INFORMATION
Specialty: BRAWLING
Fun fact: ONCE KNITTED A 25 FT SCARF AFTER GETTING DUMPED IN 1ST GRADE BY CHELSEA G.
...AND I'M IN HERE, TRAPPED IN MY HEAD, ALL THE TIME. BUT IF I HAVE TO BE STUCK IN A HIGH SCHOOL WHERE I DON'T BELONG...
TAP TAP TAP
EMMA, AGE 16
GPA: 4.0
Hobbies: CLEANING HER GUN AND COUNTING AMMUNITION
Specialty: MARKSMANSHIP
Fun fact: CAN TYPE 140 CHARACTERS IN 4.75 SECONDS

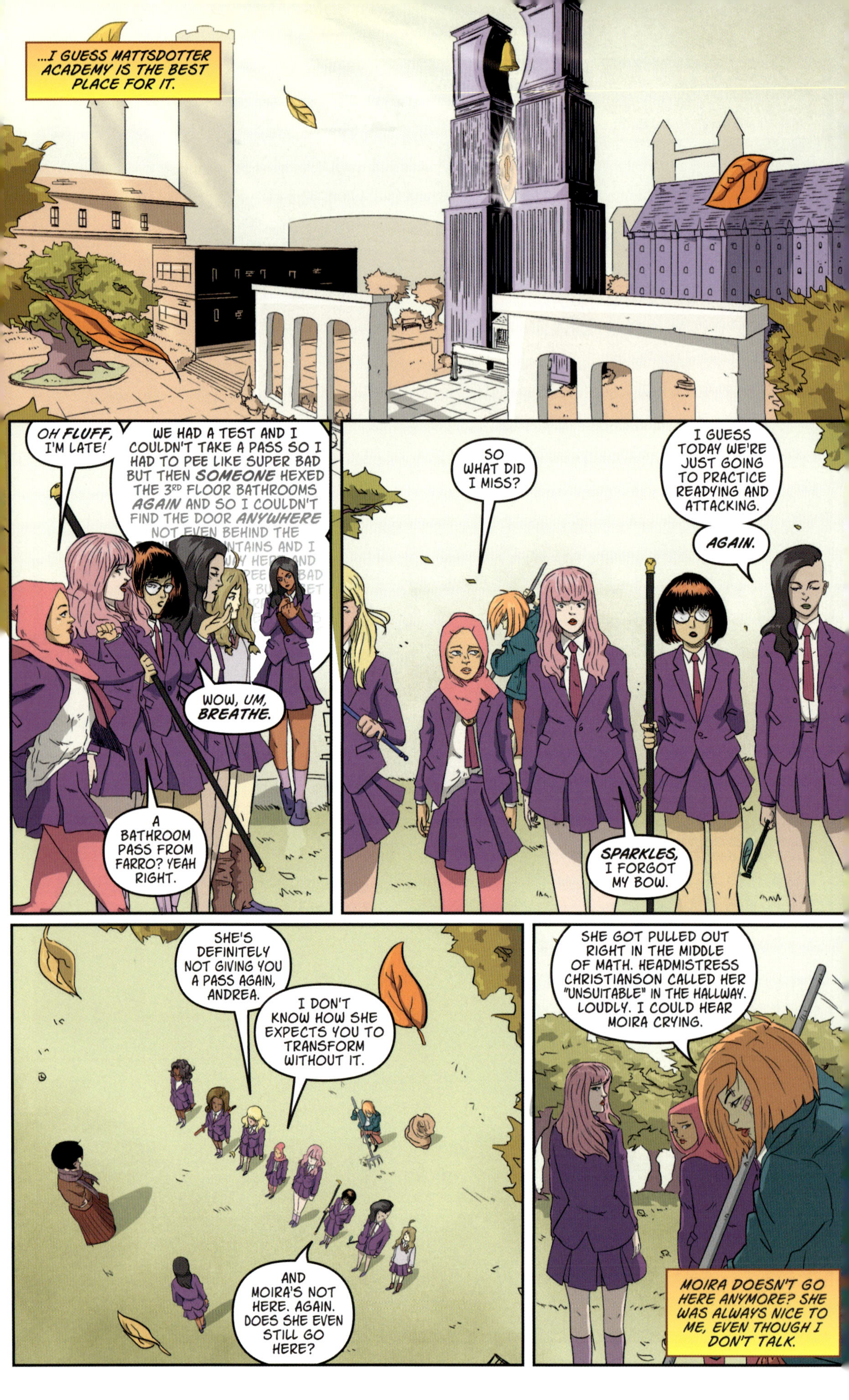
...I GUESS MATTSDOTTER ACADEMY IS THE BEST PLACE FOR IT.
OH FLUFF, I'M LATE!
WE HAD A TEST AND I COULDN'T TAKE A PASS SO I HAD TO PEE LIKE SUPER BAD BUT THEN SOMEONE HEXED THE 3RD FLOOR BATHROOMS AGAIN AND SO I COULDN'T FIND THE DOOR ANYWHERE NOT EVEN BEHIND THE
WOW, UM, BREATHE.
A BATHROOM PASS FROM FARRO? YEAH RIGHT.
SO WHAT DID I MISS?
I GUESS TODAY WE'RE JUST GOING TO PRACTICE READYING AND ATTACKING.
AGAIN.
SPARKLES, I FORGOT MY BOW.
SHE'S DEFINITELY NOT GIVING YOU A PASS AGAIN, ANDREA.
I DON'T KNOW HOW SHE EXPECTS YOU TO TRANSFORM WITHOUT IT.
AND MOIRA'S NOT HERE. AGAIN. DOES SHE EVEN STILL GO HERE?
SHE GOT PULLED OUT RIGHT IN THE MIDDLE OF MATH. HEADMISTRESS CHRISTIANSON CALLED HER "UNSUITABLE" IN THE HALLWAY. LOUDLY. I COULD HEAR MOIRA CRYING.
MOIRA DOESN'T GO HERE ANYMORE? SHE WAS ALWAYS NICE TO ME, EVEN THOUGH I DON'T TALK.

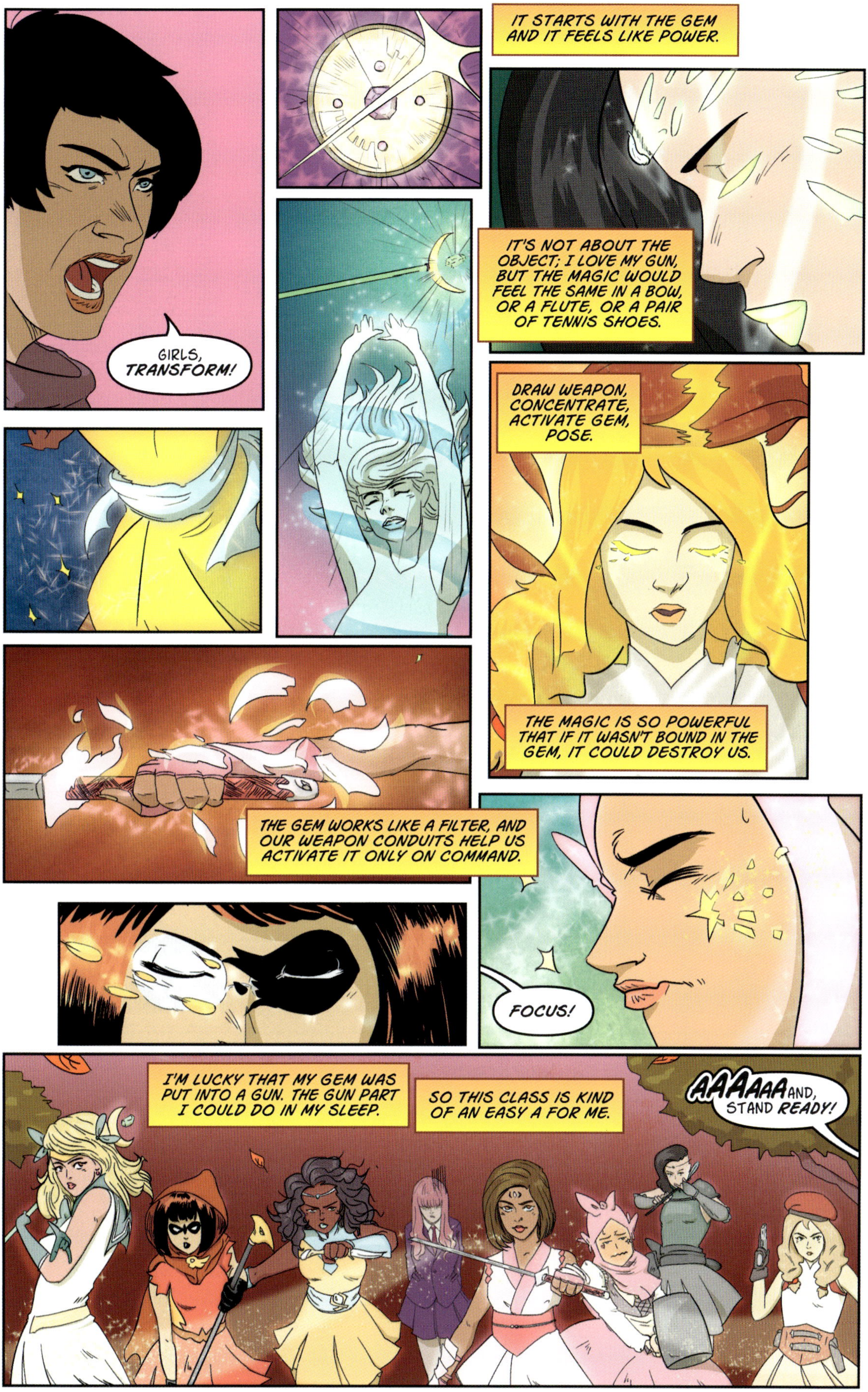
GIRLS, TRANSFORM!
IT STARTS WITH THE GEM AND IT FEELS LIKE POWER.
IT'S NOT ABOUT THE OBJECT; I LOVE MY GUN, BUT THE MAGIC WOULD FEEL THE SAME IN A BOW, OR A FLUTE, OR A PAIR OF TENNIS SHOES.
DRAW WEAPON, CONCENTRATE, ACTIVATE GEM, POSE.
THE MAGIC IS SO POWERFUL THAT IF IT WASN'T BOUND IN THE GEM, IT COULD DESTROY US.
THE GEM WORKS LIKE A FILTER, AND OUR WEAPON CONDUITS HELP US ACTIVATE IT ONLY ON COMMAND.
FOCUS!
I'M LUCKY THAT MY GEM WAS PUT INTO A GUN. THE GUN PART I COULD DO IN MY SLEEP.
SO THIS CLASS IS KIND OF AN EASY A FOR ME.
AAAAAA AND, STAND READY!

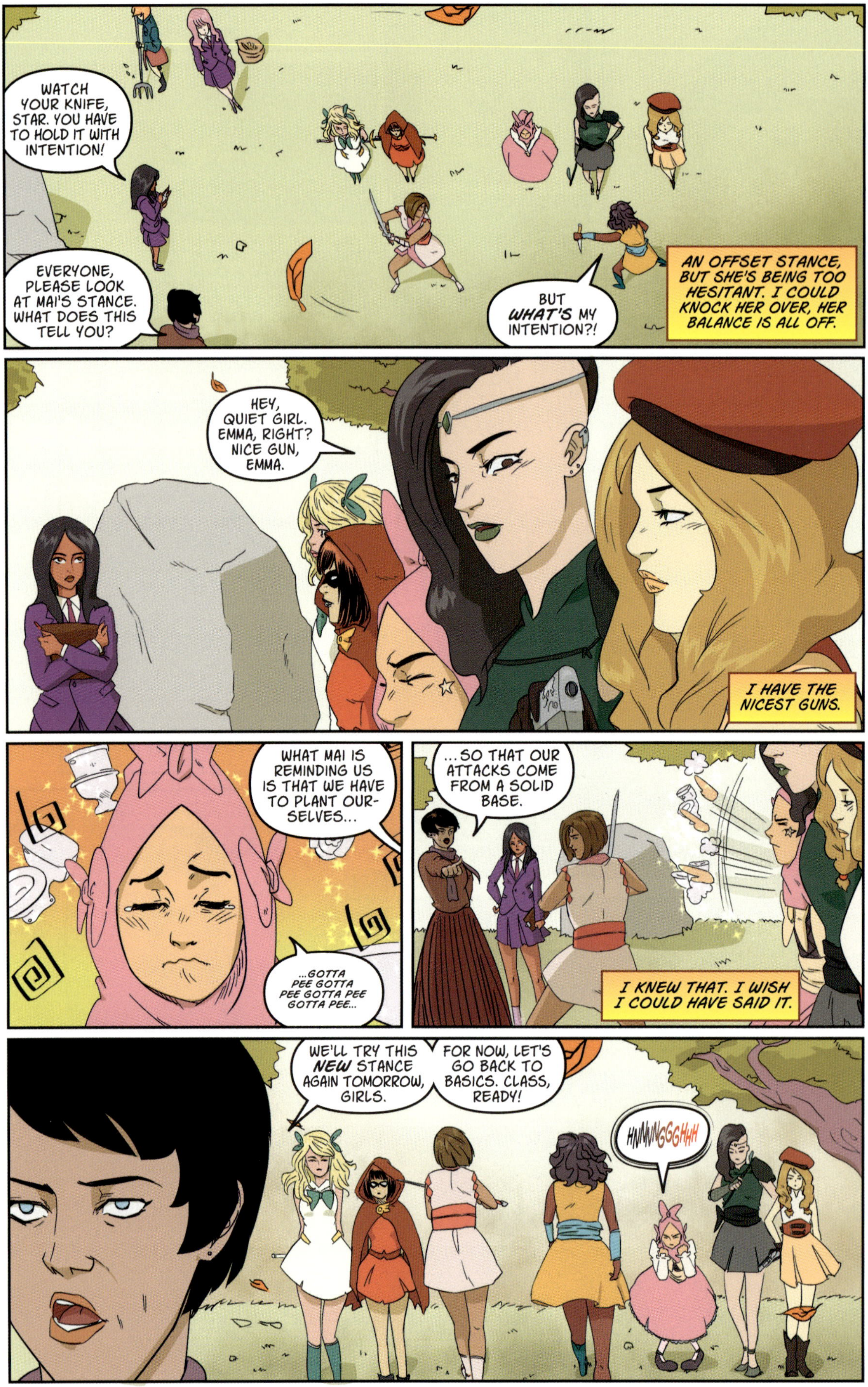
WATCH YOUR KNIFE, STAR. YOU HAVE TO HOLD IT WITH INTENTION!
EVERYONE, PLEASE LOOK AT MAI'S STANCE. WHAT DOES THIS TELL YOU?
BUT *WHAT'S* MY INTENTION?!
AN OFFSET STANCE, BUT SHE'S BEING TOO HESITANT. I COULD KNOCK HER OVER, HER BALANCE IS ALL OFF.
HEY, QUIET GIRL. EMMA, RIGHT? NICE GUN, EMMA.
I HAVE THE NICEST GUNS.
WHAT MAI IS REMINDING US IS THAT WE HAVE TO PLANT OURSELVES...
...GOTTA PEE GOTTA PEE GOTTA PEE GOTTA PEE...
...SO THAT OUR ATTACKS COME FROM A SOLID BASE.
I KNEW THAT. I WISH I COULD HAVE SAID IT.
WE'LL TRY THIS *NEW* STANCE AGAIN TOMORROW, GIRLS.
FOR NOW, LET'S GO BACK TO BASICS. CLASS, READY!
HNNNNGGGHHH

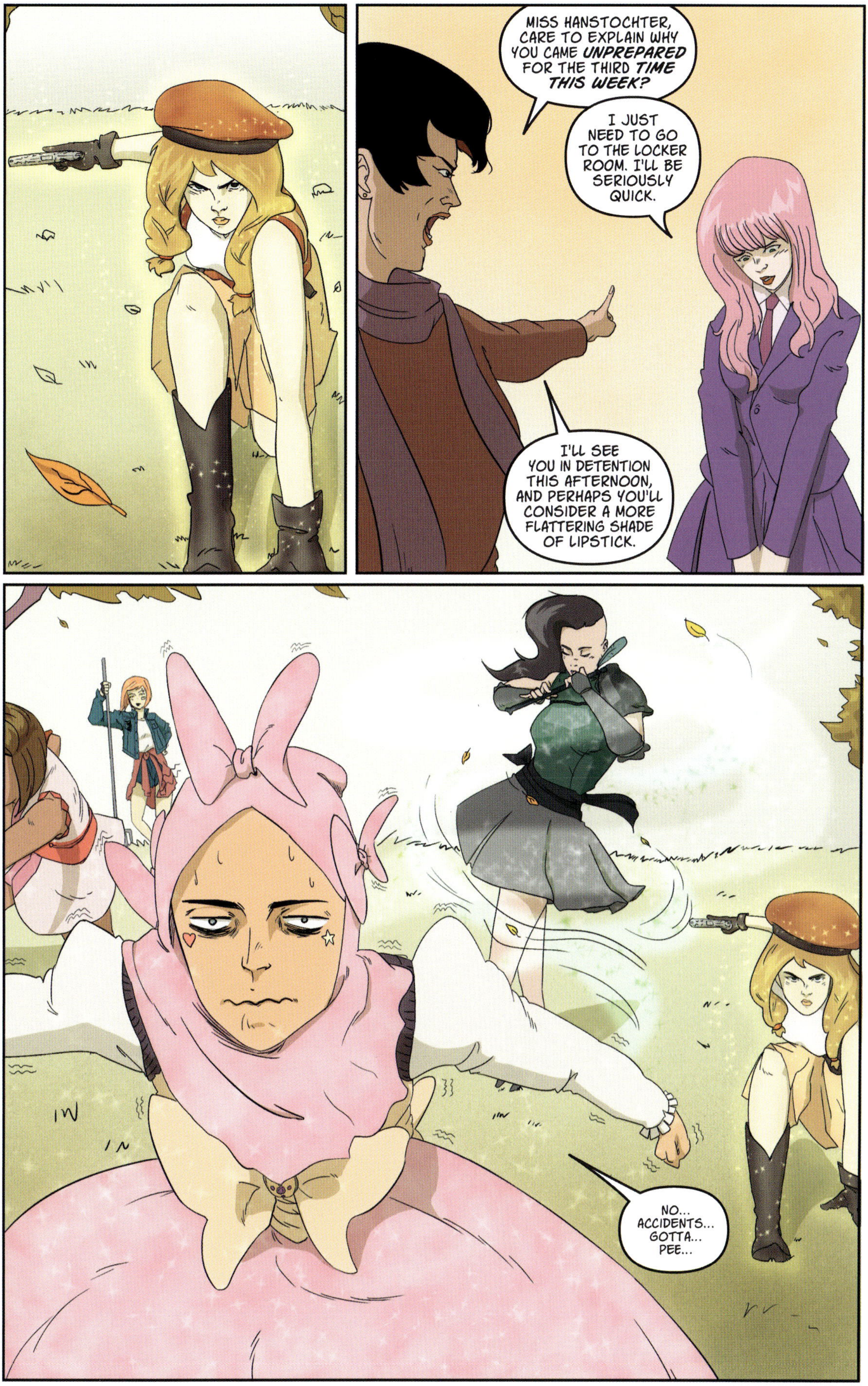
MISS HANSTOCHTER, CARE TO EXPLAIN WHY YOU CAME UNPREPARED FOR THE THIRD TIME THIS WEEK?
I JUST NEED TO GO TO THE LOCKER ROOM. I'LL BE SERIOUSLY QUICK.
I'LL SEE YOU IN DETENTION THIS AFTERNOON, AND PERHAPS YOU'LL CONSIDER A MORE FLATTERING SHADE OF LIPSTICK.
NO... ACCIDENTS... GOTTA... PEE...

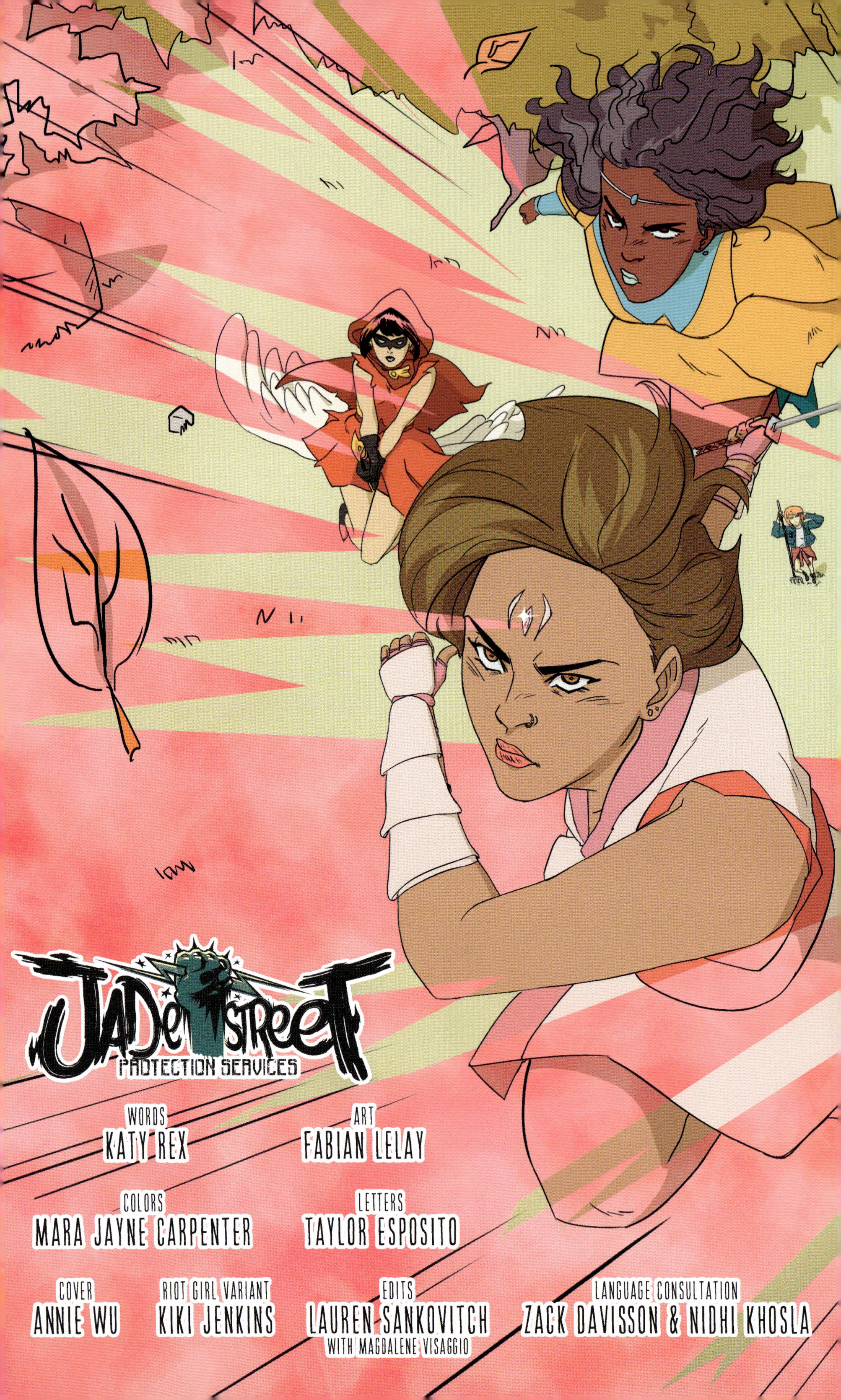

JADE STREET PROTECTION SERVICES

WORDS
KATY REX

ART
FABIAN LELAY

COLORS
MARA JAYNE CARPENTER

LETTERS
TAYLOR ESPOSITO

COVER
ANNIE WU

RIOT GIRL VARIANT
KIKI JENKINS

EDITS
LAUREN SANKOVITCH
WITH MAGDALENE VISAGGIO

LANGUAGE CONSULTATION
ZACK DAVISSON & NIDHI KHOSLA

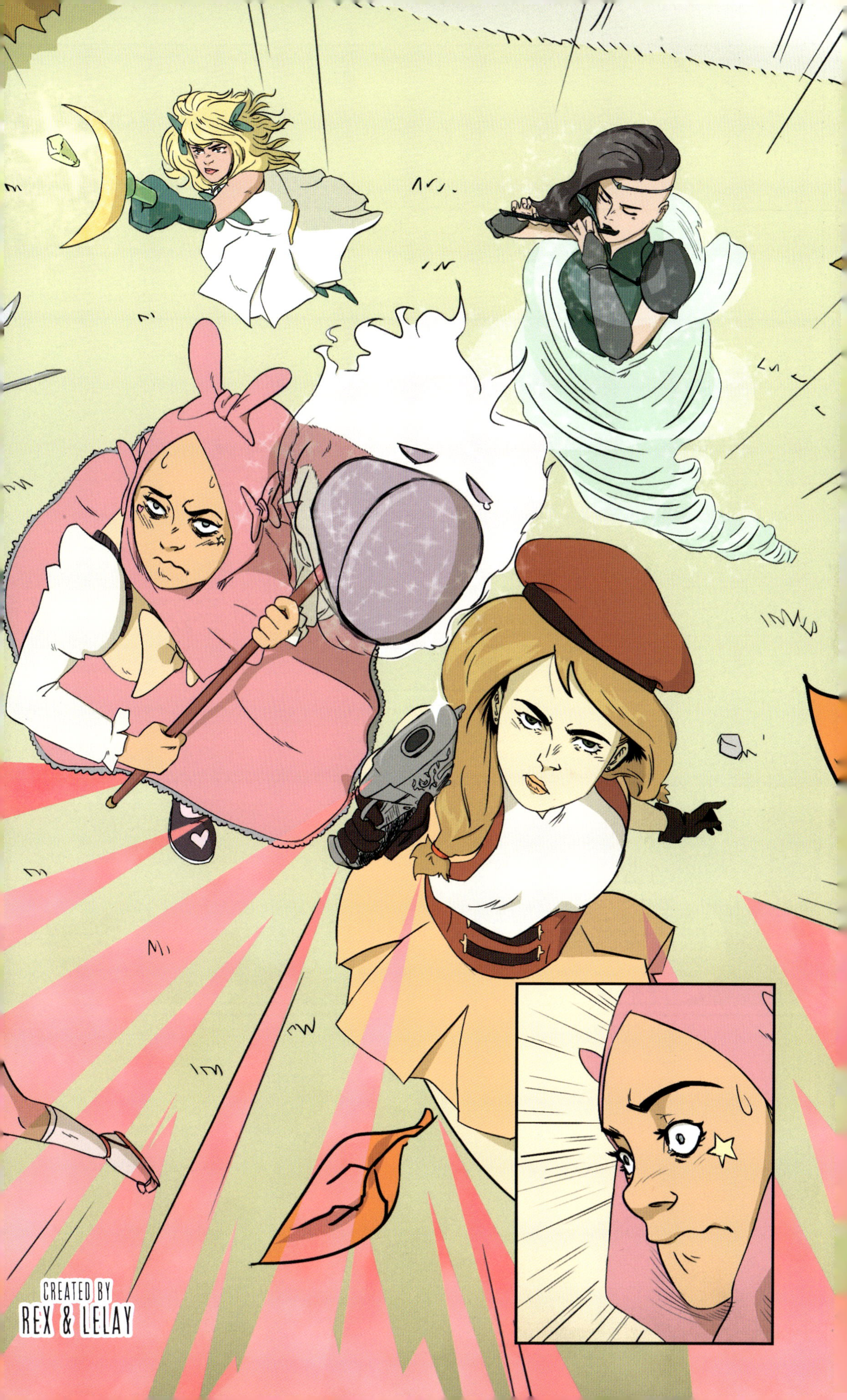
CREATED BY
REX & LELAY

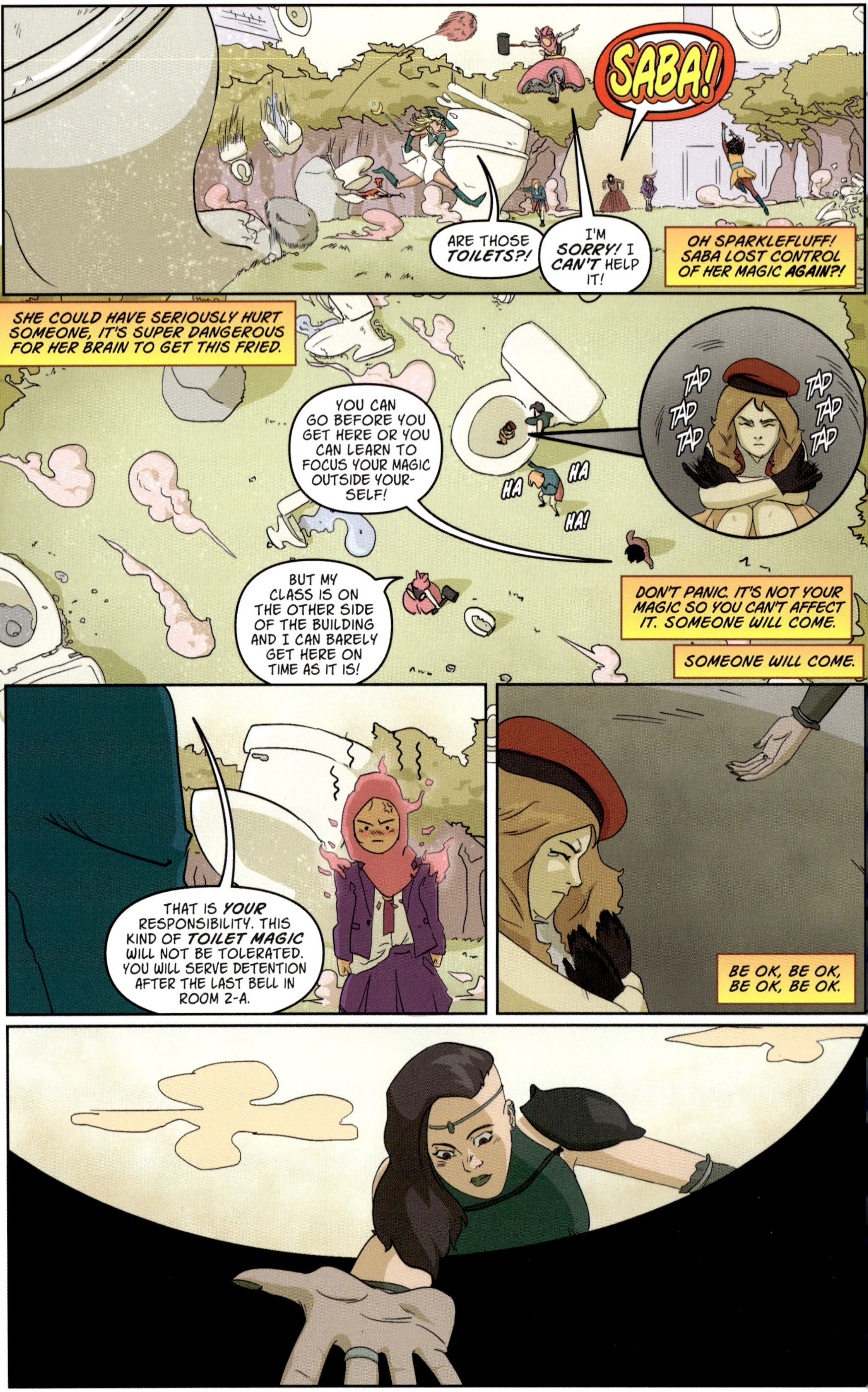
SABA!
ARE THOSE TOILETS?!
I'M SORRY! I CAN'T HELP IT!
OH SPARKLEFLUFF! SABA LOST CONTROL OF HER MAGIC AGAIN?!
SHE COULD HAVE SERIOUSLY HURT SOMEONE, IT'S SUPER DANGEROUS FOR HER BRAIN TO GET THIS FRIED.
TAP TAP TAP
TAP TAP TAP
YOU CAN GO BEFORE YOU GET HERE OR YOU CAN LEARN TO FOCUS YOUR MAGIC OUTSIDE YOURSELF!
HA HA HA!
BUT MY CLASS IS ON THE OTHER SIDE OF THE BUILDING AND I CAN BARELY GET HERE ON TIME AS IT IS!
DON'T PANIC. IT'S NOT YOUR MAGIC SO YOU CAN'T AFFECT IT. SOMEONE WILL COME.
SOMEONE WILL COME.
THAT IS YOUR RESPONSIBILITY. THIS KIND OF TOILET MAGIC WILL NOT BE TOLERATED. YOU WILL SERVE DETENTION AFTER THE LAST BELL IN ROOM 2-A.
BE OK, BE OK, BE OK, BE OK.

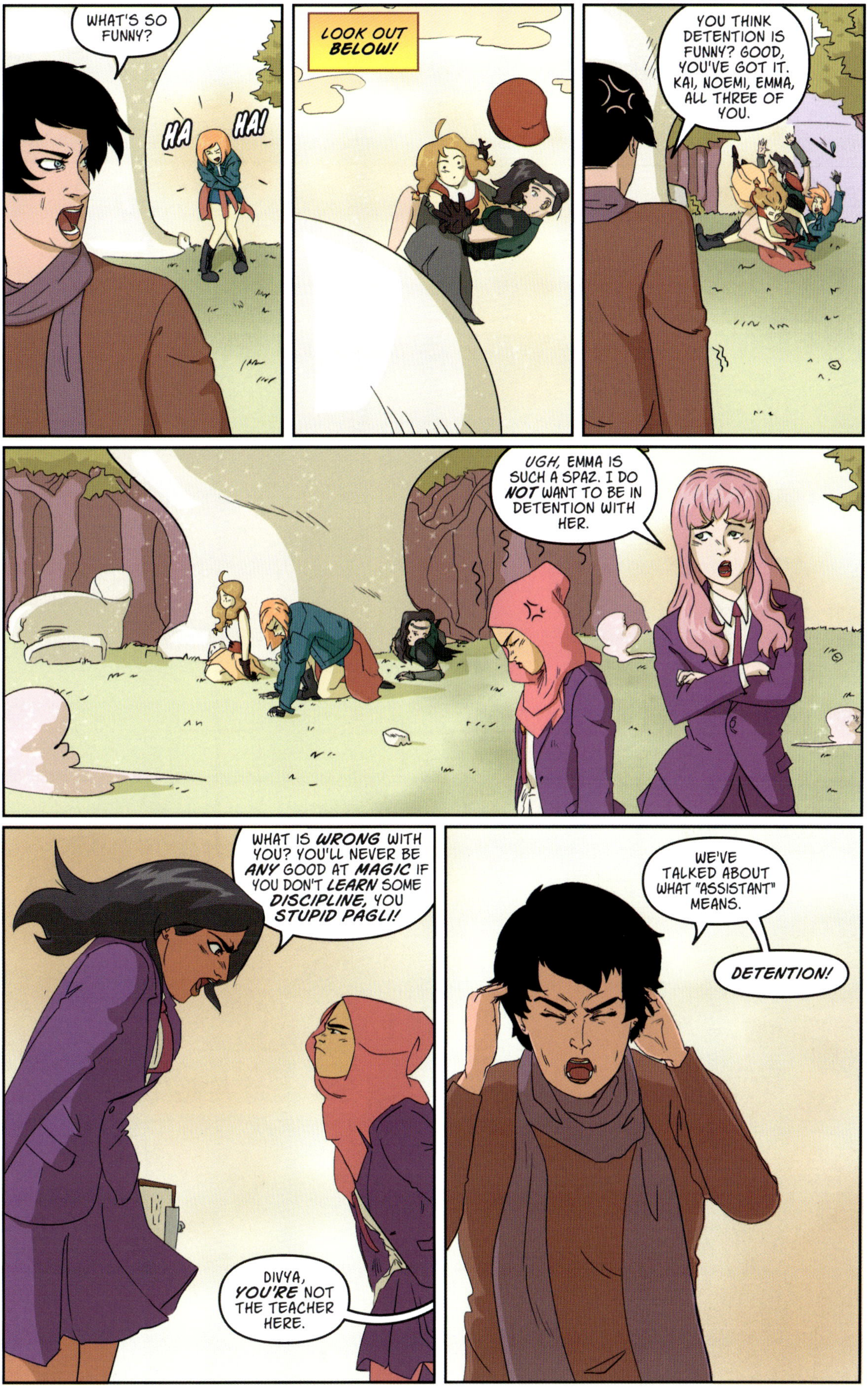
WHAT'S SO FUNNY?
HA HA!
LOOK OUT BELOW!
YOU THINK DETENTION IS FUNNY? GOOD, YOU'VE GOT IT. KAI, NOEMI, EMMA, ALL THREE OF YOU.
UGH, EMMA IS SUCH A SPAZ. I DO NOT WANT TO BE IN DETENTION WITH HER.
WHAT IS WRONG WITH YOU? YOU'LL NEVER BE ANY GOOD AT MAGIC IF YOU DON'T LEARN SOME DISCIPLINE, YOU STUPID PAGLI!
DIVYA, YOU'RE NOT THE TEACHER HERE.
WE'VE TALKED ABOUT WHAT "ASSISTANT" MEANS.
DETENTION!

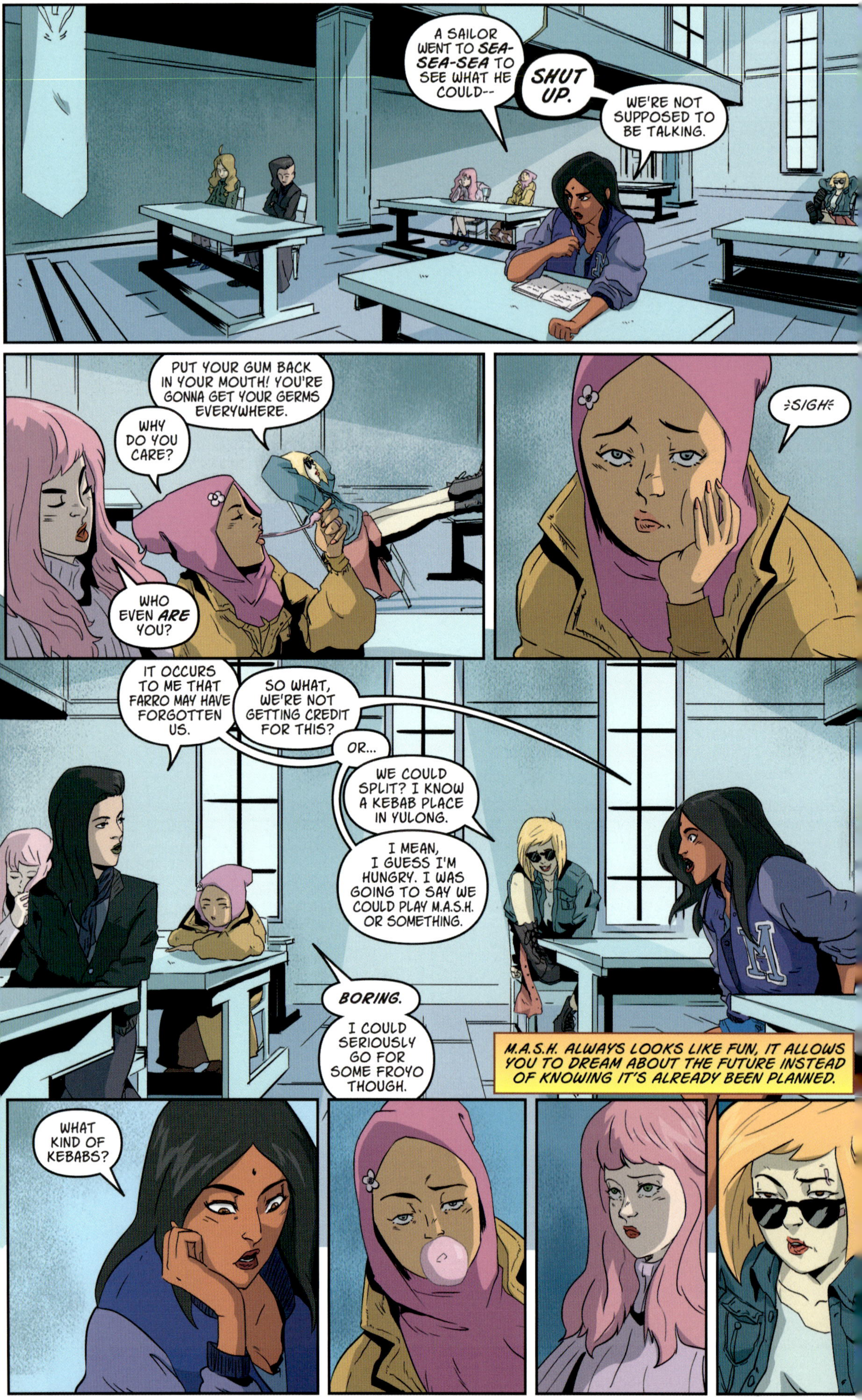
A SAILOR WENT TO SEA-SEA-SEA TO SEE WHAT HE COULD--
SHUT UP.
WE'RE NOT SUPPOSED TO BE TALKING.
PUT YOUR GUM BACK IN YOUR MOUTH! YOU'RE GONNA GET YOUR GERMS EVERYWHERE.
WHY DO YOU CARE?
WHO EVEN ARE YOU?
SIGH
IT OCCURS TO ME THAT FARRO MAY HAVE FORGOTTEN US.
SO WHAT, WE'RE NOT GETTING CREDIT FOR THIS?
OR...
WE COULD SPLIT? I KNOW A KEBAB PLACE IN YULONG.
I MEAN, I GUESS I'M HUNGRY. I WAS GOING TO SAY WE COULD PLAY M.A.S.H. OR SOMETHING.
BORING.
I COULD SERIOUSLY GO FOR SOME FROYO THOUGH.
M.A.S.H. ALWAYS LOOKS LIKE FUN, IT ALLOWS YOU TO DREAM ABOUT THE FUTURE INSTEAD OF KNOWING IT'S ALREADY BEEN PLANNED.
WHAT KIND OF KEBABS?

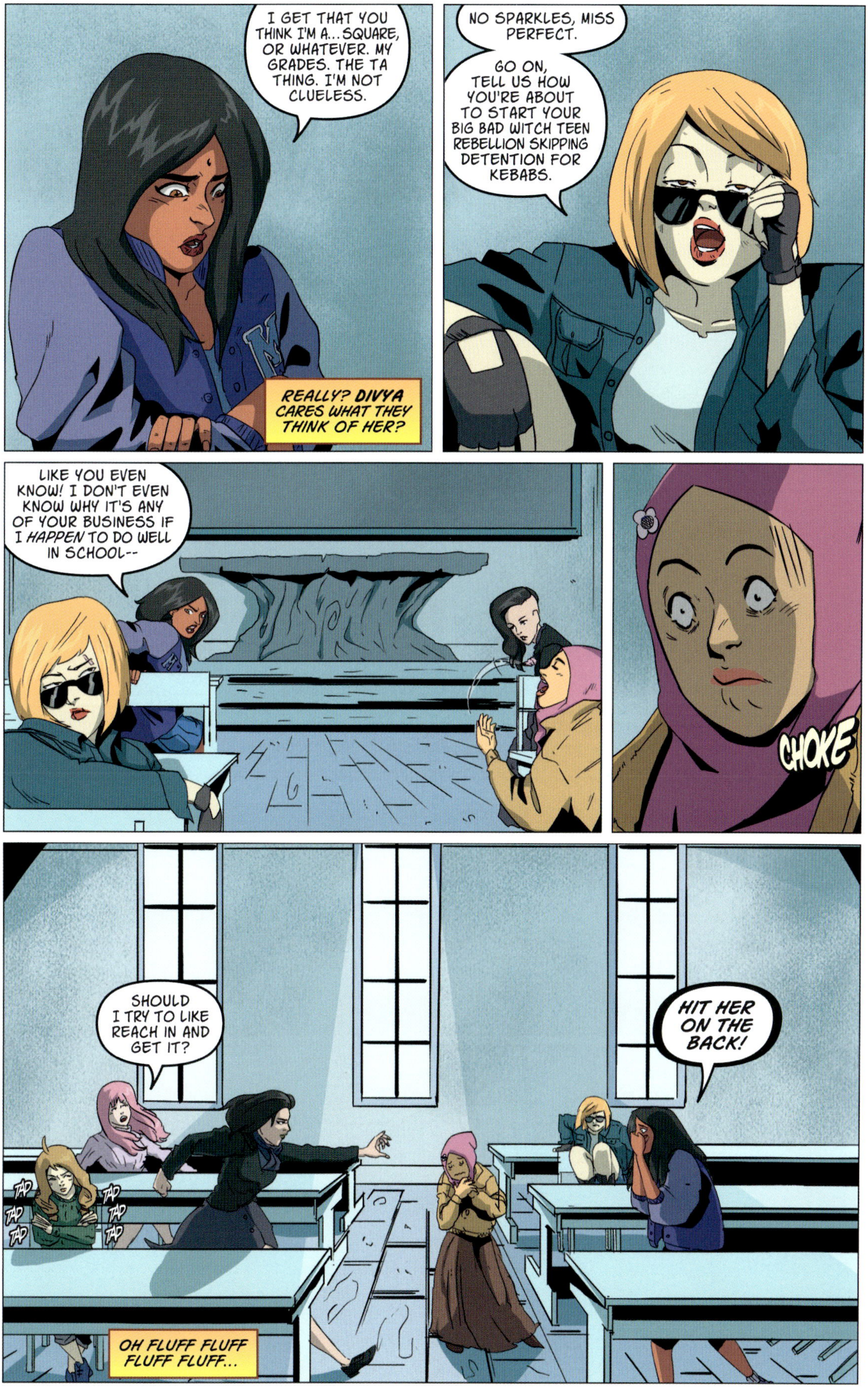
I GET THAT YOU THINK I'M A... SQUARE, OR WHATEVER. MY GRADES. THE TA THING. I'M NOT CLUELESS.
REALLY? DIVYA CARES WHAT THEY THINK OF HER?
NO SPARKLES, MISS PERFECT.
GO ON, TELL US HOW YOU'RE ABOUT TO START YOUR BIG BAD WITCH TEEN REBELLION SKIPPING DETENTION FOR KEBABS.
LIKE YOU EVEN KNOW! I DON'T EVEN KNOW WHY IT'S ANY OF YOUR BUSINESS IF I *HAPPEN* TO DO WELL IN SCHOOL--
CHOKE
SHOULD I TRY TO LIKE REACH IN AND GET IT?
HIT HER ON THE BACK!
TAP TAP TAP
TAP TAP TAP
OH FLUFF FLUFF FLUFF FLUFF...

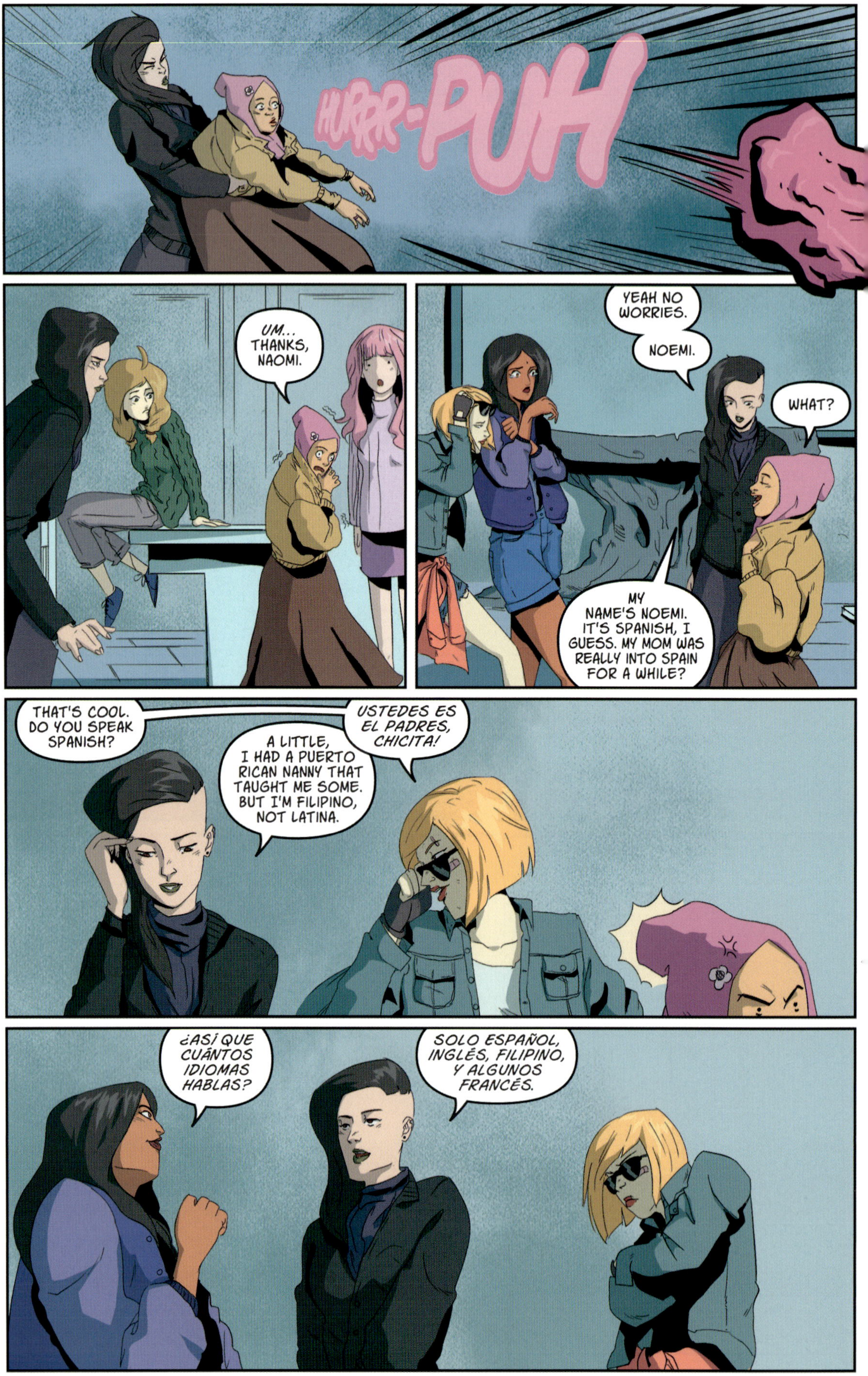
HURRR-PUH
UM... THANKS, NAOMI.
YEAH NO WORRIES.
NOEMI.
WHAT?
MY NAME'S NOEMI. IT'S SPANISH, I GUESS. MY MOM WAS REALLY INTO SPAIN FOR A WHILE?
THAT'S COOL. DO YOU SPEAK SPANISH?
A LITTLE, I HAD A PUERTO RICAN NANNY THAT TAUGHT ME SOME. BUT I'M FILIPINO, NOT LATINA.
USTEDES ES EL PADRES, CHICITA!
¿ASÍ QUE CUÁNTOS IDIOMAS HABLAS?
SOLO ESPAÑOL, INGLÉS, FILIPINO, Y ALGUNOS FRANCÉS.

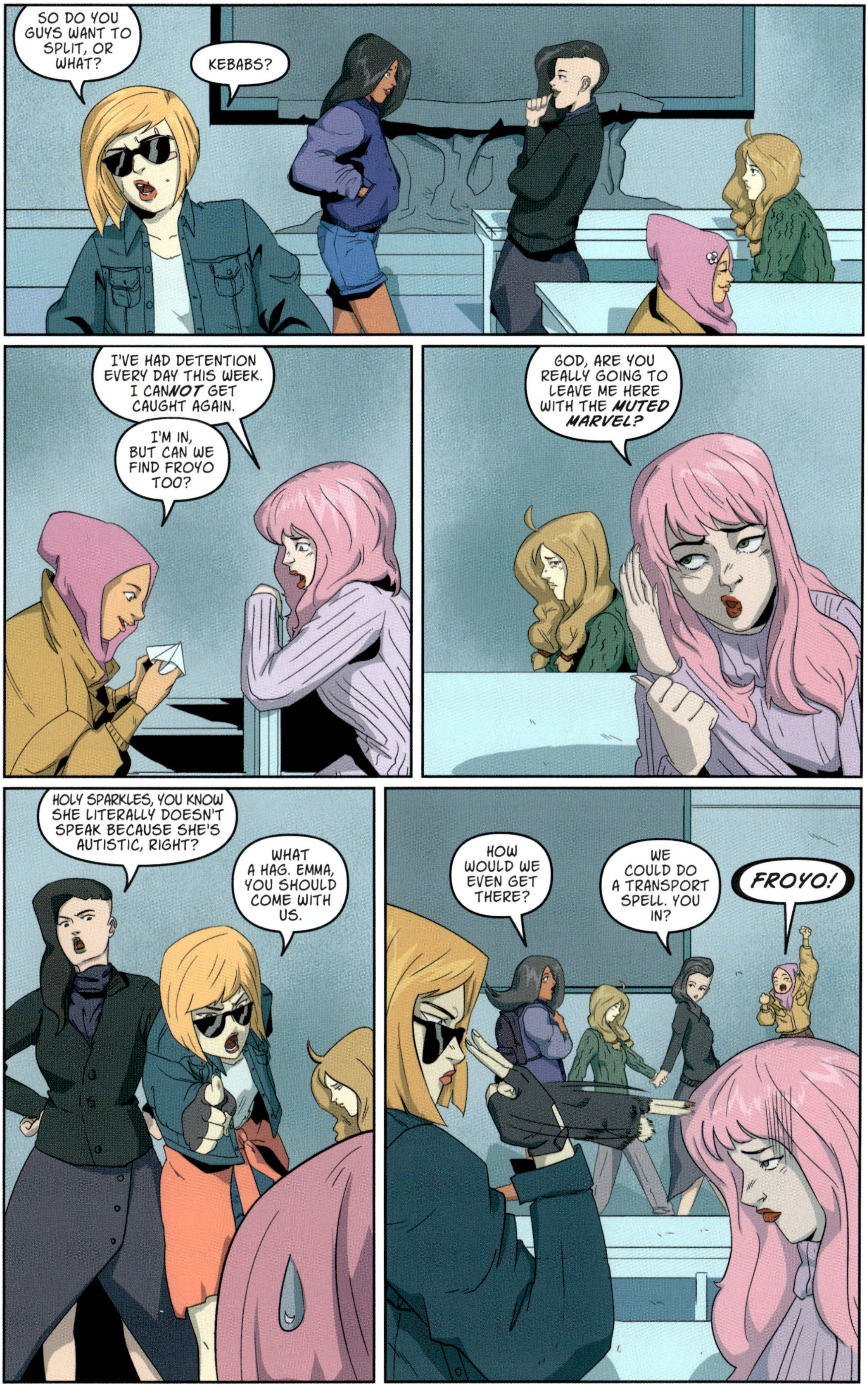

SO DO YOU GUYS WANT TO SPLIT, OR WHAT?
KEBABS?
I'VE HAD DETENTION EVERY DAY THIS WEEK. I CAN*NOT* GET CAUGHT AGAIN.
I'M IN, BUT CAN WE FIND FROYO TOO?
GOD, ARE YOU REALLY GOING TO LEAVE ME HERE WITH THE ***MUTED MARVEL?***
HOLY SPARKLES, YOU KNOW SHE LITERALLY DOESN'T SPEAK BECAUSE SHE'S AUTISTIC, RIGHT?
WHAT A HAG. EMMA, YOU SHOULD COME WITH US.
HOW WOULD WE EVEN GET THERE?
WE COULD DO A TRANSPORT SPELL. YOU IN?
FROYO!

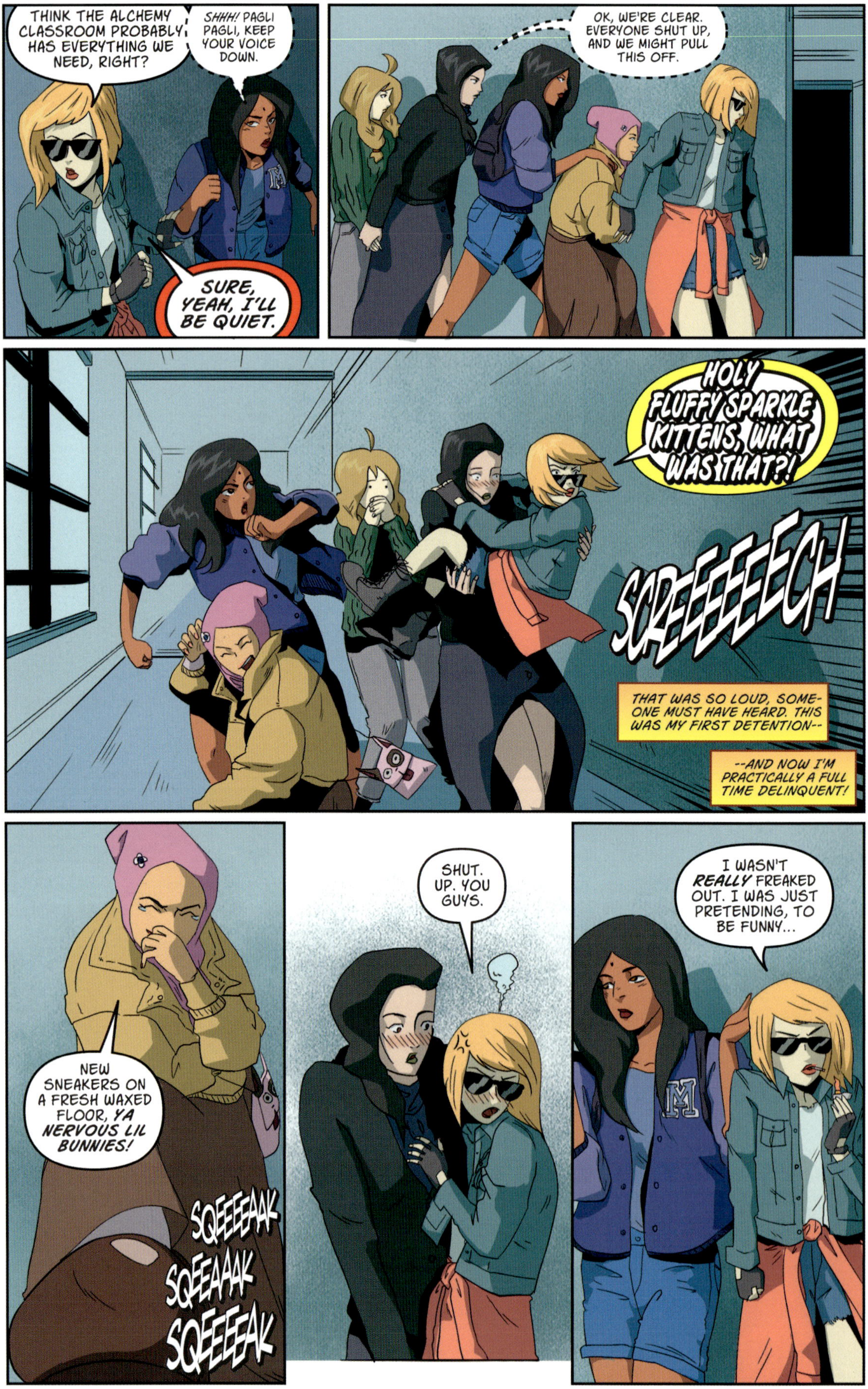

THINK THE ALCHEMY CLASSROOM PROBABLY HAS EVERYTHING WE NEED, RIGHT?
SHHH! PAGLI PAGLI, KEEP YOUR VOICE DOWN.
SURE, YEAH, I'LL BE QUIET.
OK, WE'RE CLEAR. EVERYONE SHUT UP, AND WE MIGHT PULL THIS OFF.
SCREEEEEEECH
HOLY FLUFFY SPARKLE KITTENS, WHAT WAS THAT?!
THAT WAS SO LOUD, SOMEONE MUST HAVE HEARD. THIS WAS MY FIRST DETENTION--
--AND NOW I'M PRACTICALLY A FULL TIME DELINQUENT!
NEW SNEAKERS ON A FRESH WAXED FLOOR, YA NERVOUS LIL BUNNIES!
SQEEEEAAK
SQEEAAAK
SQEEEEAK
SHUT. UP. YOU GUYS.
I WASN'T REALLY FREAKED OUT. I WAS JUST PRETENDING, TO BE FUNNY...

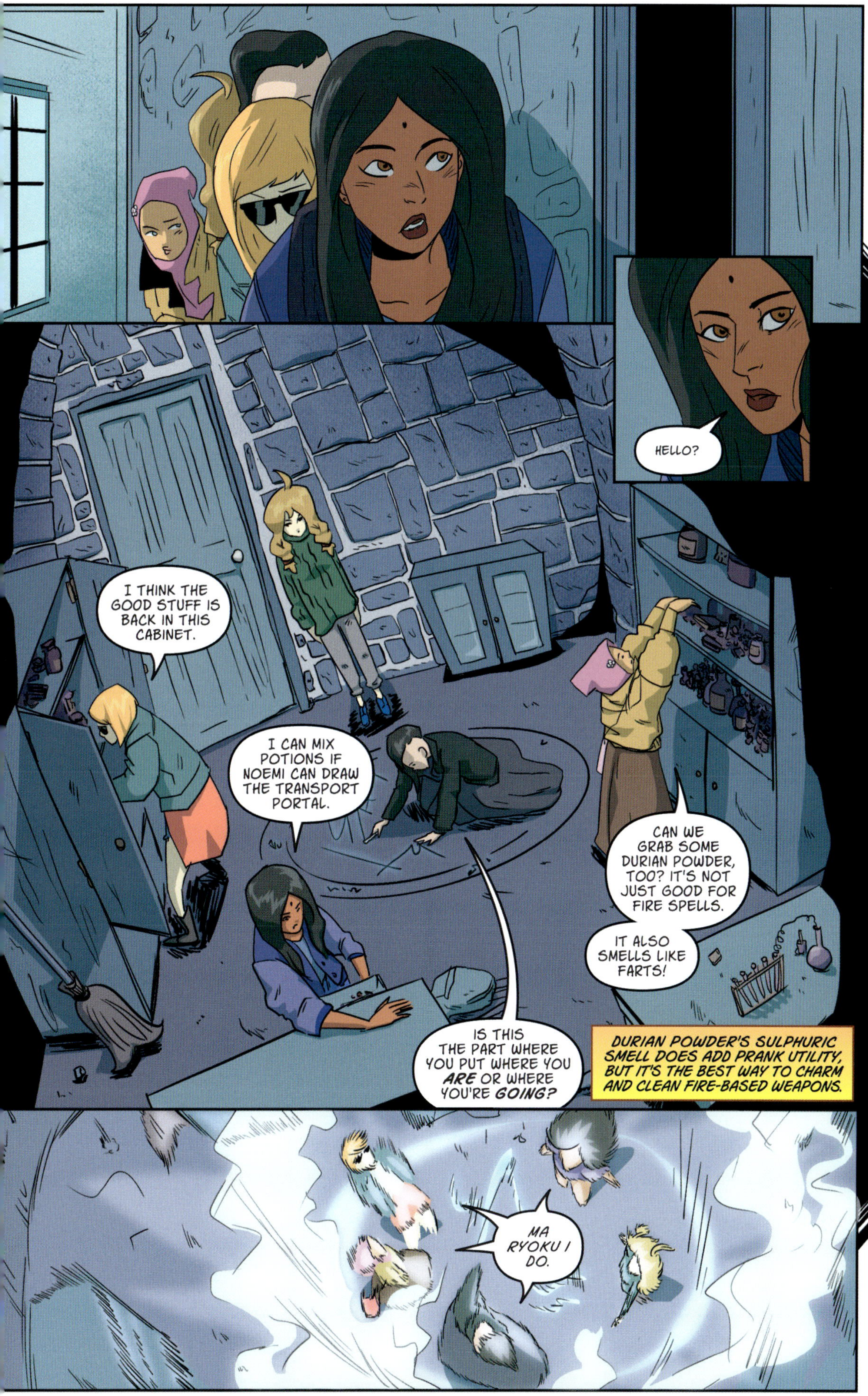
HELLO?
I THINK THE GOOD STUFF IS BACK IN THIS CABINET.
I CAN MIX POTIONS IF NOEMI CAN DRAW THE TRANSPORT PORTAL.
CAN WE GRAB SOME DURIAN POWDER, TOO? IT'S NOT JUST GOOD FOR FIRE SPELLS.
IT ALSO SMELLS LIKE FARTS!
IS THIS THE PART WHERE YOU PUT WHERE YOU ARE OR WHERE YOU'RE GOING?
DURIAN POWDER'S SULPHURIC SMELL DOES ADD PRANK UTILITY, BUT IT'S THE BEST WAY TO CHARM AND CLEAN FIRE-BASED WEAPONS.
MA RYOKU I DO.

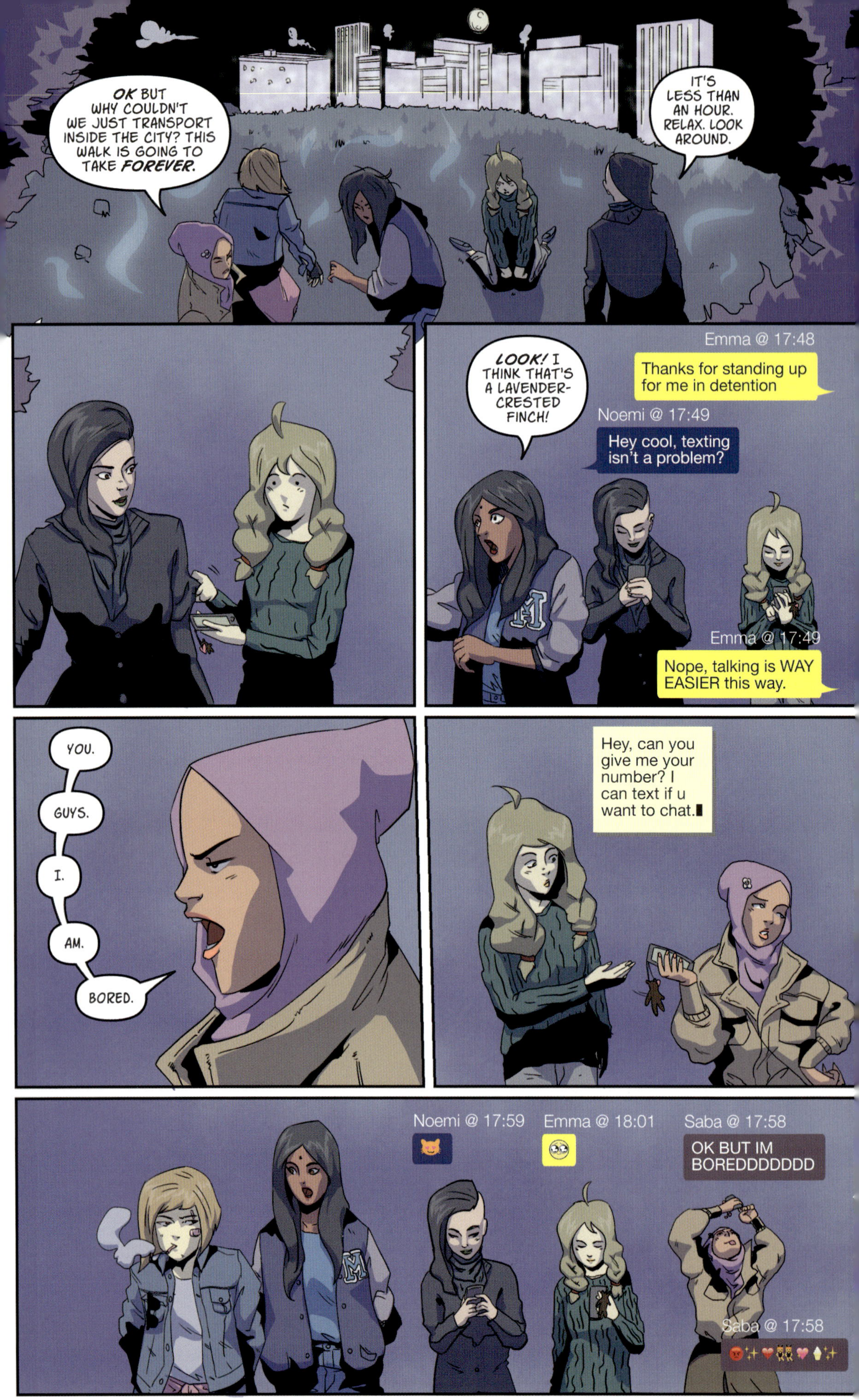

OK BUT WHY COULDN'T WE JUST TRANSPORT INSIDE THE CITY? THIS WALK IS GOING TO TAKE FOREVER.
IT'S LESS THAN AN HOUR. RELAX. LOOK AROUND.
LOOK! I THINK THAT'S A LAVENDER-CRESTED FINCH!
Emma @ 17:48
Thanks for standing up for me in detention
Noemi @ 17:49
Hey cool, texting isn't a problem?
Emma @ 17:49
Nope, talking is WAY EASIER this way.
YOU.
GUYS.
I.
AM.
BORED.
Hey, can you give me your number? I can text if u want to chat.
Noemi @ 17:59
Emma @ 18:01
Saba @ 17:58
OK BUT IM BOREDDDDDDDD
Saba @ 17:58

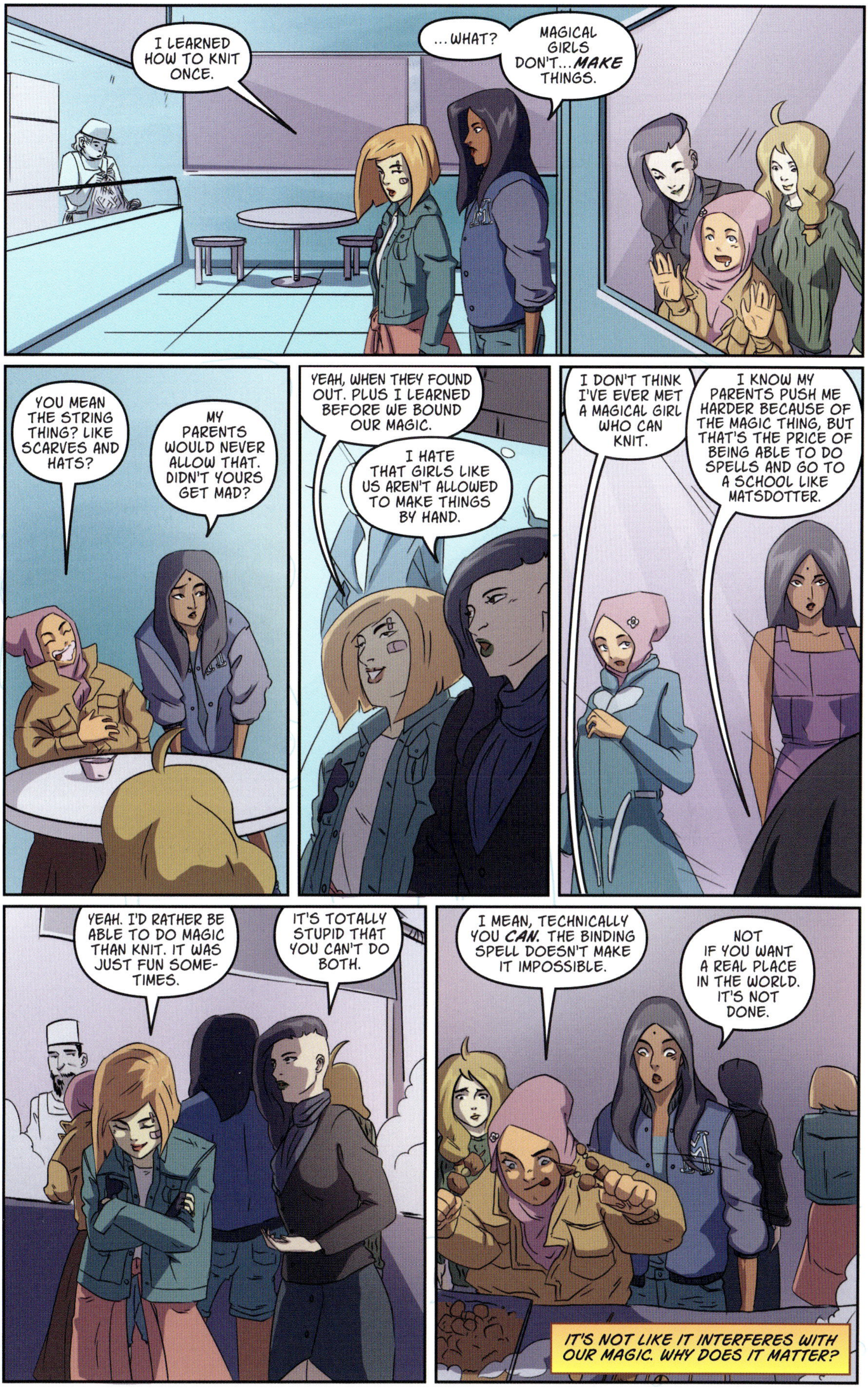
I LEARNED HOW TO KNIT ONCE.
...WHAT?
MAGICAL GIRLS DON'T...MAKE THINGS.
YOU MEAN THE STRING THING? LIKE SCARVES AND HATS?
MY PARENTS WOULD NEVER ALLOW THAT. DIDN'T YOURS GET MAD?
YEAH, WHEN THEY FOUND OUT. PLUS I LEARNED BEFORE WE BOUND OUR MAGIC.
I HATE THAT GIRLS LIKE US AREN'T ALLOWED TO MAKE THINGS BY HAND.
I DON'T THINK I'VE EVER MET A MAGICAL GIRL WHO CAN KNIT.
I KNOW MY PARENTS PUSH ME HARDER BECAUSE OF THE MAGIC THING, BUT THAT'S THE PRICE OF BEING ABLE TO DO SPELLS AND GO TO A SCHOOL LIKE MATSDOTTER.
YEAH. I'D RATHER BE ABLE TO DO MAGIC THAN KNIT. IT WAS JUST FUN SOMETIMES.
IT'S TOTALLY STUPID THAT YOU CAN'T DO BOTH.
I MEAN, TECHNICALLY YOU CAN. THE BINDING SPELL DOESN'T MAKE IT IMPOSSIBLE.
NOT IF YOU WANT A REAL PLACE IN THE WORLD. IT'S NOT DONE.
IT'S NOT LIKE IT INTERFERES WITH OUR MAGIC. WHY DOES IT MATTER?

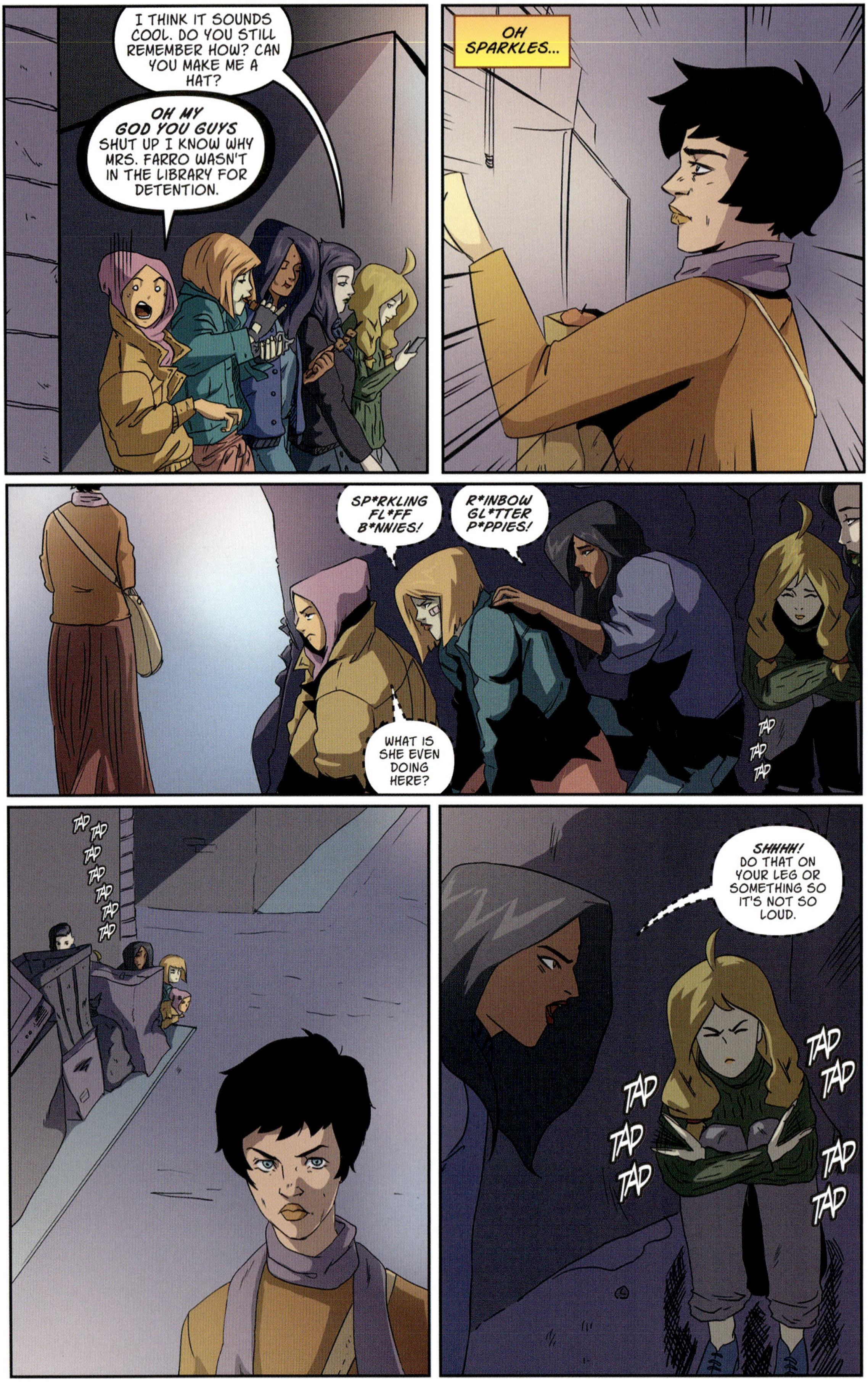

I THINK IT SOUNDS COOL. DO YOU STILL REMEMBER HOW? CAN YOU MAKE ME A HAT?
OH MY GOD YOU GUYS SHUT UP I KNOW WHY MRS. FARRO WASN'T IN THE LIBRARY FOR DETENTION.
OH SPARKLES...
SP*RKLING FL*FF B*NNIES!
R*INBOW GL*TTER P*PPIES!
WHAT IS SHE EVEN DOING HERE?
TAP TAP TAP
TAP TAP TAP TAP TAP TAP TAP
SHHHH! DO THAT ON YOUR LEG OR SOMETHING SO IT'S NOT SO LOUD.
TAP TAP TAP
TAP TAP
TAP TAP

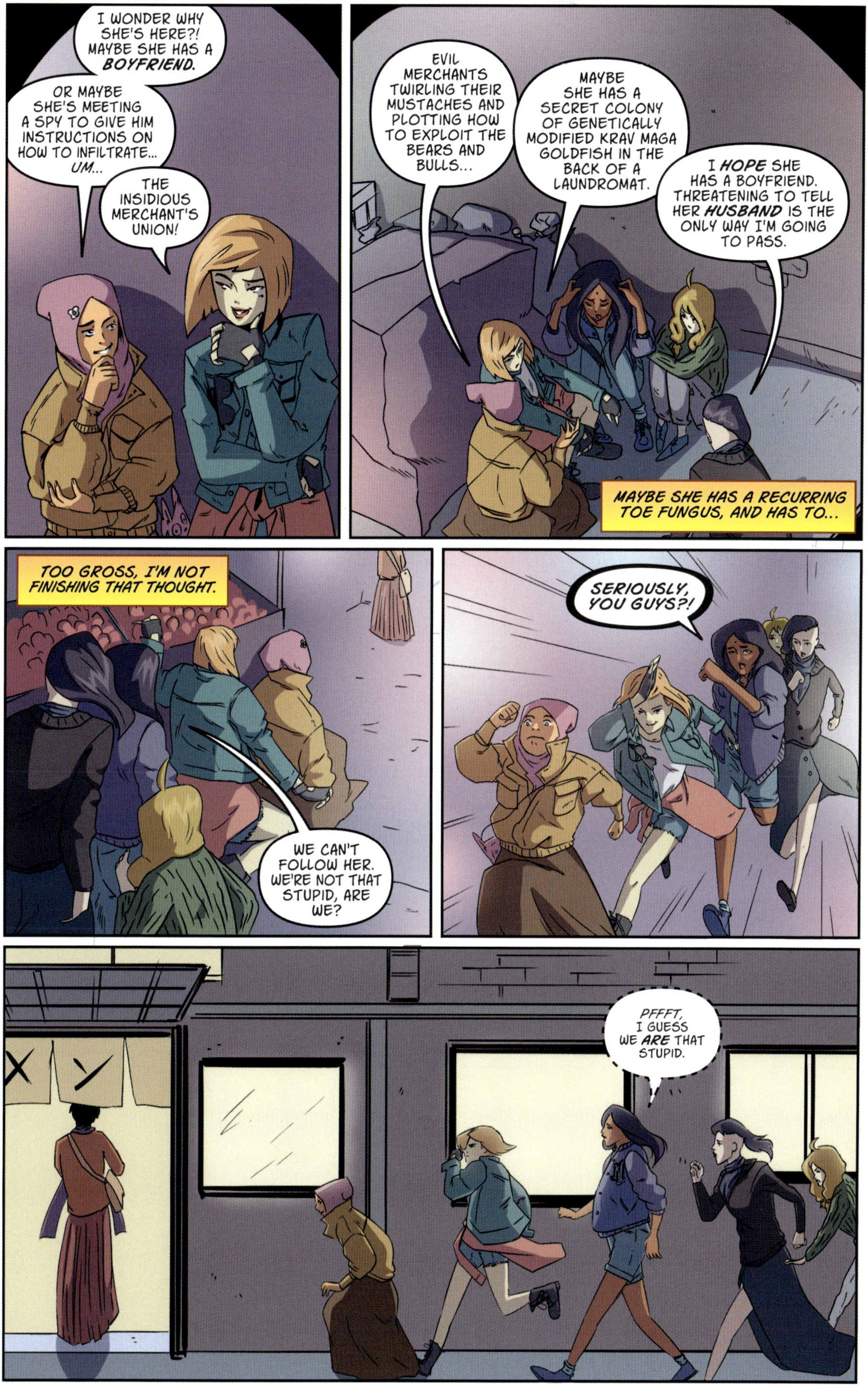
I WONDER WHY SHE'S HERE?! MAYBE SHE HAS A BOYFRIEND.
OR MAYBE SHE'S MEETING A SPY TO GIVE HIM INSTRUCTIONS ON HOW TO INFILTRATE... UM...
THE INSIDIOUS MERCHANT'S UNION!
EVIL MERCHANTS TWIRLING THEIR MUSTACHES AND PLOTTING HOW TO EXPLOIT THE BEARS AND BULLS...
MAYBE SHE HAS A SECRET COLONY OF GENETICALLY MODIFIED KRAV MAGA GOLDFISH IN THE BACK OF A LAUNDROMAT.
I HOPE SHE HAS A BOYFRIEND. THREATENING TO TELL HER HUSBAND IS THE ONLY WAY I'M GOING TO PASS.
MAYBE SHE HAS A RECURRING TOE FUNGUS, AND HAS TO...
TOO GROSS, I'M NOT FINISHING THAT THOUGHT.
WE CAN'T FOLLOW HER. WE'RE NOT THAT STUPID, ARE WE?
SERIOUSLY, YOU GUYS?!
PFFFT, I GUESS WE ARE THAT STUPID.

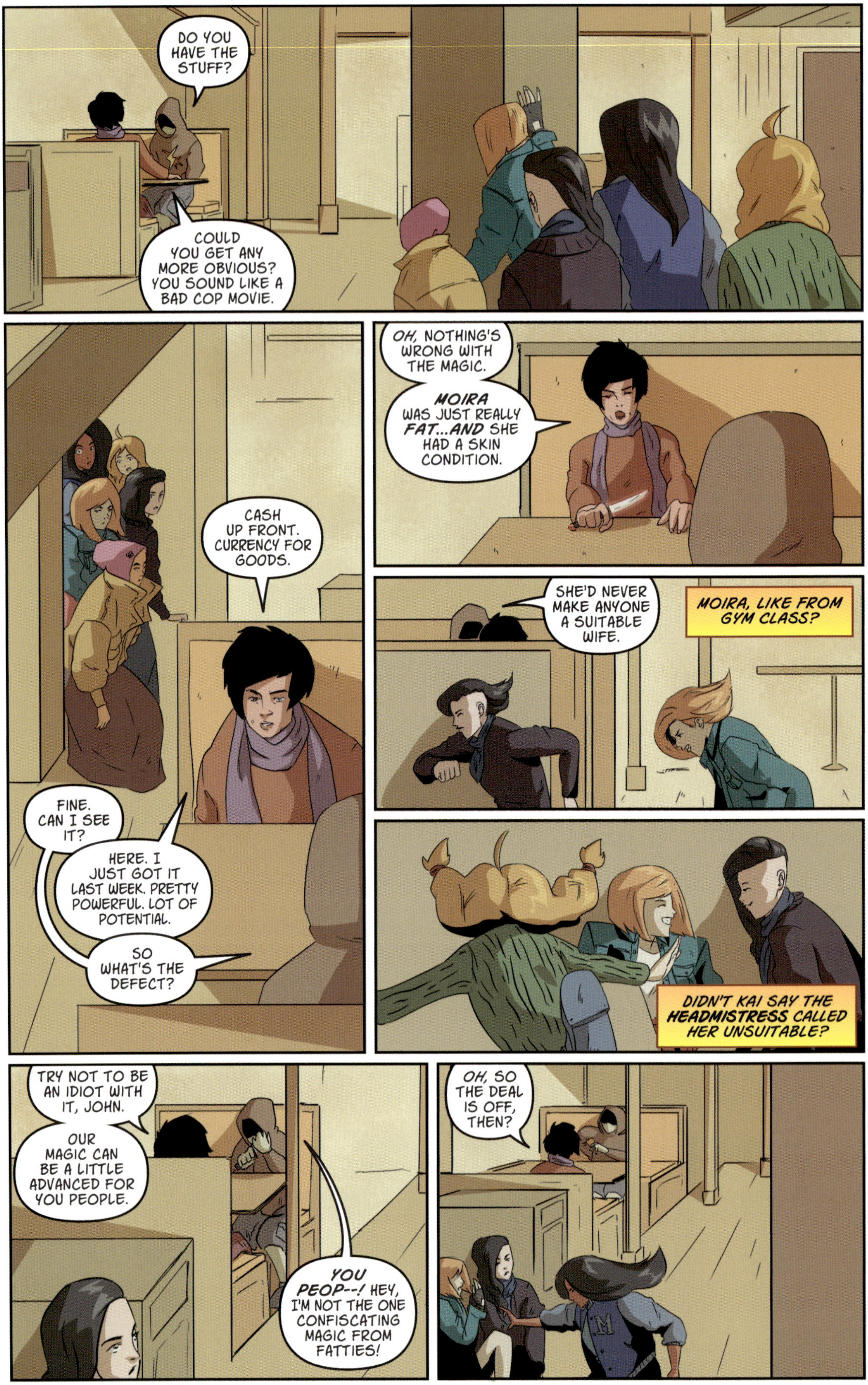
DO YOU HAVE THE STUFF?
COULD YOU GET ANY MORE OBVIOUS? YOU SOUND LIKE A BAD COP MOVIE.
CASH UP FRONT. CURRENCY FOR GOODS.
FINE. CAN I SEE IT?
HERE. I JUST GOT IT LAST WEEK. PRETTY POWERFUL. LOT OF POTENTIAL.
SO WHAT'S THE DEFECT?
OH, NOTHING'S WRONG WITH THE MAGIC.
MOIRA WAS JUST REALLY FAT...AND SHE HAD A SKIN CONDITION.
SHE'D NEVER MAKE ANYONE A SUITABLE WIFE.
MOIRA, LIKE FROM GYM CLASS?
DIDN'T KAI SAY THE HEADMISTRESS CALLED HER UNSUITABLE?
TRY NOT TO BE AN IDIOT WITH IT, JOHN.
OUR MAGIC CAN BE A LITTLE ADVANCED FOR YOU PEOPLE.
YOU PEOP--! HEY, I'M NOT THE ONE CONFISCATING MAGIC FROM FATTIES!
OH, SO THE DEAL IS OFF, THEN?

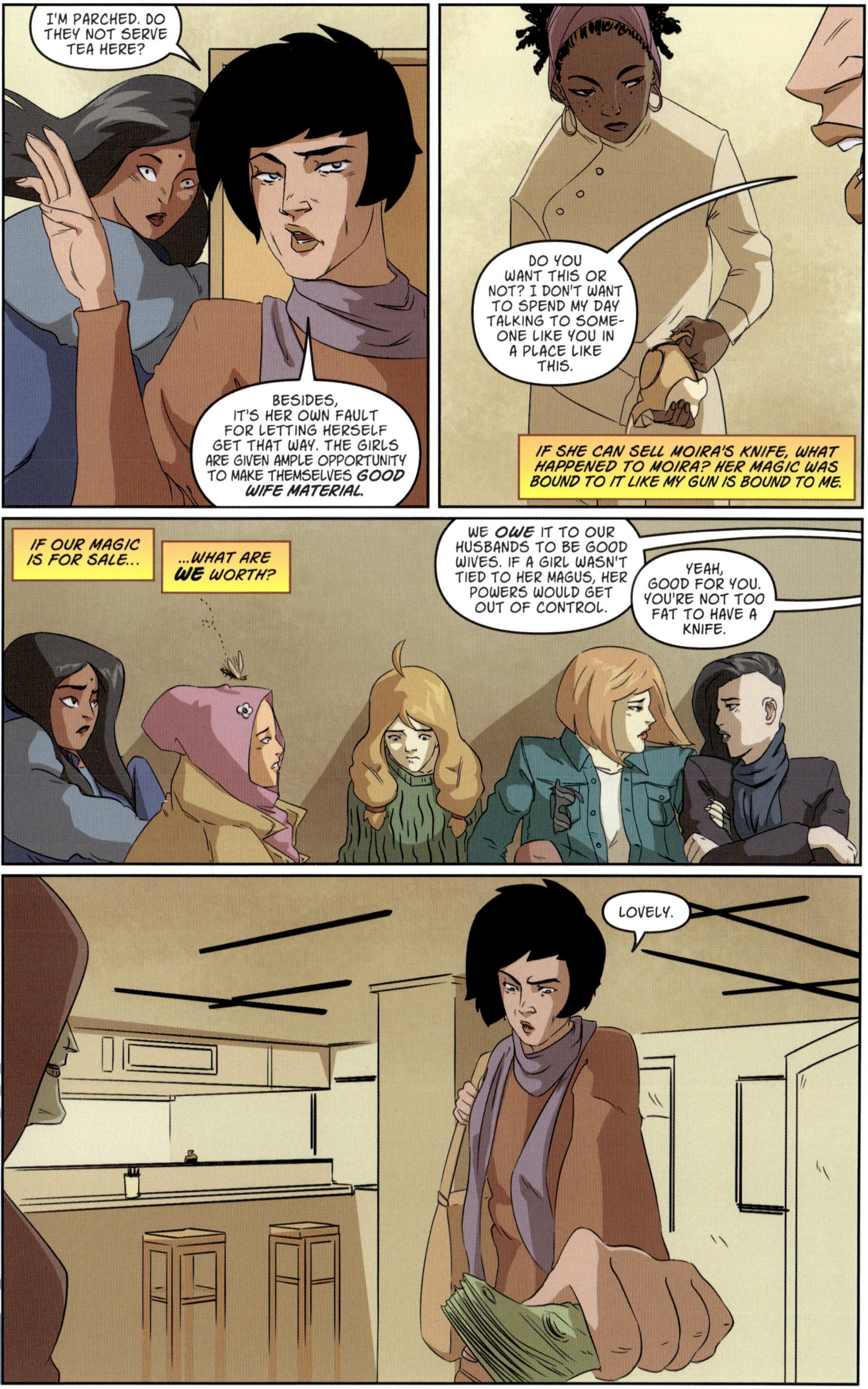
I'M PARCHED. DO THEY NOT SERVE TEA HERE?
BESIDES, IT'S HER OWN FAULT FOR LETTING HERSELF GET THAT WAY. THE GIRLS ARE GIVEN AMPLE OPPORTUNITY TO MAKE THEMSELVES GOOD WIFE MATERIAL.
DO YOU WANT THIS OR NOT? I DON'T WANT TO SPEND MY DAY TALKING TO SOME-ONE LIKE YOU IN A PLACE LIKE THIS.
IF SHE CAN SELL MOIRA'S KNIFE, WHAT HAPPENED TO MOIRA? HER MAGIC WAS BOUND TO IT LIKE MY GUN IS BOUND TO ME.
IF OUR MAGIC IS FOR SALE...
...WHAT ARE WE WORTH?
WE OWE IT TO OUR HUSBANDS TO BE GOOD WIVES. IF A GIRL WASN'T TIED TO HER MAGUS, HER POWERS WOULD GET OUT OF CONTROL.
YEAH, GOOD FOR YOU. YOU'RE NOT TOO FAT TO HAVE A KNIFE.
LOVELY.

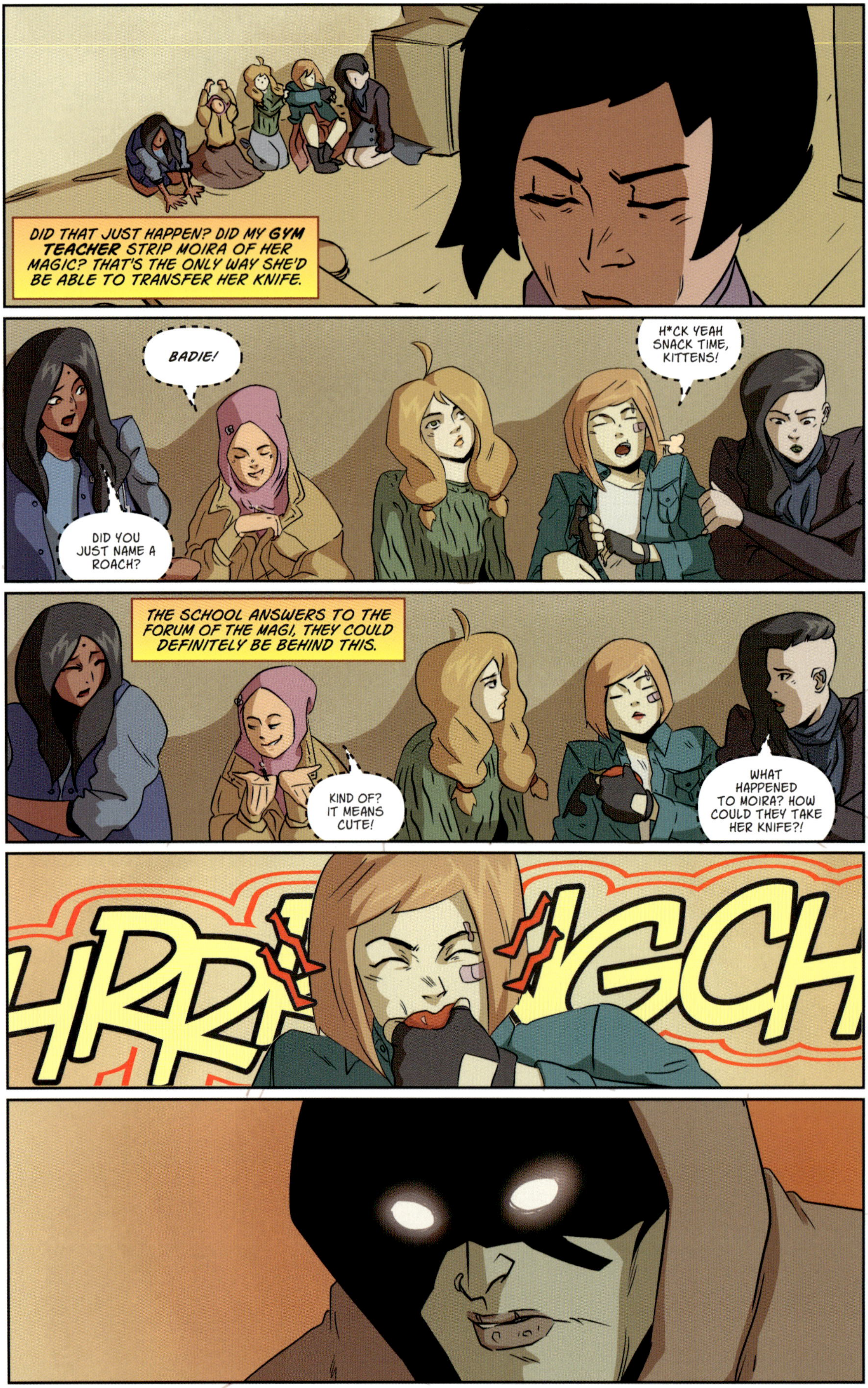
DID THAT JUST HAPPEN? DID MY GYM TEACHER STRIP MOIRA OF HER MAGIC? THAT'S THE ONLY WAY SHE'D BE ABLE TO TRANSFER HER KNIFE.
BADIE!
H*CK YEAH SNACK TIME, KITTENS!
DID YOU JUST NAME A ROACH?
THE SCHOOL ANSWERS TO THE FORUM OF THE MAGI, THEY COULD DEFINITELY BE BEHIND THIS.
KIND OF? IT MEANS CUTE!
WHAT HAPPENED TO MOIRA? HOW COULD THEY TAKE HER KNIFE?!

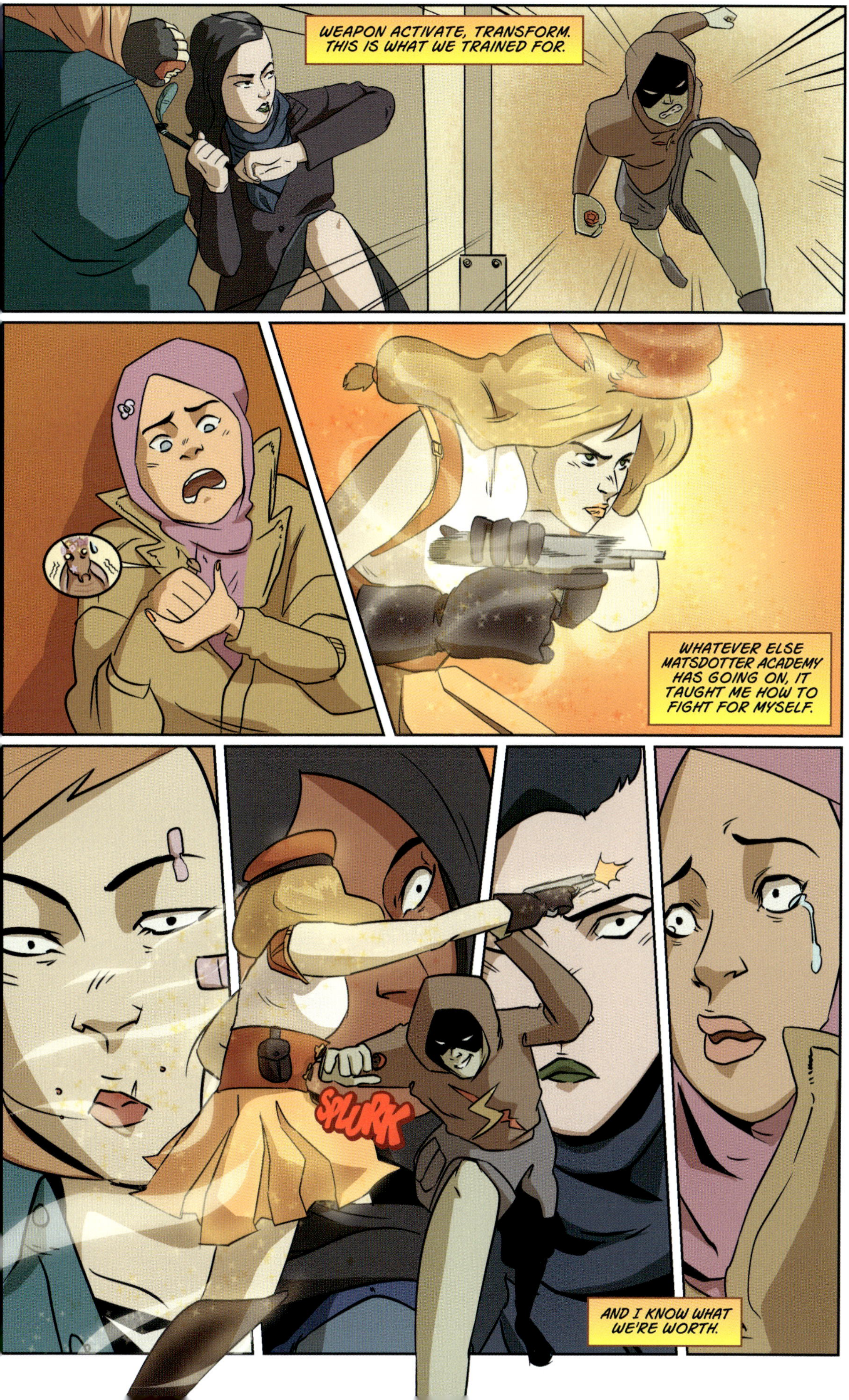
WEAPON ACTIVATE, TRANSFORM. THIS IS WHAT WE TRAINED FOR.
WHATEVER ELSE MATSDOTTER ACADEMY HAS GOING ON, IT TAUGHT ME HOW TO FIGHT FOR MYSELF.
SPLURK
AND I KNOW WHAT WE'RE WORTH.

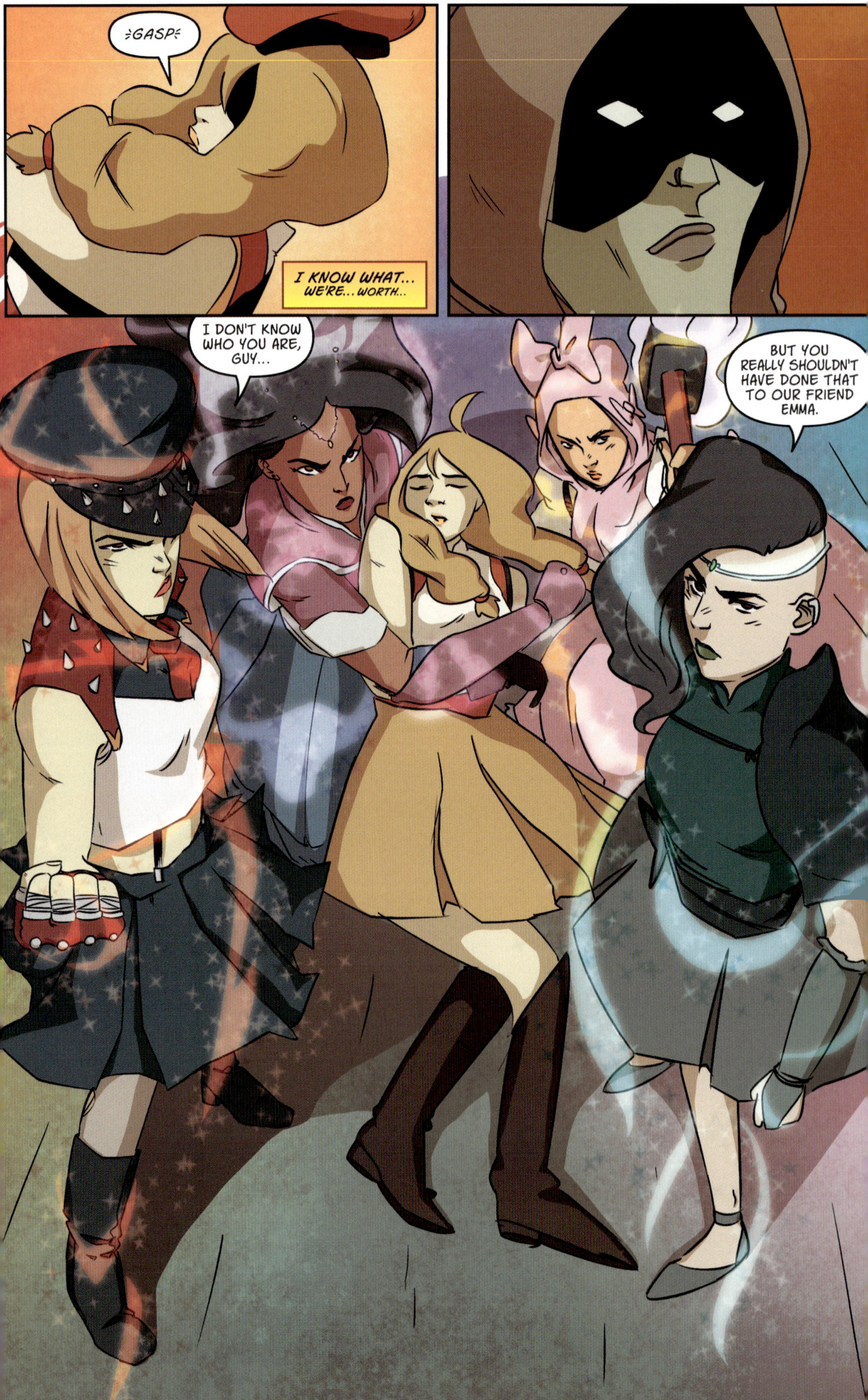

GASP
I KNOW WHAT... WE'RE... WORTH...
I DON'T KNOW WHO YOU ARE, GUY...
BUT YOU REALLY SHOULDN'T HAVE DONE THAT TO OUR FRIEND EMMA.

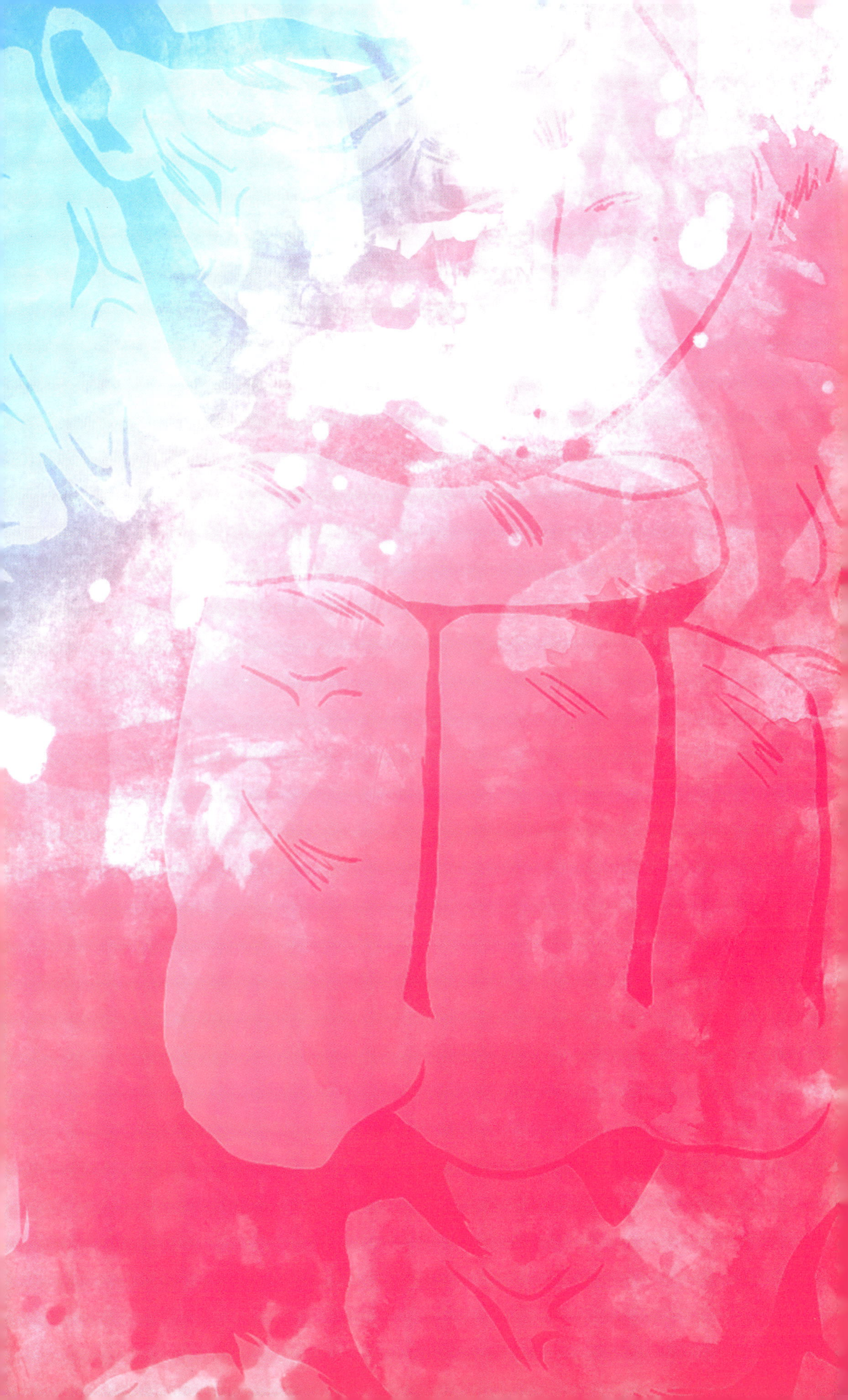

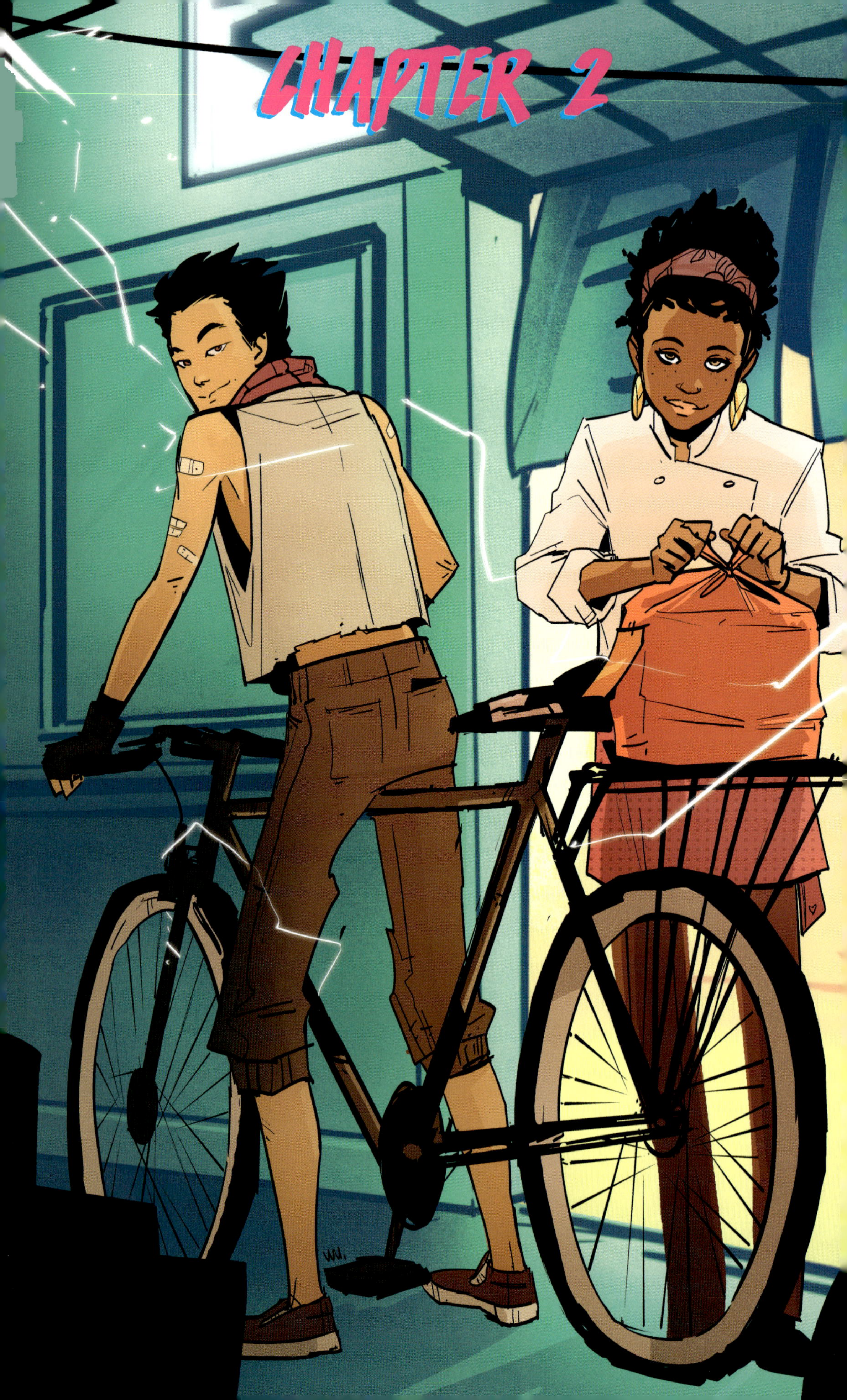
CHAPTER 2

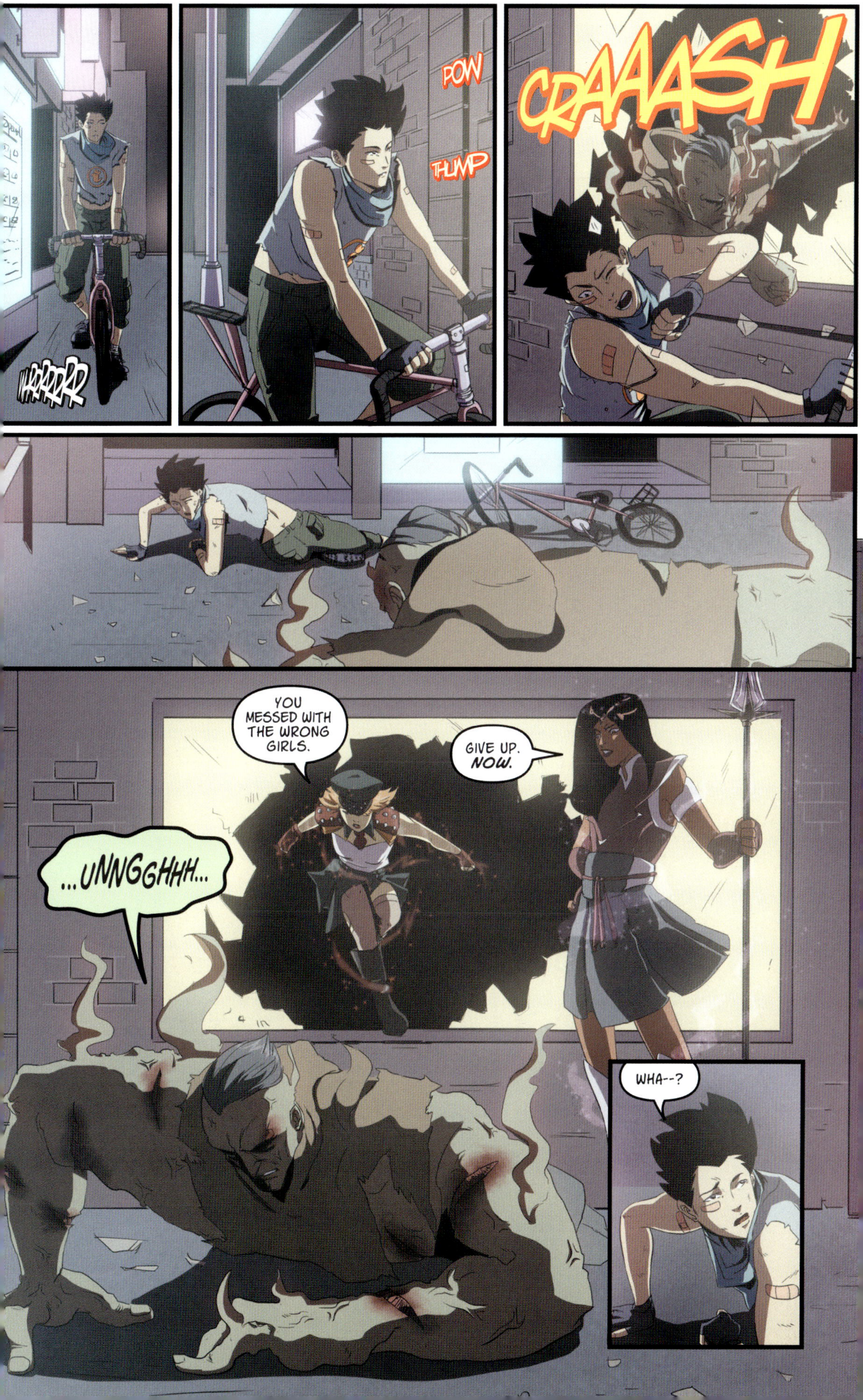
WHRRRRR
POW
THUMP
CRAAASH
YOU MESSED WITH THE WRONG GIRLS.
GIVE UP. NOW.
...UNNGGHHH...
WHA--?

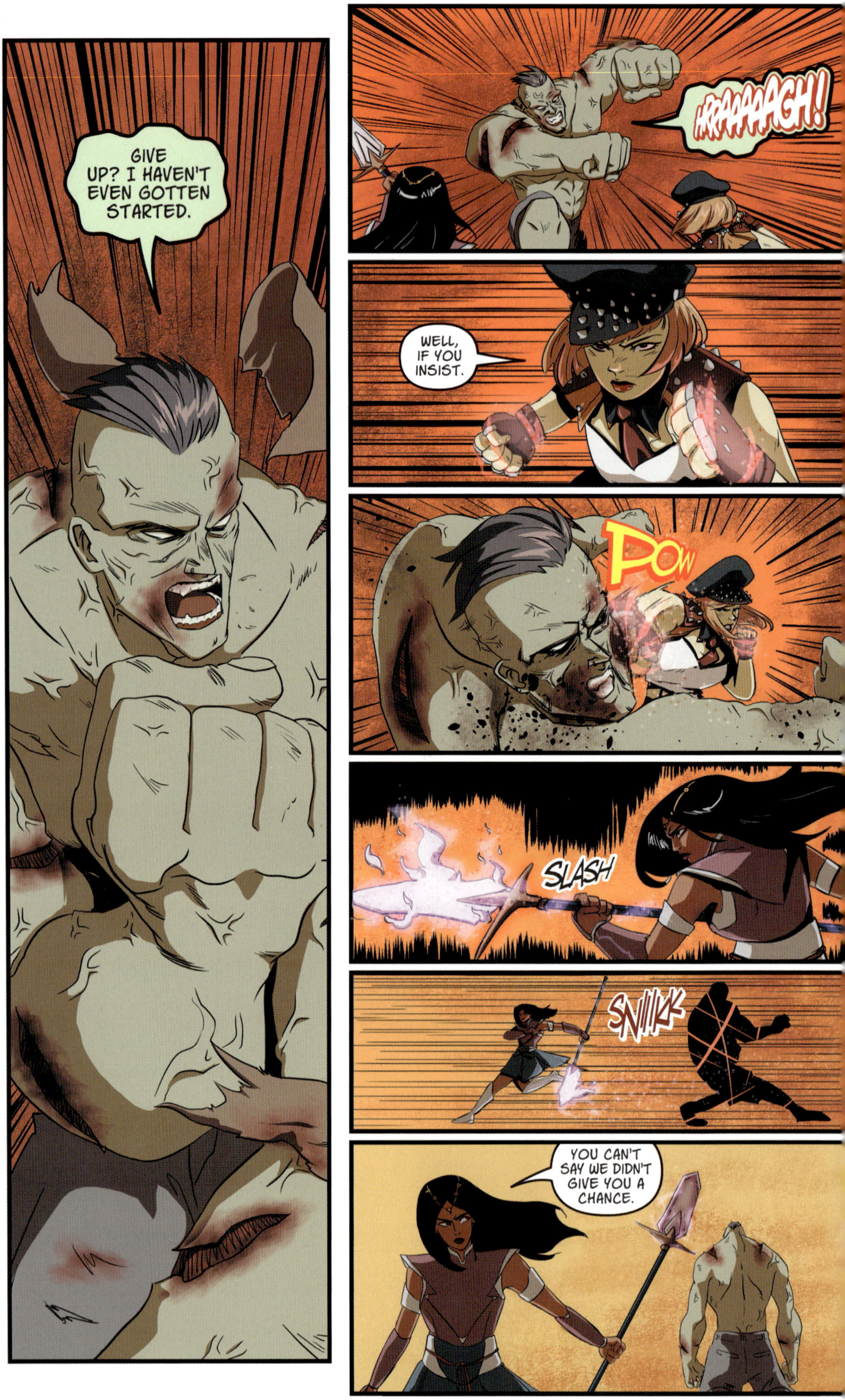
GIVE UP? I HAVEN'T EVEN GOTTEN STARTED.
HRRAAAAAGH!
WELL, IF YOU INSIST.
POW
SLASH
SNIIIKK
YOU CAN'T SAY WE DIDN'T GIVE YOU A CHANCE.

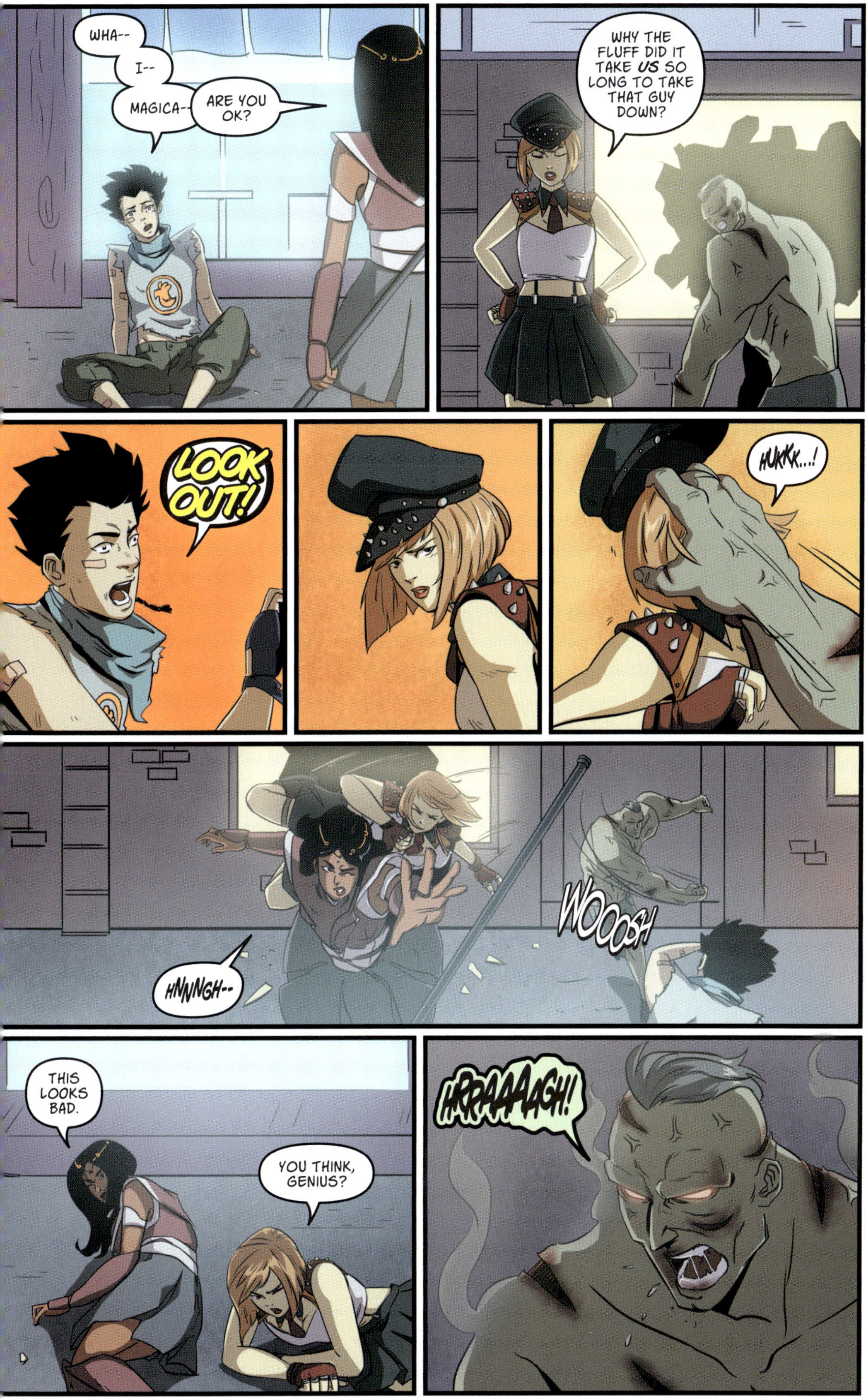
WHA--
I--
MAGICA--
ARE YOU OK?
WHY THE FLUFF DID IT TAKE US SO LONG TO TAKE THAT GUY DOWN?
LOOK OUT!
HUKKK...!
WOOOSH
HNNNGH--
THIS LOOKS BAD.
YOU THINK, GENIUS?
HRRAAAAGH!

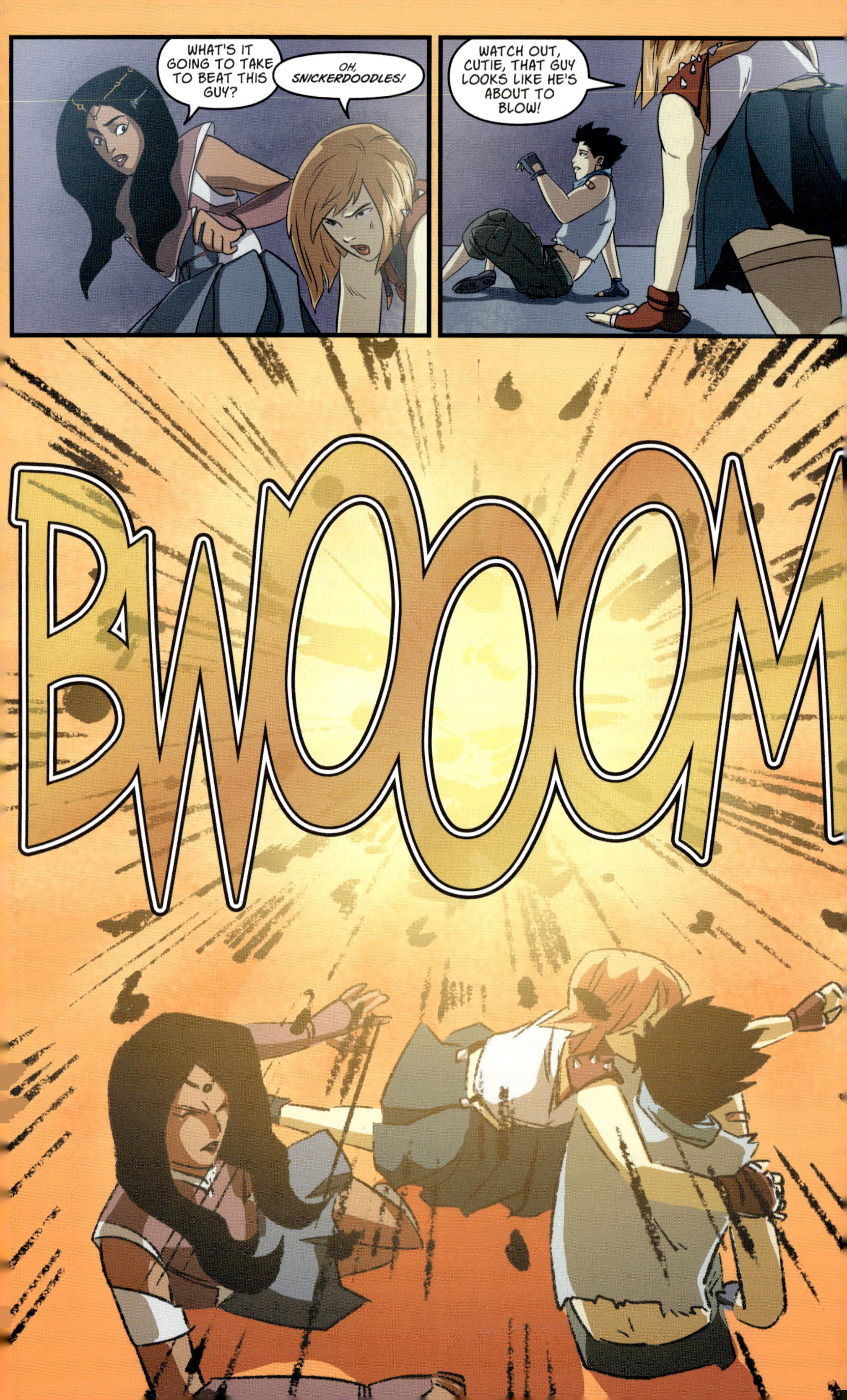
WHAT'S IT GOING TO TAKE TO BEAT THIS GUY?
OH, SNICKERDOODLES!
WATCH OUT, CUTIE, THAT GUY LOOKS LIKE HE'S ABOUT TO BLOW!
BWOOOM

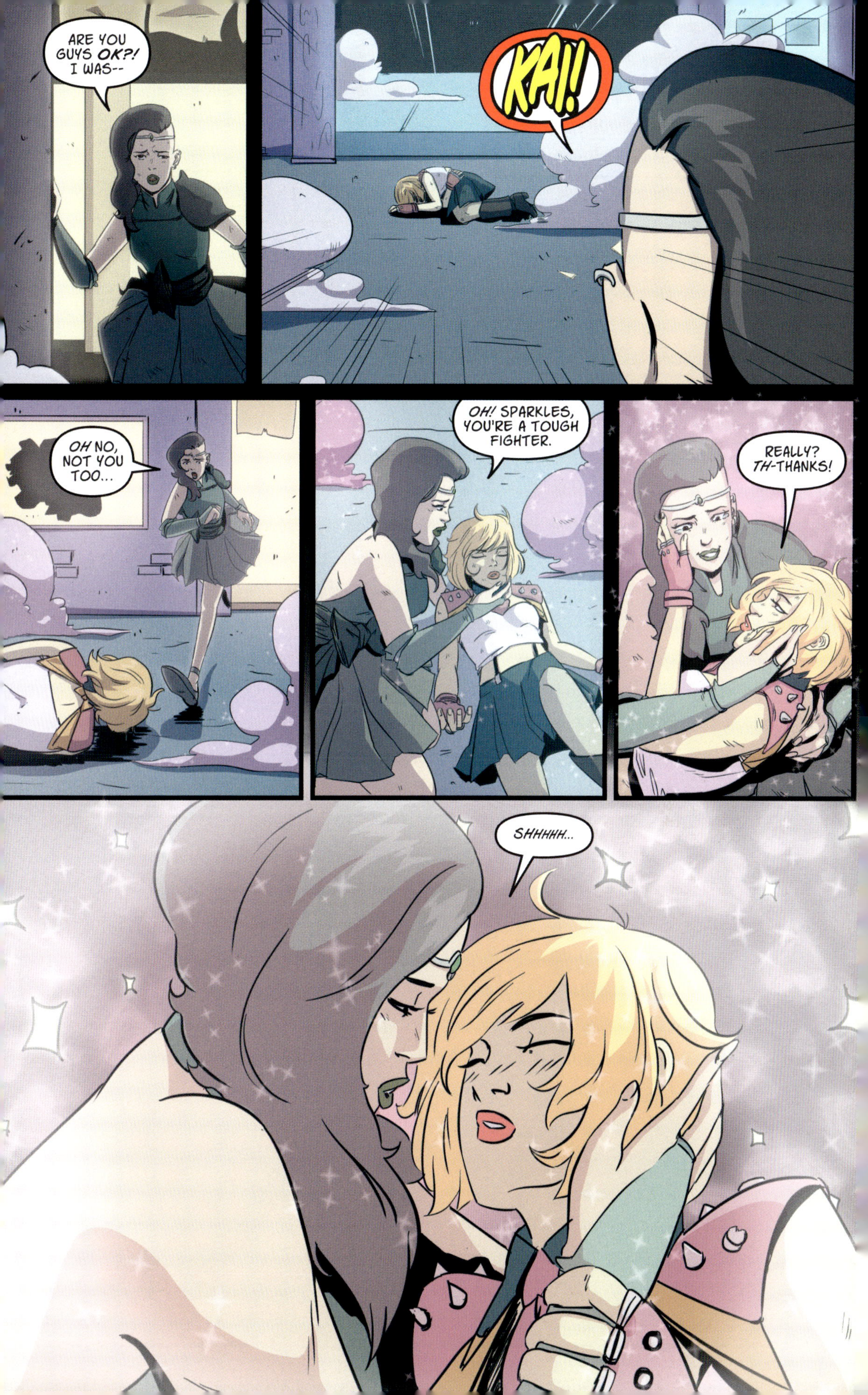
ARE YOU GUYS OK?! I WAS--
KAI!
OH NO, NOT YOU TOO...
OH! SPARKLES, YOU'RE A TOUGH FIGHTER.
REALLY? TH-THANKS!
SHHHHH...

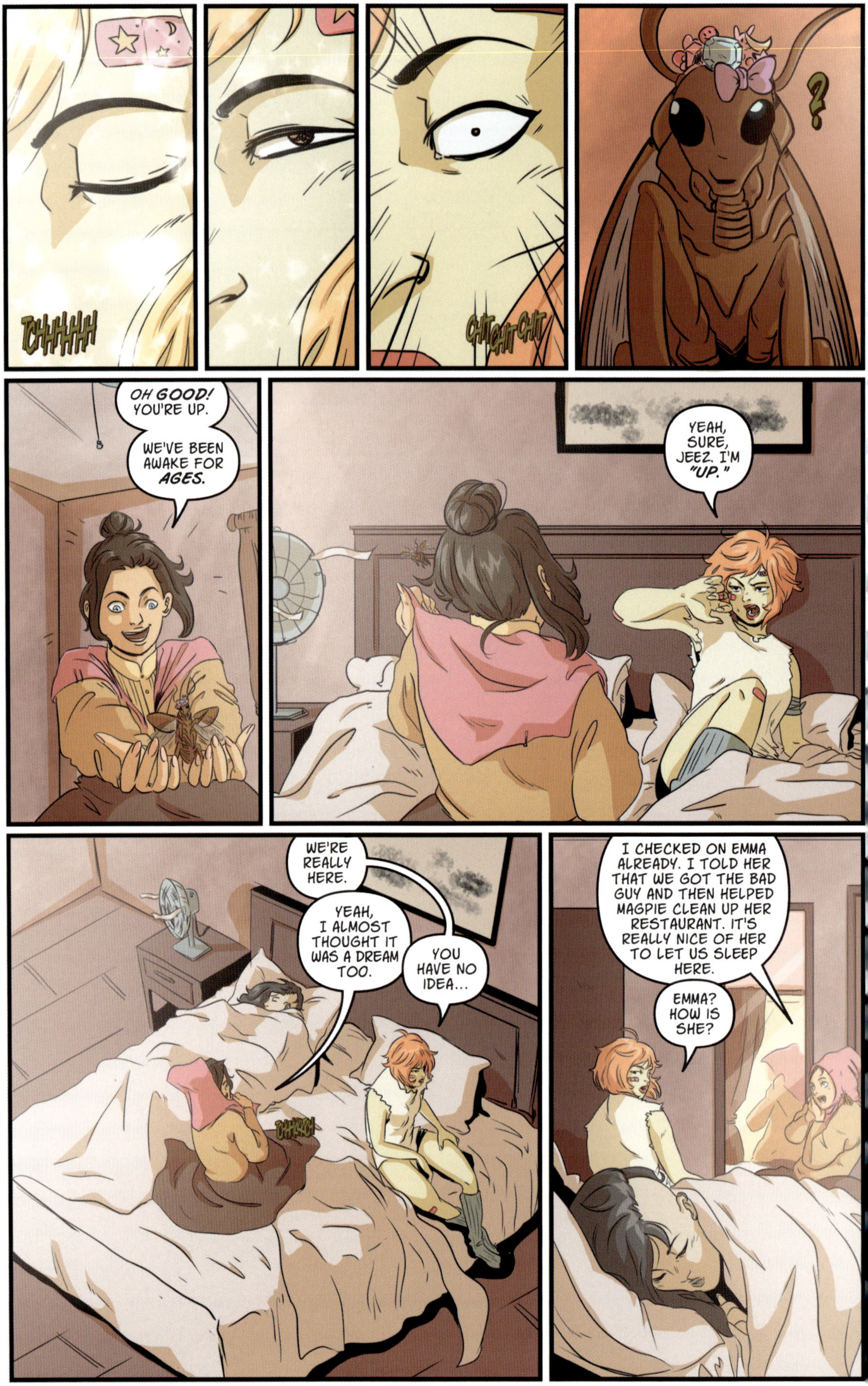
TCHHHHHH
CHIT CHIT CHIT
?
OH GOOD! YOU'RE UP.
WE'VE BEEN AWAKE FOR AGES.
YEAH, SURE, JEEZ. I'M "UP."
WE'RE REALLY HERE.
YEAH, I ALMOST THOUGHT IT WAS A DREAM TOO.
YOU HAVE NO IDEA...
I CHECKED ON EMMA ALREADY. I TOLD HER THAT WE GOT THE BAD GUY AND THEN HELPED MAGPIE CLEAN UP HER RESTAURANT. IT'S REALLY NICE OF HER TO LET US SLEEP HERE.
EMMA? HOW IS SHE?

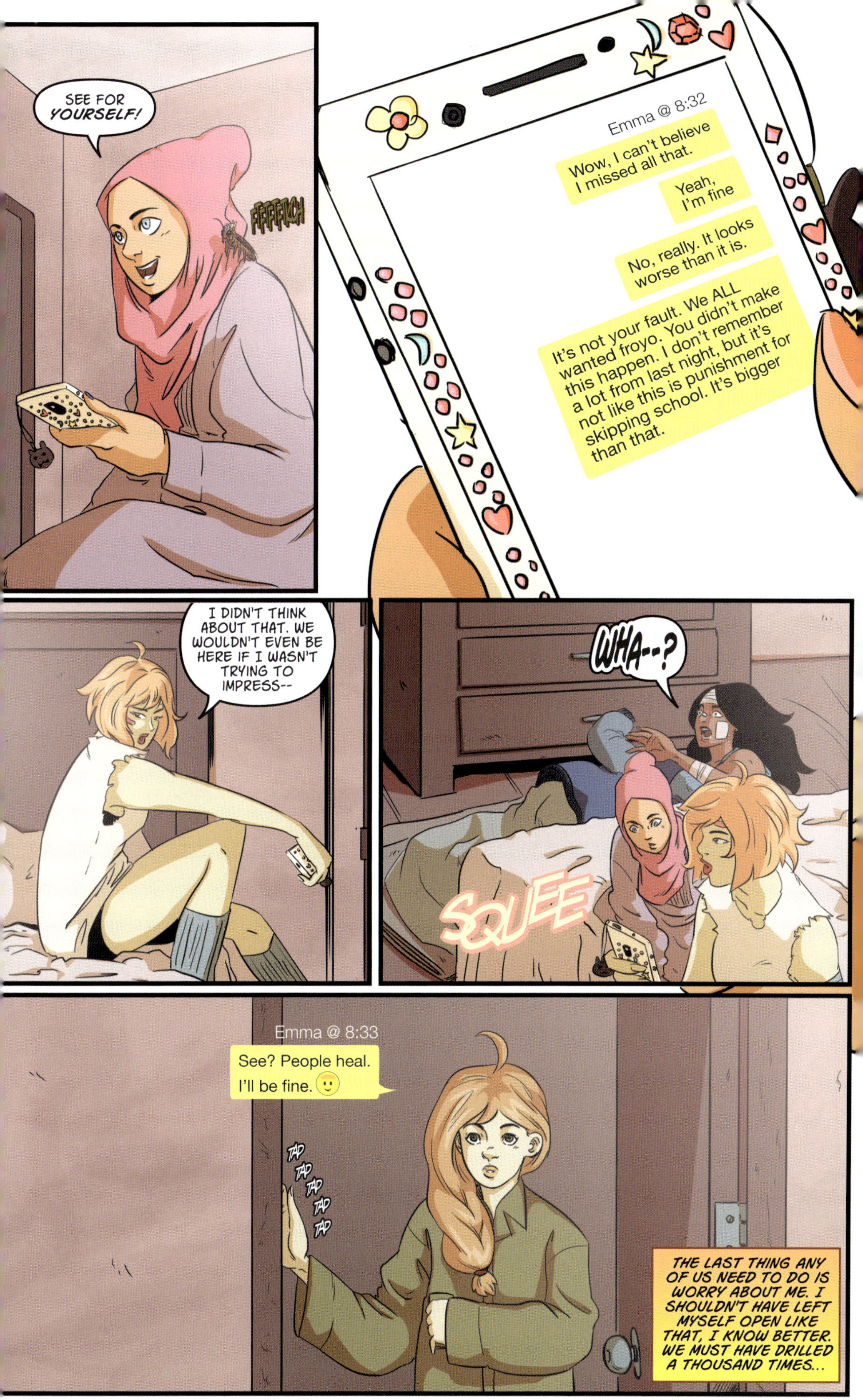
SEE FOR YOURSELF!
FFFFFTCH
Emma @ 8:32
Wow, I can't believe I missed all that.
Yeah, I'm fine
No, really. It looks worse than it is.
It's not your fault. We ALL wanted froyo. You didn't make this happen. I don't remember a lot from last night, but it's not like this is punishment for skipping school. It's bigger than that.
I DIDN'T THINK ABOUT THAT. WE WOULDN'T EVEN BE HERE IF I WASN'T TRYING TO IMPRESS--
WHA--?
SQUEE
Emma @ 8:33
See? People heal. I'll be fine. 🙂
TAP
TAP
TAP
TAP
TAP
THE LAST THING ANY OF US NEED TO DO IS WORRY ABOUT ME. I SHOULDN'T HAVE LEFT MYSELF OPEN LIKE THAT, I KNOW BETTER. WE MUST HAVE DRILLED A THOUSAND TIMES...

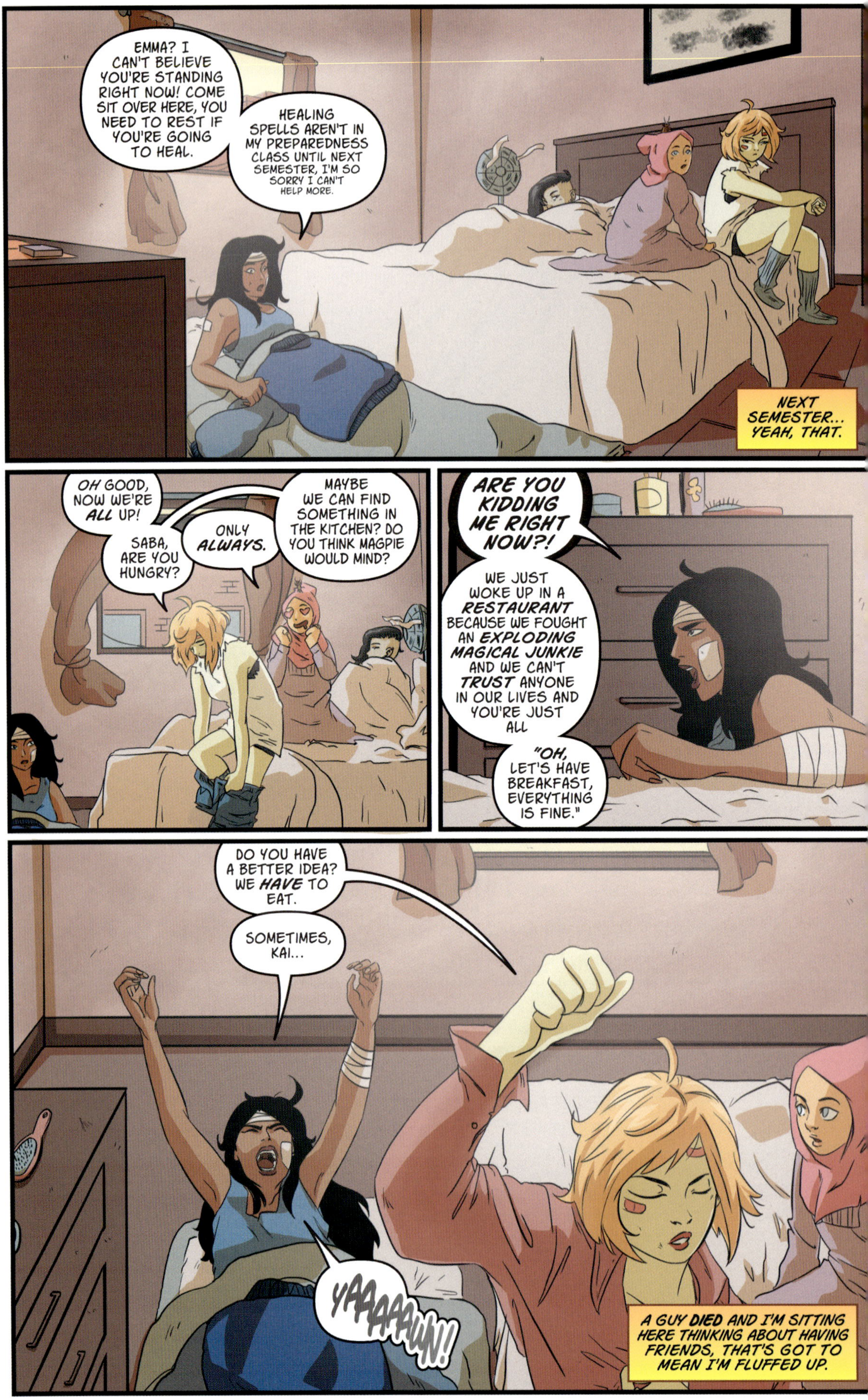
EMMA? I CAN'T BELIEVE YOU'RE STANDING RIGHT NOW! COME SIT OVER HERE, YOU NEED TO REST IF YOU'RE GOING TO HEAL.
HEALING SPELLS AREN'T IN MY PREPAREDNESS CLASS UNTIL NEXT SEMESTER, I'M SO SORRY I CAN'T HELP MORE.
NEXT SEMESTER... YEAH, THAT.
OH GOOD, NOW WE'RE ALL UP!
SABA, ARE YOU HUNGRY?
ONLY ALWAYS.
MAYBE WE CAN FIND SOMETHING IN THE KITCHEN? DO YOU THINK MAGPIE WOULD MIND?
ARE YOU KIDDING ME RIGHT NOW?!
WE JUST WOKE UP IN A RESTAURANT BECAUSE WE FOUGHT AN EXPLODING MAGICAL JUNKIE AND WE CAN'T TRUST ANYONE IN OUR LIVES AND YOU'RE JUST ALL
"OH, LET'S HAVE BREAKFAST, EVERYTHING IS FINE."
DO YOU HAVE A BETTER IDEA? WE HAVE TO EAT.
SOMETIMES, KAI...
YAAAAAAWN!
A GUY DIED AND I'M SITTING HERE THINKING ABOUT HAVING FRIENDS, THAT'S GOT TO MEAN I'M FLUFFED UP.

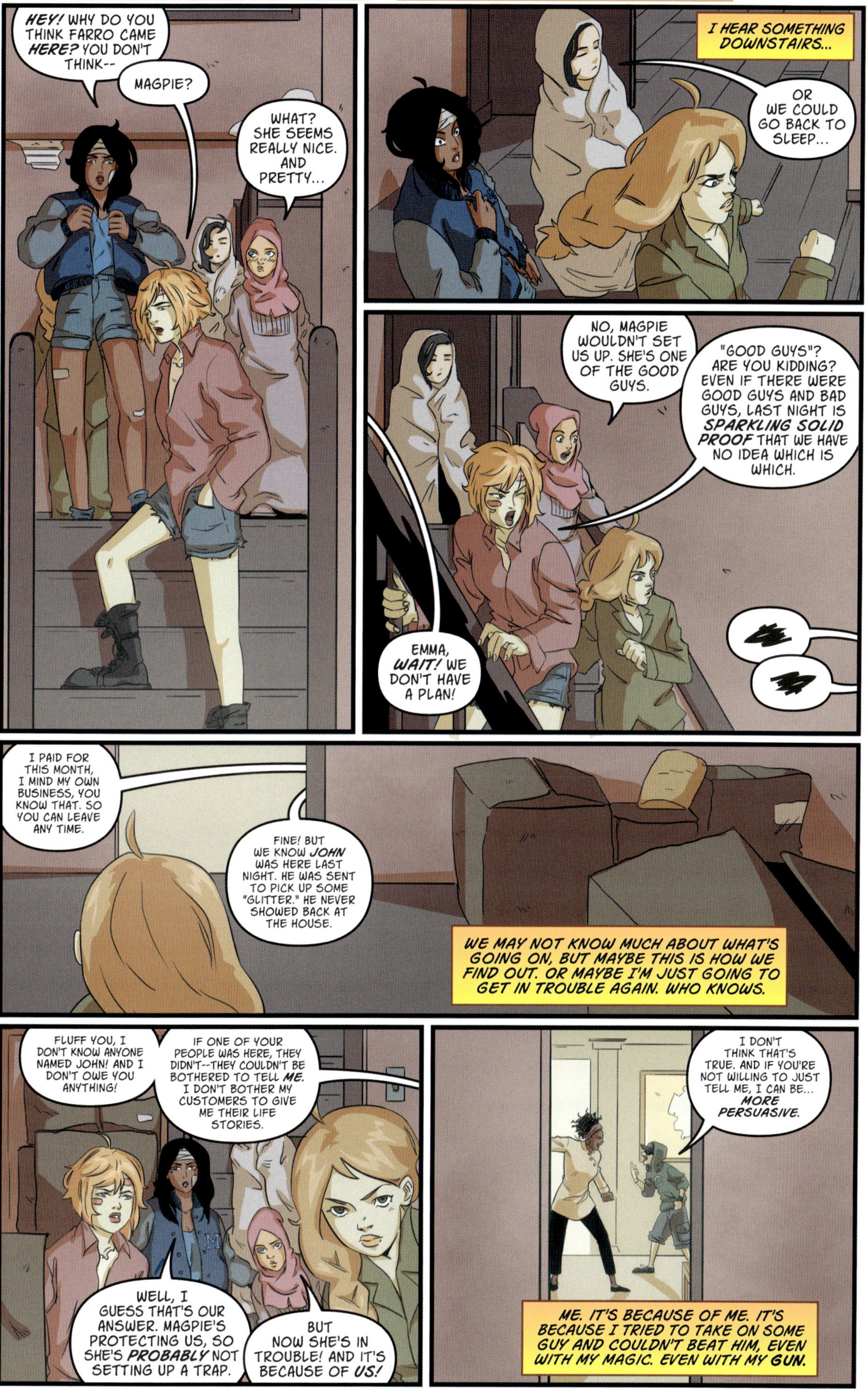

HEY! WHY DO YOU THINK FARRO CAME HERE? YOU DON'T THINK--
MAGPIE?
WHAT? SHE SEEMS REALLY NICE. AND PRETTY...
I HEAR SOMETHING DOWNSTAIRS...
OR WE COULD GO BACK TO SLEEP...
NO, MAGPIE WOULDN'T SET US UP. SHE'S ONE OF THE GOOD GUYS.
"GOOD GUYS"? ARE YOU KIDDING? EVEN IF THERE WERE GOOD GUYS AND BAD GUYS, LAST NIGHT IS SPARKLING SOLID PROOF THAT WE HAVE NO IDEA WHICH IS WHICH.
EMMA, WAIT! WE DON'T HAVE A PLAN!
I PAID FOR THIS MONTH, I MIND MY OWN BUSINESS, YOU KNOW THAT. SO YOU CAN LEAVE ANY TIME.
FINE! BUT WE KNOW JOHN WAS HERE LAST NIGHT. HE WAS SENT TO PICK UP SOME "GLITTER." HE NEVER SHOWED BACK AT THE HOUSE.
WE MAY NOT KNOW MUCH ABOUT WHAT'S GOING ON, BUT MAYBE THIS IS HOW WE FIND OUT. OR MAYBE I'M JUST GOING TO GET IN TROUBLE AGAIN. WHO KNOWS.
FLUFF YOU, I DON'T KNOW ANYONE NAMED JOHN! AND I DON'T OWE YOU ANYTHING!
IF ONE OF YOUR PEOPLE WAS HERE, THEY DIDN'T--THEY COULDN'T BE BOTHERED TO TELL ME. I DON'T BOTHER MY CUSTOMERS TO GIVE ME THEIR LIFE STORIES.
WELL, I GUESS THAT'S OUR ANSWER. MAGPIE'S PROTECTING US, SO SHE'S PROBABLY NOT SETTING UP A TRAP.
BUT NOW SHE'S IN TROUBLE! AND IT'S BECAUSE OF US!
I DON'T THINK THAT'S TRUE. AND IF YOU'RE NOT WILLING TO JUST TELL ME, I CAN BE... MORE PERSUASIVE.
ME. IT'S BECAUSE OF ME. IT'S BECAUSE I TRIED TO TAKE ON SOME GUY AND COULDN'T BEAT HIM, EVEN WITH MY MAGIC. EVEN WITH MY GUN.

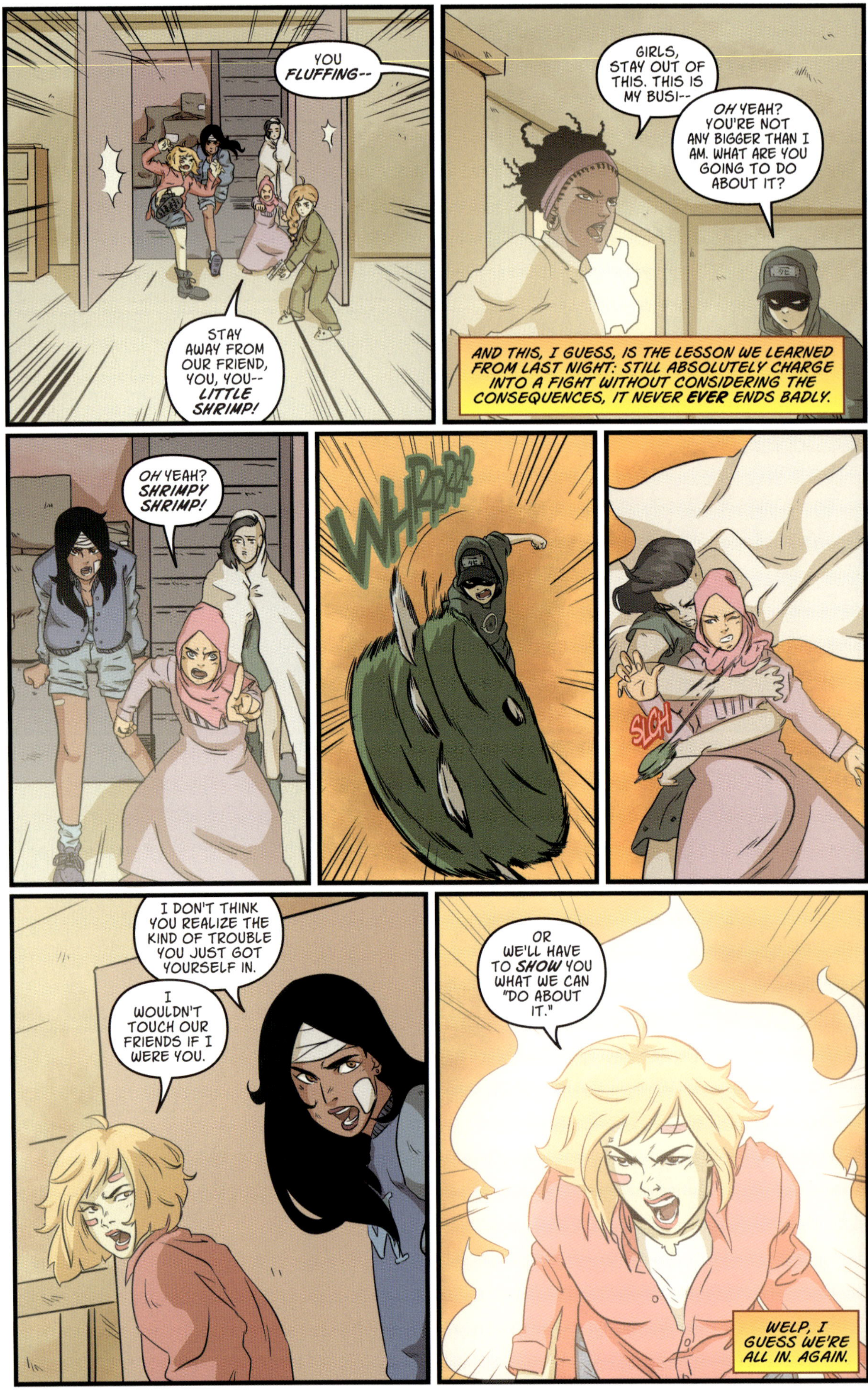
YOU FLUFFING--
STAY AWAY FROM OUR FRIEND, YOU, YOU-- LITTLE SHRIMP!
GIRLS, STAY OUT OF THIS. THIS IS MY BUSI--
OH YEAH? YOU'RE NOT ANY BIGGER THAN I AM. WHAT ARE YOU GOING TO DO ABOUT IT?
AND THIS, I GUESS, IS THE LESSON WE LEARNED FROM LAST NIGHT: STILL ABSOLUTELY CHARGE INTO A FIGHT WITHOUT CONSIDERING THE CONSEQUENCES, IT NEVER EVER ENDS BADLY.
OH YEAH? SHRIMPY SHRIMP!
WHRRRR
SLCH
I DON'T THINK YOU REALIZE THE KIND OF TROUBLE YOU JUST GOT YOURSELF IN.
I WOULDN'T TOUCH OUR FRIENDS IF I WERE YOU.
OR WE'LL HAVE TO SHOW YOU WHAT WE CAN "DO ABOUT IT."
WELP, I GUESS WE'RE ALL IN. AGAIN.

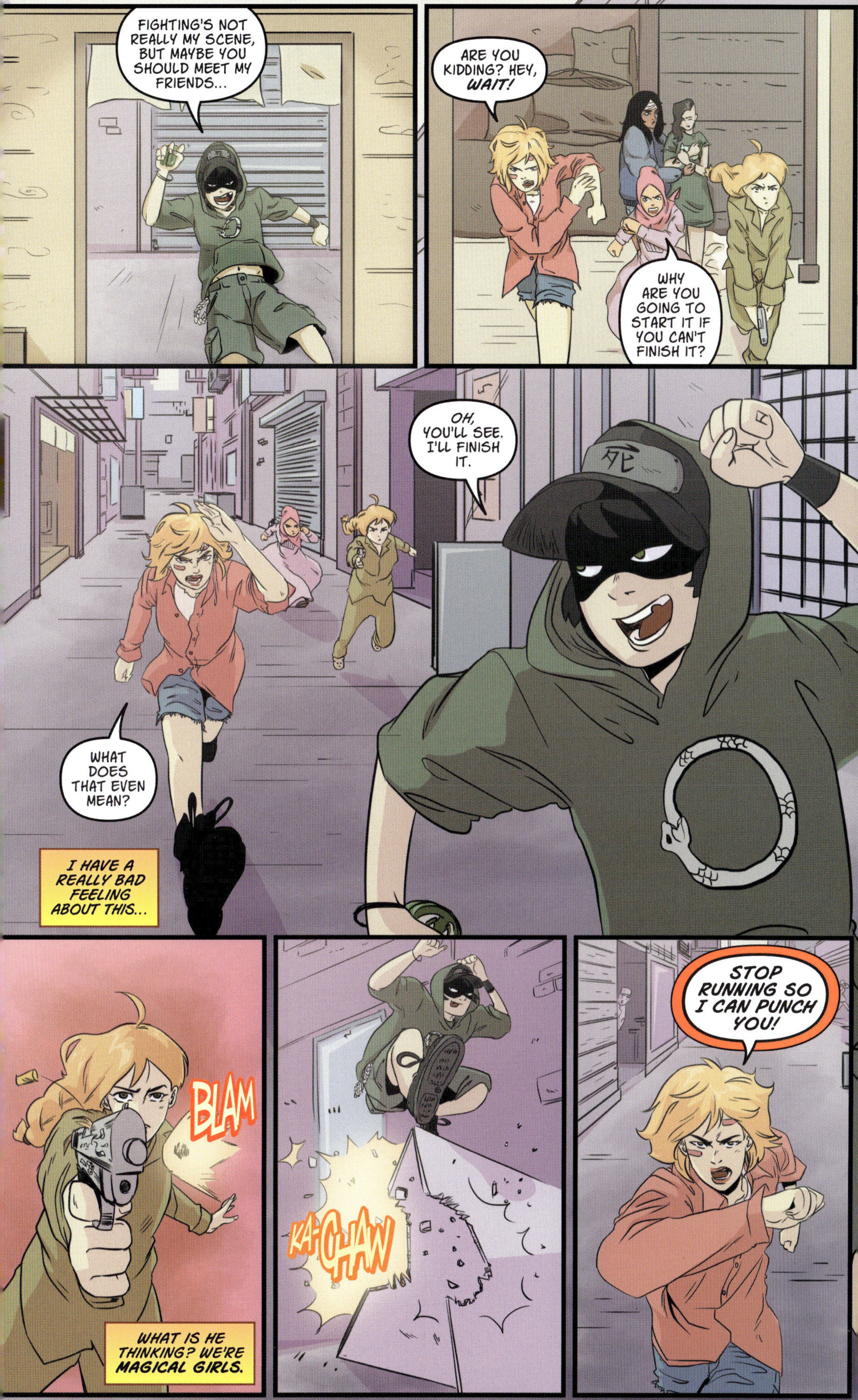
FIGHTING'S NOT REALLY MY SCENE, BUT MAYBE YOU SHOULD MEET MY FRIENDS...
ARE YOU KIDDING? HEY, WAIT!
WHY ARE YOU GOING TO START IT IF YOU CAN'T FINISH IT?
OH, YOU'LL SEE. I'LL FINISH IT.
WHAT DOES THAT EVEN MEAN?
I HAVE A REALLY BAD FEELING ABOUT THIS...
BLAM
WHAT IS HE THINKING? WE'RE MAGICAL GIRLS.
KA-CHAW
STOP RUNNING SO I CAN PUNCH YOU!

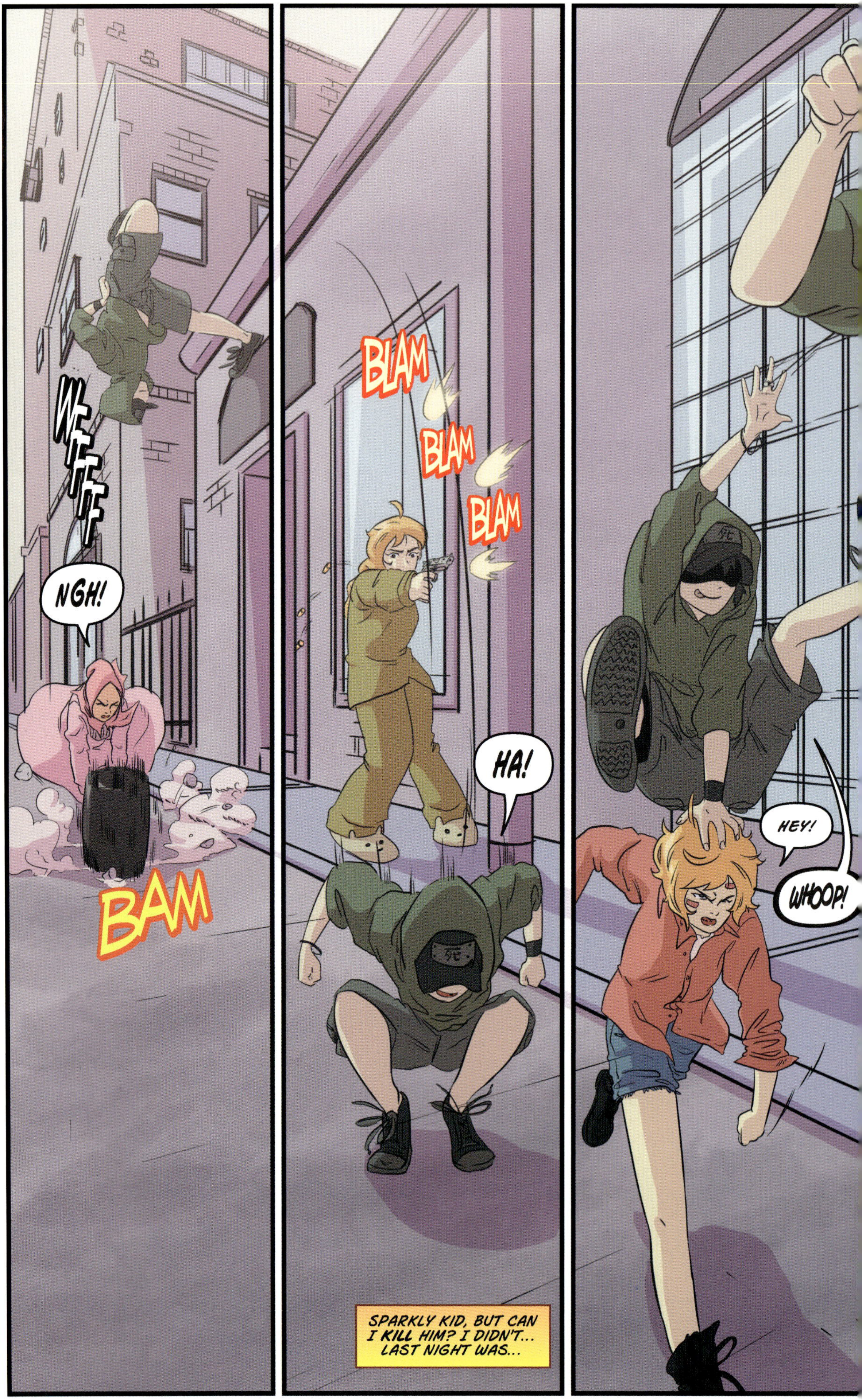
WHFFF
NGH!
BAM
BLAM
BLAM
BLAM
HA!
SPARKLY KID, BUT CAN I KILL HIM? I DIDN'T... LAST NIGHT WAS...
HEY!
WHOOP!

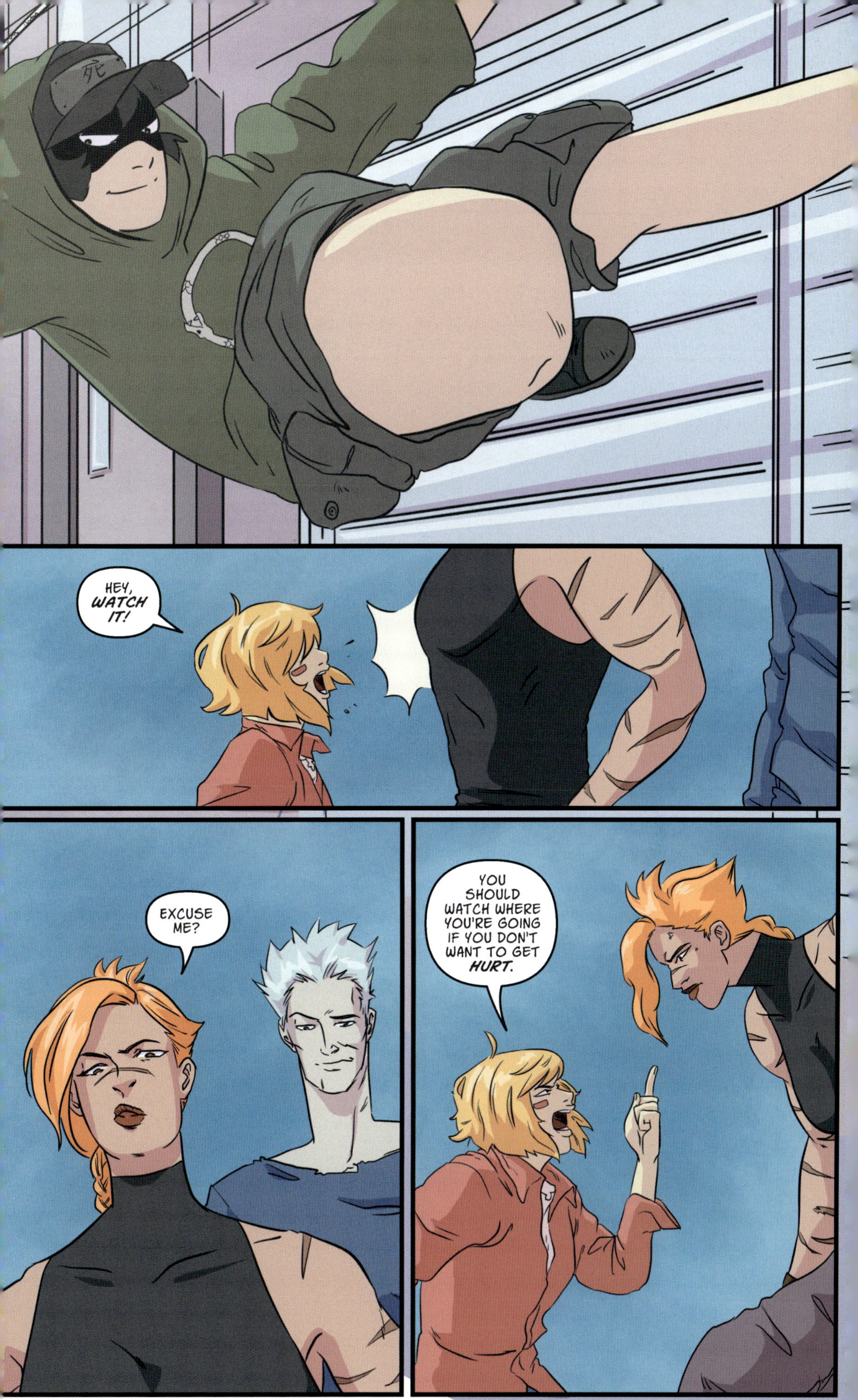
HEY, *WATCH IT!*
EXCUSE ME?
YOU SHOULD WATCH WHERE YOU'RE GOING IF YOU DON'T WANT TO GET *HURT*.

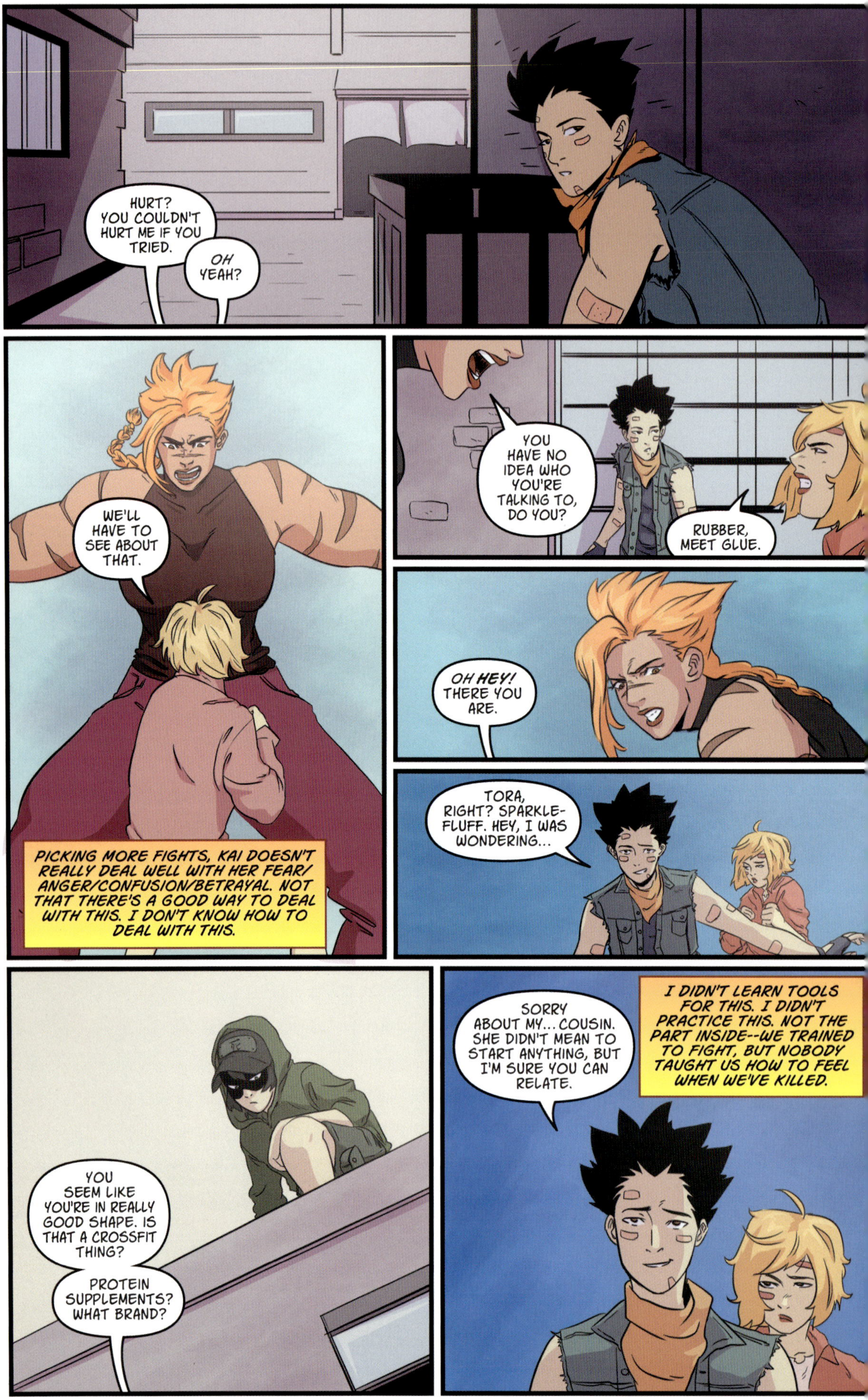
HURT? YOU COULDN'T HURT ME IF YOU TRIED.
OH YEAH?
WE'LL HAVE TO SEE ABOUT THAT.
PICKING MORE FIGHTS, KAI DOESN'T REALLY DEAL WELL WITH HER FEAR/ANGER/CONFUSION/BETRAYAL. NOT THAT THERE'S A GOOD WAY TO DEAL WITH THIS. I DON'T KNOW HOW TO DEAL WITH THIS.
YOU HAVE NO IDEA WHO YOU'RE TALKING TO, DO YOU?
RUBBER, MEET GLUE.
OH HEY! THERE YOU ARE.
TORA, RIGHT? SPARKLE-FLUFF. HEY, I WAS WONDERING...
YOU SEEM LIKE YOU'RE IN REALLY GOOD SHAPE. IS THAT A CROSSFIT THING?
PROTEIN SUPPLEMENTS? WHAT BRAND?
SORRY ABOUT MY... COUSIN. SHE DIDN'T MEAN TO START ANYTHING, BUT I'M SURE YOU CAN RELATE.
I DIDN'T LEARN TOOLS FOR THIS. I DIDN'T PRACTICE THIS. NOT THE PART INSIDE--WE TRAINED TO FIGHT, BUT NOBODY TAUGHT US HOW TO FEEL WHEN WE'VE KILLED.

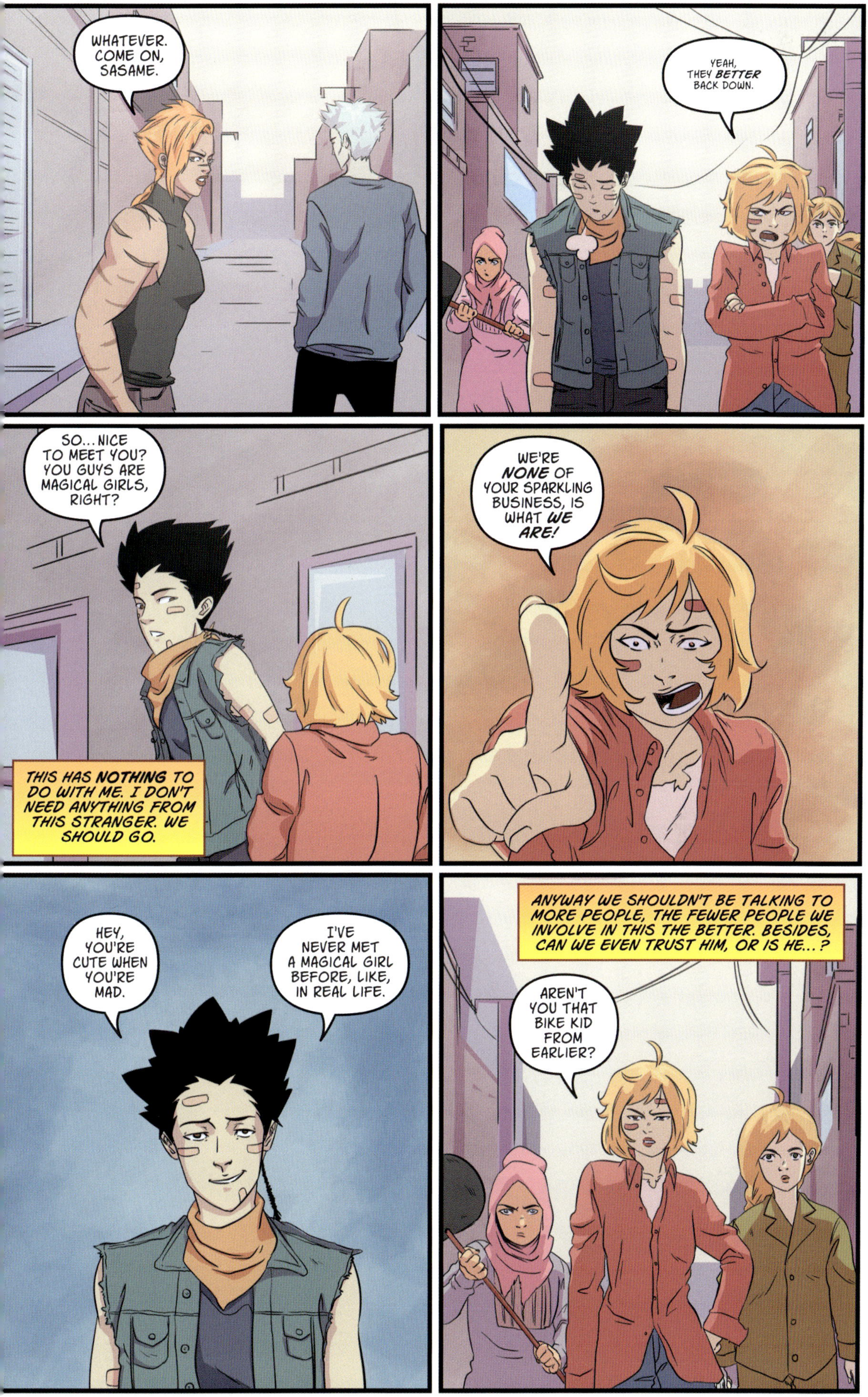
WHATEVER. COME ON, SASAME.
YEAH, THEY *BETTER* BACK DOWN.
SO... NICE TO MEET YOU? YOU GUYS ARE MAGICAL GIRLS, RIGHT?
THIS HAS **NOTHING** TO DO WITH ME. I DON'T NEED ANYTHING FROM THIS STRANGER. WE SHOULD GO.
WE'RE ***NONE*** OF YOUR SPARKLING BUSINESS, IS WHAT ***WE ARE!***
HEY, YOU'RE CUTE WHEN YOU'RE MAD.
I'VE NEVER MET A MAGICAL GIRL BEFORE, LIKE, IN REAL LIFE.
ANYWAY WE SHOULDN'T BE TALKING TO MORE PEOPLE, THE FEWER PEOPLE WE INVOLVE IN THIS THE BETTER. BESIDES, CAN WE EVEN TRUST HIM, OR IS HE...?
AREN'T YOU THAT BIKE KID FROM EARLIER?

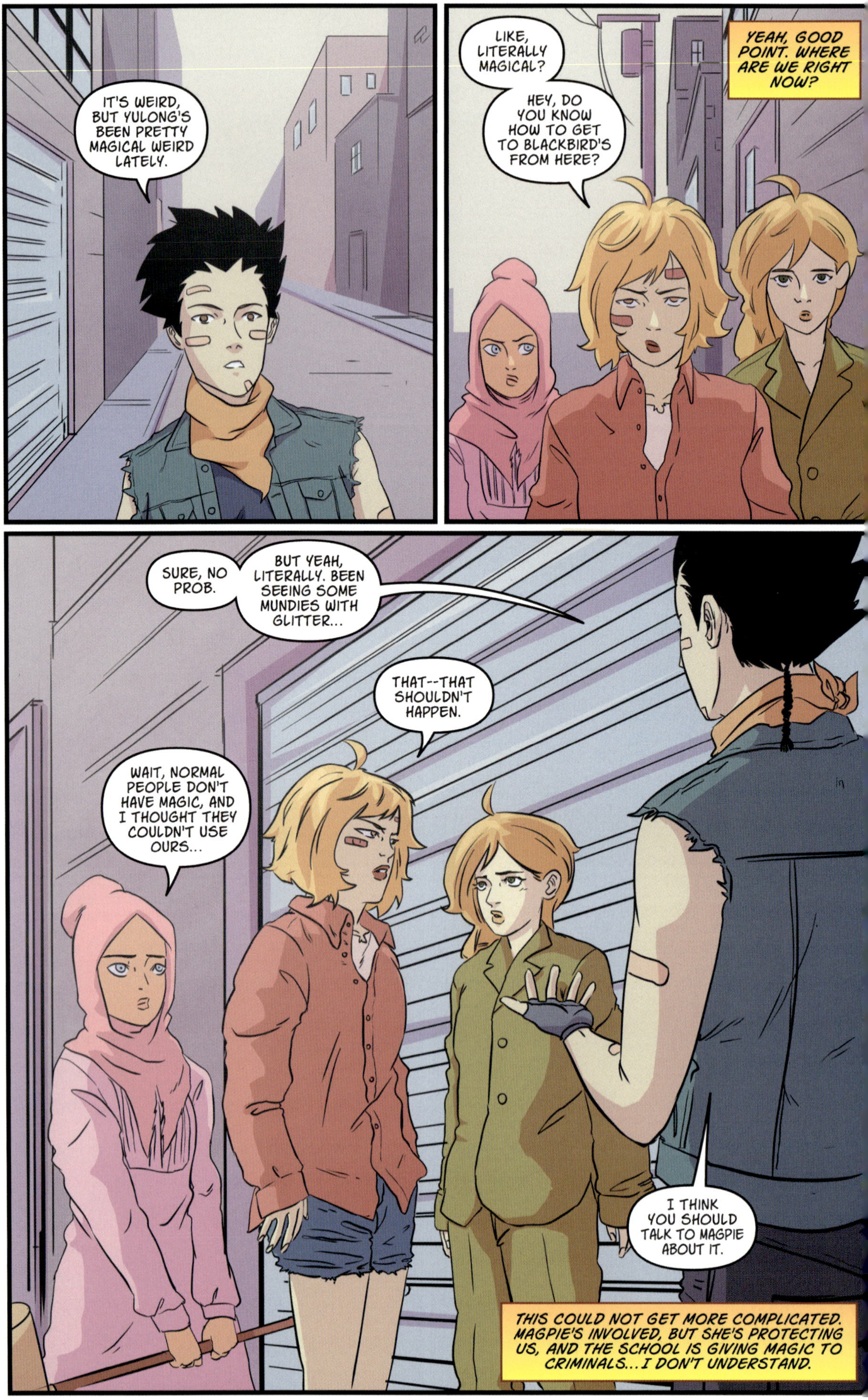
IT'S WEIRD, BUT YULONG'S BEEN PRETTY MAGICAL WEIRD LATELY.
LIKE, LITERALLY MAGICAL?
HEY, DO YOU KNOW HOW TO GET TO BLACKBIRD'S FROM HERE?
YEAH, GOOD POINT. WHERE ARE WE RIGHT NOW?
SURE, NO PROB.
BUT YEAH, LITERALLY. BEEN SEEING SOME MUNDIES WITH GLITTER...
THAT--THAT SHOULDN'T HAPPEN.
WAIT, NORMAL PEOPLE DON'T HAVE MAGIC, AND I THOUGHT THEY COULDN'T USE OURS...
I THINK YOU SHOULD TALK TO MAGPIE ABOUT IT.
THIS COULD NOT GET MORE COMPLICATED. MAGPIE'S INVOLVED, BUT SHE'S PROTECTING US, AND THE SCHOOL IS GIVING MAGIC TO CRIMINALS... I DON'T UNDERSTAND.

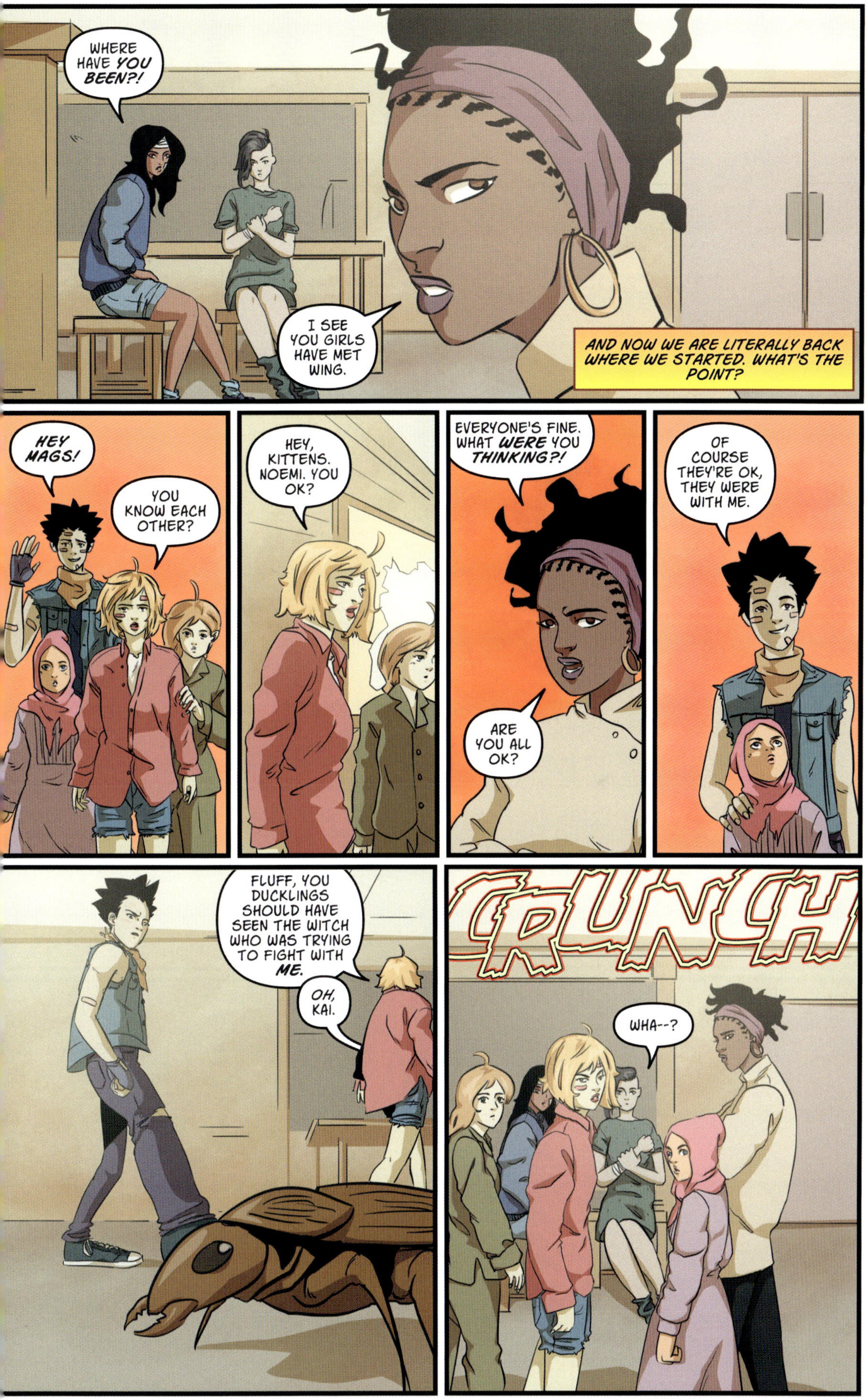
WHERE HAVE YOU BEEN?!
I SEE YOU GIRLS HAVE MET WING.
AND NOW WE ARE LITERALLY BACK WHERE WE STARTED. WHAT'S THE POINT?
HEY MAGS!
YOU KNOW EACH OTHER?
HEY, KITTENS. NOEMI. YOU OK?
EVERYONE'S FINE. WHAT WERE YOU THINKING?!
ARE YOU ALL OK?
OF COURSE THEY'RE OK, THEY WERE WITH ME.
FLUFF, YOU DUCKLINGS SHOULD HAVE SEEN THE WITCH WHO WAS TRYING TO FIGHT WITH ME.
OH, KAI.
CRUNCH
WHA--?

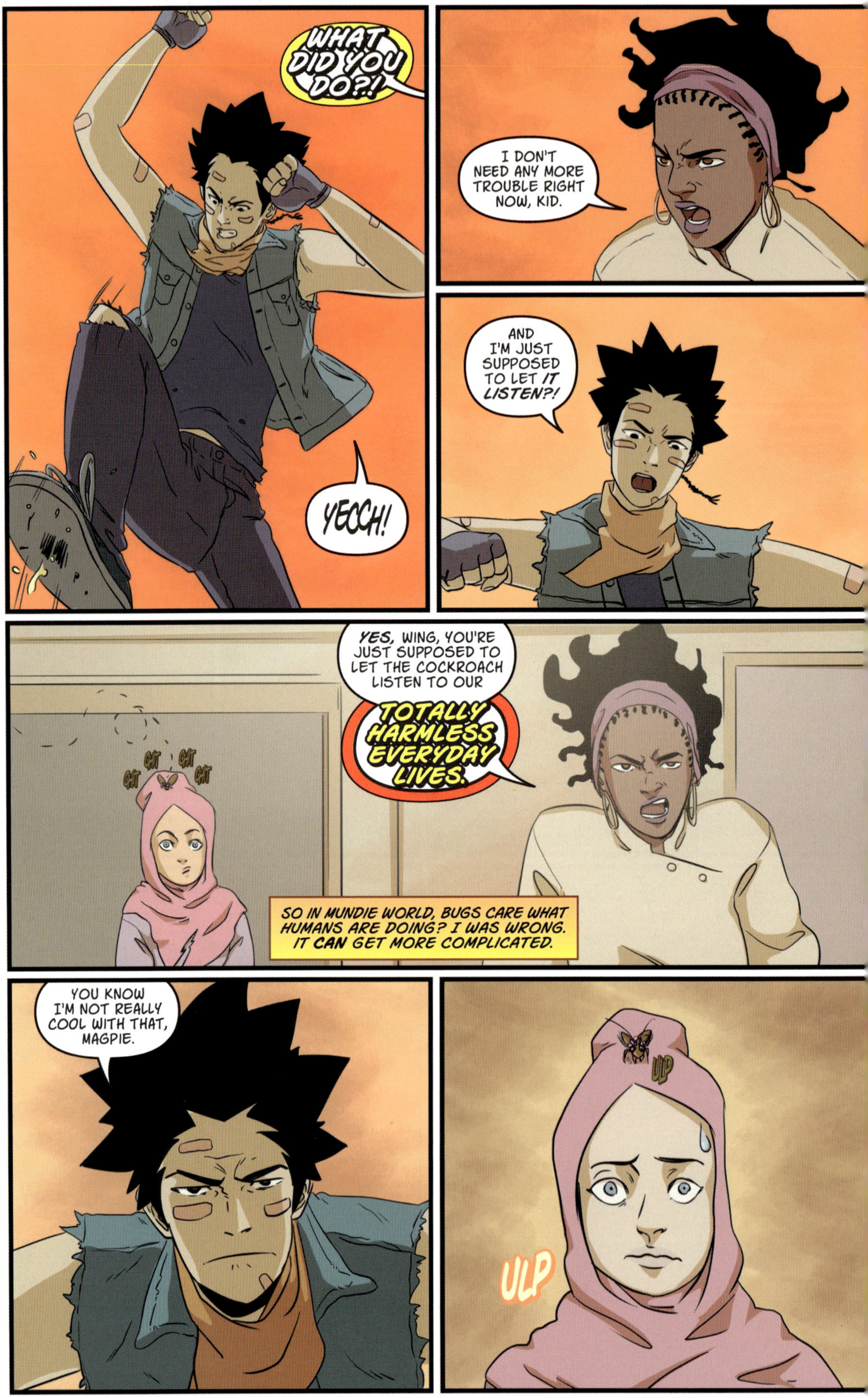
WHAT DID YOU DO?!
YECCH!
I DON'T NEED ANY MORE TROUBLE RIGHT NOW, KID.
AND I'M JUST SUPPOSED TO LET IT LISTEN?!
YES, WING, YOU'RE JUST SUPPOSED TO LET THE COCKROACH LISTEN TO OUR
TOTALLY HARMLESS EVERYDAY LIVES.
SO IN MUNDIE WORLD, BUGS CARE WHAT HUMANS ARE DOING? I WAS WRONG. IT CAN GET MORE COMPLICATED.
YOU KNOW I'M NOT REALLY COOL WITH THAT, MAGPIE.
ULP
ULP

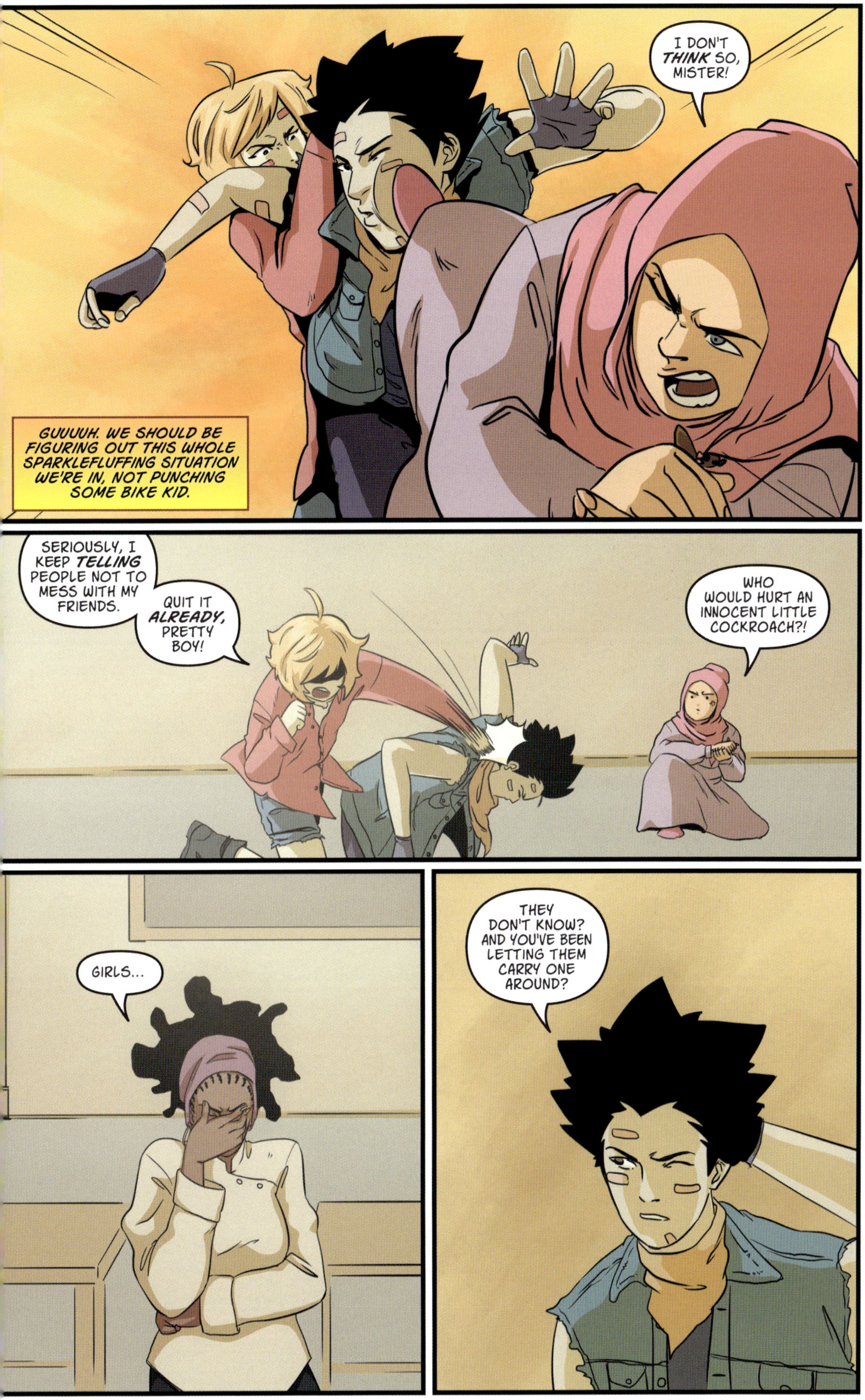
I DON'T THINK SO, MISTER!
GUUUUH. WE SHOULD BE FIGURING OUT THIS WHOLE SPARKLEFLUFFING SITUATION WE'RE IN, NOT PUNCHING SOME BIKE KID.
SERIOUSLY, I KEEP TELLING PEOPLE NOT TO MESS WITH MY FRIENDS.
QUIT IT ALREADY, PRETTY BOY!
WHO WOULD HURT AN INNOCENT LITTLE COCKROACH?!
GIRLS...
THEY DON'T KNOW? AND YOU'VE BEEN LETTING THEM CARRY ONE AROUND?

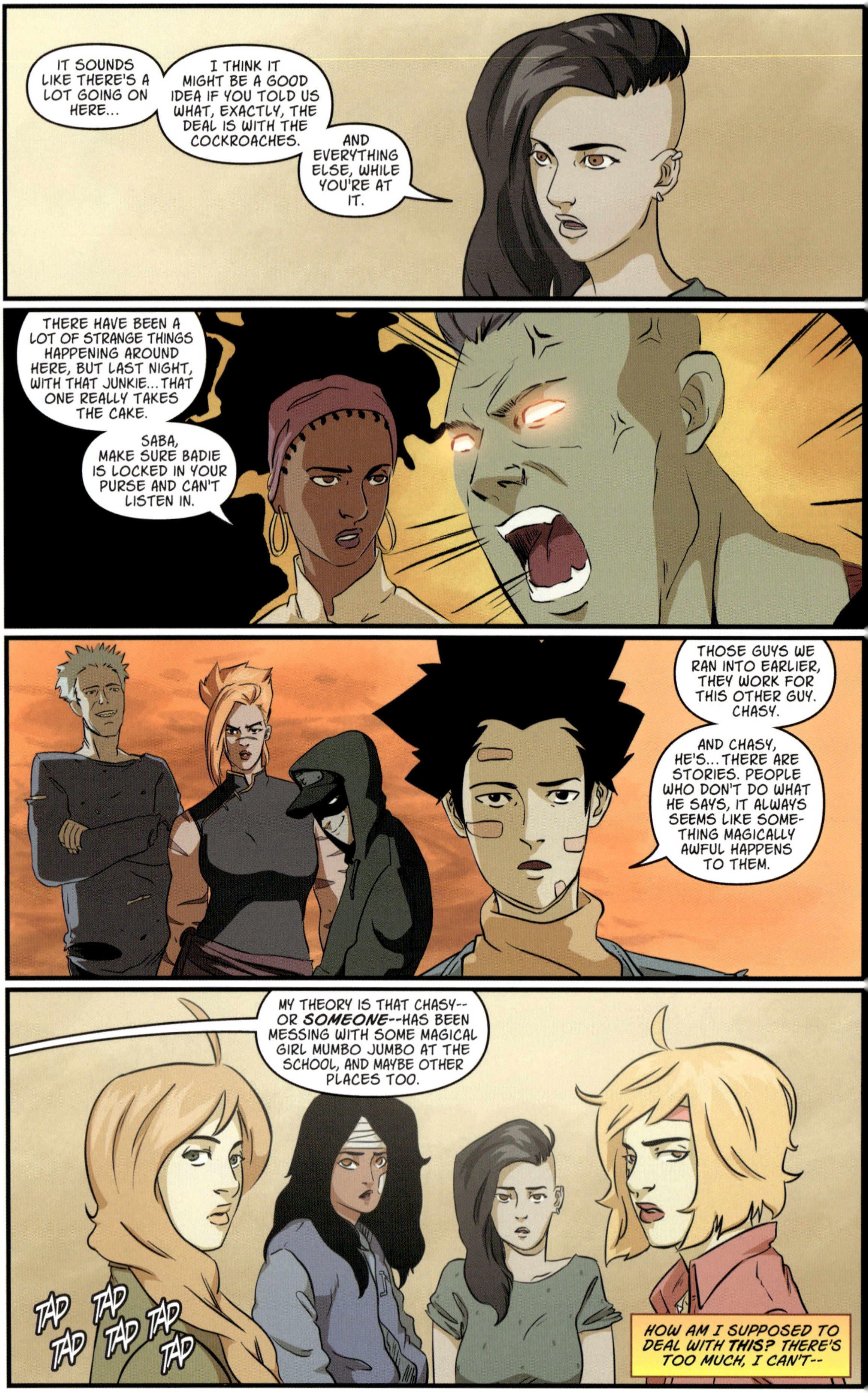
IT SOUNDS LIKE THERE'S A LOT GOING ON HERE...
I THINK IT MIGHT BE A GOOD IDEA IF YOU TOLD US WHAT, EXACTLY, THE DEAL IS WITH THE COCKROACHES.
AND EVERYTHING ELSE, WHILE YOU'RE AT IT.
THERE HAVE BEEN A LOT OF STRANGE THINGS HAPPENING AROUND HERE, BUT LAST NIGHT, WITH THAT JUNKIE...THAT ONE REALLY TAKES THE CAKE.
SABA, MAKE SURE BADIE IS LOCKED IN YOUR PURSE AND CAN'T LISTEN IN.
THOSE GUYS WE RAN INTO EARLIER, THEY WORK FOR THIS OTHER GUY. CHASY.
AND CHASY, HE'S...THERE ARE STORIES. PEOPLE WHO DON'T DO WHAT HE SAYS, IT ALWAYS SEEMS LIKE SOME-THING MAGICALLY AWFUL HAPPENS TO THEM.
MY THEORY IS THAT CHASY-- OR ***SOMEONE***--HAS BEEN MESSING WITH SOME MAGICAL GIRL MUMBO JUMBO AT THE SCHOOL, AND MAYBE OTHER PLACES TOO.
TAP TAP TAP TAP TAP TAP
*HOW AM I SUPPOSED TO DEAL WITH **THIS**? THERE'S TOO MUCH, I CAN'T--*

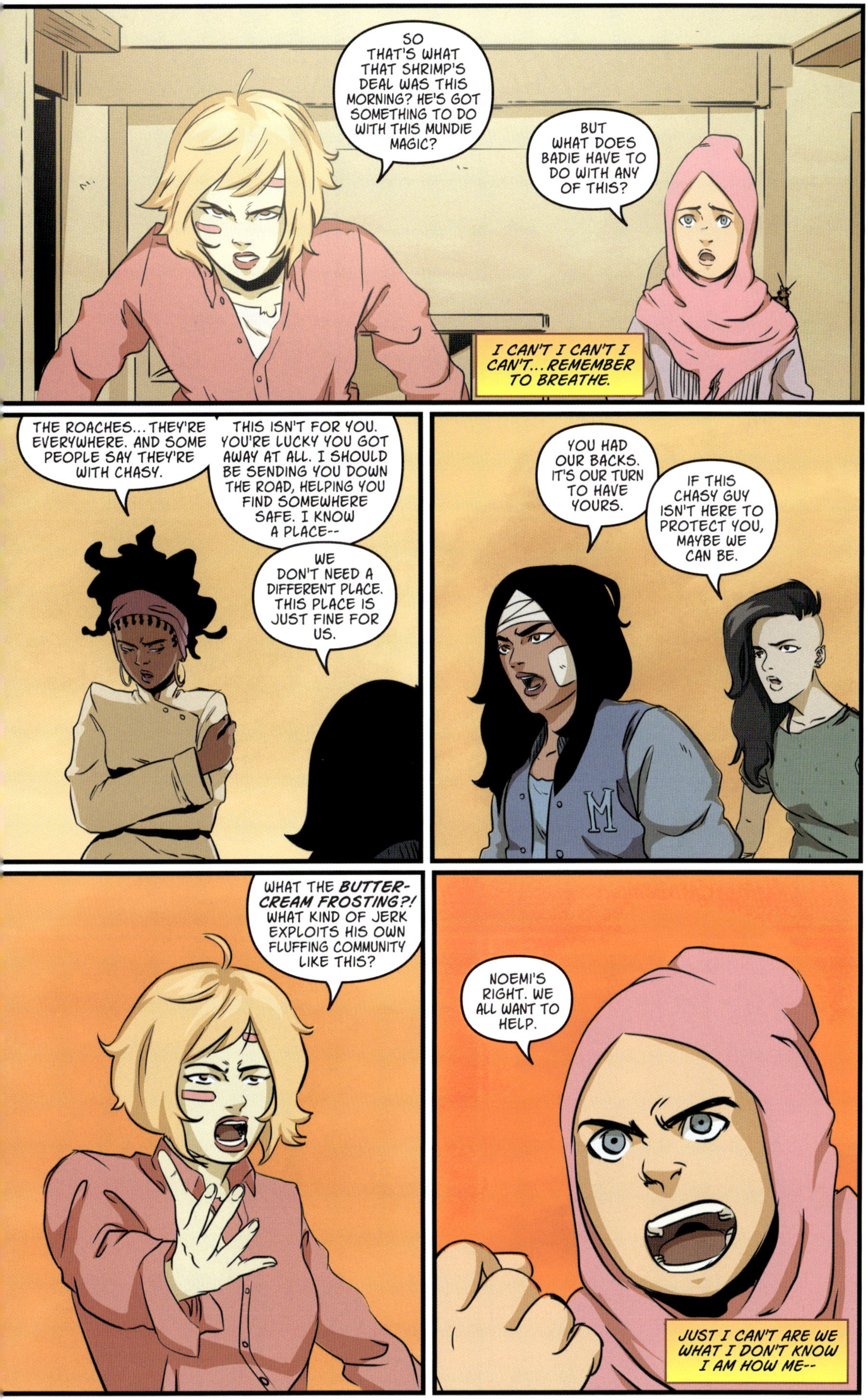

SO THAT'S WHAT THAT SHRIMP'S DEAL WAS THIS MORNING? HE'S GOT SOMETHING TO DO WITH THIS MUNDIE MAGIC?
BUT WHAT DOES BADIE HAVE TO DO WITH ANY OF THIS?
I CAN'T I CAN'T I CAN'T... REMEMBER TO BREATHE.
THE ROACHES... THEY'RE EVERYWHERE. AND SOME PEOPLE SAY THEY'RE WITH CHASY.
THIS ISN'T FOR YOU. YOU'RE LUCKY YOU GOT AWAY AT ALL. I SHOULD BE SENDING YOU DOWN THE ROAD, HELPING YOU FIND SOMEWHERE SAFE. I KNOW A PLACE--
WE DON'T NEED A DIFFERENT PLACE. THIS PLACE IS JUST FINE FOR US.
YOU HAD OUR BACKS. IT'S OUR TURN TO HAVE YOURS.
IF THIS CHASY GUY ISN'T HERE TO PROTECT YOU, MAYBE WE CAN BE.
WHAT THE **BUTTER-CREAM FROSTING?!** WHAT KIND OF JERK EXPLOITS HIS OWN FLUFFING COMMUNITY LIKE THIS?
NOEMI'S RIGHT. WE ALL WANT TO HELP.
JUST I CAN'T ARE WE WHAT I DON'T KNOW I AM HOW ME--

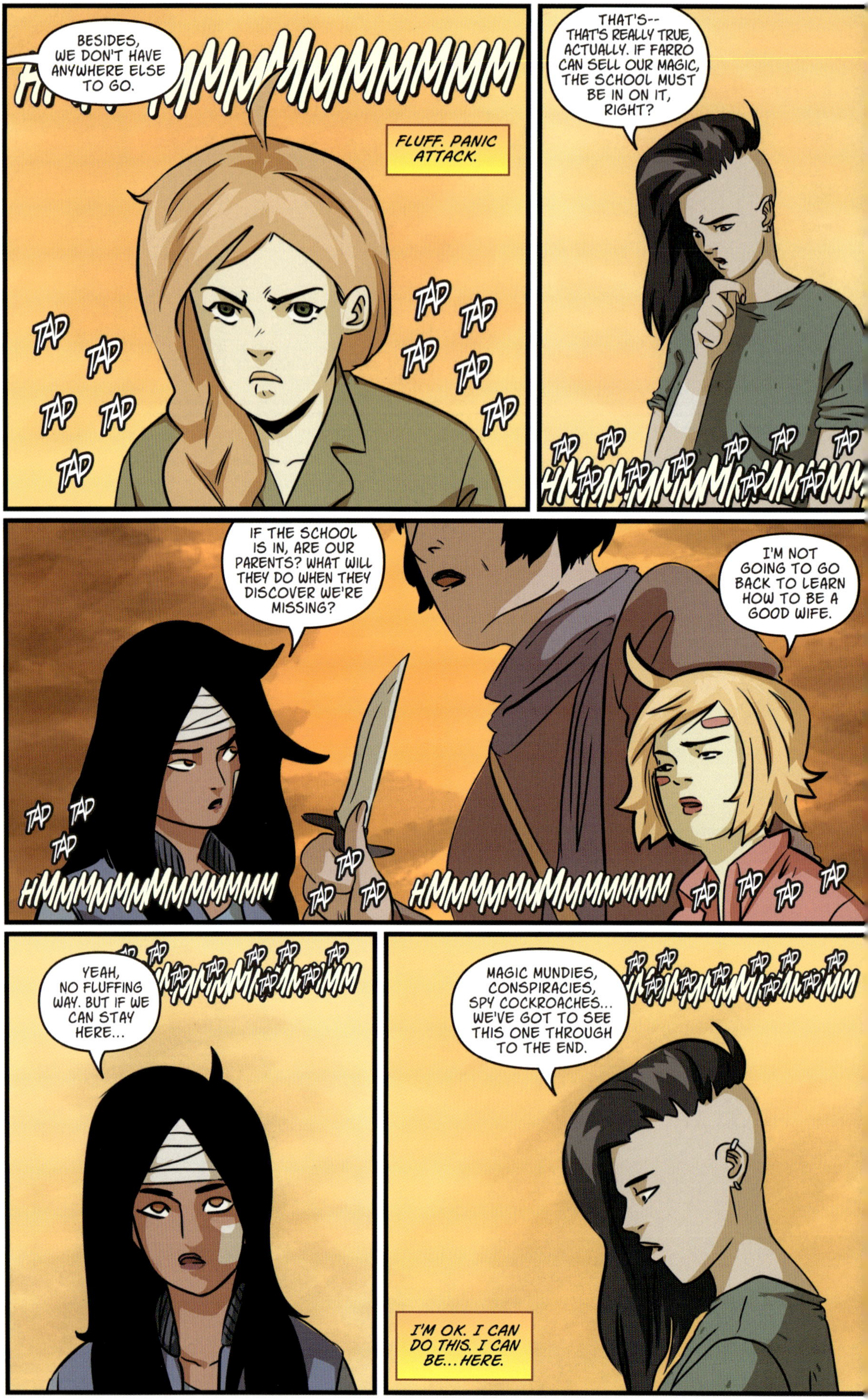
BESIDES, WE DON'T HAVE ANYWHERE ELSE TO GO.
HMMMMMMMMMMMMM
FLUFF. PANIC ATTACK.
TAD TAD TAD TAD TAD TAD TAD TAD TAD TAD TAD
THAT'S-- THAT'S REALLY TRUE, ACTUALLY. IF FARRO CAN SELL OUR MAGIC, THE SCHOOL MUST BE IN ON IT, RIGHT?
IF THE SCHOOL IS IN, ARE OUR PARENTS? WHAT WILL THEY DO WHEN THEY DISCOVER WE'RE MISSING?
I'M NOT GOING TO GO BACK TO LEARN HOW TO BE A GOOD WIFE.
HMMMMMMMMMMMMM
TAD TAD TAD
HMMMMMMMMMMMMM
TAD TAD TAD TAD TAD TAD TAD
YEAH, NO FLUFFING WAY. BUT IF WE CAN STAY HERE...
MAGIC MUNDIES, CONSPIRACIES, SPY COCKROACHES... WE'VE GOT TO SEE THIS ONE THROUGH TO THE END.
I'M OK. I CAN DO THIS. I CAN BE... HERE.

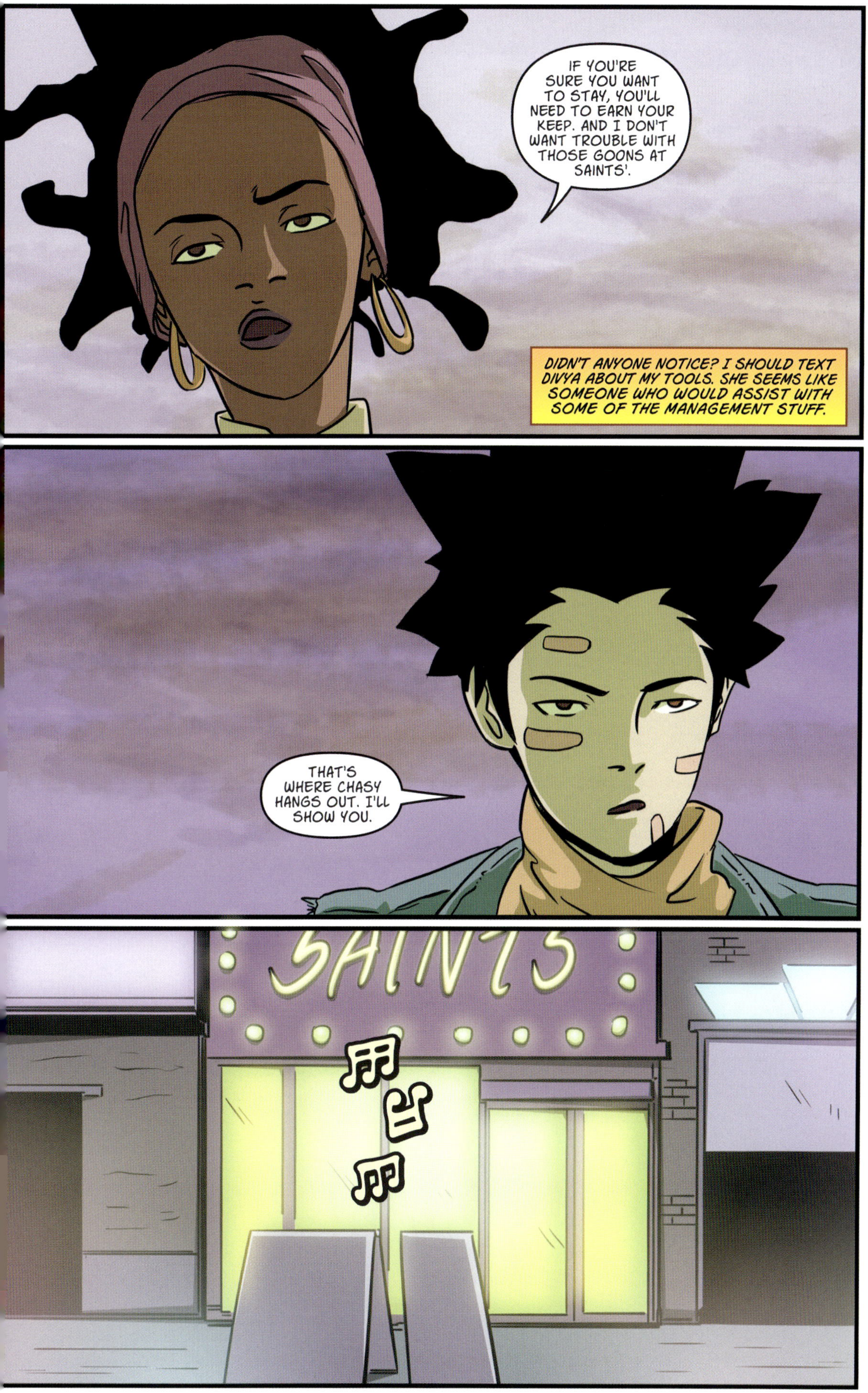
IF YOU'RE SURE YOU WANT TO STAY, YOU'LL NEED TO EARN YOUR KEEP. AND I DON'T WANT TROUBLE WITH THOSE GOONS AT SAINTS'.
DIDN'T ANYONE NOTICE? I SHOULD TEXT DIVYA ABOUT MY TOOLS. SHE SEEMS LIKE SOMEONE WHO WOULD ASSIST WITH SOME OF THE MANAGEMENT STUFF.
THAT'S WHERE CHASY HANGS OUT. I'LL SHOW YOU.
SAINTS

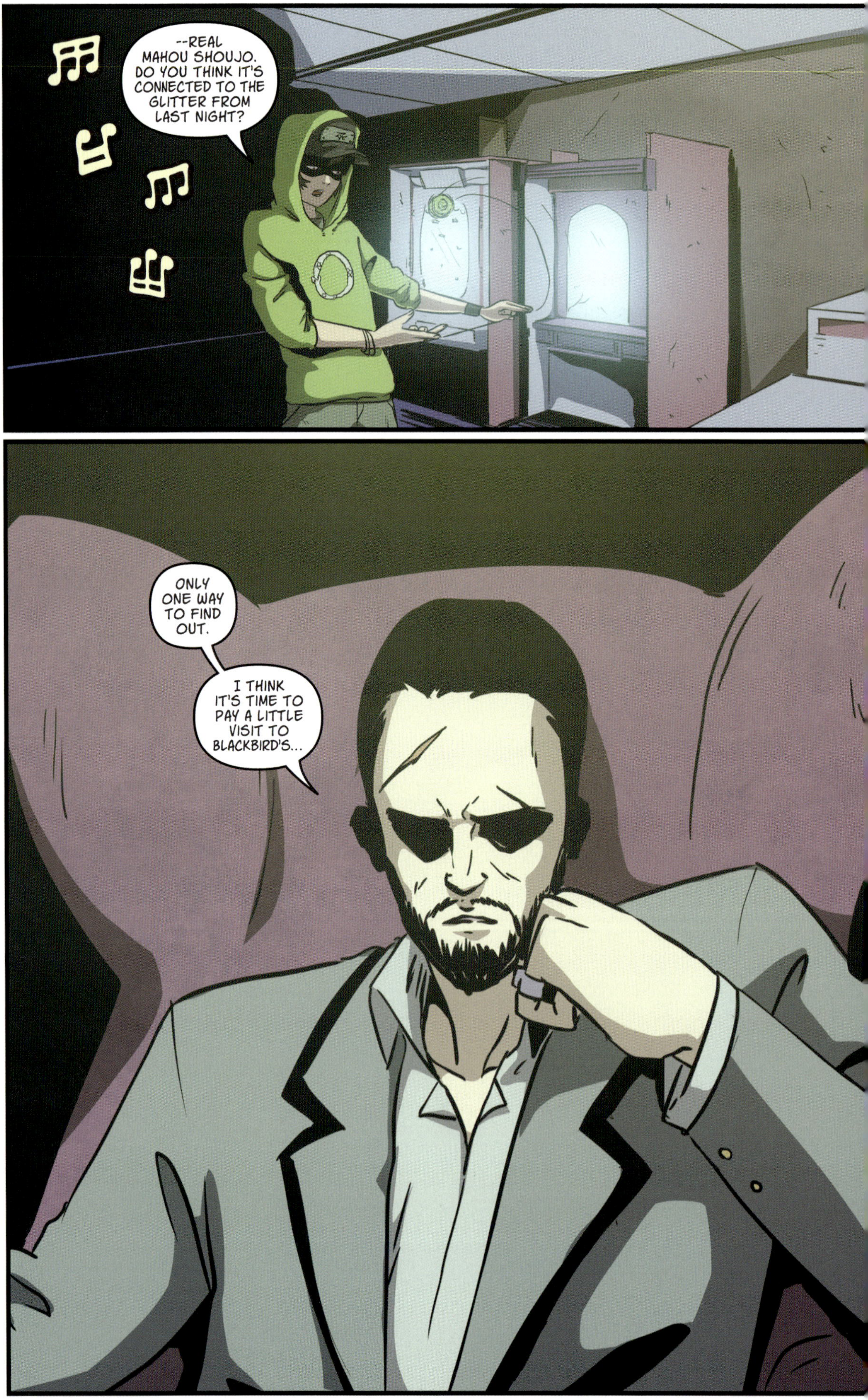
--REAL MAHOU SHOUJO. DO YOU THINK IT'S CONNECTED TO THE GLITTER FROM LAST NIGHT?
ONLY ONE WAY TO FIND OUT.
I THINK IT'S TIME TO PAY A LITTLE VISIT TO BLACKBIRD'S...

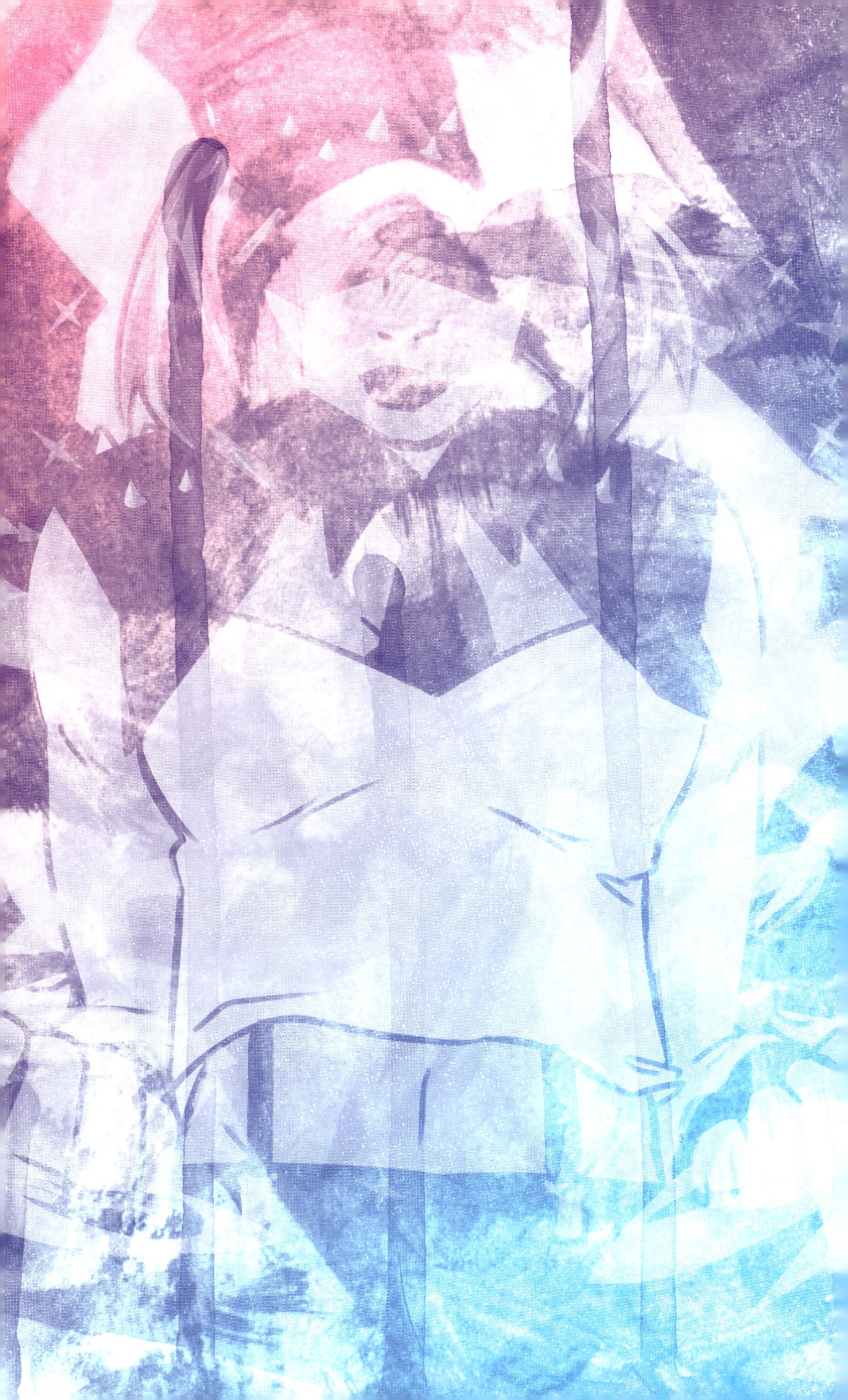

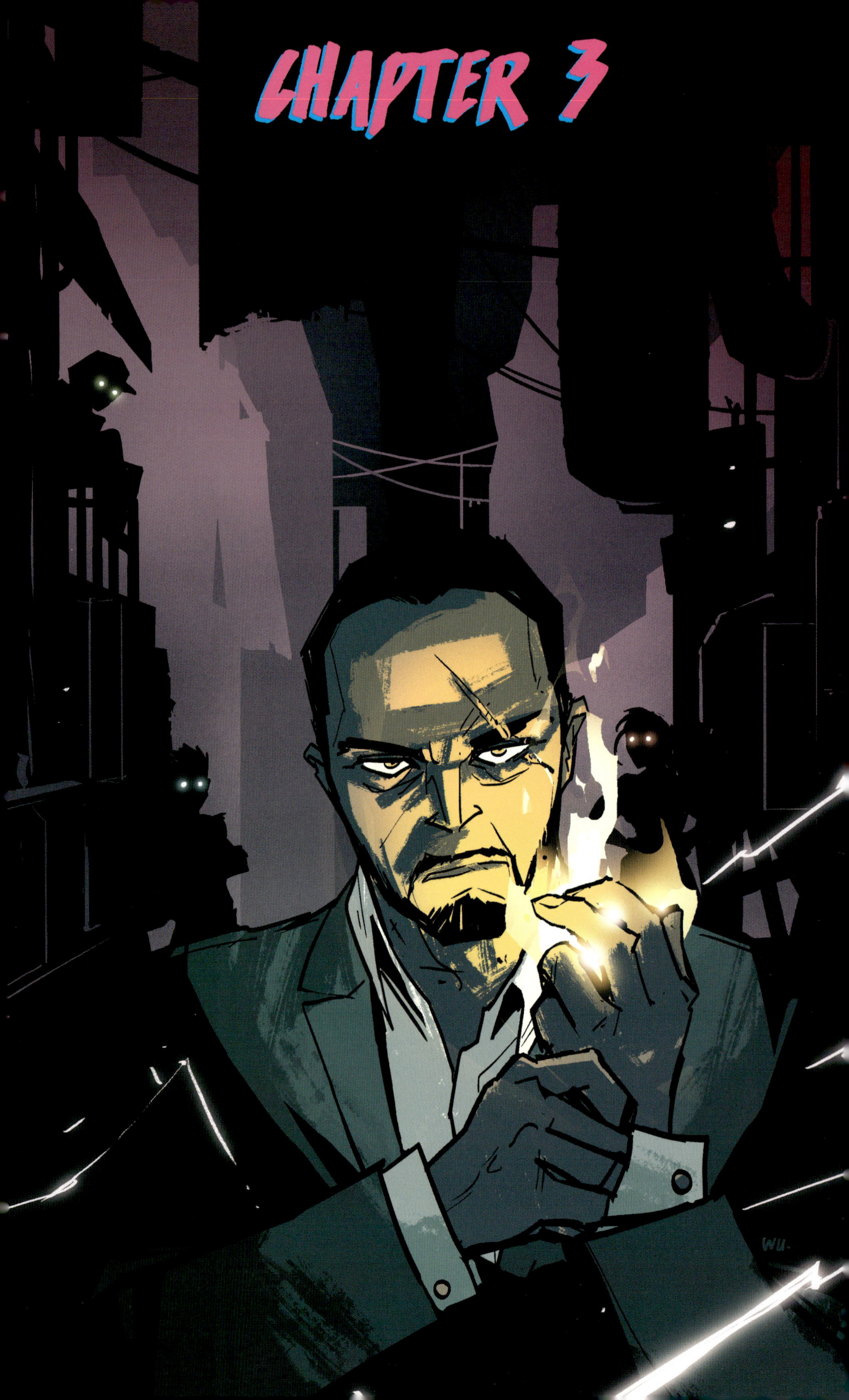
CHAPTER 3

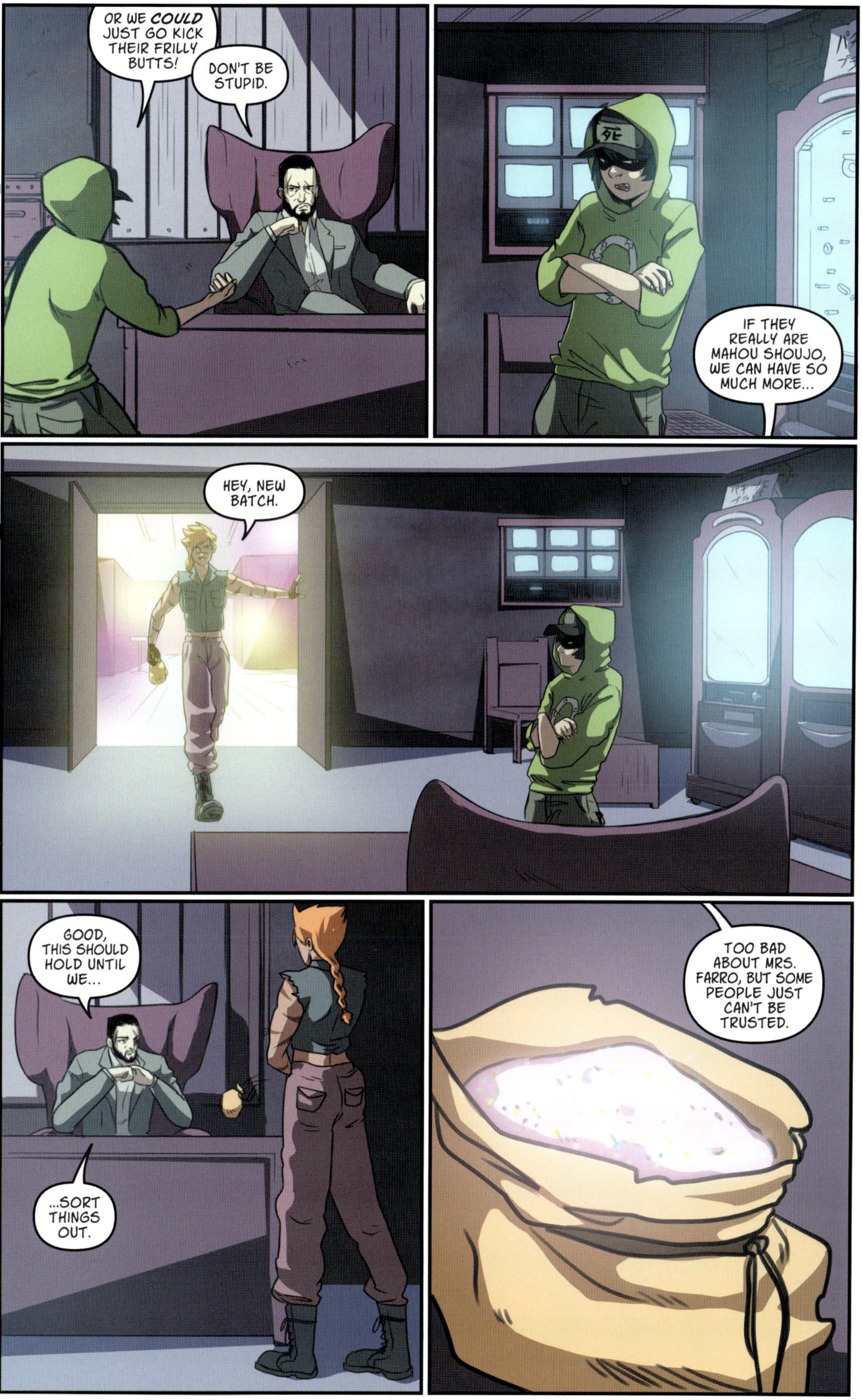
OR WE COULD JUST GO KICK THEIR FRILLY BUTTS!
DON'T BE STUPID.
IF THEY REALLY ARE MAHOU SHOUJO, WE CAN HAVE SO MUCH MORE...
HEY, NEW BATCH.
GOOD, THIS SHOULD HOLD UNTIL WE...
...SORT THINGS OUT.
TOO BAD ABOUT MRS. FARRO, BUT SOME PEOPLE JUST CAN'T BE TRUSTED.

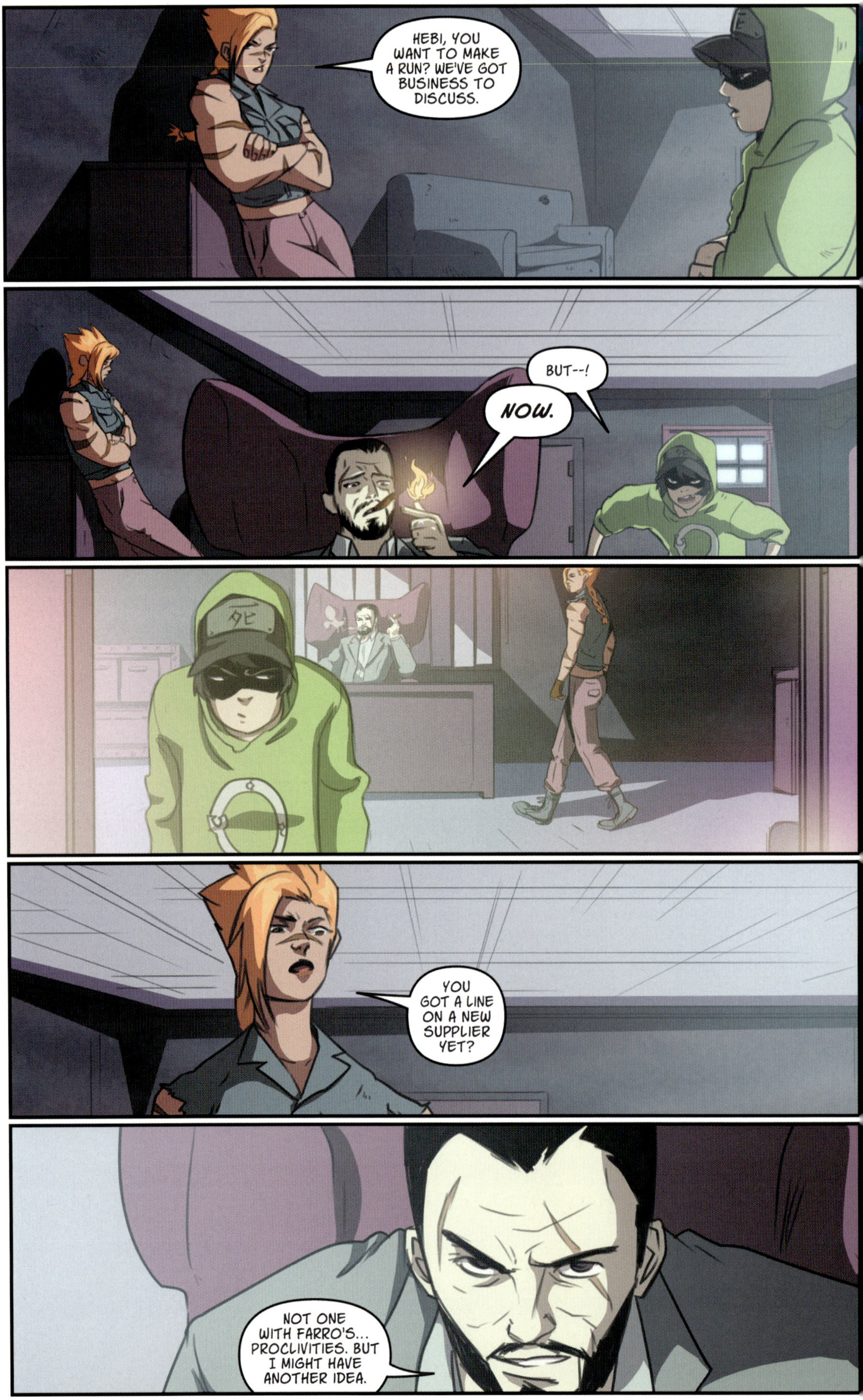
HEBI, YOU WANT TO MAKE A RUN? WE'VE GOT BUSINESS TO DISCUSS.
BUT--!
NOW.
YOU GOT A LINE ON A NEW SUPPLIER YET?
NOT ONE WITH FARRO'S... PROCLIVITIES. BUT I MIGHT HAVE ANOTHER IDEA.

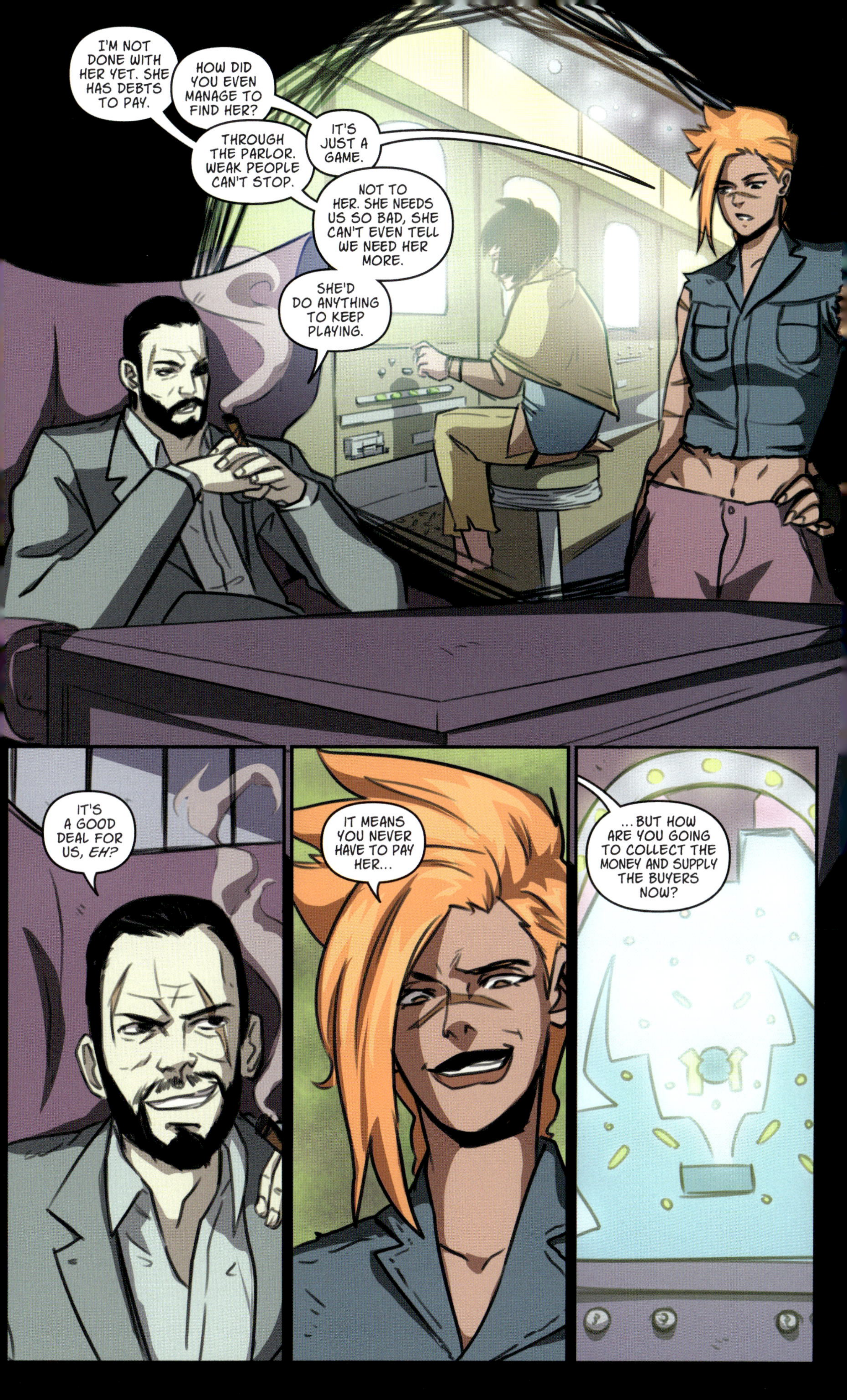
I'M NOT DONE WITH HER YET. SHE HAS DEBTS TO PAY.
HOW DID YOU EVEN MANAGE TO FIND HER?
THROUGH THE PARLOR. WEAK PEOPLE CAN'T STOP.
IT'S JUST A GAME.
NOT TO HER. SHE NEEDS US SO BAD, SHE CAN'T EVEN TELL WE NEED HER MORE.
SHE'D DO ANYTHING TO KEEP PLAYING.
IT'S A GOOD DEAL FOR US, *EH?*
IT MEANS YOU NEVER HAVE TO PAY HER...
...BUT HOW ARE YOU GOING TO COLLECT THE MONEY AND SUPPLY THE BUYERS NOW?

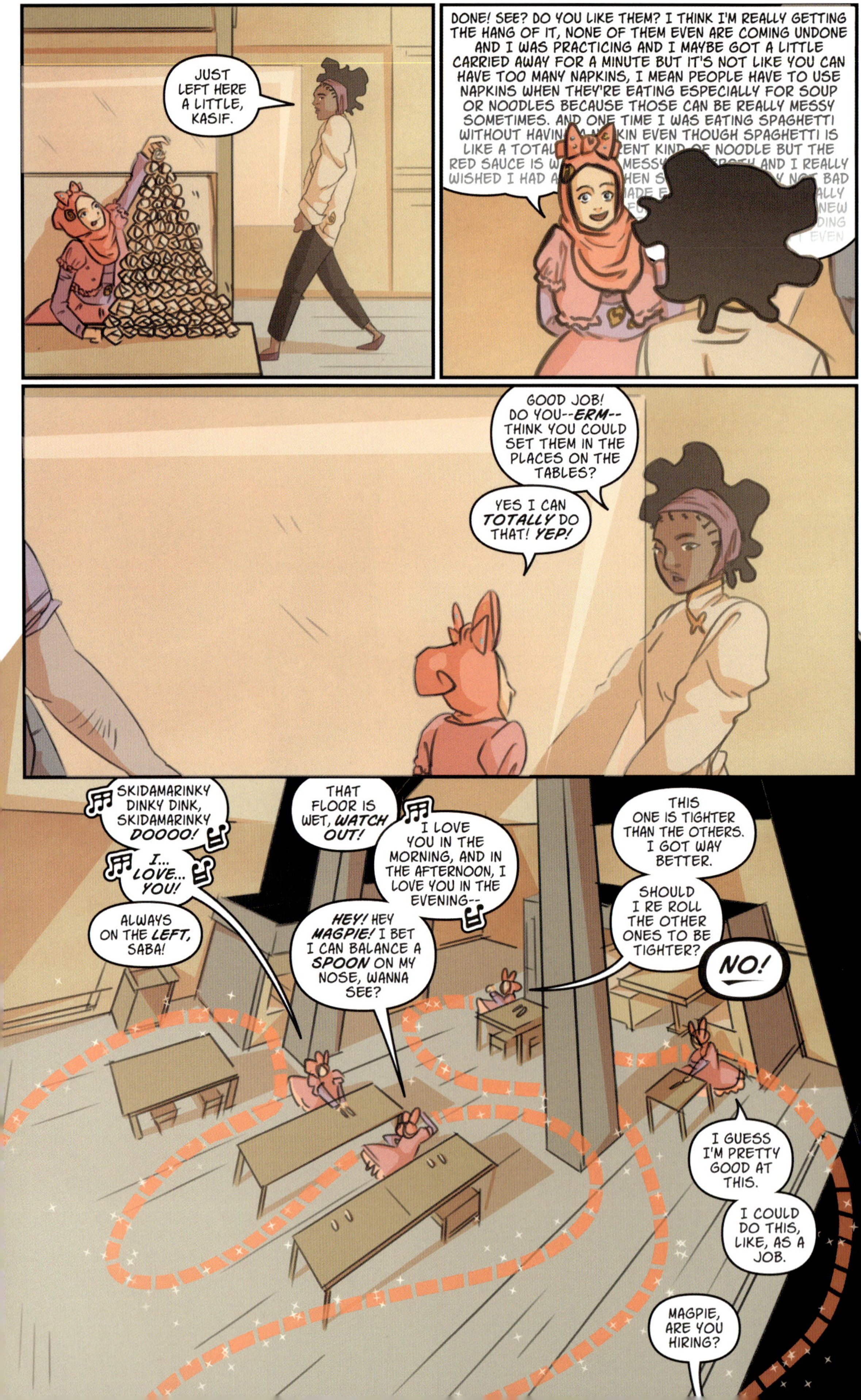
JUST LEFT HERE A LITTLE, KASIF.
DONE! SEE? DO YOU LIKE THEM? I THINK I'M REALLY GETTING THE HANG OF IT, NONE OF THEM EVEN ARE COMING UNDONE AND I WAS PRACTICING AND I MAYBE GOT A LITTLE CARRIED AWAY FOR A MINUTE BUT IT'S NOT LIKE YOU CAN HAVE TOO MANY NAPKINS, I MEAN PEOPLE HAVE TO USE NAPKINS WHEN THEY'RE EATING ESPECIALLY FOR SOUP OR NOODLES BECAUSE THOSE CAN BE REALLY MESSY SOMETIMES. AND ONE TIME I WAS EATING SPAGHETTI
GOOD JOB! DO YOU--ERM--THINK YOU COULD SET THEM IN THE PLACES ON THE TABLES?
YES I CAN TOTALLY DO THAT! YEP!
SKIDAMARINKY DINKY DINK, SKIDAMARINKY DOOOO!
I... LOVE... YOU!
ALWAYS ON THE LEFT, SABA!
THAT FLOOR IS WET, WATCH OUT!
I LOVE YOU IN THE MORNING, AND IN THE AFTERNOON, I LOVE YOU IN THE EVENING--
HEY! HEY MAGPIE! I BET I CAN BALANCE A SPOON ON MY NOSE, WANNA SEE?
THIS ONE IS TIGHTER THAN THE OTHERS. I GOT WAY BETTER.
SHOULD I RE ROLL THE OTHER ONES TO BE TIGHTER?
NO!
I GUESS I'M PRETTY GOOD AT THIS.
I COULD DO THIS, LIKE, AS A JOB.
MAGPIE, ARE YOU HIRING?

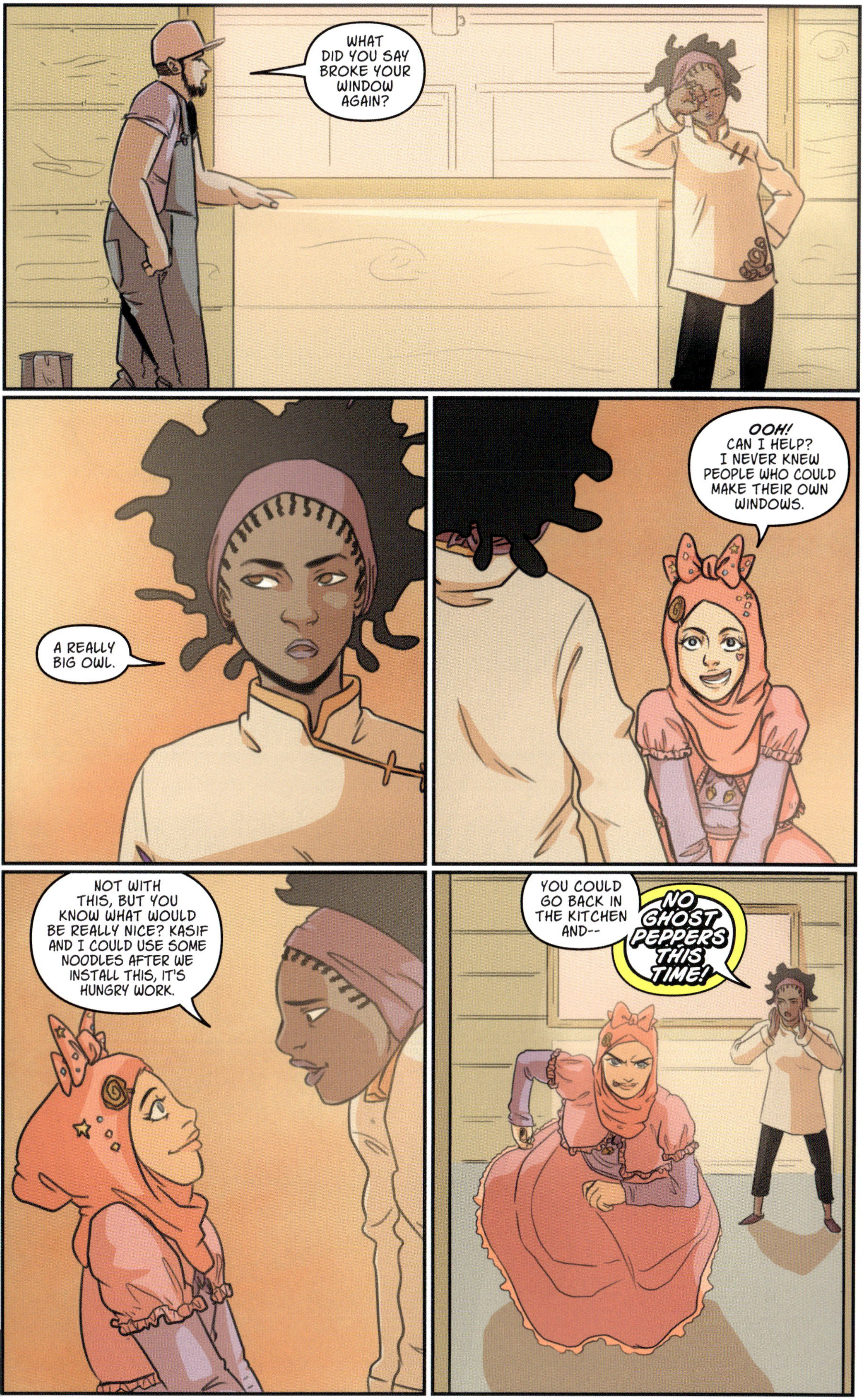
WHAT DID YOU SAY BROKE YOUR WINDOW AGAIN?
A REALLY BIG OWL.
OOH! CAN I HELP? I NEVER KNEW PEOPLE WHO COULD MAKE THEIR OWN WINDOWS.
NOT WITH THIS, BUT YOU KNOW WHAT WOULD BE REALLY NICE? KASIF AND I COULD USE SOME NOODLES AFTER WE INSTALL THIS, IT'S HUNGRY WORK.
YOU COULD GO BACK IN THE KITCHEN AND--
NO GHOST PEPPERS THIS TIME!

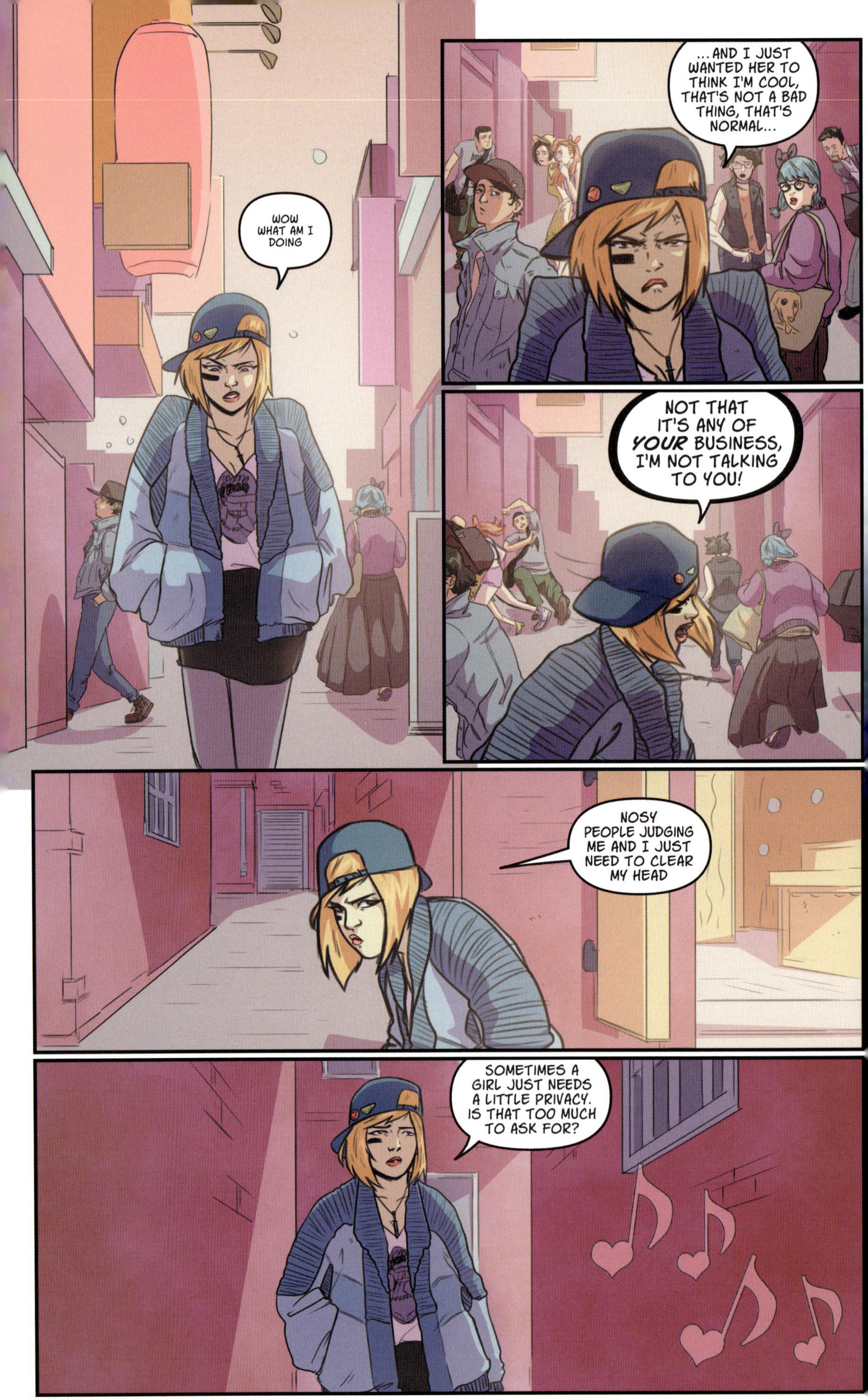
WOW WHAT AM I DOING
...AND I JUST WANTED HER TO THINK I'M COOL, THAT'S NOT A BAD THING, THAT'S NORMAL...
NOT THAT IT'S ANY OF *YOUR* BUSINESS, I'M NOT TALKING TO YOU!
NOSY PEOPLE JUDGING ME AND I JUST NEED TO CLEAR MY HEAD
SOMETIMES A GIRL JUST NEEDS A LITTLE PRIVACY. IS THAT TOO MUCH TO ASK FOR?

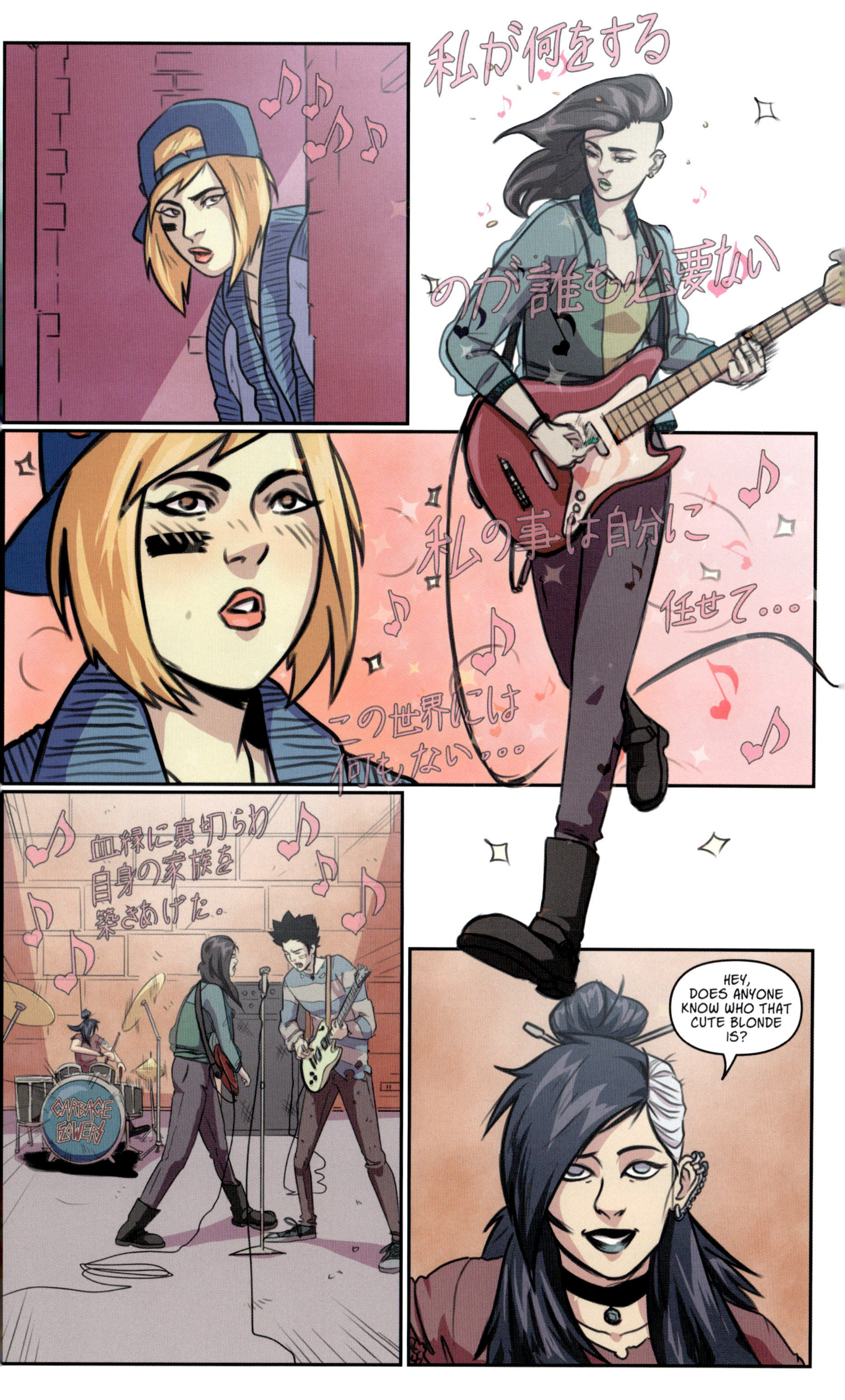
私が何をする
のが誰も必要ない
私の事は自分に
任せて...
この世界には
何もない...
血縁に裏切られ
自身の家族を
築きあげた。
GARBAGE FLOWERS
HEY, DOES ANYONE KNOW WHO THAT CUTE BLONDE IS?

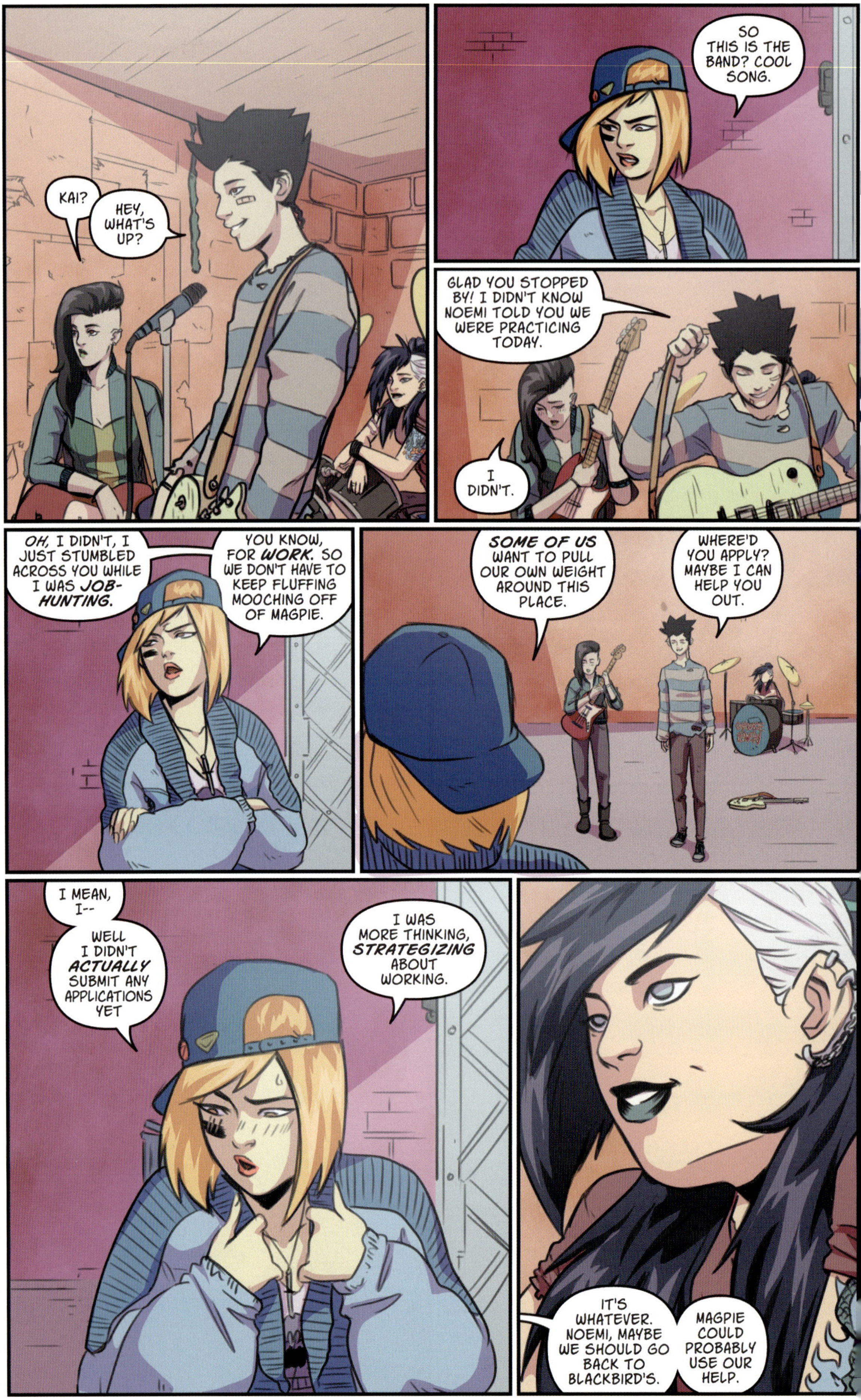
KAI?
HEY, WHAT'S UP?
SO THIS IS THE BAND? COOL SONG.
GLAD YOU STOPPED BY! I DIDN'T KNOW NOEMI TOLD YOU WE WERE PRACTICING TODAY.
I DIDN'T.
OH, I DIDN'T, I JUST STUMBLED ACROSS YOU WHILE I WAS ***JOB-HUNTING.***
YOU KNOW, FOR ***WORK.*** SO WE DON'T HAVE TO KEEP FLUFFING MOOCHING OFF OF MAGPIE.
SOME OF US WANT TO PULL OUR OWN WEIGHT AROUND THIS PLACE.
WHERE'D YOU APPLY? MAYBE I CAN HELP YOU OUT.
I MEAN, I--
WELL I DIDN'T ***ACTUALLY*** SUBMIT ANY APPLICATIONS YET
I WAS MORE THINKING, ***STRATEGIZING*** ABOUT WORKING.
IT'S WHATEVER. NOEMI, MAYBE WE SHOULD GO BACK TO BLACKBIRD'S.
MAGPIE COULD PROBABLY USE OUR HELP.

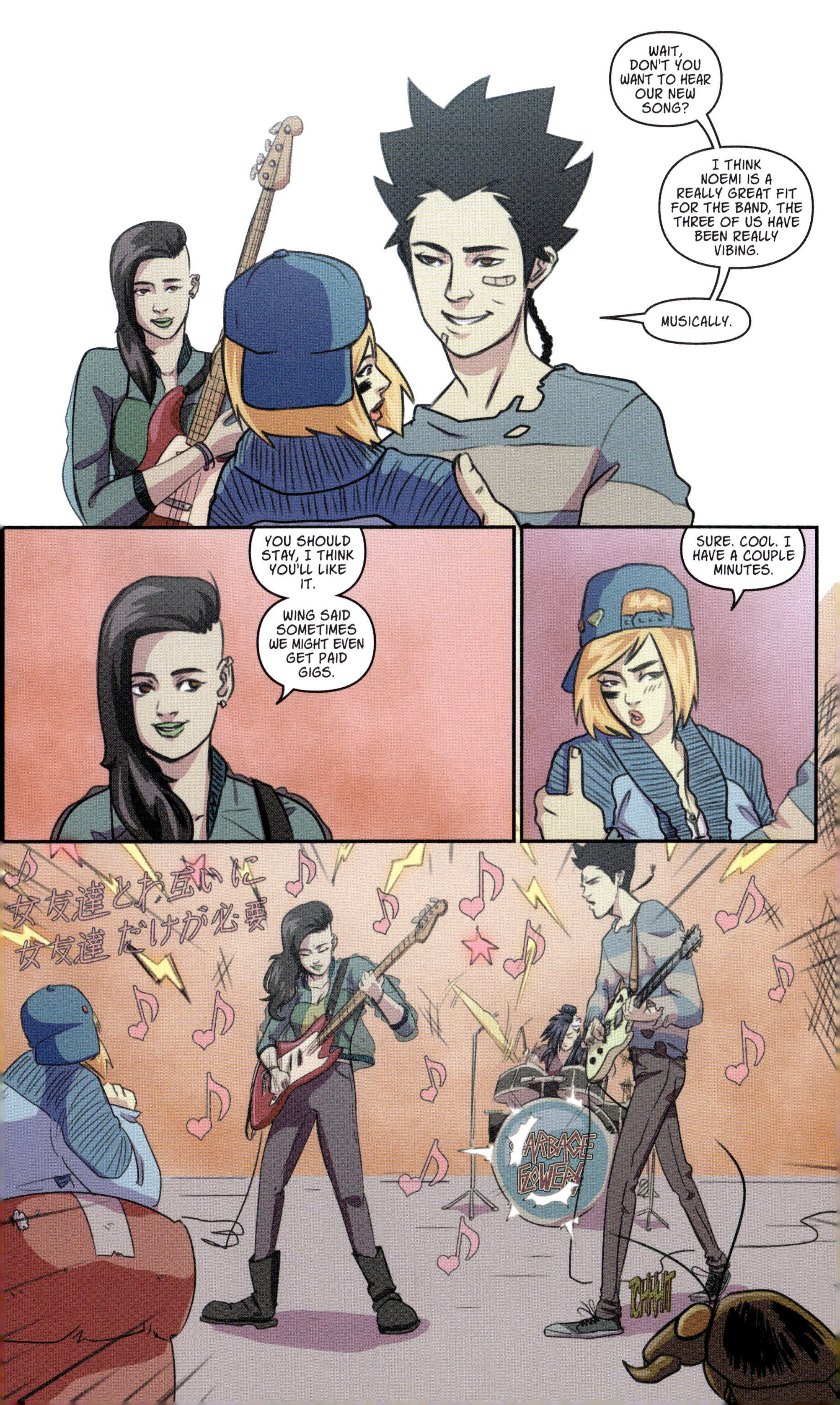
WAIT, DON'T YOU WANT TO HEAR OUR NEW SONG?
I THINK NOEMI IS A REALLY GREAT FIT FOR THE BAND, THE THREE OF US HAVE BEEN REALLY VIBING.
MUSICALLY.
YOU SHOULD STAY, I THINK YOU'LL LIKE IT.
WING SAID SOMETIMES WE MIGHT EVEN GET PAID GIGS.
SURE. COOL. I HAVE A COUPLE MINUTES.
女友達とお互いに
女友達だけが必要
TCHHHT

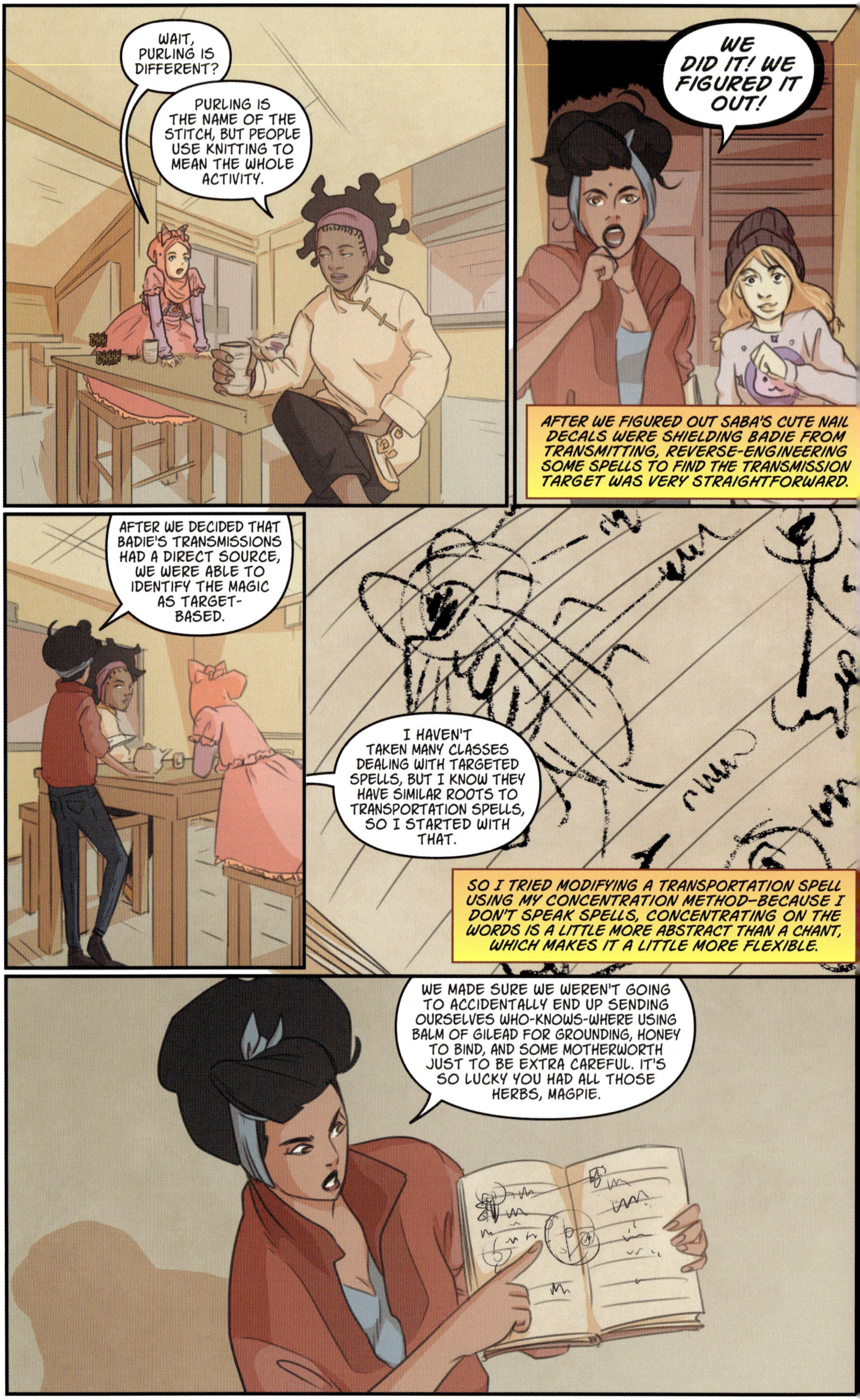
WAIT, PURLING IS DIFFERENT?
PURLING IS THE NAME OF THE STITCH, BUT PEOPLE USE KNITTING TO MEAN THE WHOLE ACTIVITY.
WE DID IT! WE FIGURED IT OUT!
AFTER WE FIGURED OUT SABA'S CUTE NAIL DECALS WERE SHIELDING BADIE FROM TRANSMITTING, REVERSE-ENGINEERING SOME SPELLS TO FIND THE TRANSMISSION TARGET WAS VERY STRAIGHTFORWARD.
AFTER WE DECIDED THAT BADIE'S TRANSMISSIONS HAD A DIRECT SOURCE, WE WERE ABLE TO IDENTIFY THE MAGIC AS TARGET-BASED.
I HAVEN'T TAKEN MANY CLASSES DEALING WITH TARGETED SPELLS, BUT I KNOW THEY HAVE SIMILAR ROOTS TO TRANSPORTATION SPELLS, SO I STARTED WITH THAT.
SO I TRIED MODIFYING A TRANSPORTATION SPELL USING MY CONCENTRATION METHOD—BECAUSE I DON'T SPEAK SPELLS, CONCENTRATING ON THE WORDS IS A LITTLE MORE ABSTRACT THAN A CHANT, WHICH MAKES IT A LITTLE MORE FLEXIBLE.
WE MADE SURE WE WEREN'T GOING TO ACCIDENTALLY END UP SENDING OURSELVES WHO-KNOWS-WHERE USING BALM OF GILEAD FOR GROUNDING, HONEY TO BIND, AND SOME MOTHERWORTH JUST TO BE EXTRA CAREFUL. IT'S SO LUCKY YOU HAD ALL THOSE HERBS, MAGPIE.

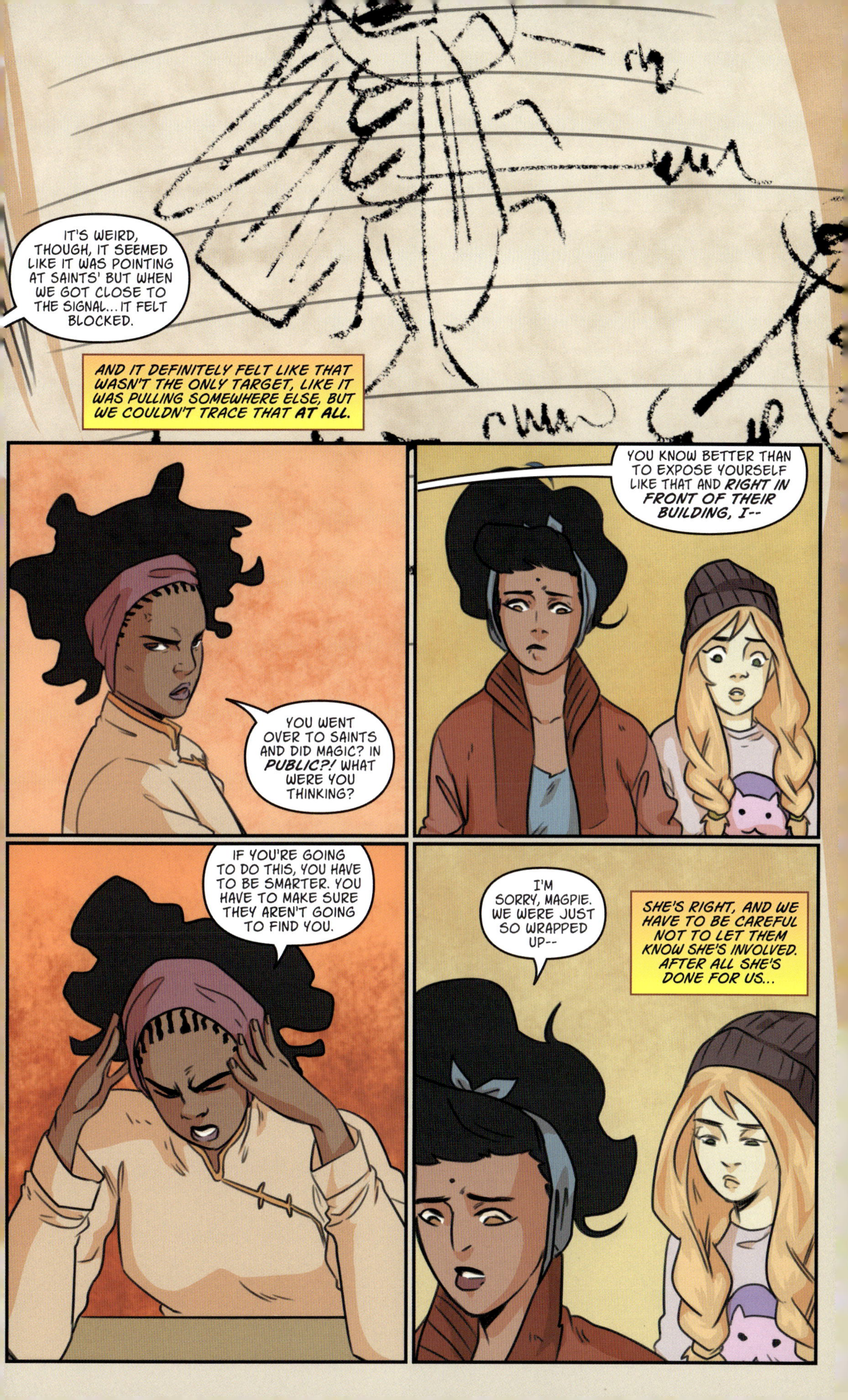
IT'S WEIRD, THOUGH, IT SEEMED LIKE IT WAS POINTING AT SAINTS' BUT WHEN WE GOT CLOSE TO THE SIGNAL... IT FELT BLOCKED.
AND IT DEFINITELY FELT LIKE THAT WASN'T THE ONLY TARGET, LIKE IT WAS PULLING SOMEWHERE ELSE, BUT WE COULDN'T TRACE THAT AT ALL.
YOU WENT OVER TO SAINTS AND DID MAGIC? IN PUBLIC?! WHAT WERE YOU THINKING?
YOU KNOW BETTER THAN TO EXPOSE YOURSELF LIKE THAT AND RIGHT IN FRONT OF THEIR BUILDING, I--
IF YOU'RE GOING TO DO THIS, YOU HAVE TO BE SMARTER. YOU HAVE TO MAKE SURE THEY AREN'T GOING TO FIND YOU.
I'M SORRY, MAGPIE. WE WERE JUST SO WRAPPED UP--
SHE'S RIGHT, AND WE HAVE TO BE CAREFUL NOT TO LET THEM KNOW SHE'S INVOLVED. AFTER ALL SHE'S DONE FOR US...

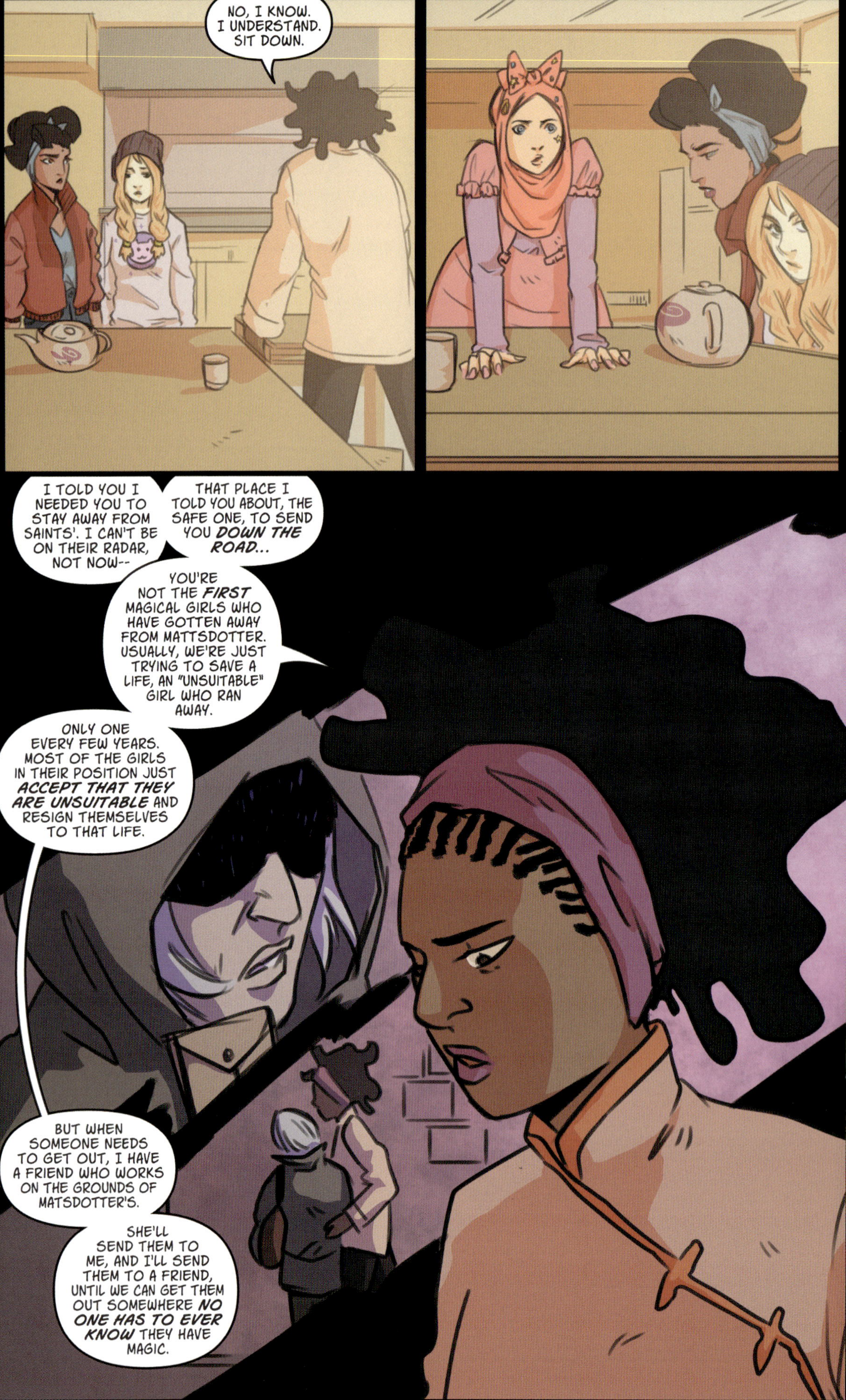
NO, I KNOW. I UNDERSTAND. SIT DOWN.
I TOLD YOU I NEEDED YOU TO STAY AWAY FROM SAINTS'. I CAN'T BE ON THEIR RADAR, NOT NOW--
THAT PLACE I TOLD YOU ABOUT, THE SAFE ONE, TO SEND YOU **DOWN THE ROAD...**
YOU'RE NOT THE **FIRST** MAGICAL GIRLS WHO HAVE GOTTEN AWAY FROM MATTSDOTTER. USUALLY, WE'RE JUST TRYING TO SAVE A LIFE, AN "UNSUITABLE" GIRL WHO RAN AWAY.
ONLY ONE EVERY FEW YEARS. MOST OF THE GIRLS IN THEIR POSITION JUST **ACCEPT THAT THEY ARE UNSUITABLE** AND RESIGN THEMSELVES TO THAT LIFE.
BUT WHEN SOMEONE NEEDS TO GET OUT, I HAVE A FRIEND WHO WORKS ON THE GROUNDS OF MATSDOTTER'S.
SHE'LL SEND THEM TO ME, AND I'LL SEND THEM TO A FRIEND, UNTIL WE CAN GET THEM OUT SOMEWHERE **NO ONE HAS TO EVER KNOW** THEY HAVE MAGIC.

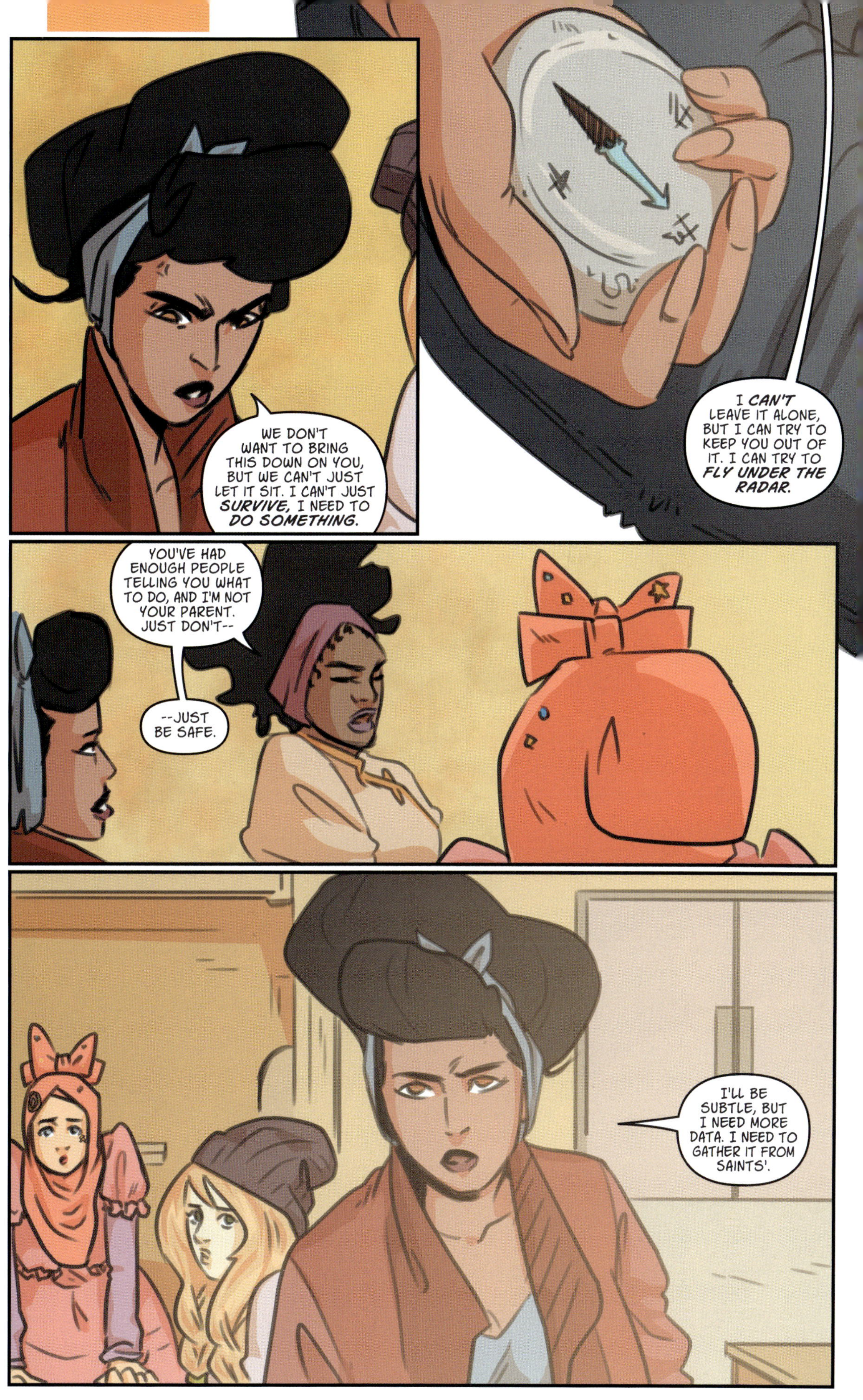
WE DON'T WANT TO BRING THIS DOWN ON YOU, BUT WE CAN'T JUST LET IT SIT. I CAN'T JUST SURVIVE, I NEED TO DO SOMETHING.
I CAN'T LEAVE IT ALONE, BUT I CAN TRY TO KEEP YOU OUT OF IT. I CAN TRY TO FLY UNDER THE RADAR.
YOU'VE HAD ENOUGH PEOPLE TELLING YOU WHAT TO DO, AND I'M NOT YOUR PARENT. JUST DON'T--
--JUST BE SAFE.
I'LL BE SUBTLE, BUT I NEED MORE DATA. I NEED TO GATHER IT FROM SAINTS'.

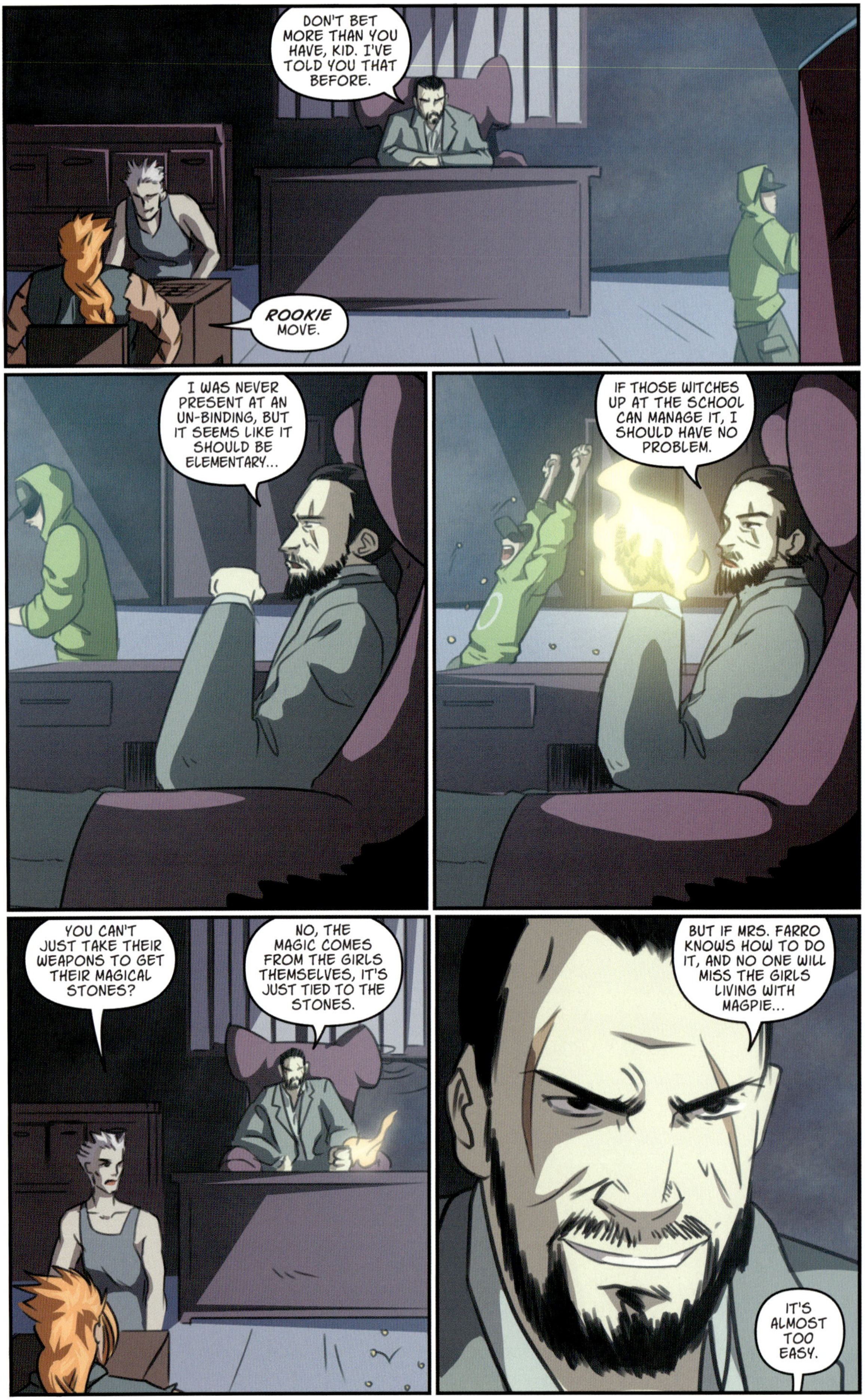
DON'T BET MORE THAN YOU HAVE, KID. I'VE TOLD YOU THAT BEFORE.
ROOKIE MOVE.
I WAS NEVER PRESENT AT AN UN-BINDING, BUT IT SEEMS LIKE IT SHOULD BE ELEMENTARY...
IF THOSE WITCHES UP AT THE SCHOOL CAN MANAGE IT, I SHOULD HAVE NO PROBLEM.
YOU CAN'T JUST TAKE THEIR WEAPONS TO GET THEIR MAGICAL STONES?
NO, THE MAGIC COMES FROM THE GIRLS THEMSELVES, IT'S JUST TIED TO THE STONES.
BUT IF MRS. FARRO KNOWS HOW TO DO IT, AND NO ONE WILL MISS THE GIRLS LIVING WITH MAGPIE...
IT'S ALMOST TOO EASY.

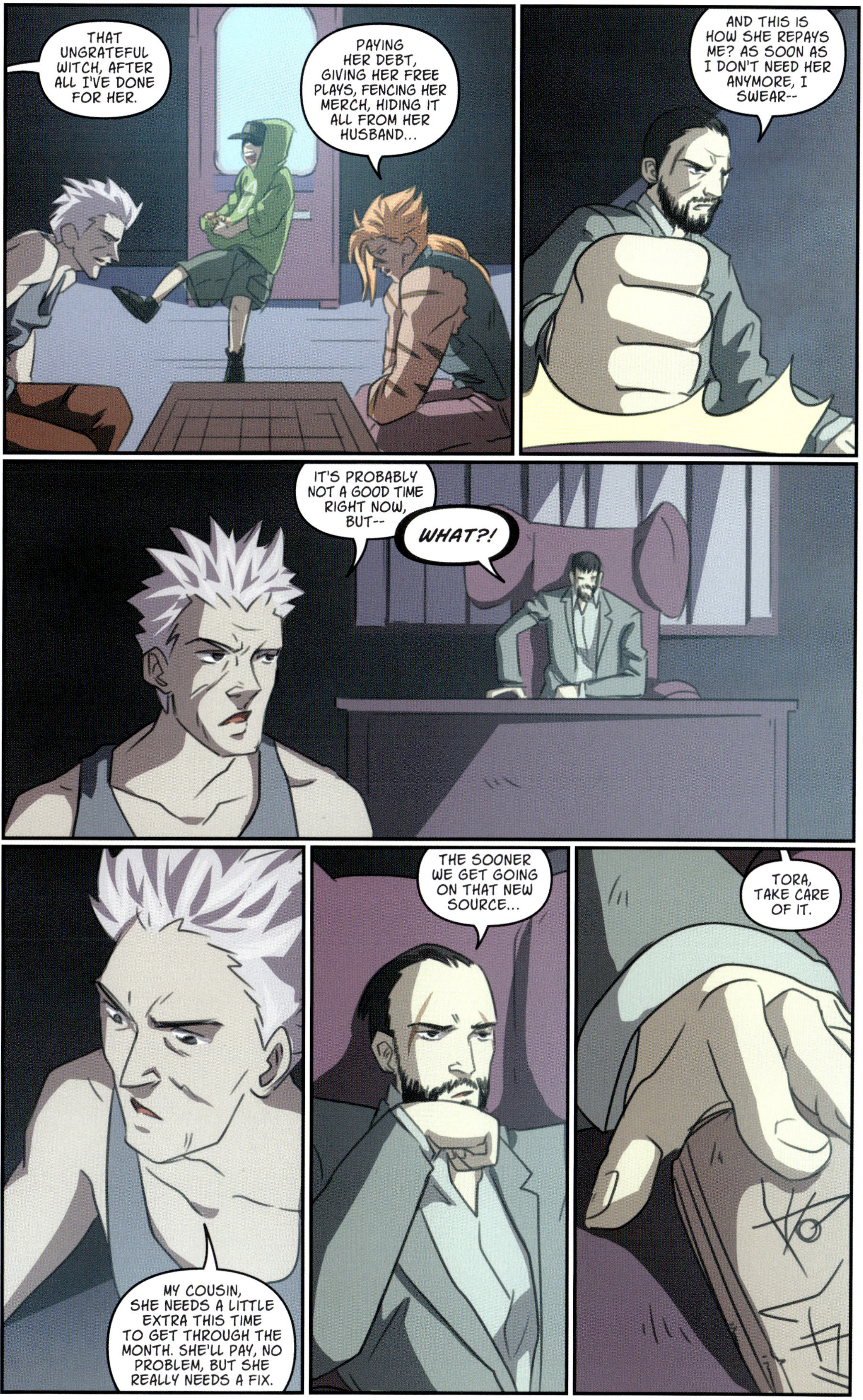
THAT UNGRATEFUL WITCH, AFTER ALL I'VE DONE FOR HER.
PAYING HER DEBT, GIVING HER FREE PLAYS, FENCING HER MERCH, HIDING IT ALL FROM HER HUSBAND...
AND THIS IS HOW SHE REPAYS ME? AS SOON AS I DON'T NEED HER ANYMORE, I SWEAR--
IT'S PROBABLY NOT A GOOD TIME RIGHT NOW, BUT--
WHAT?!
MY COUSIN, SHE NEEDS A LITTLE EXTRA THIS TIME TO GET THROUGH THE MONTH. SHE'LL PAY, NO PROBLEM, BUT SHE REALLY NEEDS A FIX.
THE SOONER WE GET GOING ON THAT NEW SOURCE...
TORA, TAKE CARE OF IT.

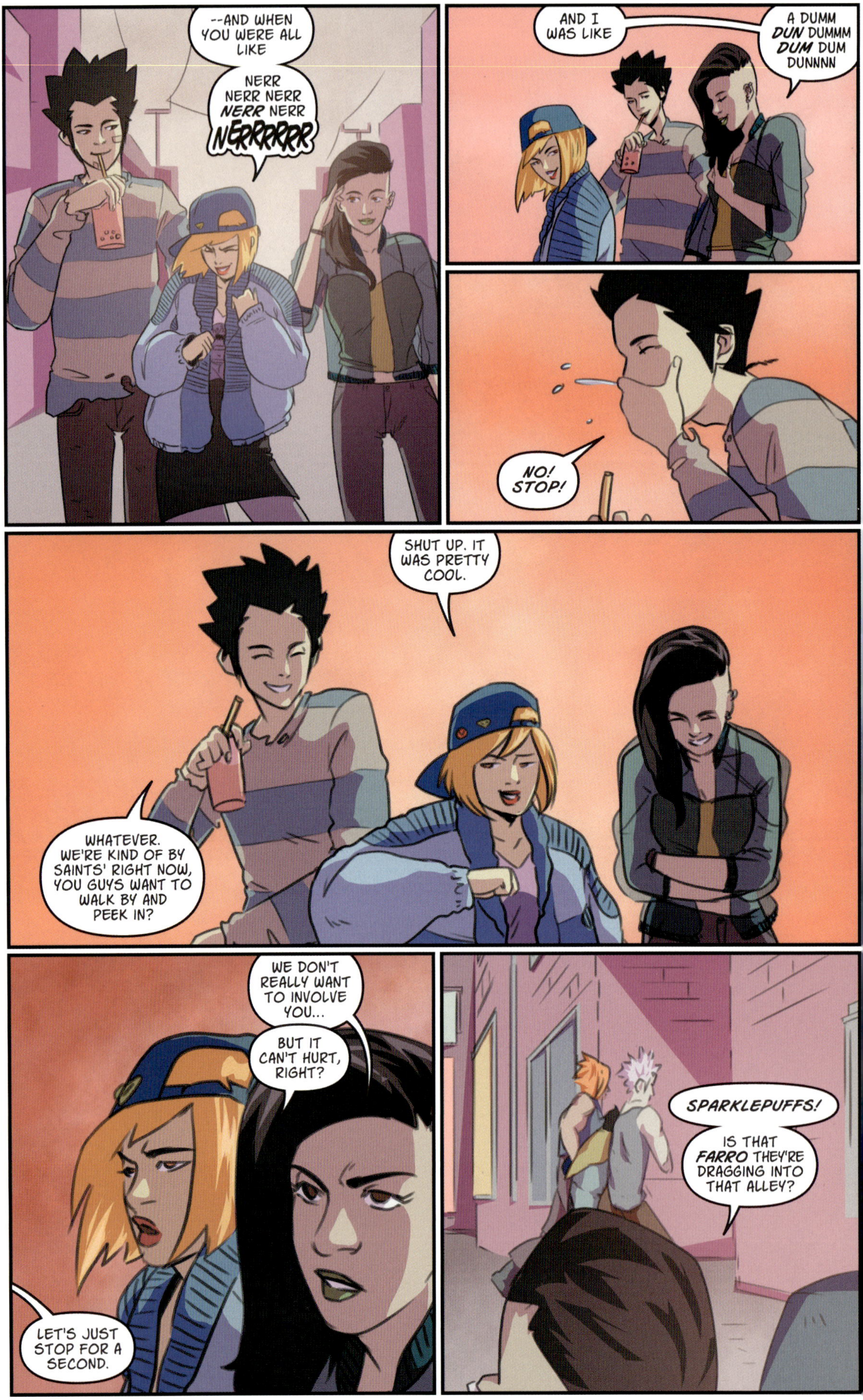
--AND WHEN YOU WERE ALL LIKE
NERR NERR NERR *NERR* NERR
NERRRRRR
AND I WAS LIKE
A DUMM *DUN* DUMMM *DUM* DUM DUNNNN
NO! STOP!
SHUT UP. IT WAS PRETTY COOL.
WHATEVER. WE'RE KIND OF BY SAINTS' RIGHT NOW, YOU GUYS WANT TO WALK BY AND PEEK IN?
WE DON'T REALLY WANT TO INVOLVE YOU...
BUT IT CAN'T HURT, RIGHT?
LET'S JUST STOP FOR A SECOND.
SPARKLEPUFFS!
IS THAT *FARRO* THEY'RE DRAGGING INTO THAT ALLEY?

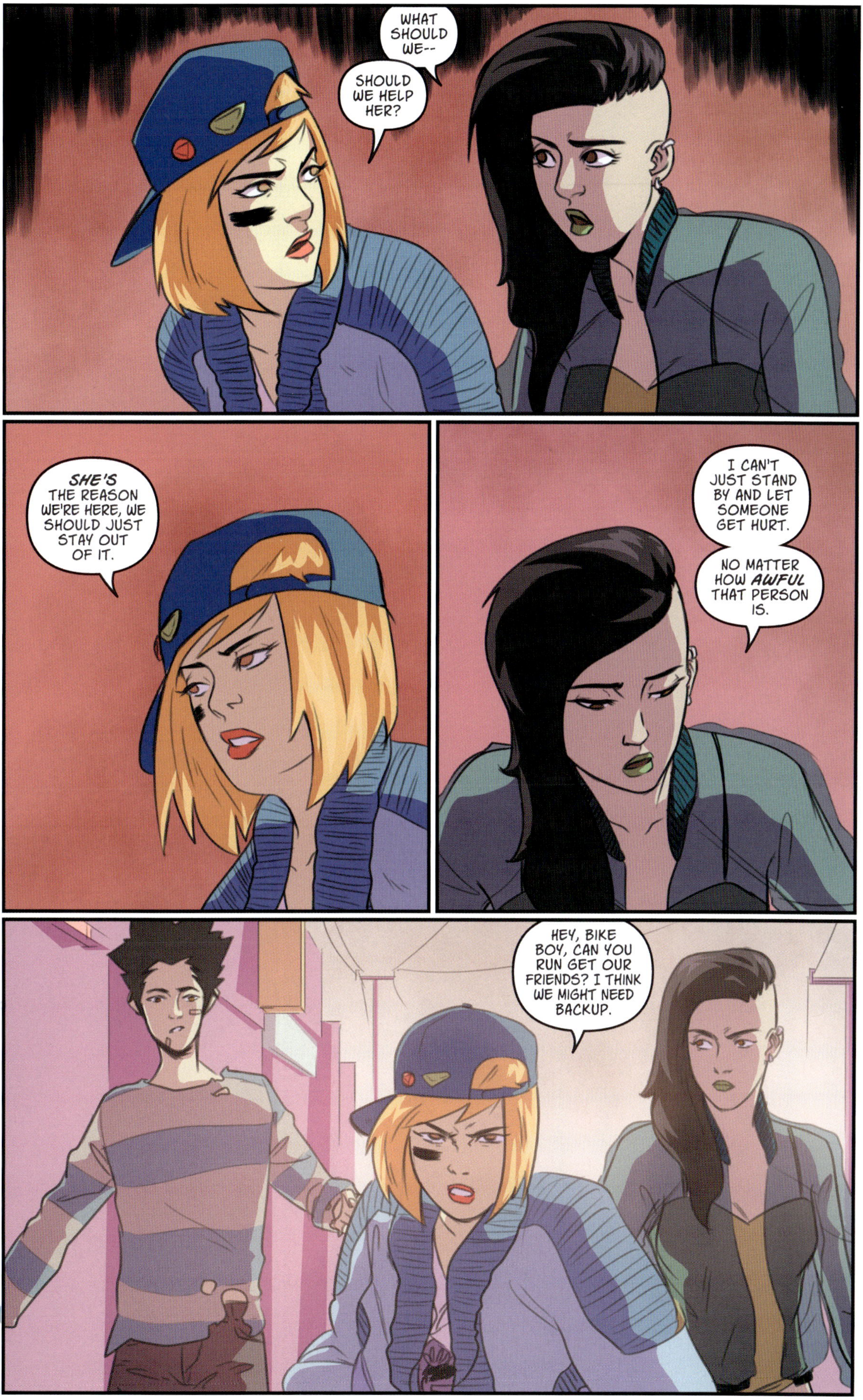
WHAT SHOULD WE--
SHOULD WE HELP HER?
SHE'S THE REASON WE'RE HERE, WE SHOULD JUST STAY OUT OF IT.
I CAN'T JUST STAND BY AND LET SOMEONE GET HURT.
NO MATTER HOW *AWFUL* THAT PERSON IS.
HEY, BIKE BOY, CAN YOU RUN GET OUR FRIENDS? I THINK WE MIGHT NEED BACKUP.

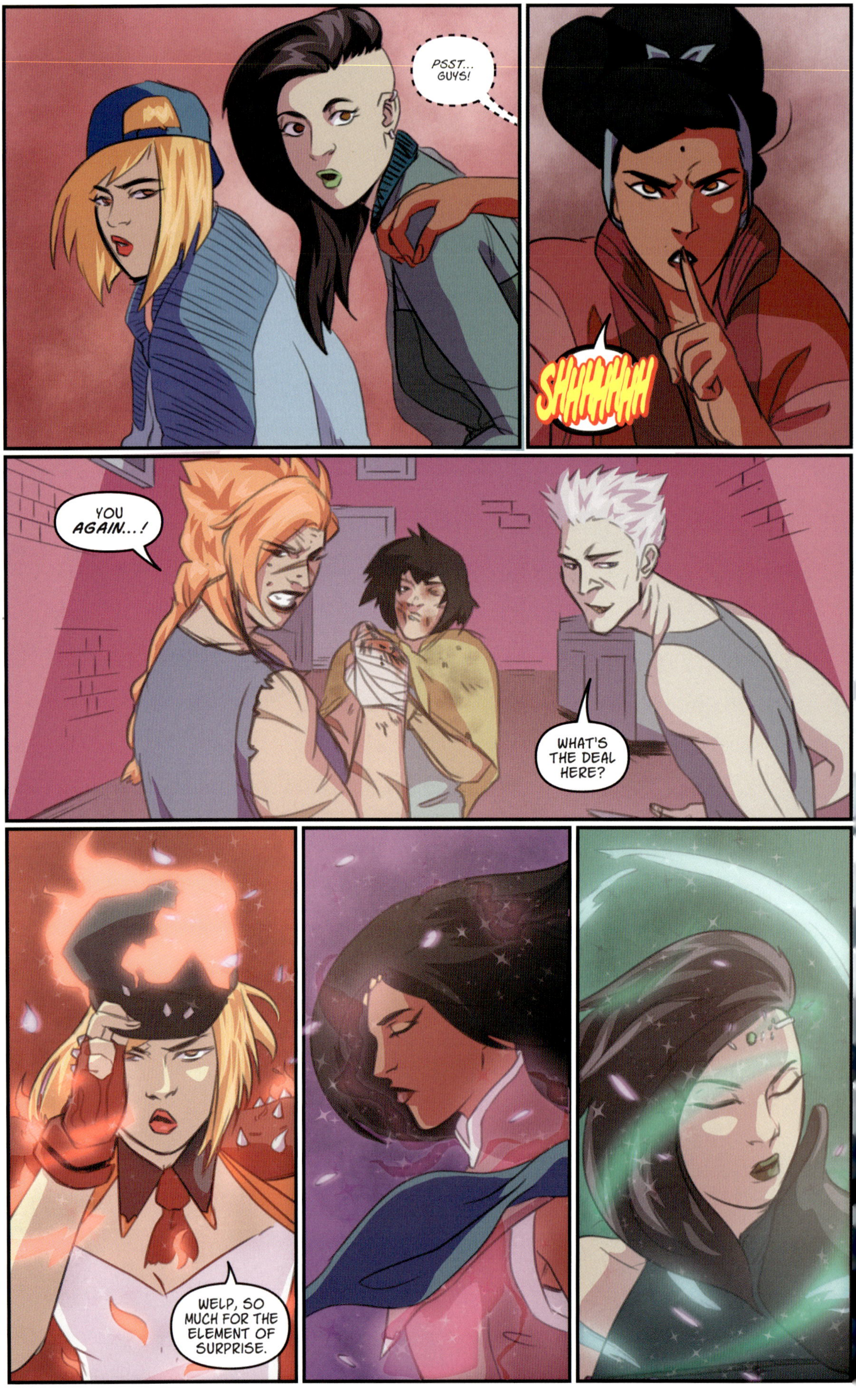
PSST... GUYS!
SHHHHHH
YOU AGAIN...!
WHAT'S THE DEAL HERE?
WELP, SO MUCH FOR THE ELEMENT OF SURPRISE.

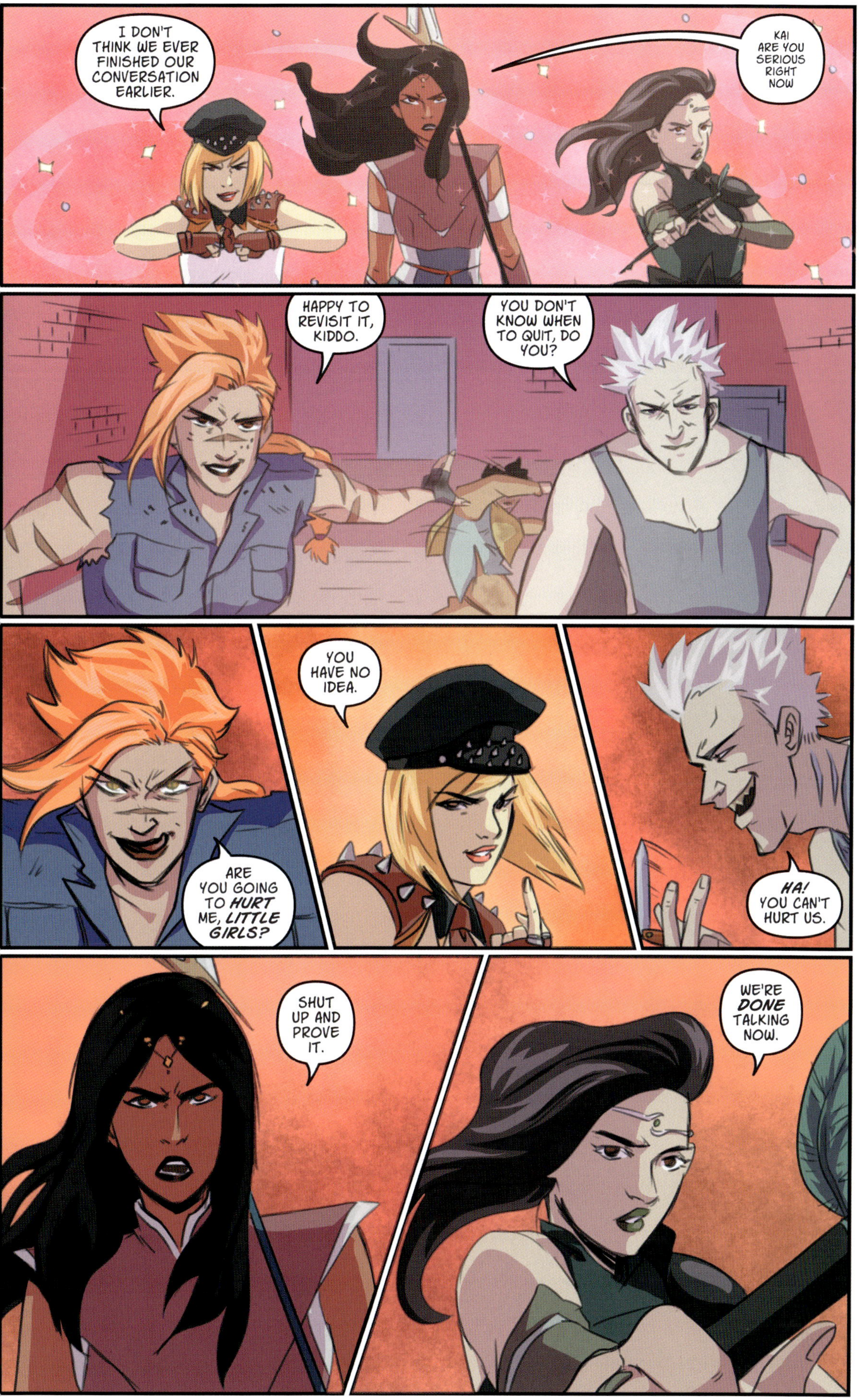
I DON'T THINK WE EVER FINISHED OUR CONVERSATION EARLIER.
KAI ARE YOU SERIOUS RIGHT NOW
HAPPY TO REVISIT IT, KIDDO.
YOU DON'T KNOW WHEN TO QUIT, DO YOU?
ARE YOU GOING TO HURT ME, LITTLE GIRLS?
YOU HAVE NO IDEA.
HA! YOU CAN'T HURT US.
SHUT UP AND PROVE IT.
WE'RE DONE TALKING NOW.

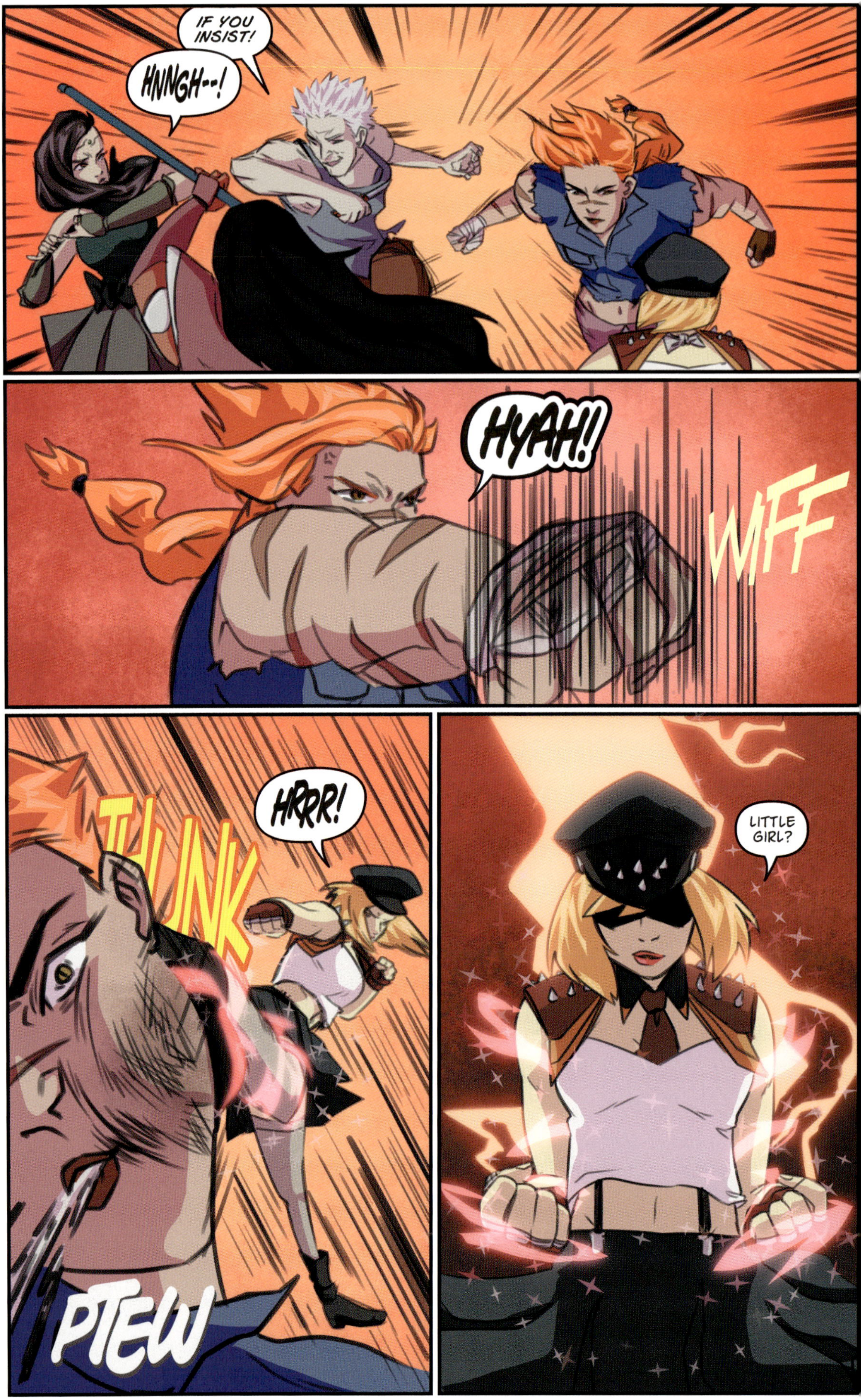
IF YOU INSIST!
HNNGH--!
HYAH!
WIFF
HRRR!
THUNK
PTEW
LITTLE GIRL?

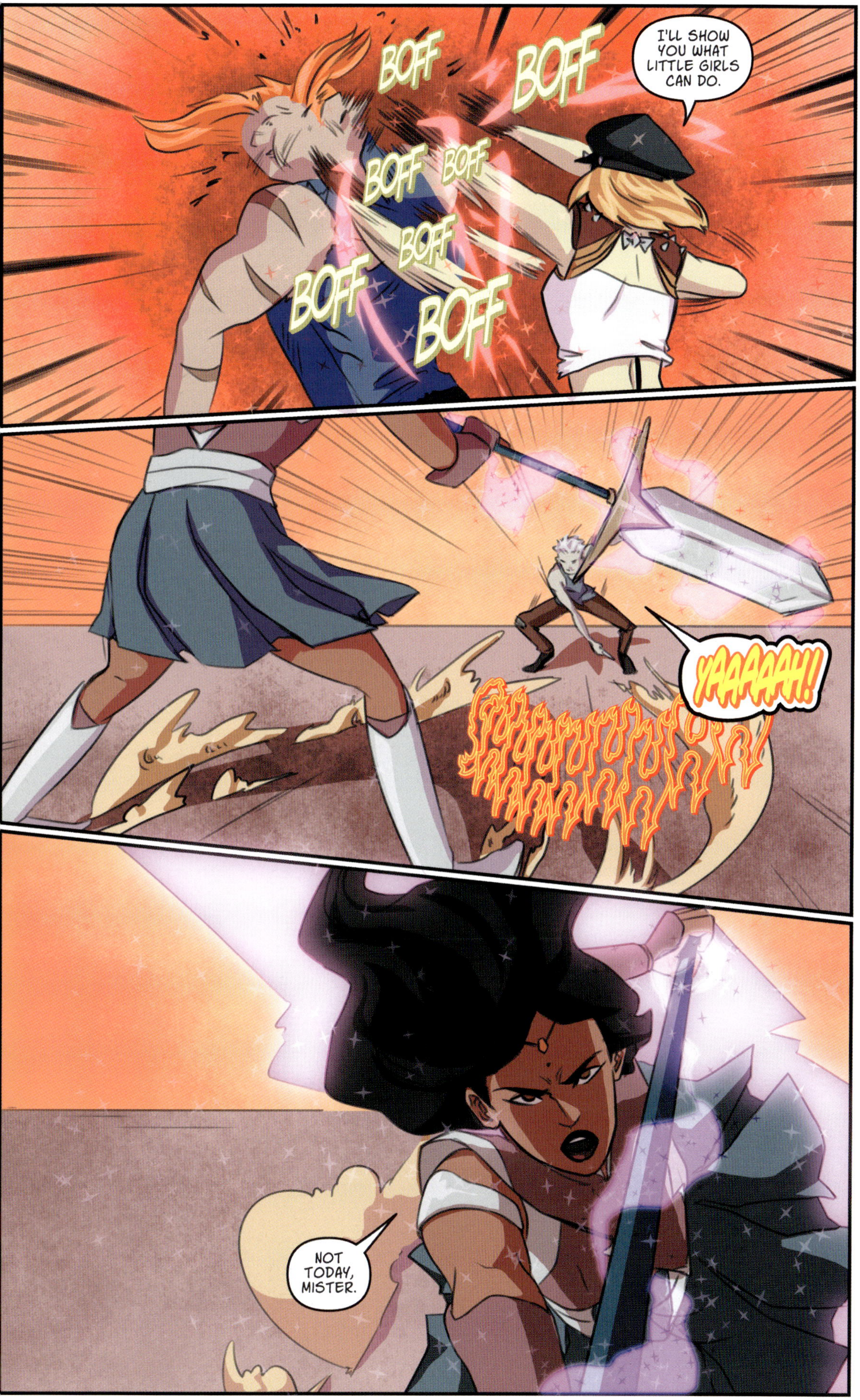
BOFF
BOFF
I'LL SHOW YOU WHAT LITTLE GIRLS CAN DO.
BOFF
BOFF
BOFF
BOFF
BOFF
YAAAAAH!
NOT TODAY, MISTER.

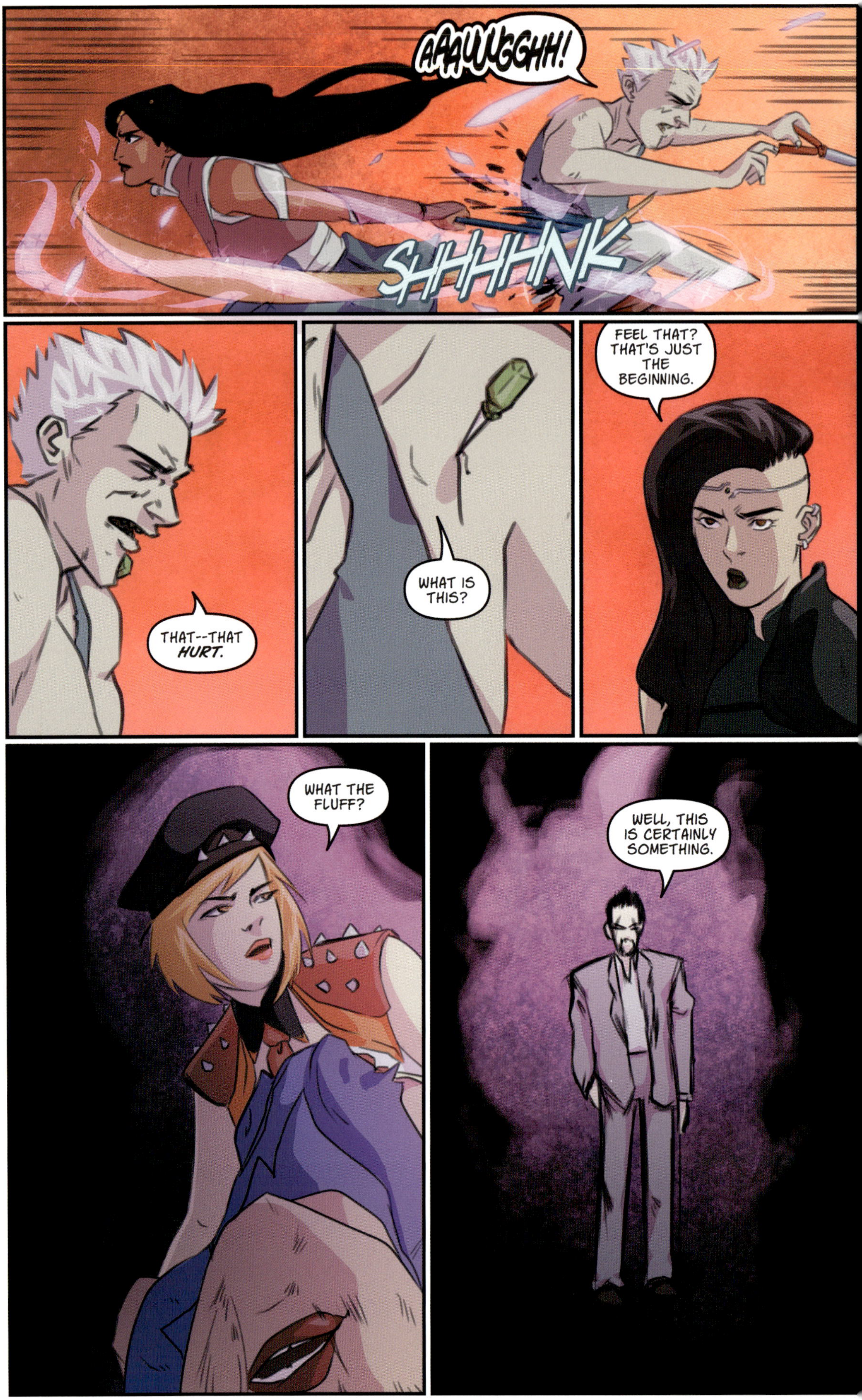
AAAUUUGGHH!
SHHHHNK
THAT--THAT *HURT.*
WHAT IS THIS?
FEEL THAT? THAT'S JUST THE BEGINNING.
WHAT THE FLUFF?
WELL, THIS IS CERTAINLY SOMETHING.

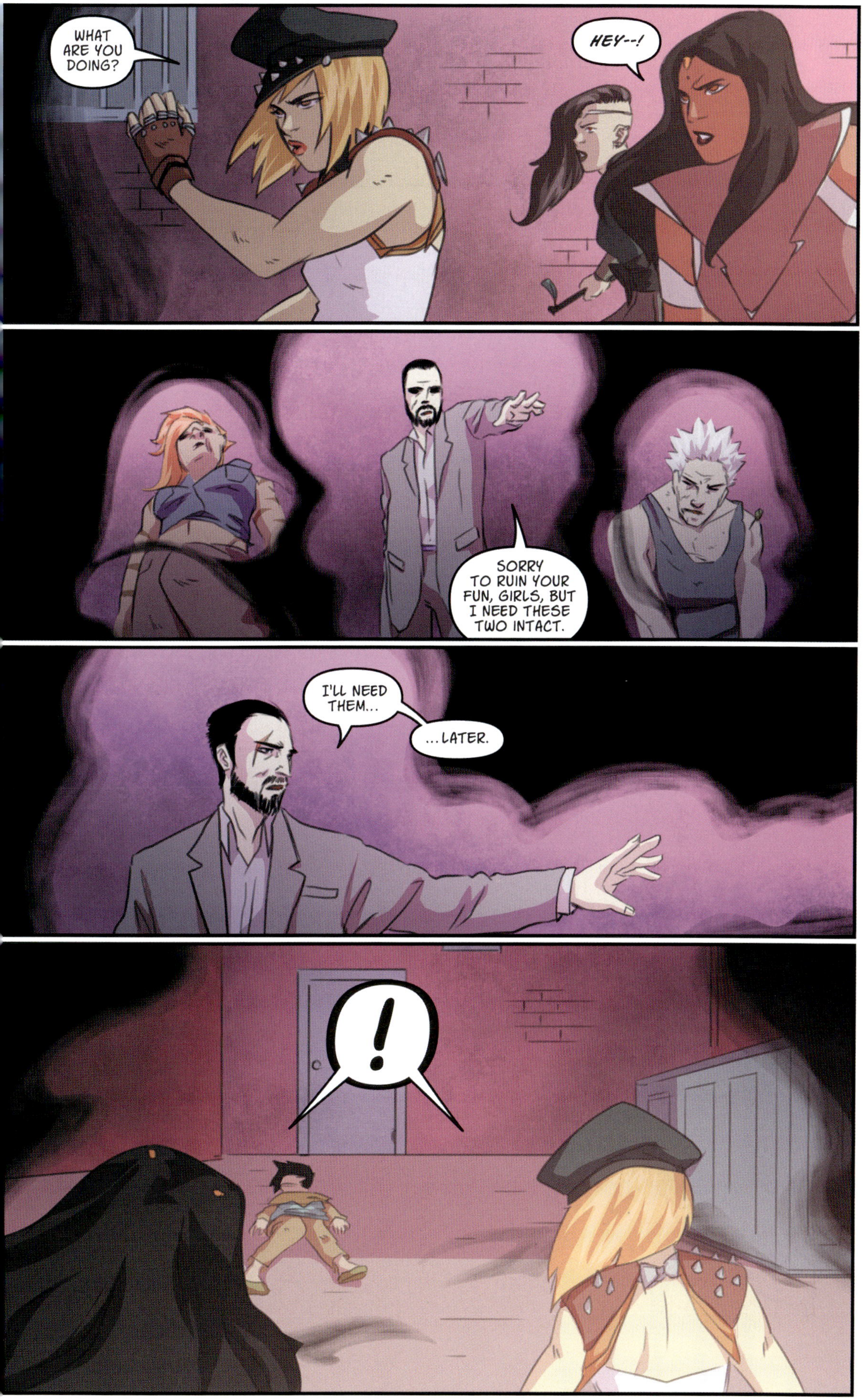
WHAT ARE YOU DOING?
HEY--!
SORRY TO RUIN YOUR FUN, GIRLS, BUT I NEED THESE TWO INTACT.
I'LL NEED THEM...
...LATER.
!

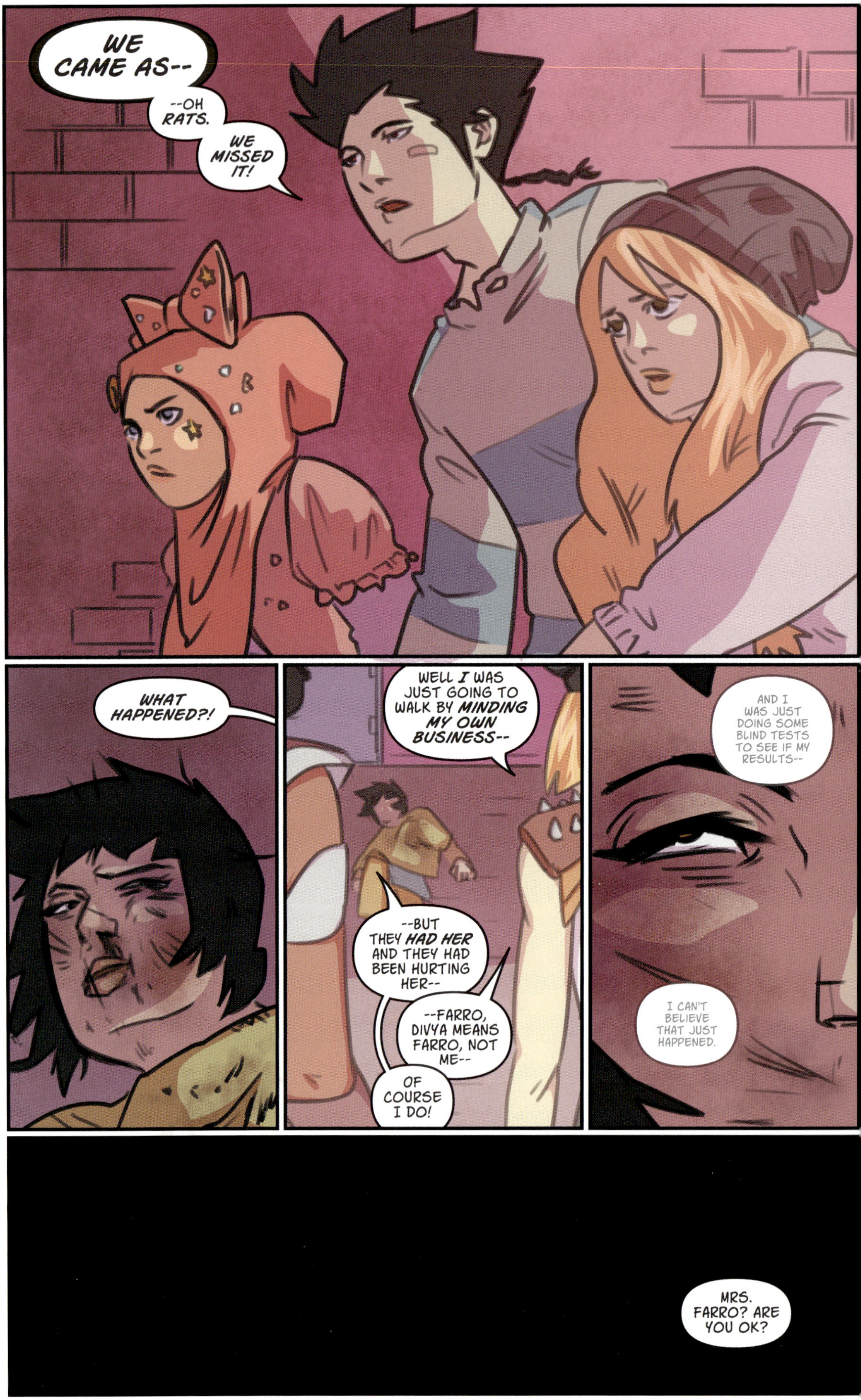
WE CAME AS--
--OH RATS.
WE MISSED IT!
WHAT HAPPENED?!
WELL I WAS JUST GOING TO WALK BY MINDING MY OWN BUSINESS--
--BUT THEY HAD HER AND THEY HAD BEEN HURTING HER--
--FARRO, DIVYA MEANS FARRO, NOT ME--
OF COURSE I DO!
AND I WAS JUST DOING SOME BLIND TESTS TO SEE IF MY RESULTS--
I CAN'T BELIEVE THAT JUST HAPPENED.
MRS. FARRO? ARE YOU OK?

CHAPTER 4

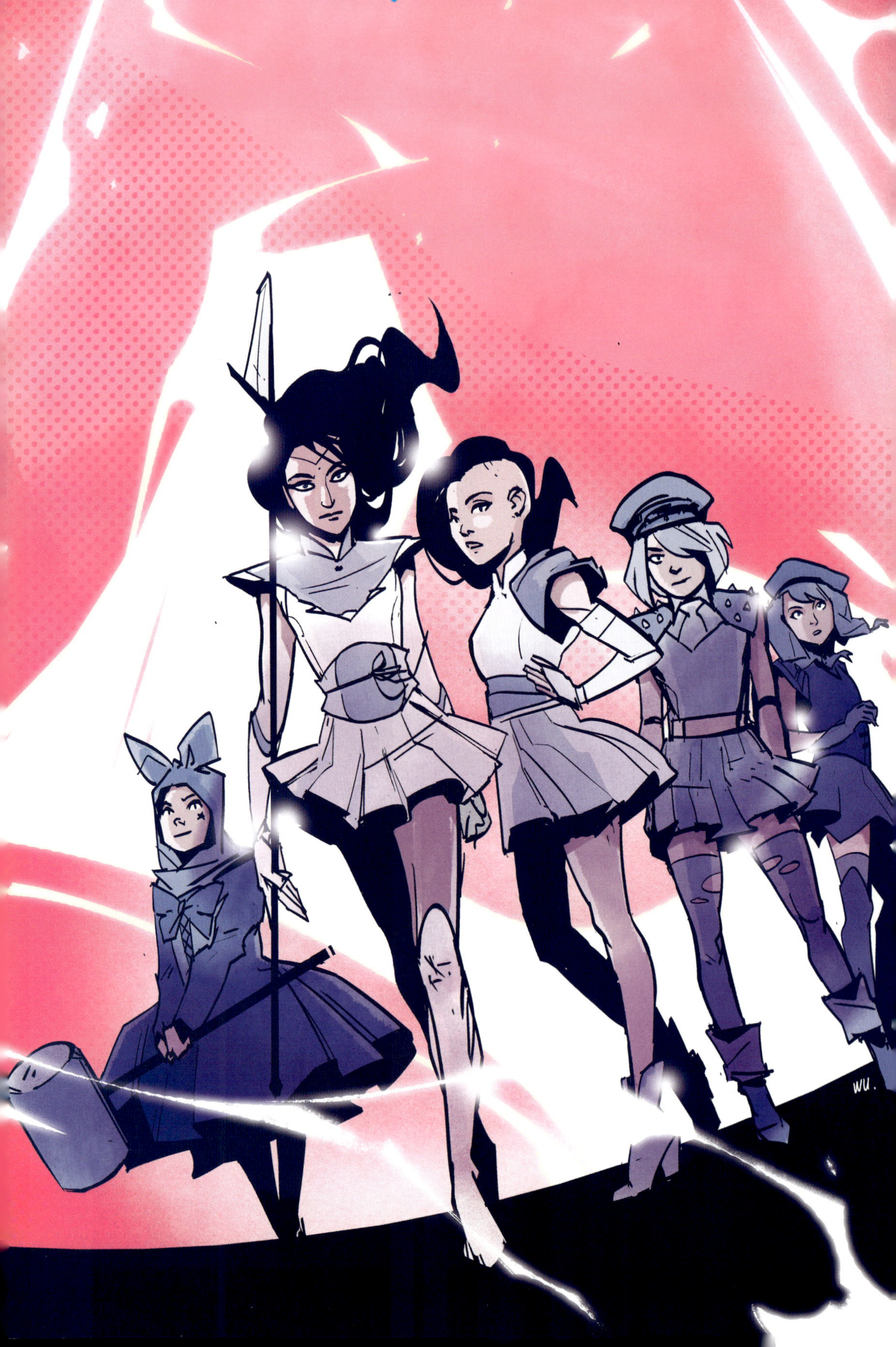
WU.

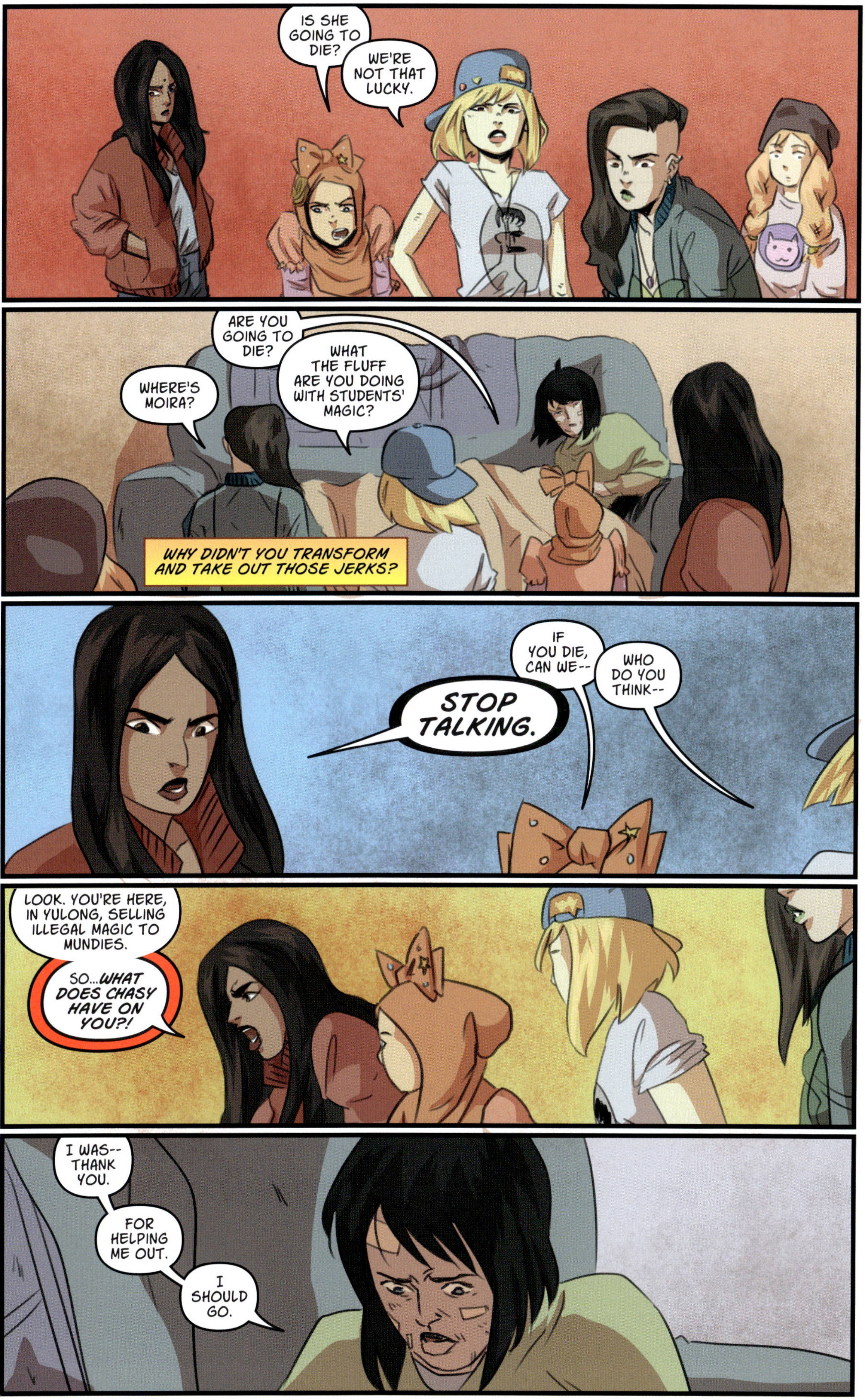
IS SHE GOING TO DIE?
WE'RE NOT THAT LUCKY.
ARE YOU GOING TO DIE?
WHERE'S MOIRA?
WHAT THE FLUFF ARE YOU DOING WITH STUDENTS' MAGIC?
WHY DIDN'T YOU TRANSFORM AND TAKE OUT THOSE JERKS?
IF YOU DIE, CAN WE--
WHO DO YOU THINK--
STOP TALKING.
LOOK. YOU'RE HERE, IN YULONG, SELLING ILLEGAL MAGIC TO MUNDIES.
SO...WHAT DOES CHASY HAVE ON YOU?!
I WAS-- THANK YOU.
FOR HELPING ME OUT.
I SHOULD GO.

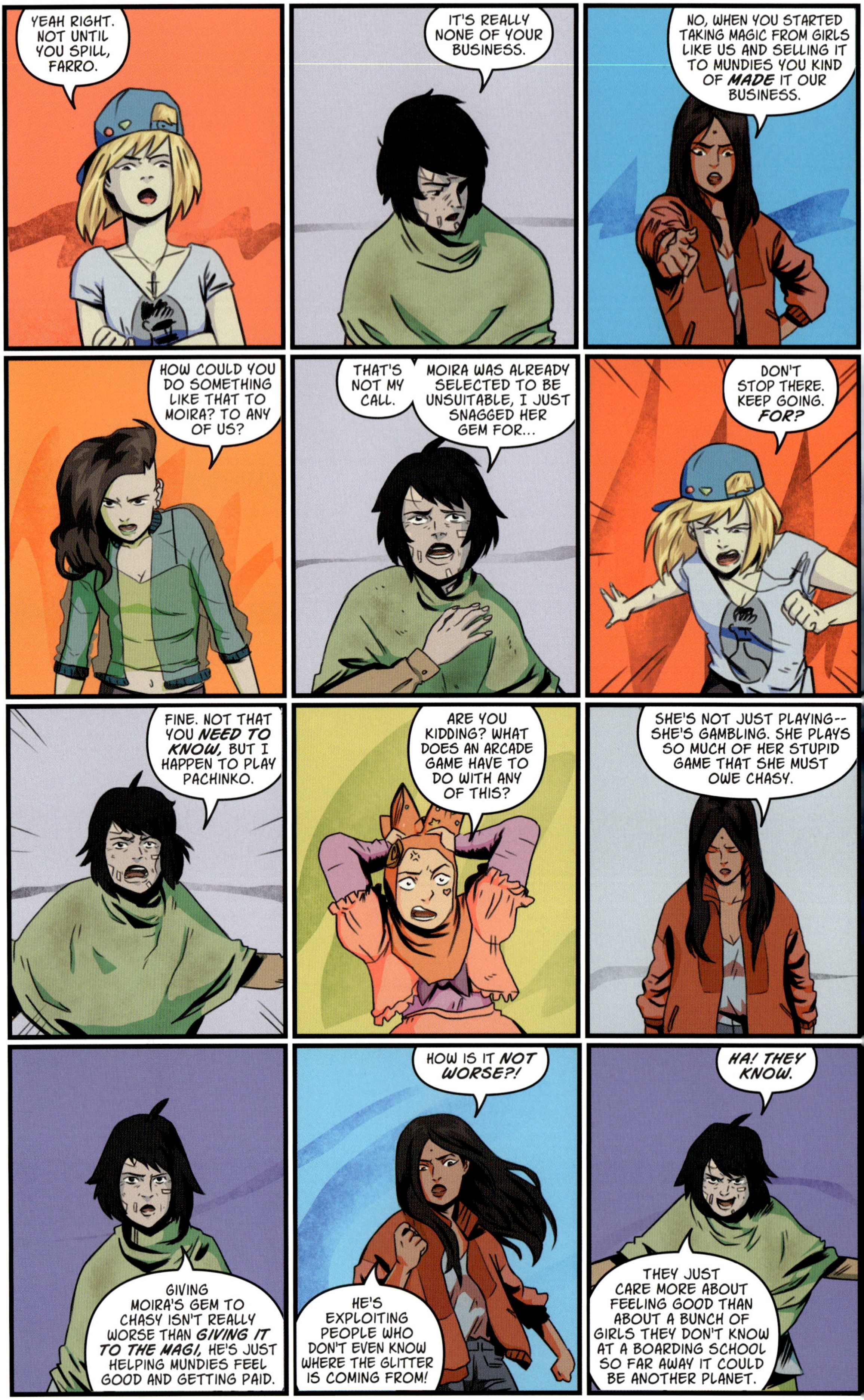
YEAH RIGHT. NOT UNTIL YOU SPILL, FARRO.
IT'S REALLY NONE OF YOUR BUSINESS.
NO, WHEN YOU STARTED TAKING MAGIC FROM GIRLS LIKE US AND SELLING IT TO MUNDIES YOU KIND OF *MADE* IT OUR BUSINESS.
HOW COULD YOU DO SOMETHING LIKE THAT TO MOIRA? TO ANY OF US?
THAT'S NOT MY CALL.
MOIRA WAS ALREADY SELECTED TO BE UNSUITABLE, I JUST SNAGGED HER GEM FOR...
DON'T STOP THERE. KEEP GOING. *FOR?*
FINE. NOT THAT YOU *NEED TO KNOW,* BUT I HAPPEN TO PLAY PACHINKO.
ARE YOU KIDDING? WHAT DOES AN ARCADE GAME HAVE TO DO WITH ANY OF THIS?
SHE'S NOT JUST PLAYING-- SHE'S GAMBLING. SHE PLAYS SO MUCH OF HER STUPID GAME THAT SHE MUST OWE CHASY.
GIVING MOIRA'S GEM TO CHASY ISN'T REALLY WORSE THAN *GIVING IT TO THE MAGI,* HE'S JUST HELPING MUNDIES FEEL GOOD AND GETTING PAID.
HOW IS IT *NOT WORSE?!*
HE'S EXPLOITING PEOPLE WHO DON'T EVEN KNOW WHERE THE GLITTER IS COMING FROM!
HA! THEY KNOW.
THEY JUST CARE MORE ABOUT FEELING GOOD THAN ABOUT A BUNCH OF GIRLS THEY DON'T KNOW AT A BOARDING SCHOOL SO FAR AWAY IT COULD BE ANOTHER PLANET.

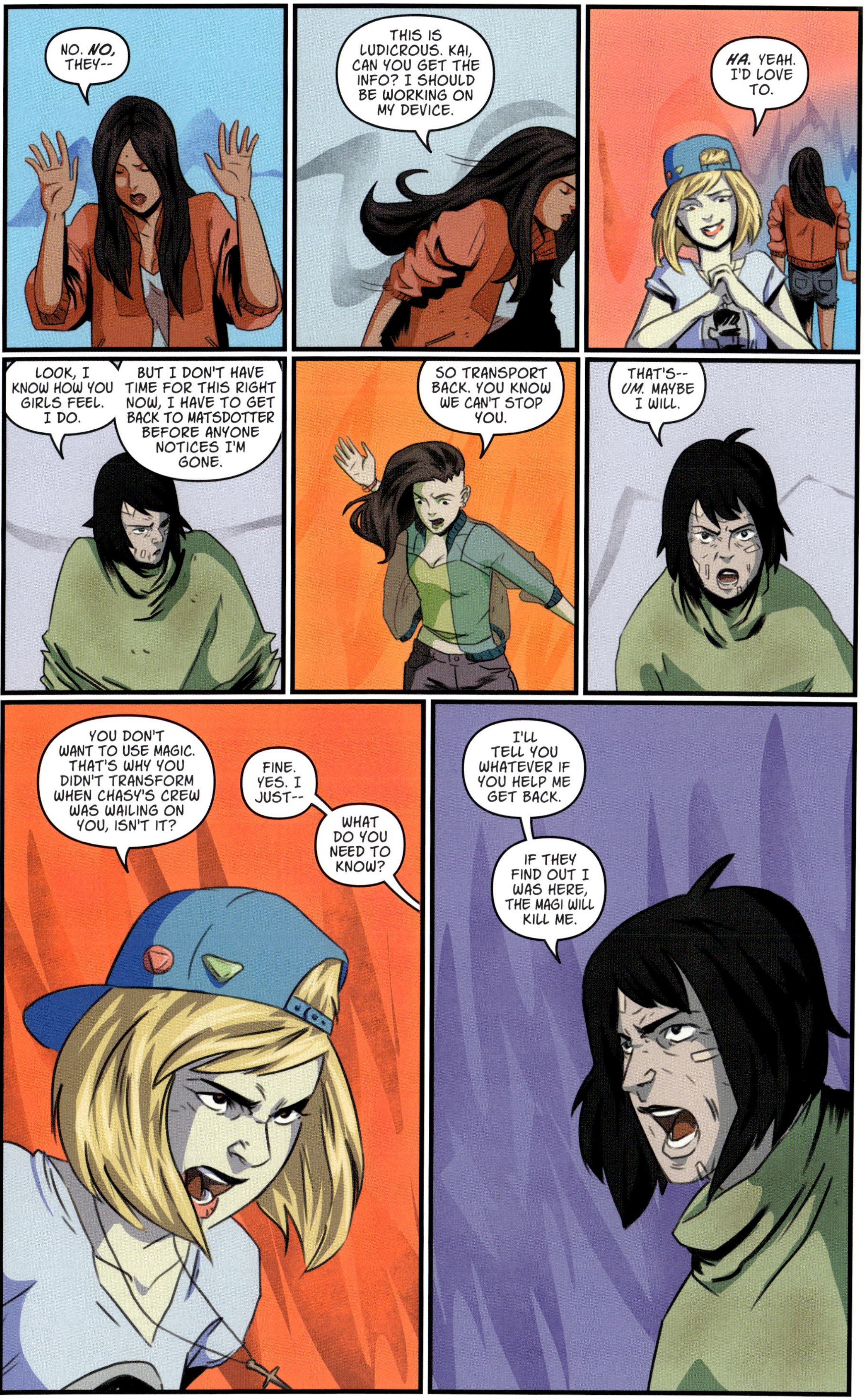
NO. *NO,* THEY--
THIS IS LUDICROUS. KAI, CAN YOU GET THE INFO? I SHOULD BE WORKING ON MY DEVICE.
HA. YEAH. I'D LOVE TO.
LOOK, I KNOW HOW YOU GIRLS FEEL. I DO.
BUT I DON'T HAVE TIME FOR THIS RIGHT NOW, I HAVE TO GET BACK TO MATSDOTTER BEFORE ANYONE NOTICES I'M GONE.
SO TRANSPORT BACK. YOU KNOW WE CAN'T STOP YOU.
THAT'S-- *UM.* MAYBE I WILL.
YOU DON'T WANT TO USE MAGIC. THAT'S WHY YOU DIDN'T TRANSFORM WHEN CHASY'S CREW WAS WAILING ON YOU, ISN'T IT?
FINE. YES. I JUST--
WHAT DO YOU NEED TO KNOW?
I'LL TELL YOU WHATEVER IF YOU HELP ME GET BACK.
IF THEY FIND OUT I WAS HERE, THE MAGI WILL KILL ME.

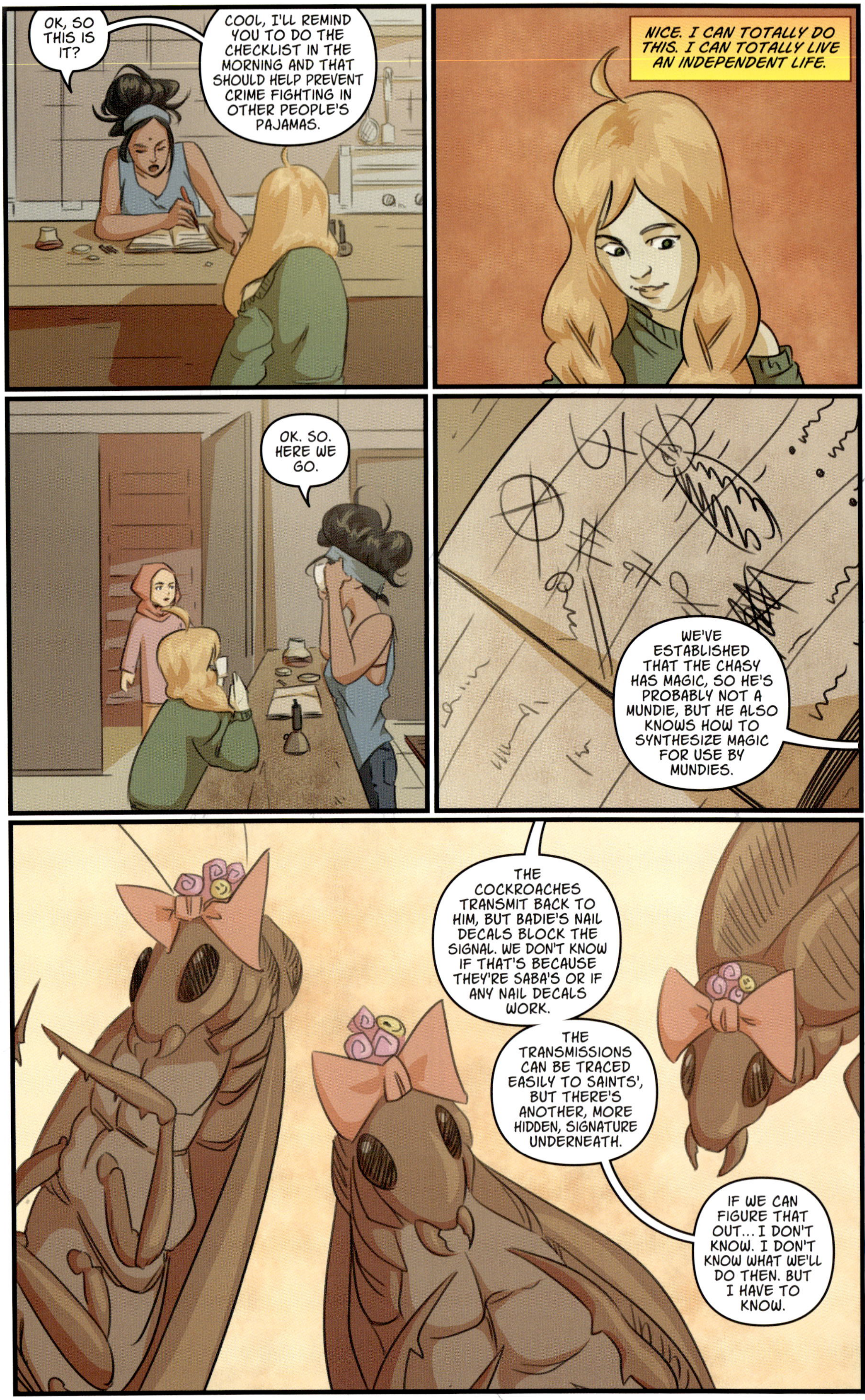
OK, SO THIS IS IT?
COOL, I'LL REMIND YOU TO DO THE CHECKLIST IN THE MORNING AND THAT SHOULD HELP PREVENT CRIME FIGHTING IN OTHER PEOPLE'S PAJAMAS.
NICE. I CAN TOTALLY DO THIS. I CAN TOTALLY LIVE AN INDEPENDENT LIFE.
OK. SO. HERE WE GO.
WE'VE ESTABLISHED THAT THE CHASY HAS MAGIC, SO HE'S PROBABLY NOT A MUNDIE, BUT HE ALSO KNOWS HOW TO SYNTHESIZE MAGIC FOR USE BY MUNDIES.
THE COCKROACHES TRANSMIT BACK TO HIM, BUT BADIE'S NAIL DECALS BLOCK THE SIGNAL. WE DON'T KNOW IF THAT'S BECAUSE THEY'RE SABA'S OR IF ANY NAIL DECALS WORK.
THE TRANSMISSIONS CAN BE TRACED EASILY TO SAINTS', BUT THERE'S ANOTHER, MORE HIDDEN, SIGNATURE UNDERNEATH.
IF WE CAN FIGURE THAT OUT... I DON'T KNOW. I DON'T KNOW WHAT WE'LL DO THEN. BUT I HAVE TO KNOW.

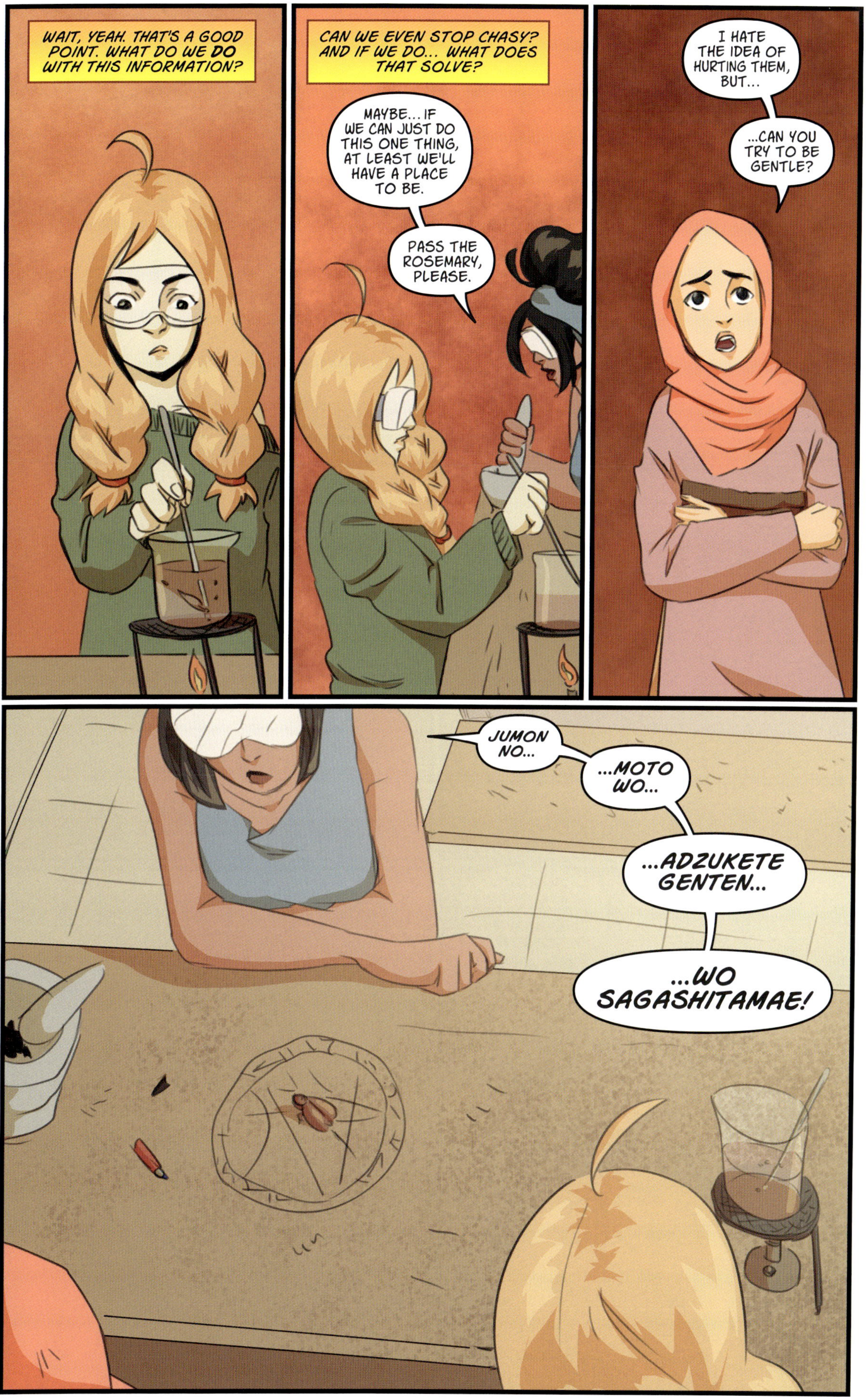
WAIT, YEAH. THAT'S A GOOD POINT. WHAT DO WE DO WITH THIS INFORMATION?
CAN WE EVEN STOP CHASY? AND IF WE DO... WHAT DOES THAT SOLVE?
MAYBE... IF WE CAN JUST DO THIS ONE THING, AT LEAST WE'LL HAVE A PLACE TO BE.
PASS THE ROSEMARY, PLEASE.
I HATE THE IDEA OF HURTING THEM, BUT...
...CAN YOU TRY TO BE GENTLE?
JUMON NO...
...MOTO WO...
...ADZUKETE GENTEN...
...WO SAGASHITAMAE!

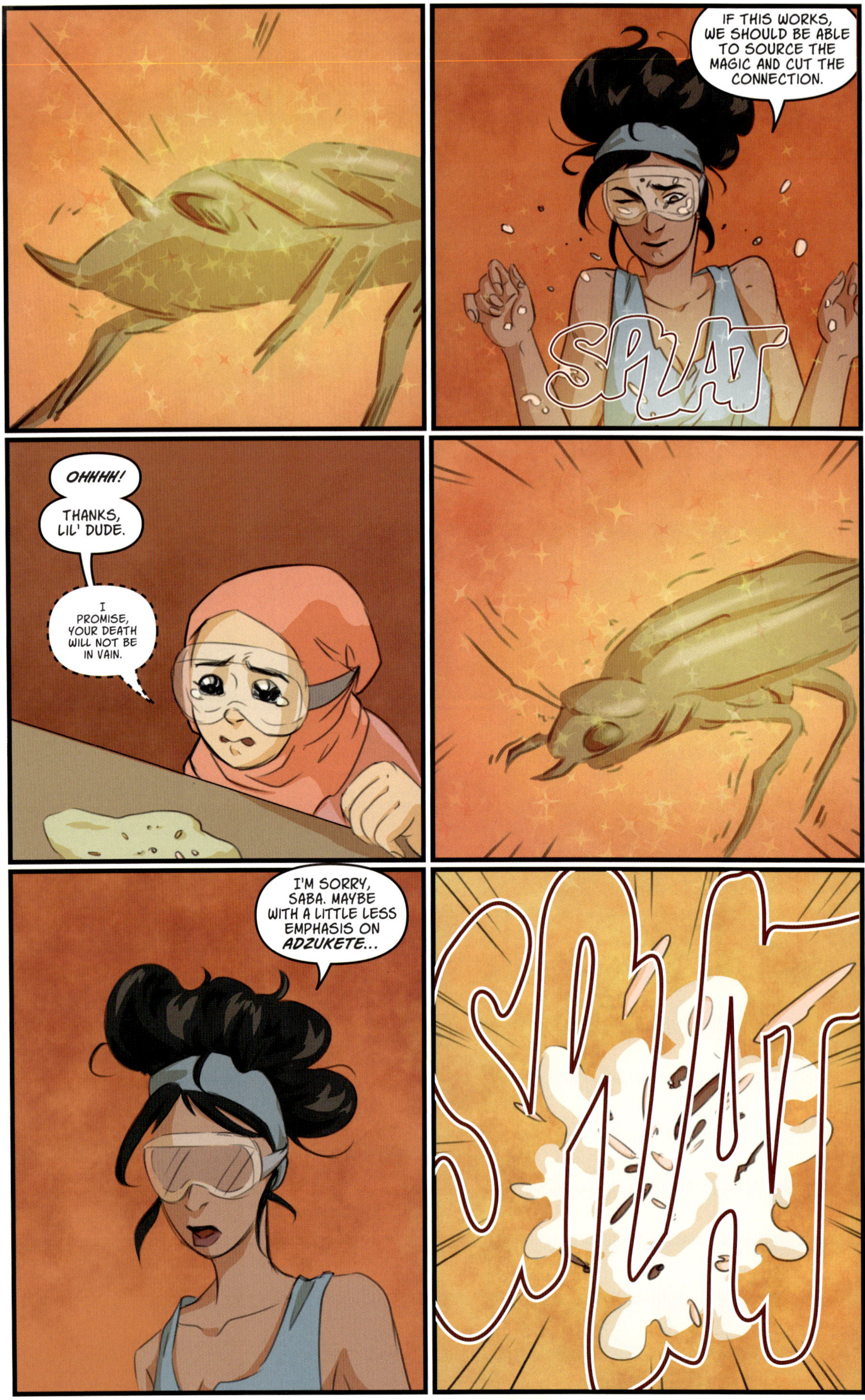
IF THIS WORKS, WE SHOULD BE ABLE TO SOURCE THE MAGIC AND CUT THE CONNECTION.
SPLAT
OHHHH!
THANKS, LIL' DUDE.
I PROMISE, YOUR DEATH WILL NOT BE IN VAIN.
I'M SORRY, SABA. MAYBE WITH A LITTLE LESS EMPHASIS ON *ADZUKETE*...
SPLAT

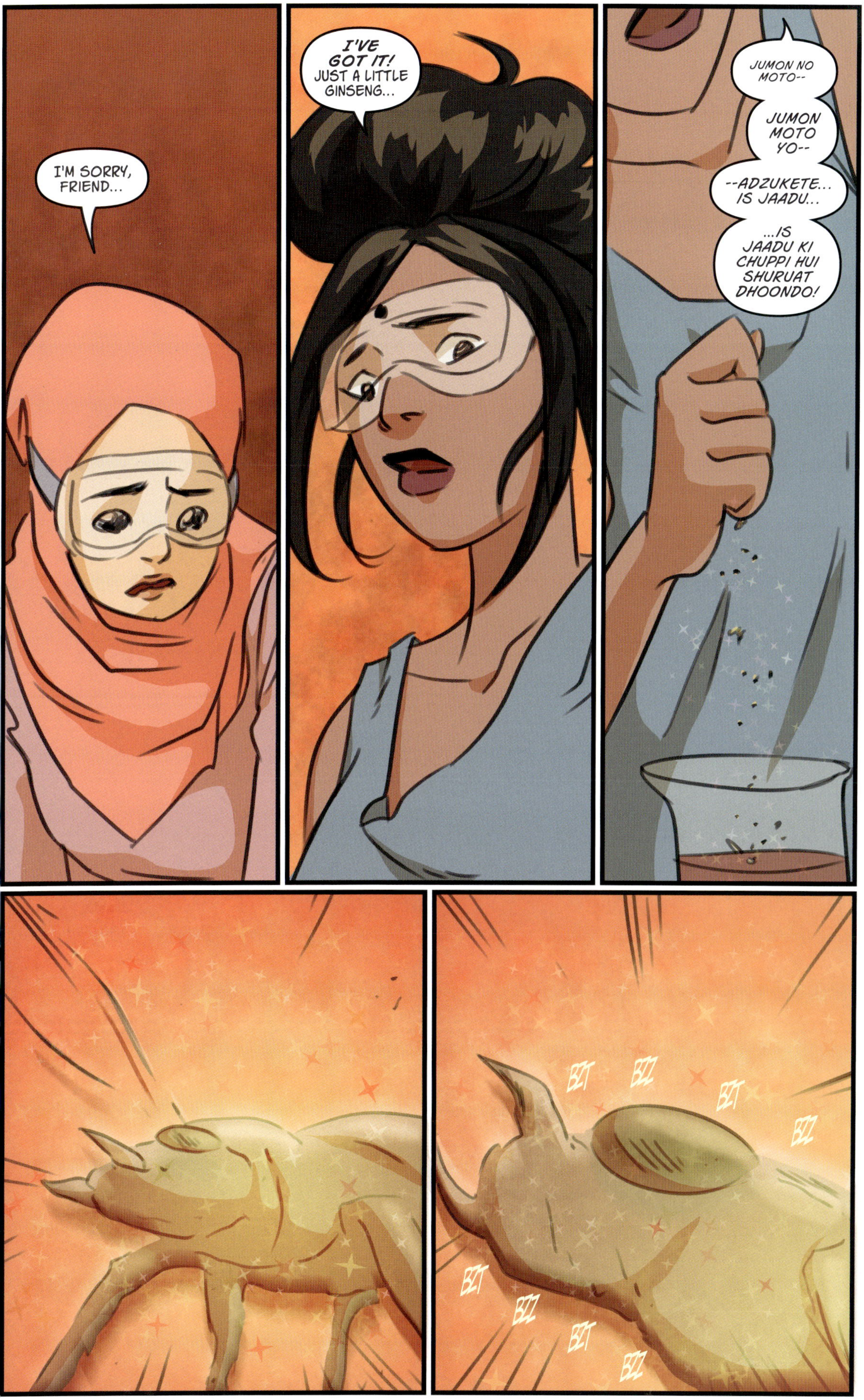
I'M SORRY, FRIEND...
I'VE GOT IT! JUST A LITTLE GINSENG...
JUMON NO MOTO--
JUMON MOTO YO--
--ADZUKETE... IS JAADU...
...IS JAADU KI CHUPPI HUI SHURUAT DHOONDO!
BZT
BZZ
BZT
BZZ
BZT
BZZ
BZT
BZZ

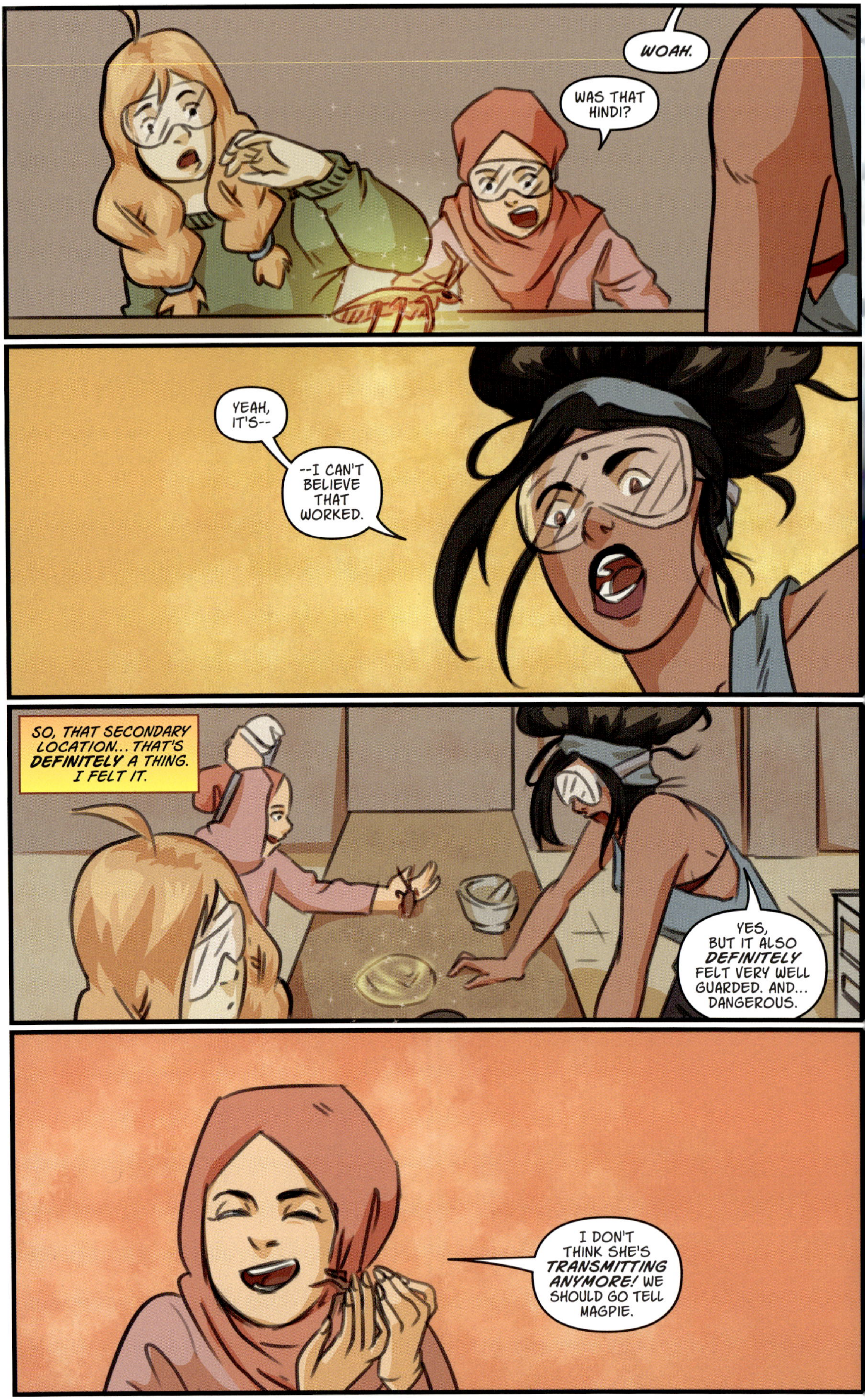
WOAH.
WAS THAT HINDI?
YEAH, IT'S--
--I CAN'T BELIEVE THAT WORKED.
SO, THAT SECONDARY LOCATION... THAT'S DEFINITELY A THING. I FELT IT.
YES, BUT IT ALSO DEFINITELY FELT VERY WELL GUARDED. AND... DANGEROUS.
I DON'T THINK SHE'S TRANSMITTING ANYMORE! WE SHOULD GO TELL MAGPIE.

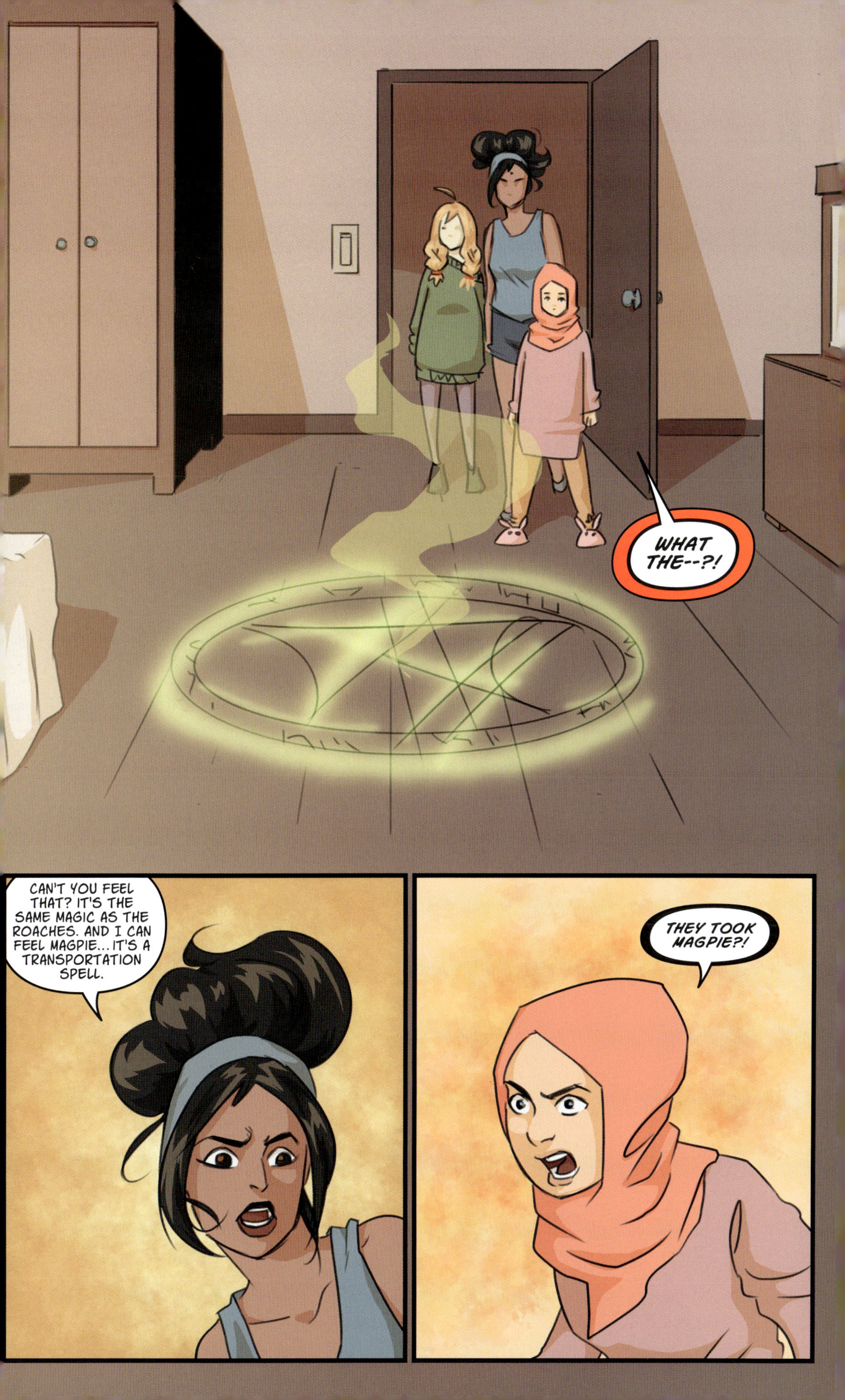
WHAT THE--?!
CAN'T YOU FEEL THAT? IT'S THE SAME MAGIC AS THE ROACHES. AND I CAN FEEL MAGPIE... IT'S A TRANSPORTATION SPELL.
THEY TOOK MAGPIE?!

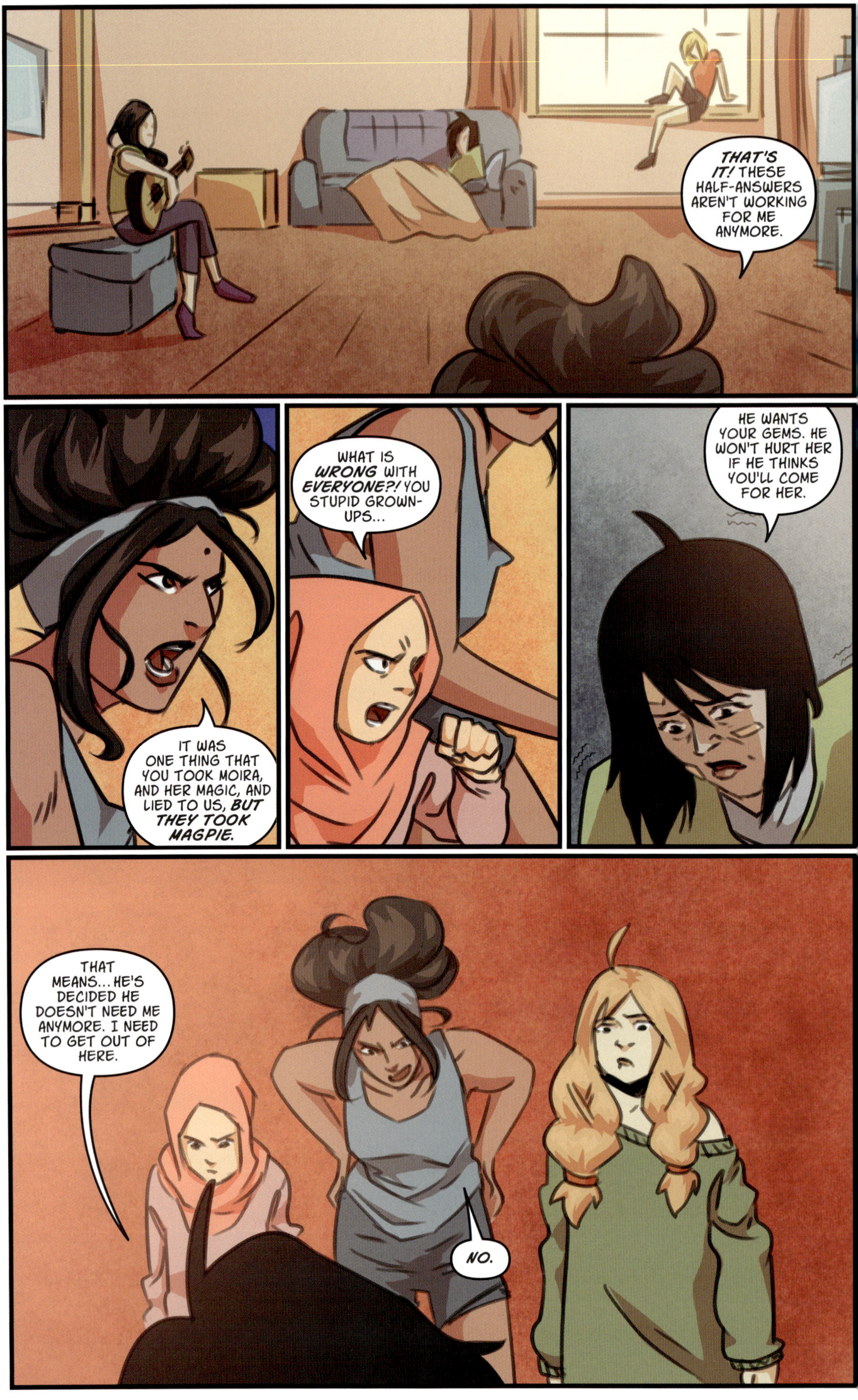
THAT'S IT! THESE HALF-ANSWERS AREN'T WORKING FOR ME ANYMORE.
IT WAS ONE THING THAT YOU TOOK MOIRA, AND HER MAGIC, AND LIED TO US, BUT THEY TOOK MAGPIE.
WHAT IS WRONG WITH EVERYONE?! YOU STUPID GROWN-UPS...
HE WANTS YOUR GEMS. HE WON'T HURT HER IF HE THINKS YOU'LL COME FOR HER.
THAT MEANS... HE'S DECIDED HE DOESN'T NEED ME ANYMORE. I NEED TO GET OUT OF HERE.
NO.

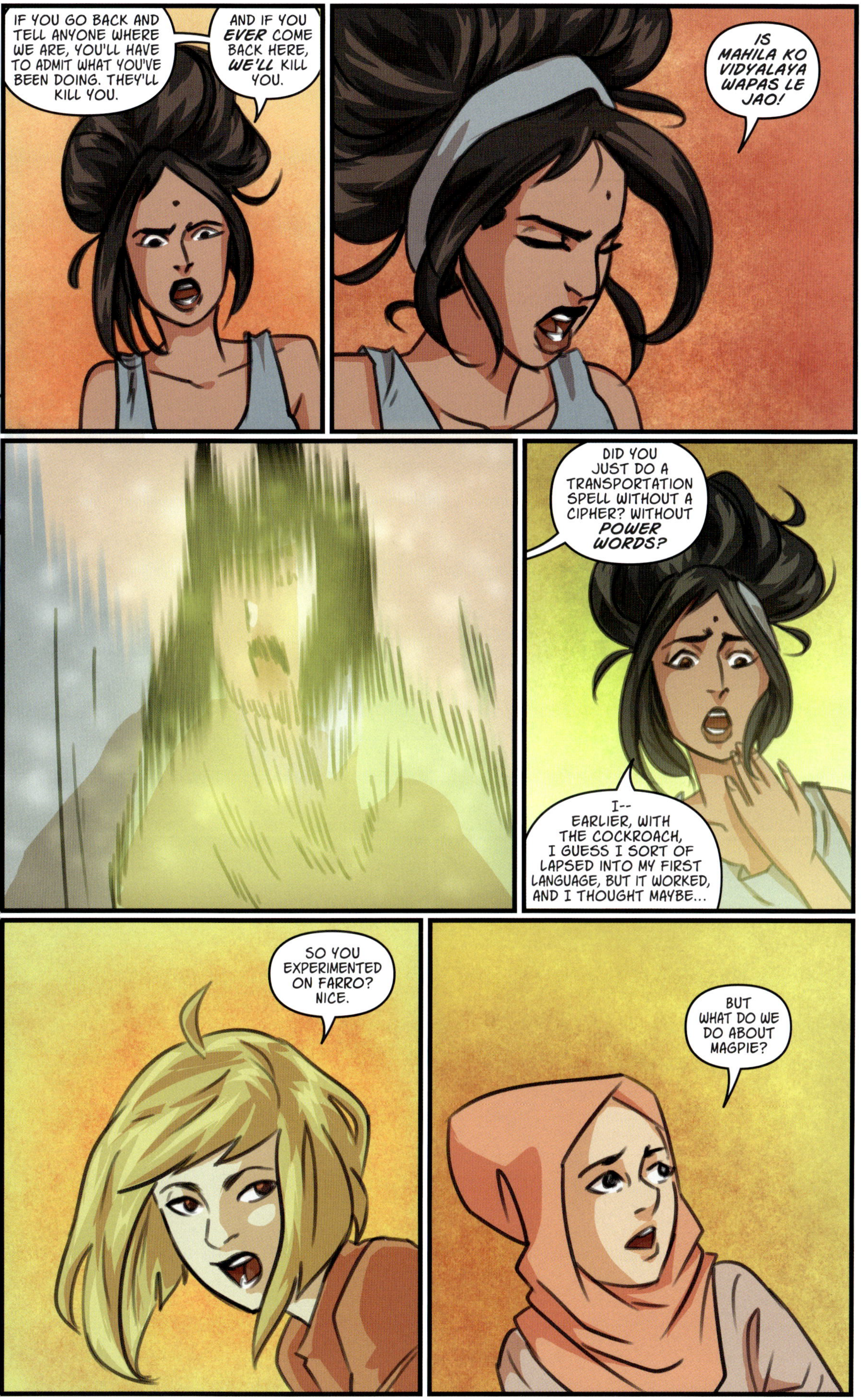
IF YOU GO BACK AND TELL ANYONE WHERE WE ARE, YOU'LL HAVE TO ADMIT WHAT YOU'VE BEEN DOING. THEY'LL KILL YOU.
AND IF YOU EVER COME BACK HERE, WE'LL KILL YOU.
IS MAHILA KO VIDYALAYA WAPAS LE JAO!
DID YOU JUST DO A TRANSPORTATION SPELL WITHOUT A CIPHER? WITHOUT POWER WORDS?
I-- EARLIER, WITH THE COCKROACH, I GUESS I SORT OF LAPSED INTO MY FIRST LANGUAGE, BUT IT WORKED, AND I THOUGHT MAYBE...
SO YOU EXPERIMENTED ON FARRO? NICE.
BUT WHAT DO WE DO ABOUT MAGPIE?

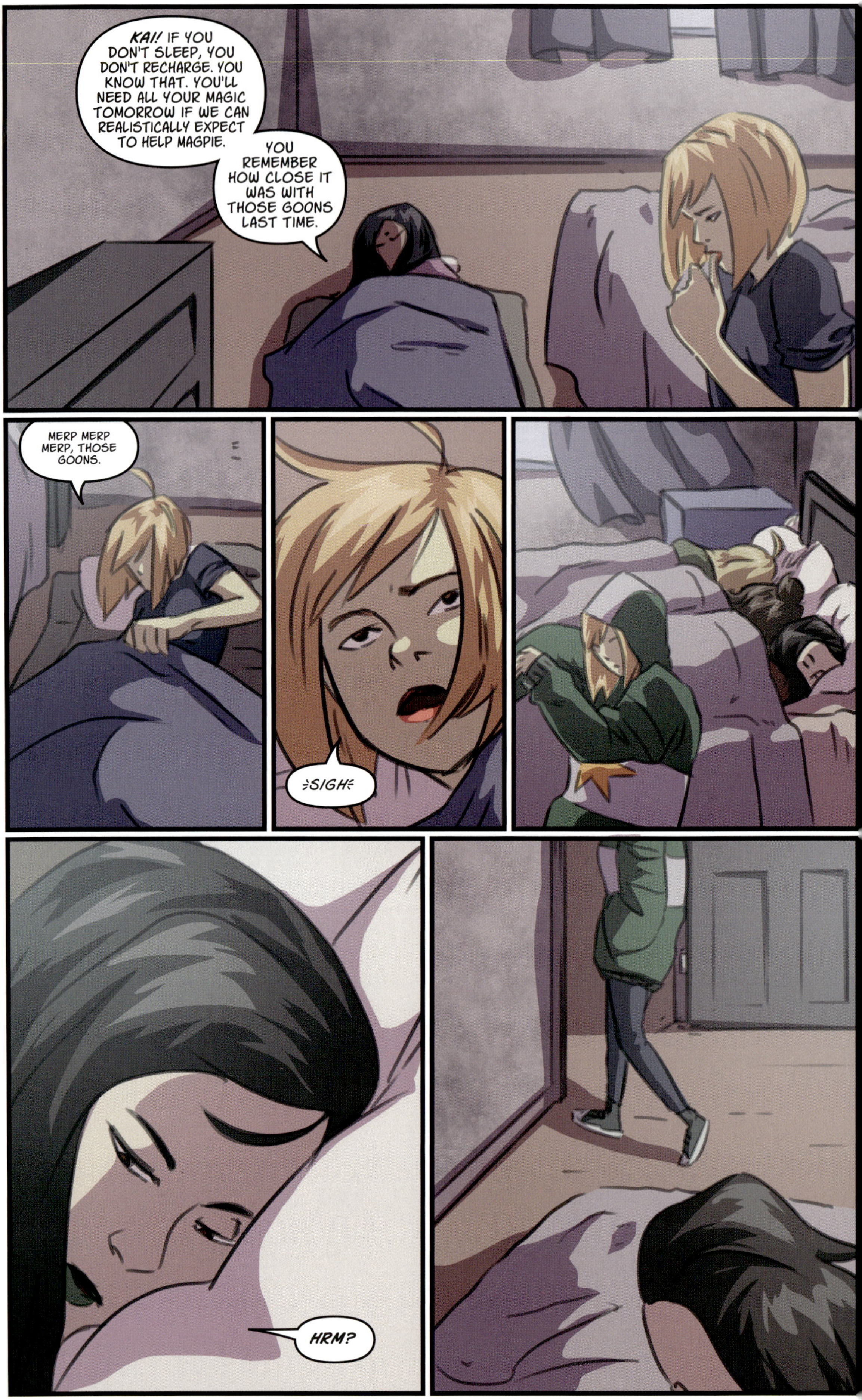
KAI! IF YOU DON'T SLEEP, YOU DON'T RECHARGE. YOU KNOW THAT. YOU'LL NEED ALL YOUR MAGIC TOMORROW IF WE CAN REALISTICALLY EXPECT TO HELP MAGPIE.
YOU REMEMBER HOW CLOSE IT WAS WITH THOSE GOONS LAST TIME.
MERP MERP MERP, THOSE GOONS.
SIGH
HRM?

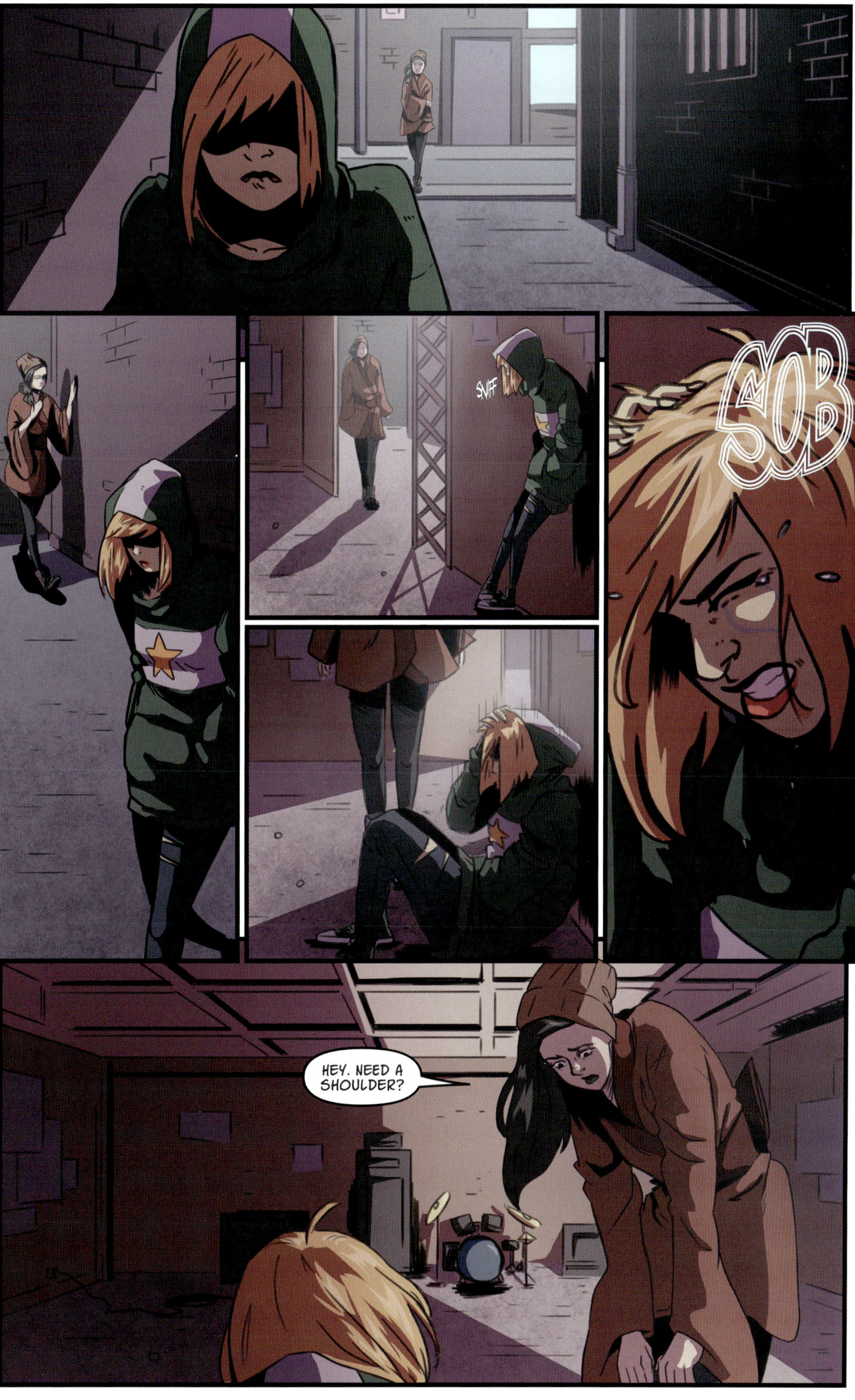
SNIFF
SOB
HEY. NEED A SHOULDER?

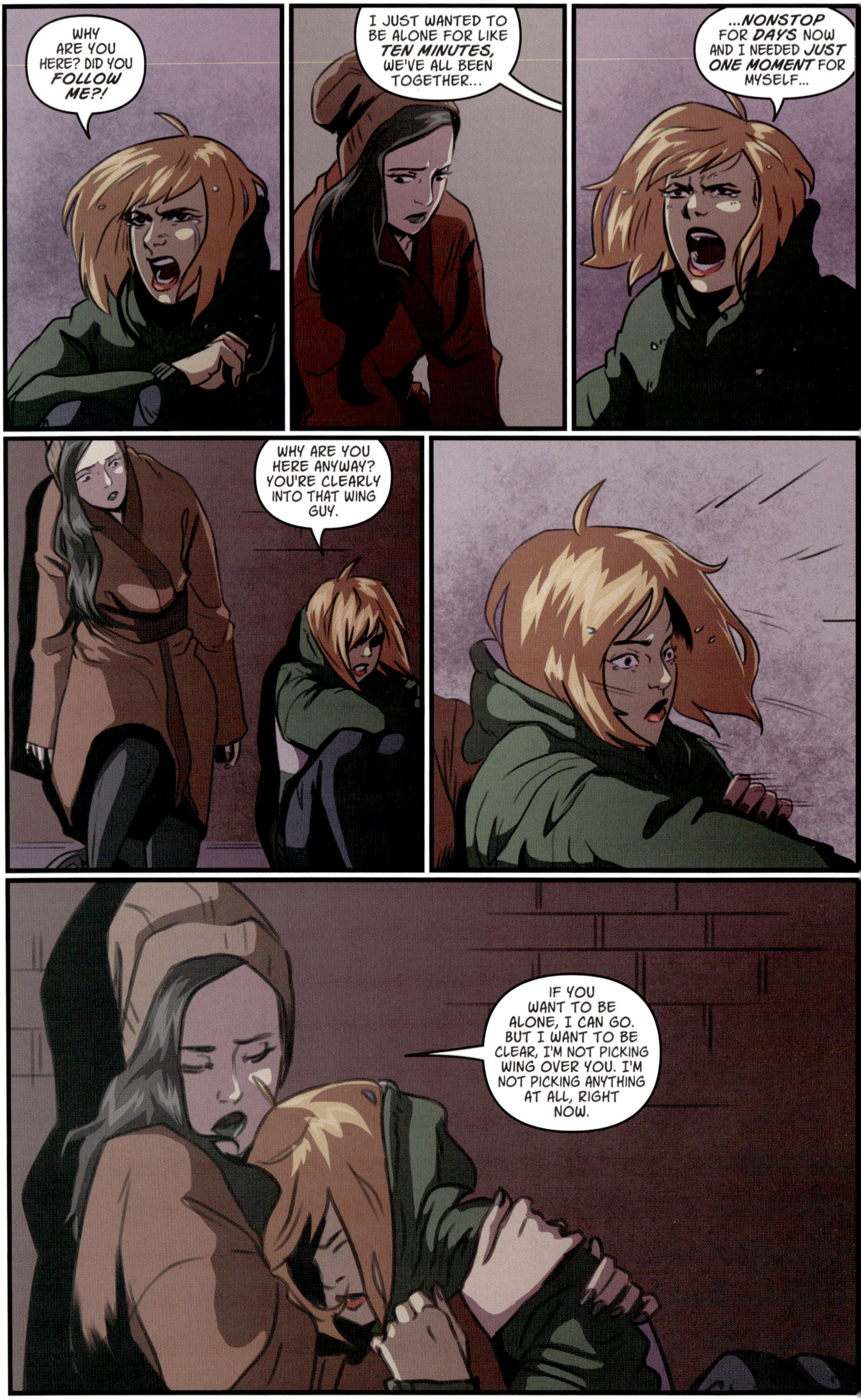
WHY ARE YOU HERE? DID YOU FOLLOW ME?!
I JUST WANTED TO BE ALONE FOR LIKE TEN MINUTES, WE'VE ALL BEEN TOGETHER...
...NONSTOP FOR DAYS NOW AND I NEEDED JUST ONE MOMENT FOR MYSELF...
WHY ARE YOU HERE ANYWAY? YOU'RE CLEARLY INTO THAT WING GUY.
IF YOU WANT TO BE ALONE, I CAN GO. BUT I WANT TO BE CLEAR, I'M NOT PICKING WING OVER YOU. I'M NOT PICKING ANYTHING AT ALL, RIGHT NOW.

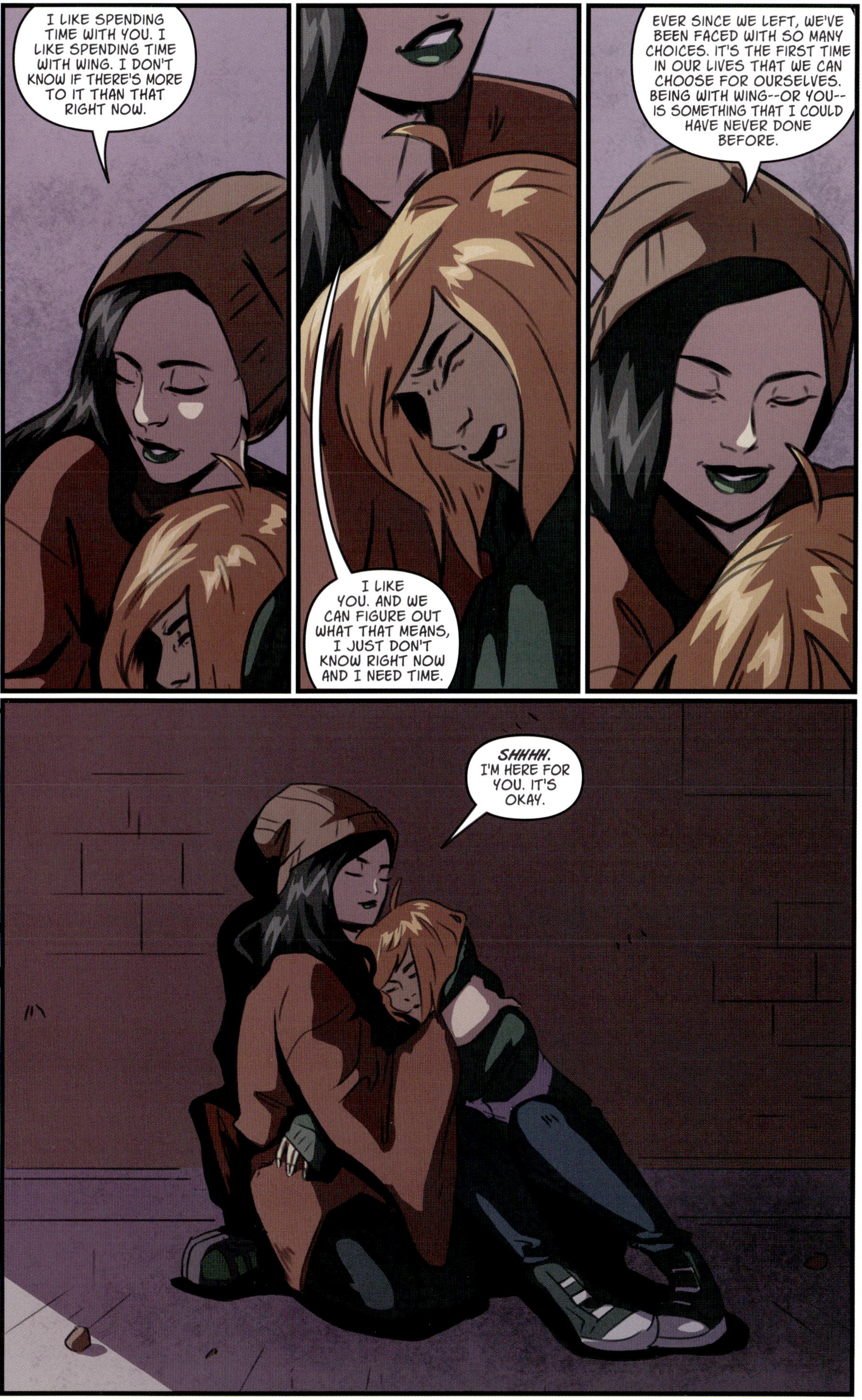
I LIKE SPENDING TIME WITH YOU. I LIKE SPENDING TIME WITH WING. I DON'T KNOW IF THERE'S MORE TO IT THAN THAT RIGHT NOW.
I LIKE YOU. AND WE CAN FIGURE OUT WHAT THAT MEANS, I JUST DON'T KNOW RIGHT NOW AND I NEED TIME.
EVER SINCE WE LEFT, WE'VE BEEN FACED WITH SO MANY CHOICES. IT'S THE FIRST TIME IN OUR LIVES THAT WE CAN CHOOSE FOR OURSELVES. BEING WITH WING--OR YOU--IS SOMETHING THAT I COULD HAVE NEVER DONE BEFORE.
SHHHH. I'M HERE FOR YOU. IT'S OKAY.

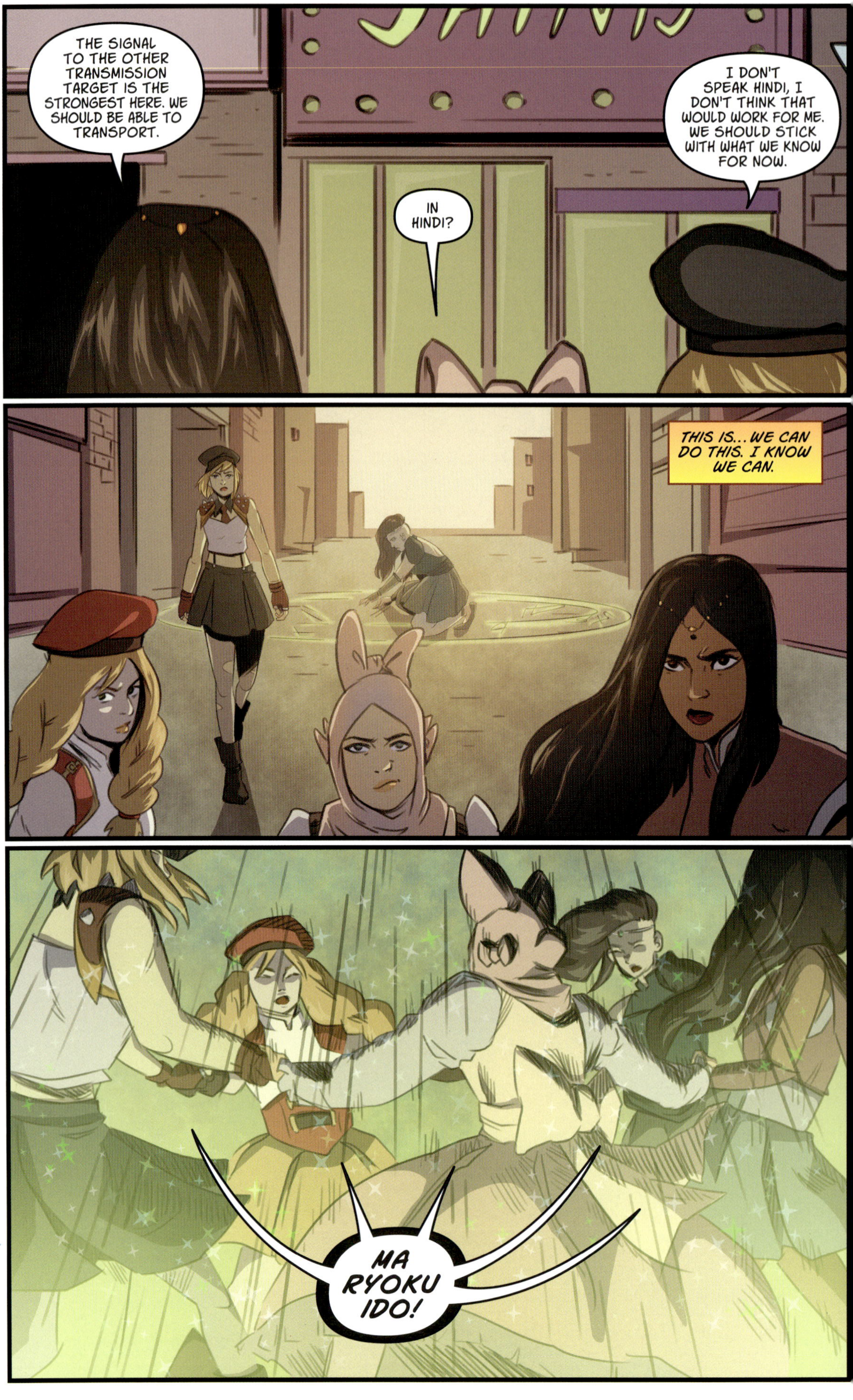
THE SIGNAL TO THE OTHER TRANSMISSION TARGET IS THE STRONGEST HERE. WE SHOULD BE ABLE TO TRANSPORT.
IN HINDI?
I DON'T SPEAK HINDI, I DON'T THINK THAT WOULD WORK FOR ME. WE SHOULD STICK WITH WHAT WE KNOW FOR NOW.
THIS IS... WE CAN DO THIS. I KNOW WE CAN.
MA RYOKU IDO!

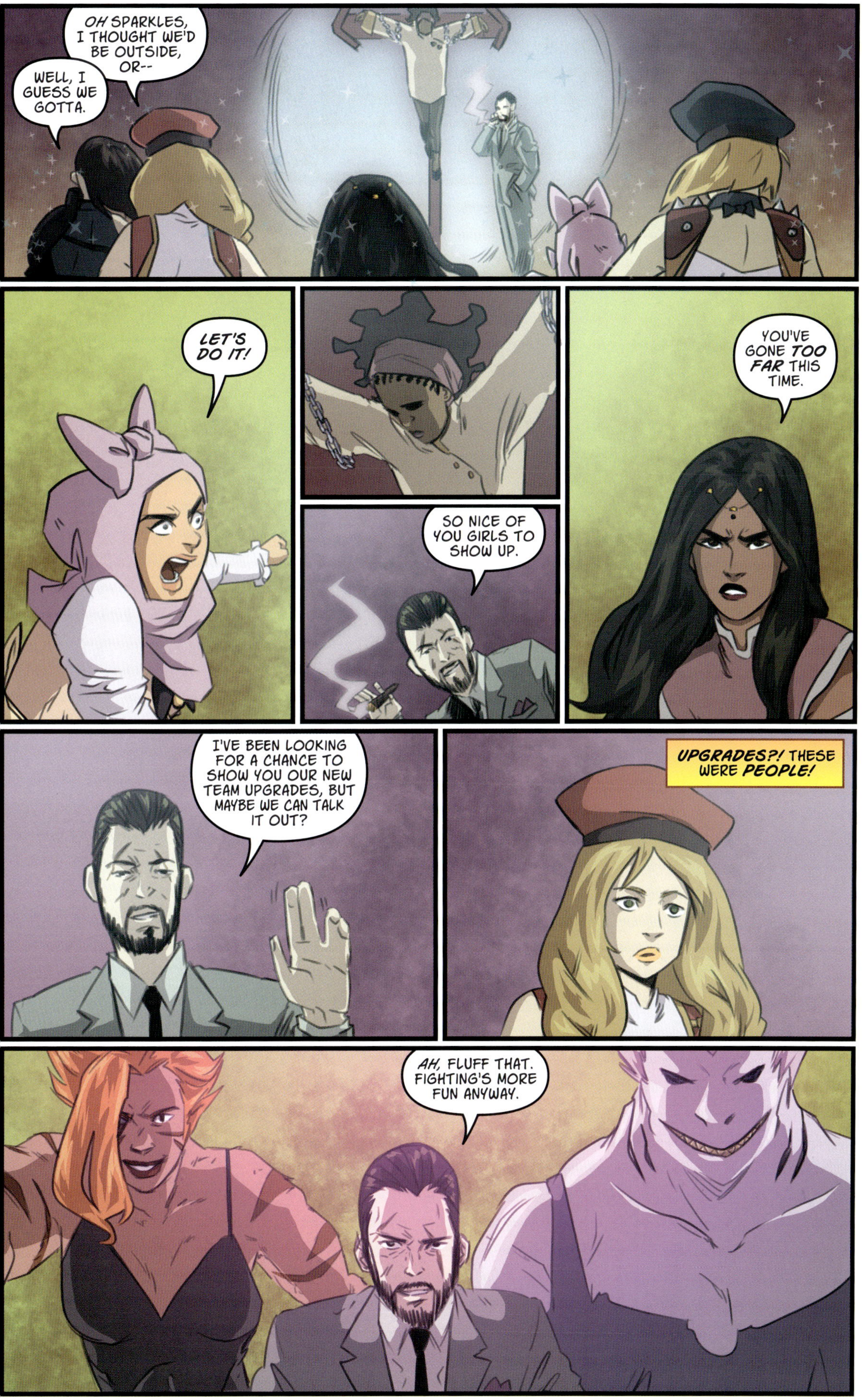
OH SPARKLES, I THOUGHT WE'D BE OUTSIDE, OR--
WELL, I GUESS WE GOTTA.
LET'S DO IT!
YOU'VE GONE TOO FAR THIS TIME.
SO NICE OF YOU GIRLS TO SHOW UP.
I'VE BEEN LOOKING FOR A CHANCE TO SHOW YOU OUR NEW TEAM UPGRADES, BUT MAYBE WE CAN TALK IT OUT?
UPGRADES?! THESE WERE PEOPLE!
AH, FLUFF THAT. FIGHTING'S MORE FUN ANYWAY.

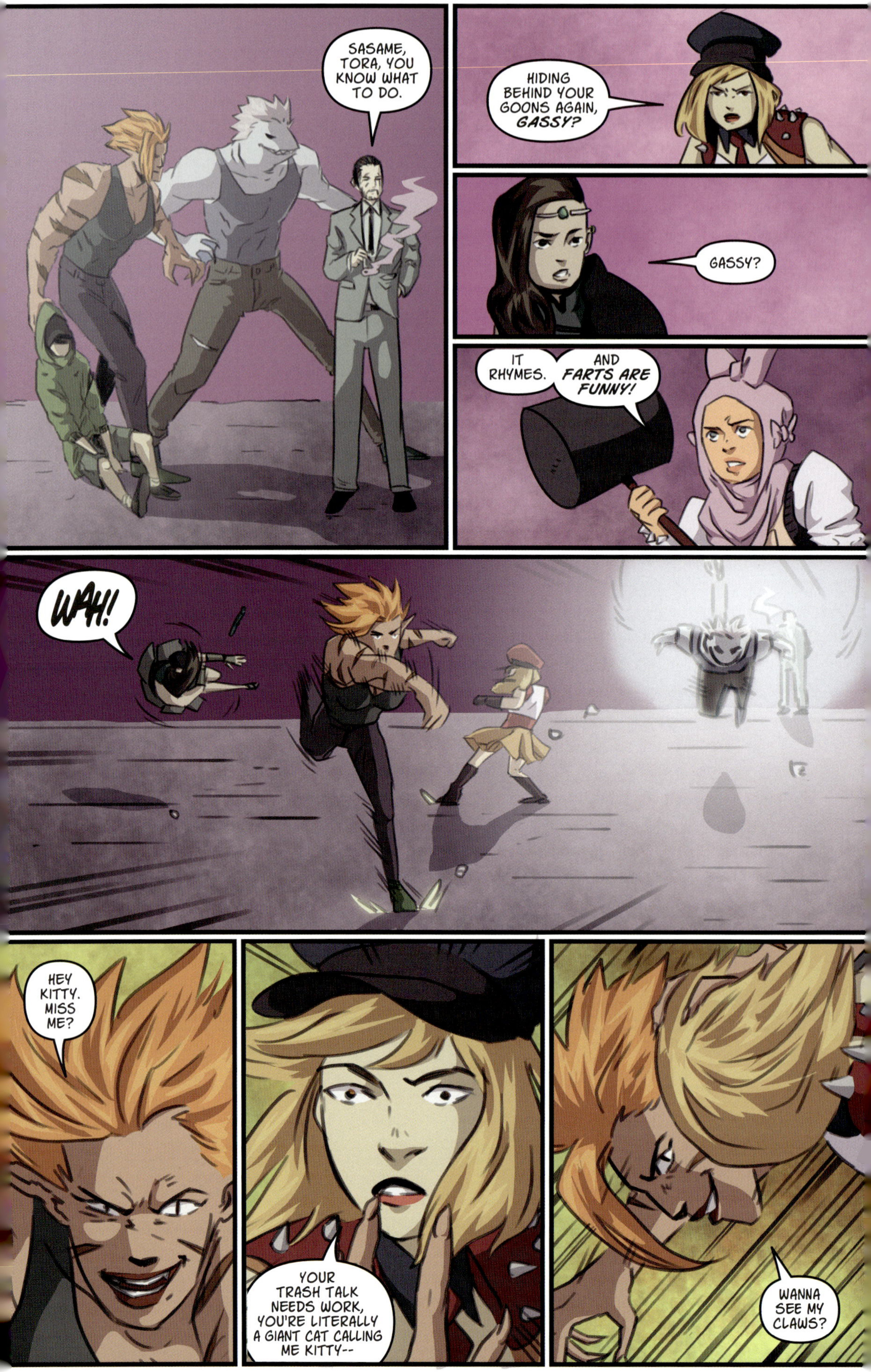
SASAME, TORA, YOU KNOW WHAT TO DO.
HIDING BEHIND YOUR GOONS AGAIN, GASSY?
GASSY?
IT RHYMES.
AND FARTS ARE FUNNY!
WAH!
HEY KITTY. MISS ME?
YOUR TRASH TALK NEEDS WORK, YOU'RE LITERALLY A GIANT CAT CALLING ME KITTY--
WANNA SEE MY CLAWS?

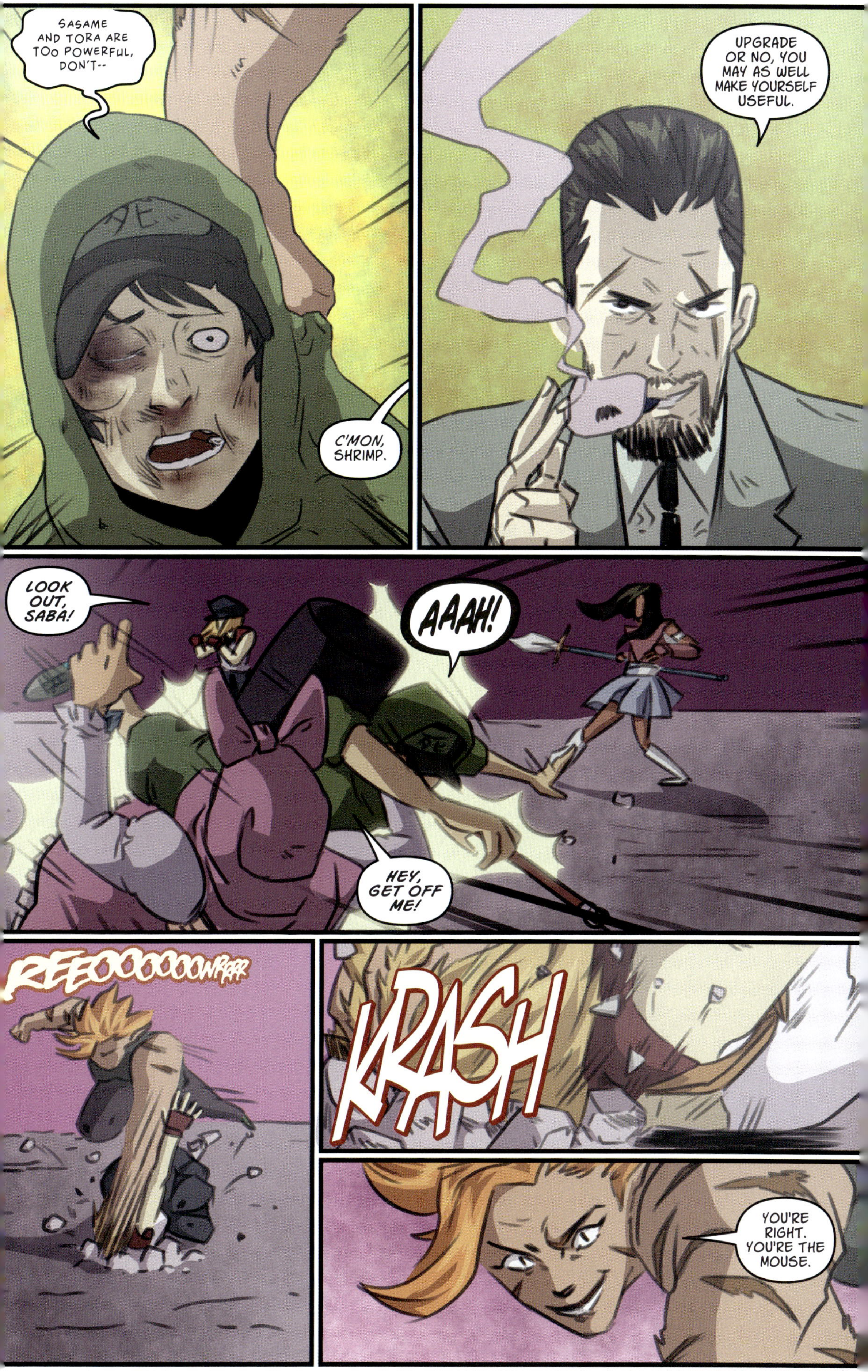
SASAME AND TORA ARE TOO POWERFUL, DON'T--
C'MON, SHRIMP.
UPGRADE OR NO, YOU MAY AS WELL MAKE YOURSELF USEFUL.
LOOK OUT, SABA!
AAAH!
HEY, GET OFF ME!
REEOOOOOOWRRR
KRASH
YOU'RE RIGHT. YOU'RE THE MOUSE.

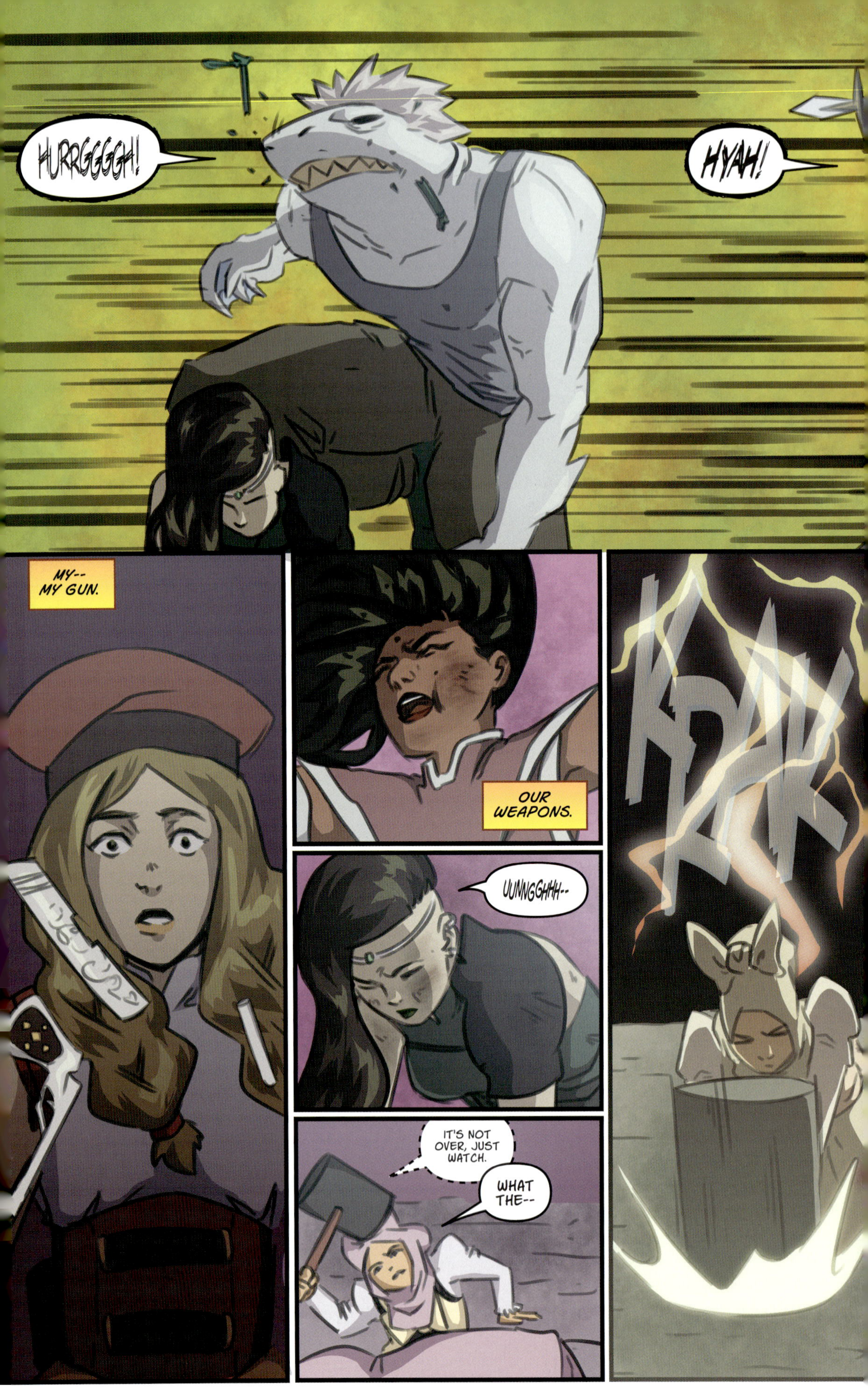
HURRGGGGH!
HYAH!
MY-- MY GUN.
OUR WEAPONS.
UUNNGGHHH--
IT'S NOT OVER, JUST WATCH.
WHAT THE--
KRAKKK

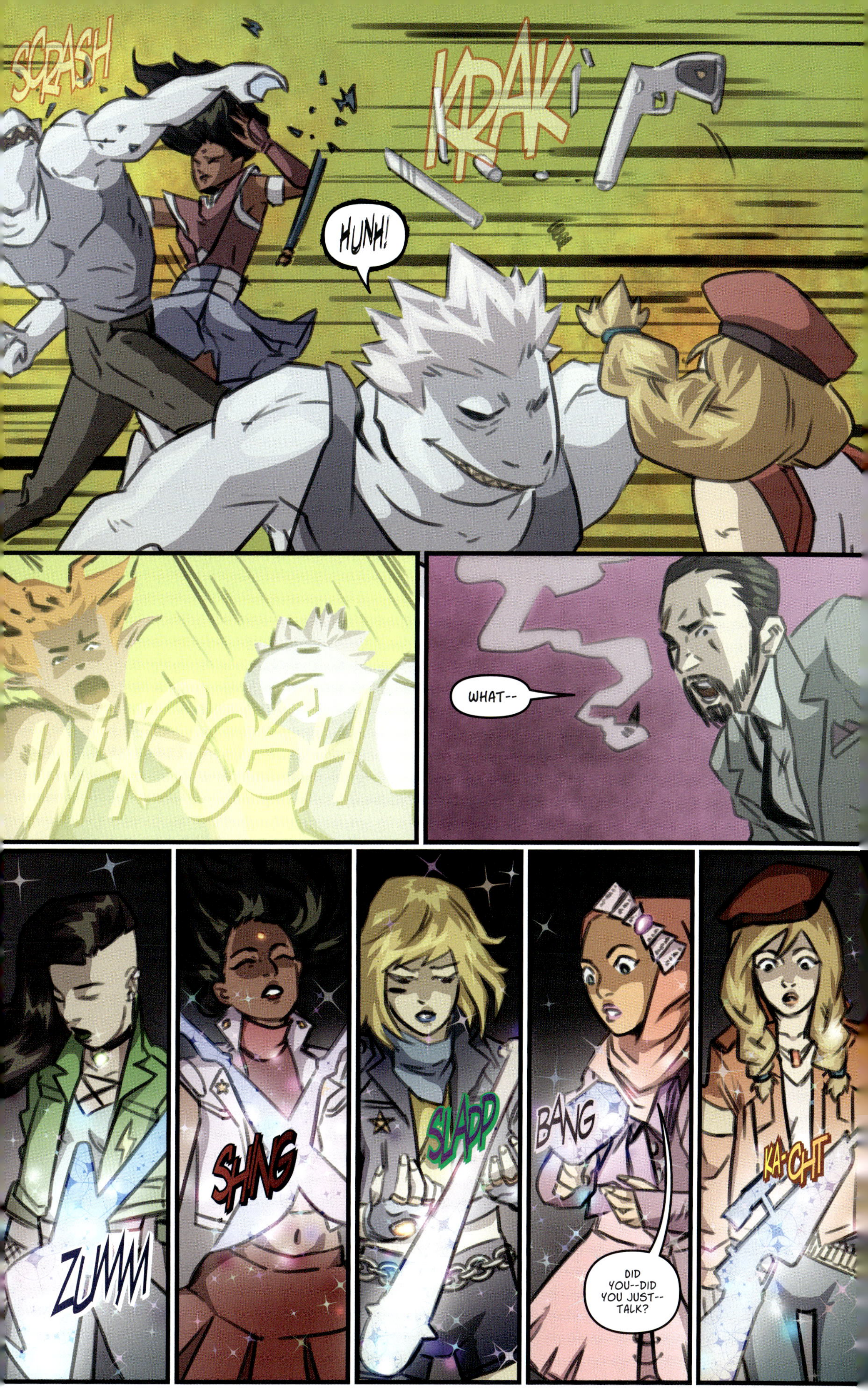
SCRASH
KRAK
HUNH!
WHOOSH
WHAT--
ZUMM
SHING
SLADP
BANG
DID YOU--DID YOU JUST--TALK?
KA-CHT

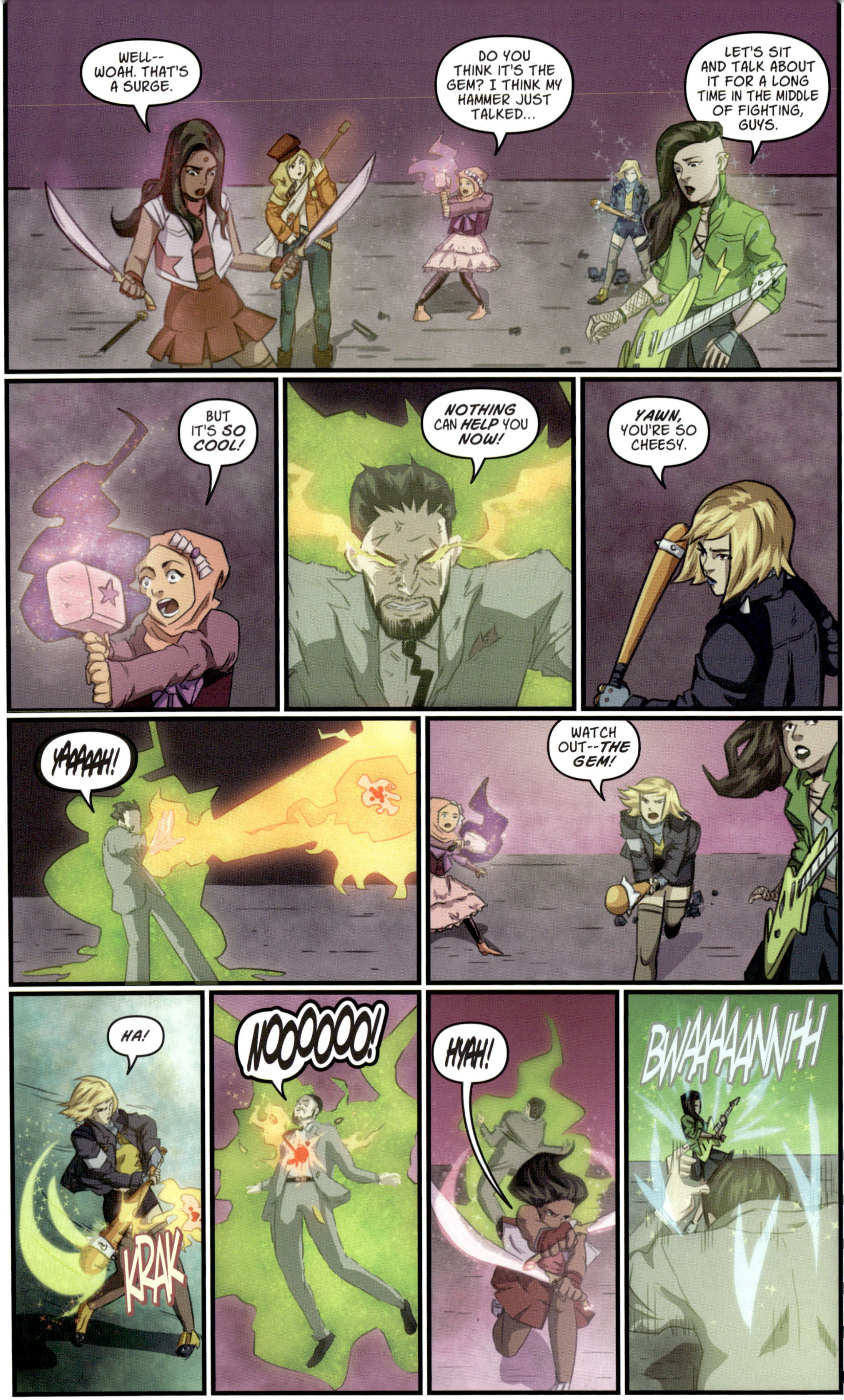
WELL-- WOAH. THAT'S A SURGE.
DO YOU THINK IT'S THE GEM? I THINK MY HAMMER JUST TALKED...
LET'S SIT AND TALK ABOUT IT FOR A LONG TIME IN THE MIDDLE OF FIGHTING, GUYS.
BUT IT'S SO COOL!
NOTHING CAN HELP YOU NOW!
YAWN, YOU'RE SO CHEESY.
YAAAAH!
WATCH OUT--THE GEM!
HA!
KRAK
NOOOOOO!
HYAH!
BWAAAAANNHH

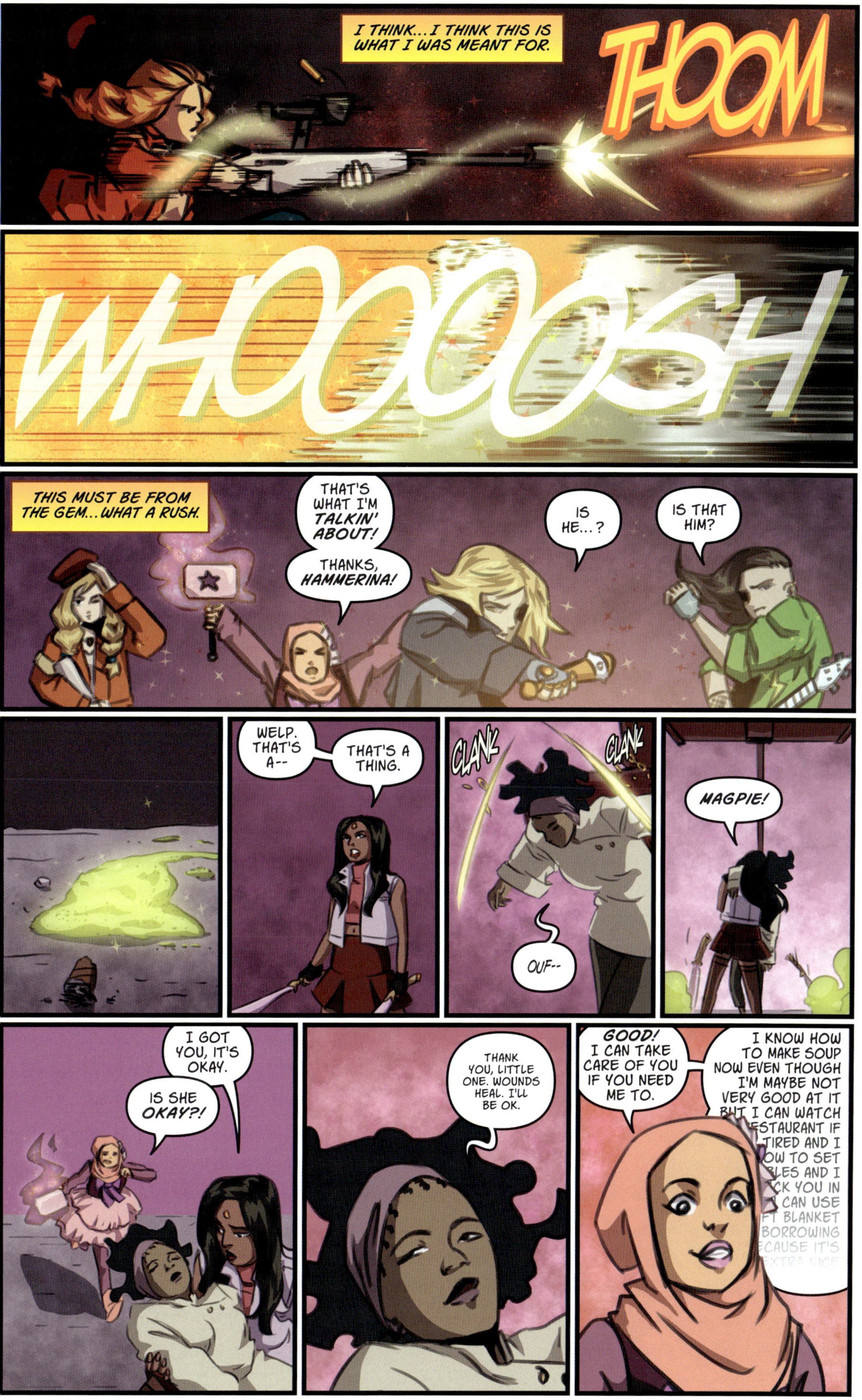

I THINK... I THINK THIS IS WHAT I WAS MEANT FOR.
THOOM
WHOOOOSH
THIS MUST BE FROM THE GEM... WHAT A RUSH.
THAT'S WHAT I'M TALKIN' ABOUT!
THANKS, HAMMERINA!
IS HE...?
IS THAT HIM?
WELP. THAT'S A--
THAT'S A THING.
CLANK
CLANK
OUF--
MAGPIE!
I GOT YOU, IT'S OKAY.
IS SHE OKAY?!
THANK YOU, LITTLE ONE. WOUNDS HEAL. I'LL BE OK.
GOOD! I CAN TAKE CARE OF YOU IF YOU NEED ME TO.
I KNOW HOW TO MAKE SOUP NOW EVEN THOUGH I'M MAYBE NOT VERY GOOD AT IT BUT I CAN WATCH

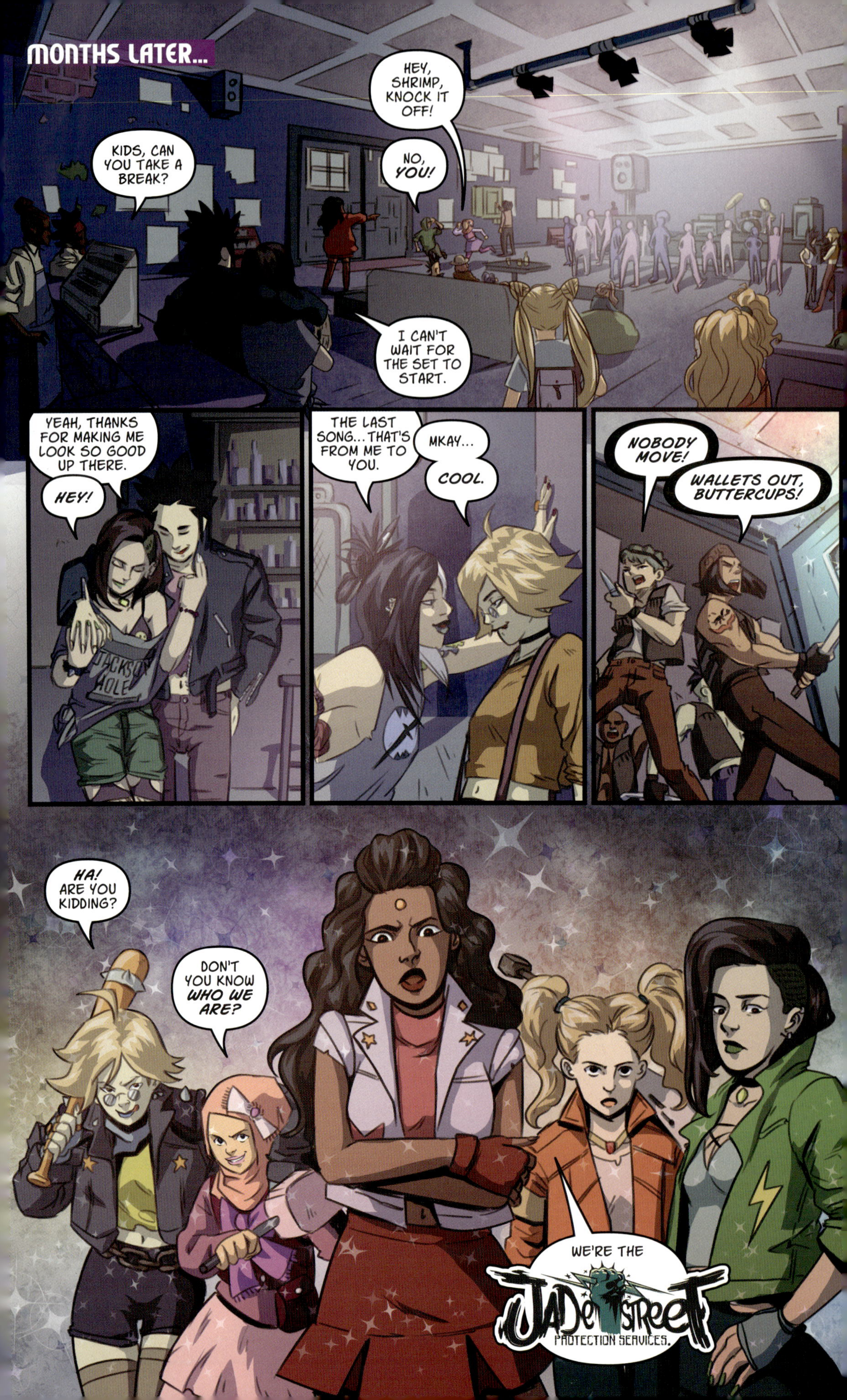
MONTHS LATER...
HEY, SHRIMP, KNOCK IT OFF!
KIDS, CAN YOU TAKE A BREAK?
NO, YOU!
I CAN'T WAIT FOR THE SET TO START.
YEAH, THANKS FOR MAKING ME LOOK SO GOOD UP THERE.
HEY!
JACKSON HOLE
THE LAST SONG... THAT'S FROM ME TO YOU.
MKAY...
COOL.
NOBODY MOVE!
WALLETS OUT, BUTTERCUPS!
HA! ARE YOU KIDDING?
DON'T YOU KNOW WHO WE ARE?
WE'RE THE
JADE STREET
PROTECTION SERVICES.

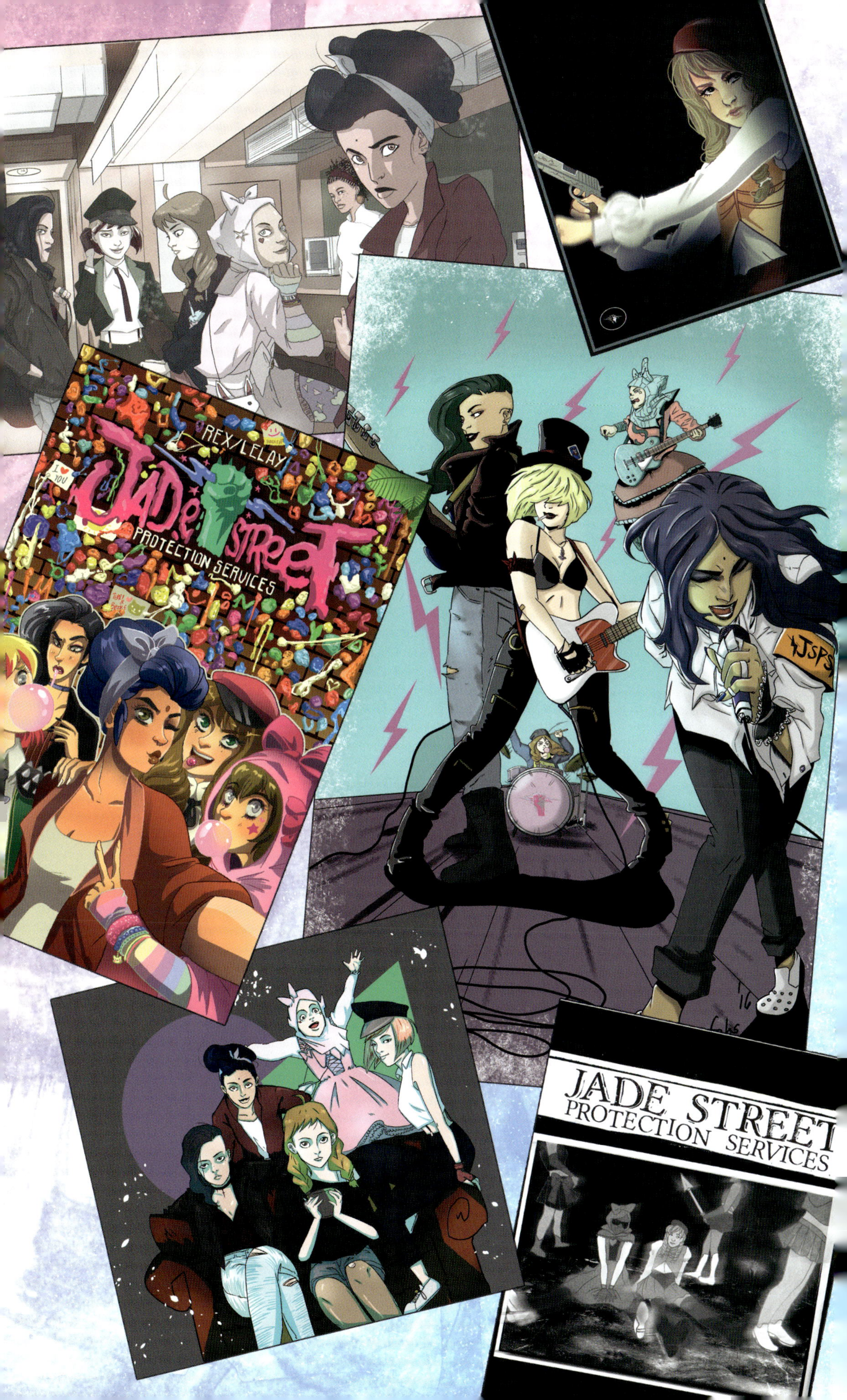
REX/LELAY
JADE STREET
PROTECTION SERVICES
JSPS
JADE STREET
PROTECTION SERVICES

RETAILER VARIANTS

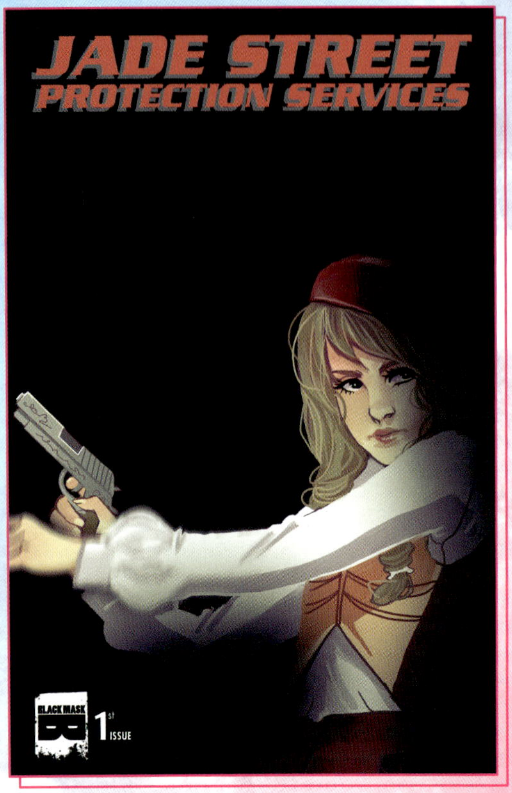
JADE STREET
PROTECTION SERVICES
BLACK MASK
1st ISSUE

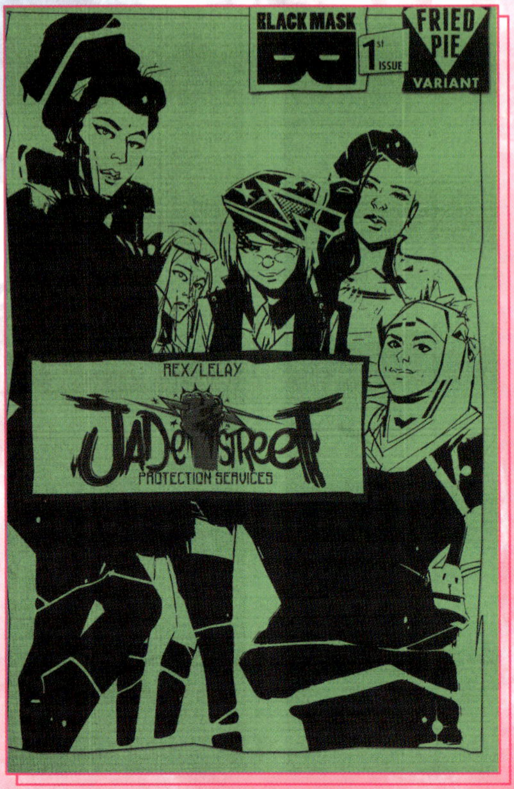
BLACK MASK
1st ISSUE
FRIED PIE
VARIANT
REX/LELAY
JADE STREET
PROTECTION SERVICES

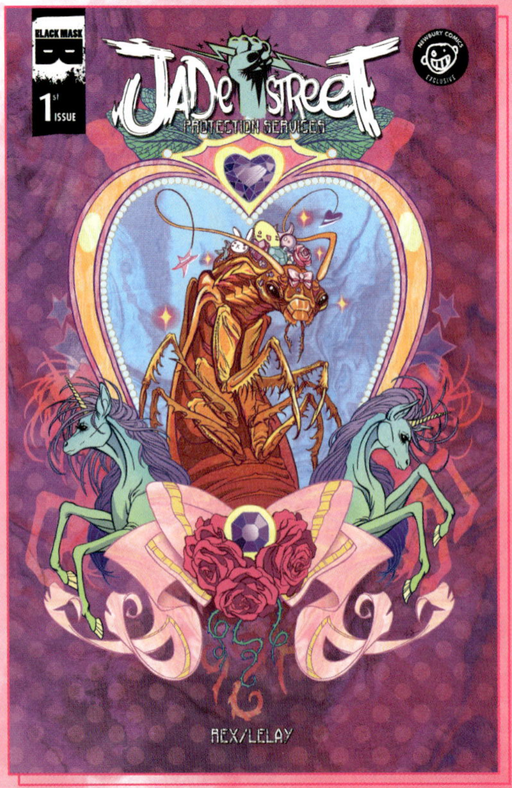
BLACK MASK
1st ISSUE
JADE STREET
PROTECTION SERVICES
NEWBURY COMICS
EXCLUSIVE
REX/LELAY

RETAILER VARIANTS

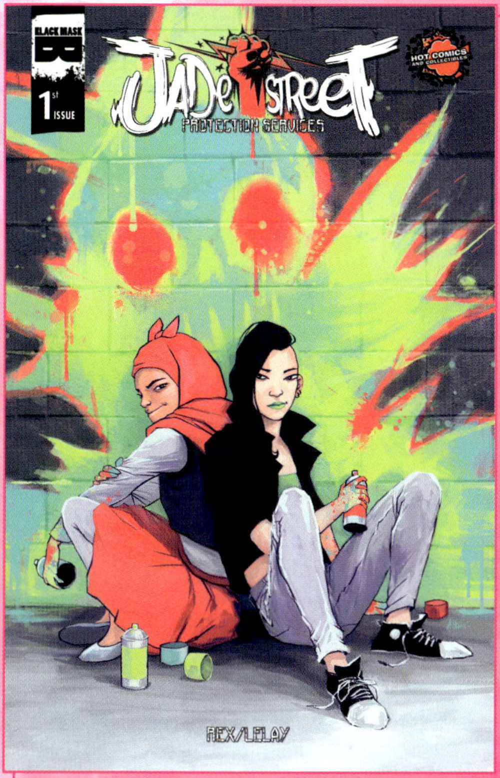
BLACK MASK
1st ISSUE
JADE STREET
PROTECTION SERVICES
HOT COMICS AND COLLECTIBLES
REX/LELAY

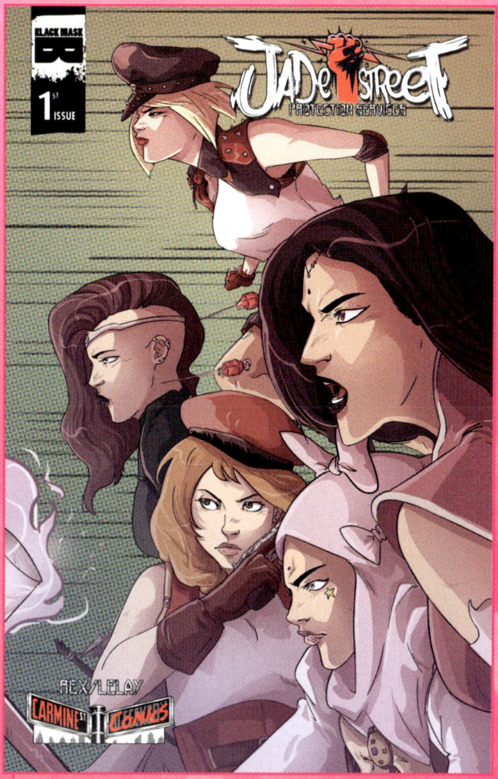
BLACK MASK
1st ISSUE
JADE STREET
PROTECTION SERVICES
REX/LELAY
CARMINE ST COMICS

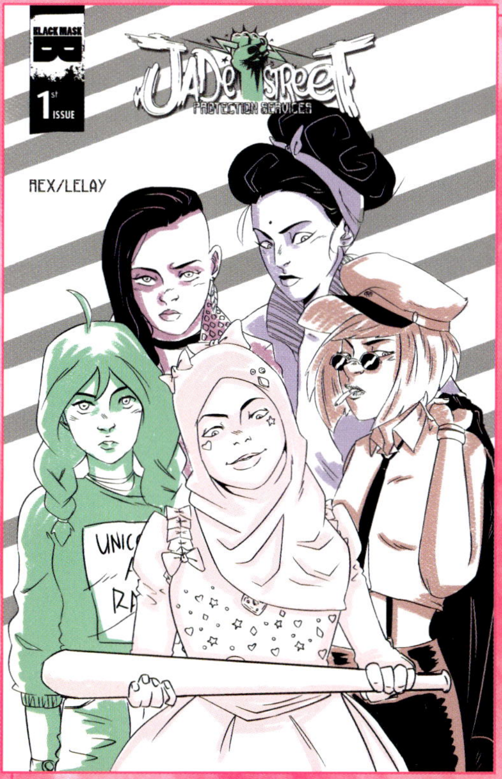
BLACK MASK
1st ISSUE
JADE STREET
PROTECTION SERVICES
REX/LELAY

Katy Rex is a comic book writer and the editor of *Kim & Kim*, also from Black Mask Studios. She is a former reviewer for sites such as Comics Bulletin and Bloody Disgusting, and has written about comics academically for pop culture conferences in Providence, RI, and Chicago, IL. She currently resides in the bitterly cold Minnesota. Her credits include *Jade Street Protection Services* and *Strange Wit*. She is on Twitter as @thekatyrex and her website is www.katyrex.com.

Katy thanks:
I would like to extend a special thank you to friends and family who have supported me through this new exciting journey, first and foremost my team and my publisher, but also especially all the Valkyries, Tini Howard, Jess Camacho, Matt Miner, JP, the Michigan uncles, and my dog Dax who has had to listen to more than her fair share of dramatic sighs while I write.

Fabian Lelay is a Brooklyn based creator imported from the Philippines. He began drawing comics with his friends at the age of 13 and briefly tried to venture into fashion when he set foot in college. He has used his fashion experience to design characters. And after meeting Magdalene and Katy he decided to jump headfirst into comics with *Jade Street Protection Services* and has a number of other exciting creator-owned stories in the works. You can find more of his work on his website rocketsandpens.com and you can follow more of his updates on twitter under @rocketsandpens and his patreon /rocketsandpens.

Fabs thanks:
It goes without saying, how much I am thankful for Black Mask and my wonderful teammates. I'd also like to specially thank Adrian Sta. Maria, Gmenier Mendoza and Stanley Adecla for their support and the clutch assists behind the scenes. And to everyone who picked up our book: You are the bee's knees.

Taylor Esposito is a comic book lettering professional and owner of Ghost Glyph Studios. As a staff letterer at DC, he lettered titles such as *Red Hood and The Outlaws, Constantine, Bodies, CMYK, The New 52: Future's End*, and *New Suicide Squad*. Prior to this, Taylor was credited on numerous titles for Marvel as a production artist. He is currently working on a new batch of creator-owned titles, such as *The Paybacks* and *Interceptor* (Heavy Metal Comics), *Heroine Chic, Dents, Mirror,* and *Finality* (Line Webtoon). Other publishers he has worked with include First Second, Zenescope, Valiant, and Dynamite. He can be reached at @TaylorEspo or @GhostGlyph on Twitter and taylor@ghostglyphstudios.com

Taylor thanks:
Thanks to two of my closest comics family members: Fabian, my brother and Katy, my comics wife. Love you both and it's been a pleasure to be part of this experience with you both. And thanks to Mara, with me in the trenches at the Eleventh hour. We made it.

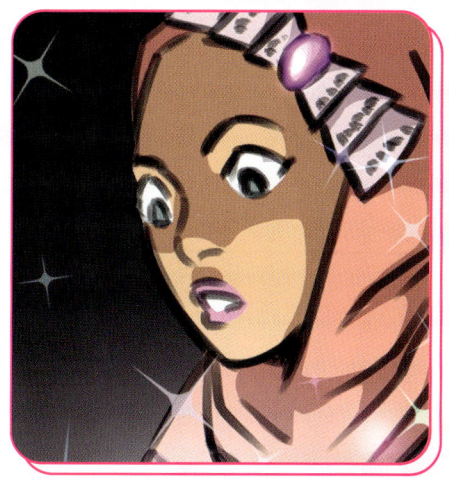

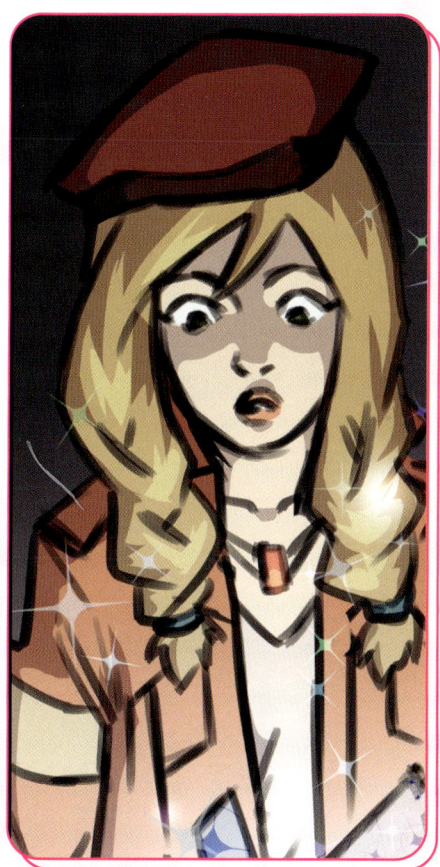

Magdalene Visaggio is the writer and creator of *Kim & Kim* and *Quantum Teens Are Go* for Black Mask Studios. A former wannabe academic theologian, she turned to writing comics after dropping out of graduate school. She actually started writing comics when she was eight, but honestly, those were pretty terrible. She has contributed work to DC Comics' *Shade the Changing Girl,* alongside her participation in the *Dirty Diamonds* comic anthology. She is also a contributing writer at Paste Magazine. Magdalene lives in Manhattan. Her twitter is @MagsVisaggs.

Mags thanks:
Big thanks to the fabulous team on Jade Street Protection Services for bringing me on as a member of the family.

Mara Jayne Carpenter is a graphic designer during the day, colorist by night. Her palettes are her superpower, basically. She's based in Connecticut and is addicted to coffee and anime. Jade Street is the first nationally published book she has colored, and she looks forward to many comic projects in the future. You can find her on twitter at @Gingerjujju.

Mara Jayne thanks:
I'd like to thank Andy Earwaker, Bethany Peckham, and Jude Vigants. And the JSPS team.

Additional dedication:
Katy would like to dedicate her work on the book to Grammie (a.k.a. Eileen Leider) who has always been behind Katy 100% even when she thought comics writing was 'Superman on tissue paper.' She was the first in line to buy Jade Street and this book could not have happened without her.
April 12, 1928 - September 22, 2016

HB2 covers:
As a response to the HB2 "bathroom bill" signed in mid-2016 by North Carolina governor Pat McCrory, Katy Rex and Magdalene Visaggio decided to turn their appearance at HeroesCon in Charlotte, NC into a charity fundraiser for local NC LGBT organizations. JSPS and Kim & Kim swapped artists, and the resulting special limited-edition covers raised over $700 to support these pro-LGBT causes.

JADE STREET
PROTECTION SERVICES

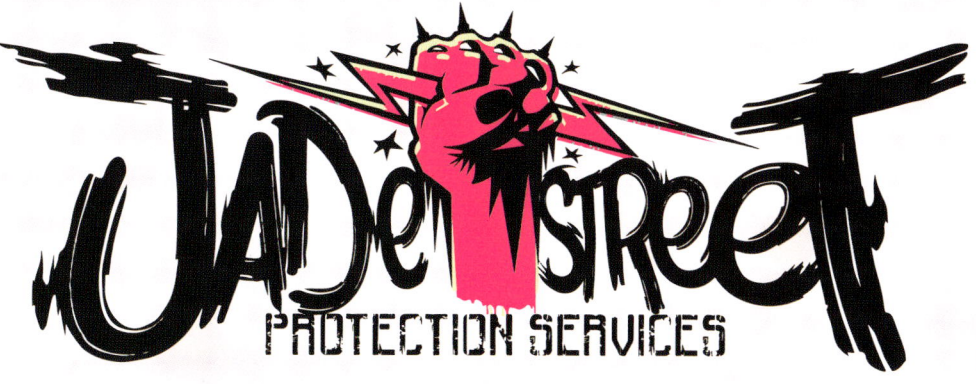

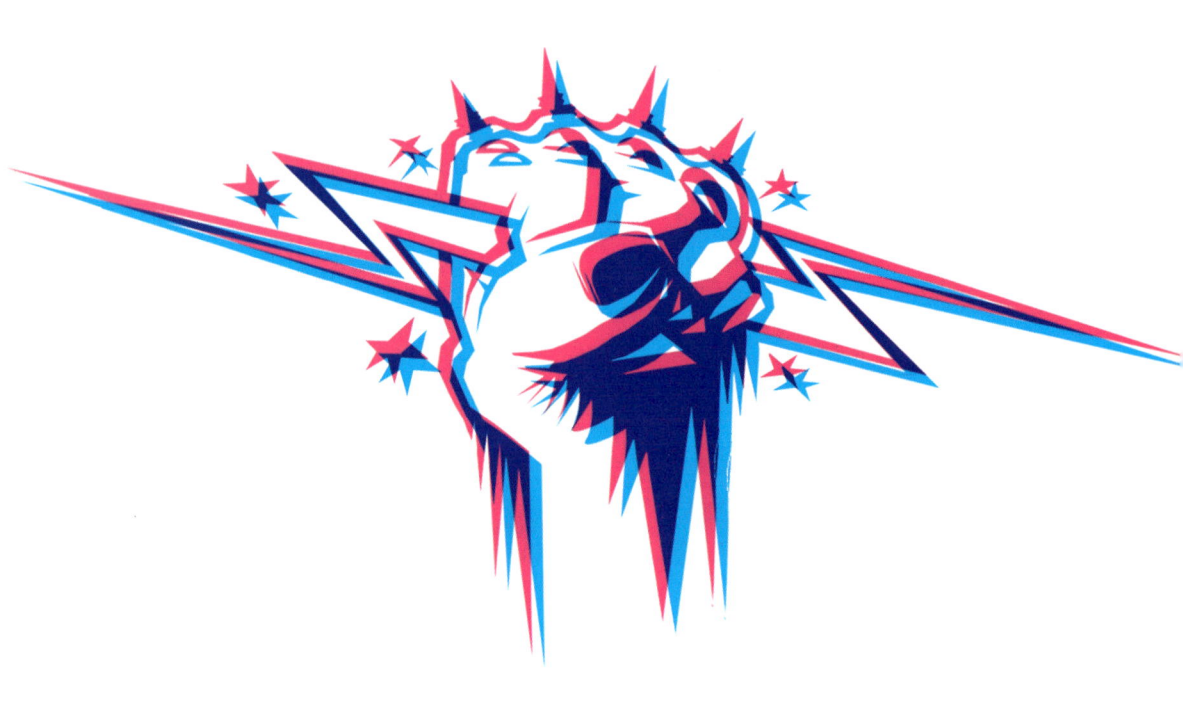